EYES ONLY

JASON TRAPP
BOOK 10

JACK SLATER

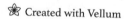

1

Pyongyang, North Korea

IT WAS ANOTHER SWELTERING MORNING, which Supreme Guard Commander Hwa Yung-Gi knew would turn into a suffocating afternoon since the Democratic People's Republic of Korea was scorching under a record-breaking heat streak reminiscent of the Australian outback.

Keeping to the shadow for its fractional coolness rather than stealth, he watched his principal, Myo Il-Song, crouch to embrace her daughters. At thirty-seven, she still moved with the lithe muscularity of a woman half her age. He suspected that her elderly father's almost constant ill health throughout her life had prompted her to keep as wholesome and active a regimen as she could, though naturally he would never ask. The girls, Soo-Yun and Min-Seo, clung to her like baby monkeys, their faces buried in the soft material of her business suit.

"*Eomma* will be back soon," Myo said, pretending to shake them off, faking horror at their claws digging into her. "Be good for your evil brother!"

Sixteen-year-old Sung-Min stood at attention nearby, his posture military-taut, the boy desiring to appear mature in his general-father's absence, especially in the presence of Yung-Gi and the other guards in the fortress-like grounds of Myo's home. When Myo finally convinced the girls to disengage, Sung-Min bowed. "Safe travels, *Eomma*. I'll take care of everything."

Myo answered with a smile, and Yung-Gi sensed a flash of pride. She gripped Sung-Min's shoulder, then turned to give the girls a final, fierce monkey-hug.

Having recently turned sixty, Yung-Gi had long since given up any dreams of family. His life belonged to the Republic, to Myo Il-Song and her father, President Kuk.

Shouldering her bag, Myo snapped out orders to the security detail, her brusque manner practiced to brook no dissent. As she passed Yung-Gi to board the helicopter waiting on the designated 'H' pad at the far end of her lawn, he caught an uncharacteristic worried pinch to her eyes. She quickly masked it, as if she sensed his eyes on her.

Yung-Gi ducked into the fat-bellied helicopter behind her, taking his place at her side, no words needed as the engines powered up and the rotors whined to life. Six other security officers joined them.

As they rose over Pyongyang, he studied Myo's profile, heavy with responsibility, not only for her family—her father's failing health had thrust her into a political spotlight she'd never sought. Her determination to succeed where other leaders had failed was born of reluctant necessity.

For her children. For their country. She would do what needed to be done.

FIELDS OF WITHERED crops flashed by beneath the helicopter, a bleak portrait of usually lush countryside. In the distance, smokestacks belched gray plumes. A grim canvas of industry and famine.

Myo leaned forward, surveying the landscape with a forlorn frown, as if longing for the brown land to suddenly brighten and declare the failed crop yield a sick joke. The suffering of vast swathes of the population had weighed visibly upon her even before her father appointed her head of resource allocation and distribution, and that burden had seemingly doubled.

"We fought so hard for independence," she said, her words crackling through the headset. "Only to starve slowly in the shadow of our allies. Or kowtow to our enemies."

Yung-Gi remained silent. He didn't know what to make of the proposed treaty with the West. Pride and disgust melted together, burning hot in his belly at the thought of capitulating to either America or the UN. But his loyalty to Myo and her wider family transcended personal feelings, and they had a duty to feed their people. After all, a man could not fight on an empty belly. At least, not for long.

They had flown for over an hour before the village appeared on the horizon, a colorless sprawl of small, concrete buildings and cramped hanok-style houses. The big difference here compared to the areas they'd flown over was its greenery, its blossoms; this southwest corner of the country was the only region not suffering from blight or from the searing heat that had wrecked the rest of the country's harvest.

Yung-Gi checked his pistol as they began their descent. Myo had said she was optimistic for a swift diplomatic resolution to the standoff over the crop reserves, but Yung-Gi had to prepare for the worst. He'd been a soldier long enough to know that hope and optimism were the flimsiest of shields.

They put down on a flat, green field on the village's boundary and disembarked onto a dirt road. It was cooler here, almost comfortable. The six-strong security in plain civilian clothes were under orders to keep all weapons stowed on their backs and to paint on friendly faces throughout; only if Myo's life was in danger were they to engage in anything other than compassion and benevolence. Inside the village, a group of thin civilians watched their approach.

Myo Il-Song straightened her jacket and strode forward to meet them. Yung-Gi and the other guards fanned out, trying to look casual but remaining watchful beside her. A frail-looking man with a stringy beard stepped forward and bowed.

"Welcome, Comrade Myo. Thank you for coming." His words were deferential, but an undercurrent of suspicion underpinned his tone.

Myo inclined her head. "Thank you for receiving me, Comrade...?"

"Comrade Kwan," the man said. "Please, this way."

As the group strode into the central part of the village, Yung-Gi's hand never strayed far from his firearm. Dozens of eyes tracked their passage from shadowed doorways and narrow alleys, pitched downward to avoid insulting with direct stares. Market stalls stood empty but were in good repair, a fountain with an ornate surround had run dry, while other businesses—a garage, a café, a small supermarket—were active but empty as the owners and customers gathered to receive their guests. The tang of dried fish and fermented vegetables alternated with the ever-present stench of exhaust fumes.

Not an affluent village but getting by reasonably well. It was unfortunate that the heat had forced them into this desperate standoff, which they could not hope to win by force.

Myo's shoulders pulled back taut beneath her suit as she surveyed the gathered village leadership assembled on the steps of the squat administrative building. Yung-Gi counted at least thirty local officials, their expressions a delicate balance of deference and defiance.

"Steady," Myo murmured for Yung-Gi's ears alone. "Reason will prevail."

Yung-Gi acknowledged her, keenly aware of the rifles slung on the backs of their security personnel. A show of force, but one he hoped would prove unnecessary.

Hope...

They drew to a halt before the village leaders. Myo stepped forward, inclining her head in a carefully measured show of respect that avoided verging on supplication.

"Comrades," she said, "I am here in the spirit of unity. As loyal citizens of the Republic, we must find a path forward."

The villagers' backs were straight with stubborn pride as Myo accepted their invitation to sit at a table with four men who appeared to have been trusted to lead the negotiation. In years past, the village would have had no voice; soldiers with semiautomatic weapons would have jumped off the back of trucks and ransacked the prosperous village for its surplus, as was only fair and right. Yung-Gi knew that Myo wanted to do things differently. Just as he knew that if she failed, her younger male cousin would take matters into his own hands.

Yung-Gi stood close by as Myo engaged the local leadership in terse negotiations in the shadow of the administrative building, speaking across a wooden table placed there in full view of dozens of witnesses. He could not hear the business discussed, but he didn't need to; his senses remained attuned to the crowd's every shift and noise.

Most seemed to be simple farmers or laborers, their faces weathered by long days in the sun. They seemed to watch the proceedings with a sense of resignation. But as the talks dragged on, Yung-Gi felt the crowd's restlessness deepen.

Another tiny flash of movement caught his eye, and his hand twitched toward his gun. A young girl, around six or seven in a cute sundress, slipped between several adults' legs. She held a trio of faded pink flowers in her tiny, grubby hand, their petals ready to fall. Yung-Gi moved to stop her, by Myo told him to let her through. The child darted up to Myo, holding out her wilted offering.

"For you, Comrade Myo! My *eomma* says you are wiser than the men. You won't take everything from us."

Crouching down off her chair, Myo accepted the flowers with a smile that lit up her thoughtful dark eyes.

"Thank you, little comrade. Your *eomma* is very wise, too. I will do all I can to help your village."

The girl then reached into her pocket to pull out two braided strings, pink like the flowers, and shyly held one out to Yung-Gi.

"For you too, *ahjussi*. To keep you safe."

Yung-Gi hesitated before Myo raised her eyebrows his way. He accepted the small bracelet with a gruff nod of thanks. The girl flashed him a smile, then scampered back into the crowd.

"Now," Myo said calmly, the flowers still in hand, "let us find a solution. For all our children's sake."

By the time the negotiations began, Yung-Gi could feel the sweat trailing down his spine beneath his suit, but he maintained his unbending posture, directing his team with his eyes. The village elders remained an intimidating presence, but their lined faces had softened somewhat. Myo met their gazes respectfully but firmly as she laid out her final proposal.

The eldest of the village leaders, a stooped man with a face like a withered apple but clothes that were not as dirty as most of the watching civilians, stepped forward. He bowed deeply to Myo, his hands trembling slightly as he clasped them before him.

"Comrade Myo," he began, his voice a dry rasp. "We are loyal citizens of the Republic. We want only to serve our people. But our children are hungry. Our elders are weak. How can we give what little we have and hope to survive until winter?"

Myo's expression drifted to the flowers from the little girl, still in her hand. "I understand your fears, Comrade Kang. But I ask you to have faith. My father's treaty with the West will bring new resources. Your region, and the others who peacefully volunteer their excess yields, will be the first to reap the benefits. You have my word."

Yung-Gi could sense the villagers' uncertainty, an ingrained distrust of the enemy in the West warring with the prospect of concluding matters here peacefully. Not to mention prosperously.

The old man held Myo's gaze for a long moment, searching her face for any hint of deception. Finally, he bowed again, deeper than before.

"We will discuss your proposal, Comrade Myo. Please wait here while we confer."

As twelve of the leaders shuffled away to a nearby building —some unspoken hierarchy coming into play—Yung-Gi leaned in close to Myo's ear.

"Do you think they'll agree?" he asked.

Myo's lips thinned, her eyes distant. "The alternative would be terrible. For all of us."

Yung-Gi forced himself to breathe steadily, his expression neutral. The crowd milled restlessly in the heat, keeping their distance, wary of the armed men eyeballing them.

When the elders finally emerged from their impromptu council, Comrade Kang approached Myo, his steps heavy with the burden of his people's fate.

"Comrade Myo," he said formally, his voice carrying across the hushed square. "We accept your proposal. The harvest will be shared, as requested. But we request a formal declaration before we relinquish it, signed by our beloved president."

A sigh rippled through the crowd, the reaction difficult to read. Some relief, some resignation, some outright distrust.

Myo gave a shallow bow and shook the elder's hand.

"Thank you, Comrade Kang. Your trust will be rewarded. I will ensure that the president—"

The crack of a gunshot shattered the peace, a thunderclap echoing off the concrete walls. Yung-Gi drew his sidearm before the sound fully registered, moving on instinct honed by a lifetime of training, covering Myo as chaos erupted in the square. Panicked villagers screamed and scattered. The security team whipped the guns from their stowed position faster than seemed possible, folding stocks to their shoulders as they spread out.

Yung-Gi scanned the rooftops, the alleys, the windows and doorways, his heart pounding in his ears but his hand steady.

"There!" one of the other guards shouted, pointing at a figure bedded in behind a van with no wheels as panicked citizens zipped back and forth all around.

Yung-Gi aimed, finger on his trigger, ready to fire, but Myo's hand rested on his arm.

"No," she said, her voice steely calm. "Don't risk the innocents."

Another shot rang out, the bullet gouging a chunk out of the building by Myo's ear. Yung-Gi swore, torn between his duty and Myo's orders.

"Get her to safety!" he shouted at the other guards, moving toward the shooter, keeping himself dead center of the line between the danger and Myo. "I'll handle this."

More figures emerged from the shadows, eight, then ten young men in rags for clothing with wild eyes and outdated weapons. They formed a loose pincer around the square, cutting off escape.

This was no lone wolf attack. It was an ambush. And they were outnumbered.

"They are not with us!" cried one of the council leaders, lying on the floor rather than running. "Bandits! They want our crops as you do."

As the first of the rebels charged forward, Yung-Gi breathed a silent prayer for strength and took aim. It was going to be a bloodbath.

The flash of muzzle fire.

The acrid smell of gunpowder.

The racket of firearms discharging.

His men were trained professionals, selected from the Supreme Guard Command's elite protection unit, and they picked off the attackers as they spread in a ragged line. The rebels were young and had little skill in this incursion, but they made up for their shortcomings in ferocity.

Bullets zinged past Yung-Gi, one slug singeing his hair as he dragged Myo into the meager cover of a locked doorway. Splinters flew as the wood took a barrage of gunfire, but it gave him the seconds he needed.

"Stay down," he ordered Myo, folding her into a ball and using his body as a shield to cover her.

Yung-Gi risked a glance around the concrete wall. Even ten years ago, he might have spotted the first shooter. Twenty years ago, he would have ordered the helicopter with its armaments to circle the village, maybe raze one of the outbuildings to the ground with a hail of rockets, but that was bad optics—Myo wanted their trust, not their submission.

Two of his unit were already down, their bodies sprawled on the dusty ground along with several villagers, one of which was still moving, bloodied and moaning for help. Dozens of civilians had hidden, using market stalls, tables, and vehicles as cover, not risking a dash in the open. The rest of Yung-Gi's team was pinned down behind buildings, doorways, and the parched fountain.

New movement caught Yung-Gi's eye. A trio of gunmen was

circling around, trying to flank them, keeping out of range of the remaining protection detail. They carried crude explosives, likely acquired from raids on mining or quarrying sites. Fuses sparked like firecrackers.

Dynamite.

Yung-Gi had to end this—now.

"When I say run," he told Myo, "you run like hell for the helicopter. Don't look back."

Myo's mouth tightened, but Yung-Gi took off before she could object, firing as he went. Two rebels went down, their dynamite falling near one of Yung-Gi's men, who yanked out the fuse.

The third rebel let out a howl and charged at Yung-Gi. Yung-Gi dropped him with a single shot, but not before the lad managed to lob his bomb forward.

It arced through the air, tumbling end over end, the fuse fizzing and sparking close to the detonator. Too close to disarm, even if Yung-Gi leapt up and caught it. Age and direction meant it wasn't an option. The explosive spun through the air toward a group of villagers cowering by an upended market stall.

"Run, Myo!" he roared and threw himself toward the bomb, hoping forlornly that he could snap the fuse out in time.

He failed.

The explosion shook the earth. The searing heat, the percussive force, slammed into him like a giant fist. For a moment, everything was waves alternating numbness and pain, his vision whiting out as his body landed in a position it was not meant to assume.

Dazed, ears ringing, Yung-Gi struggled to push himself upright. A warm trickle of blood soaked his face. But he was alive.

Yung-Gi staggered to his feet. Smoke stung his eyes, copper and ash coated his tongue. The square was a tableau of destruction, the once-orderly rows of stalls reduced to splintered kindling, the windows shattered, and a small, scorched crater smoldered. But it was the bodies that turned his stomach. Not the rebels; he cared not a jot for them. A group of innocent villagers, limbs torn off, bodies limp. One man dragging himself along with one leg just a bloody stump, the other burned and blistered.

And there, crumpled like a broken doll amid the rubble, was a horrifying swath of pink. The little girl who had given him the bracelet stared sightlessly at the sky.

Yung-Gi screwed his eyes tight. Swayed on his feet. Grief threatened to tear from his throat, but he choked it down along with the rising bile.

He was a professional.

He tamped the emotion down ruthlessly; he couldn't afford to fall apart. Not when Myo still needed him.

Ignoring the protest of his battered body, Yung-Gi picked his way through the devastation, searching desperately for any sign of Myo. The smoke-filled air echoed with the moans of the wounded. But there was no sign of his principal.

She must have gotten away.

"Hold them off," he told the nearest security agent.

There were four left alive, able to fight. They acknowledged the order; they would hold off any remaining attackers. They would not shirk their task, even at the cost of their lives.

All men had families, after all.

Pushing on to the outskirts of the village, the ringing in Yung-Gi's ears had faded to a dull roar, like waves breaking on rocks. His legs were lead weights, but he forced himself onward.

As he stumbled past the final houses, slow figures caught his eye. He whirled around, gun ready, only to find himself aiming at a shell-shocked family, huddled together, the father holding his back to Yung-Gi—a voluntary human shield. Their faces were streaked with soot and tears, their eyes hollow.

For a moment, they just stared at each other, the villagers

and the blood-spattered soldier. Then, slowly, their expressions began to change.

This is your fault, their eyes seemed to say. *You brought this upon us.*

Backing away, Yung-Gi's heel caught on a rock, and he stumbled. The family came forward, the father spotting a chance to protect his family, picking up a length of wood as he surged forward.

Yung-Gi braced himself for the impact, refusing to shoot, accepting that he was guilty of bringing death to their doorstep.

"Enough!"

Myo stood close by, her hair disheveled and her clothes dusty. But alive. Mercifully alive. She supported a young woman who was sobbing uncontrollably, Myo's hand around her back, the girl's arm on her shoulder.

"Stand down," she said. "Please. This man is not your enemy."

The father hesitated, his anger and instinct to protect his family simmering.

"The enemy," she said, "is hunger. Desperation. It's what created the people who murdered your friends. We cannot let more children starve."

The man dropped the makeshift weapon and came slowly forward, neither cowed nor satisfied. He accepted the injured young woman from Myo, his nod promising to take care of her.

Yung-Gi struggled to his feet, wincing as his injuries made themselves known. For a moment, he and Myo just stared at each other, the weight of the day hanging over them.

Without a word, they made the rest of the journey to the waiting helicopter, where the four surviving bodyguards accompanied them, their faces grim and blood-spattered.

As the helicopter lifted into the air, Yung-Gi looked down at the village. From this perspective, it looked almost peaceful, the scars of violence hidden by distance.

He felt a touch on his arm and turned to find Myo watching him.

"This can't happen again," she said, her voice again distorted in his headset. "We can't let it."

Yung-Gi nodded. "Will it be enough? The treaty?"

Myo sighed, her gaze distant. "It has to be." Her hands still clutched the pink flowers from the dead little girl. "For my children. For all our children."

Yung-Gi reached out to hold her hand, completely against protocol, the first time he had ever made the gesture. She did not pull away as the braided pink bracelet hung from his wrist against hers.

He would do what needed to be done.

2

B oston, Massachusetts

WHILE THE PRICE tag of the twenty-five-year-old single malt attested to its pedigree, the promised "light, peaty notes" were much stronger than expected, filling Jason Trapp's throat with whisky-flavored ash.

The first time Trapp had drunk in Joshua Price's bar, he would have described it as a dive. He remembered nursing a beer at one in the afternoon, surrounded by worn-out American flags and military memorabilia adorning the walls.

Now almost five years later, amid the buzz of patrons drinking a little too much on a night closed to the public, the flags were bright, hung with care and stretched taut, as if standing to attention. Decommissioned handguns lived in illuminated glass cabinets alongside an arrangement of World War One medals and other military knickknacks. Last of all, an ancient M1903 rifle kept its vigil over the well-lit bar, mounted where all could admire it. The bullet scar on its varnished stock shone lighter than the rest, a reminder of how it had allegedly saved a soldier's life—none other than the grandfather to Joshua and his brother, Ryan.

Ryan Price.

Why his name stung as much today as it had when Trapp had delivered Ryan's money to Joshua, he couldn't say. He'd lost others close to him—friends, comrades, even his mother—but none of their deaths lingered the way Ryan's had. Perhaps it was what followed that had burrowed this grief deep in Trapp's psyche—the violence and tragedy of Black Monday. Or it could simply be that Trapp still blamed himself.

He sipped his peat-infused whisky, served neat.

People who proclaimed themselves whisky connoisseurs often advised drinking it with ice or to follow the Scots' way, adding a dribble of water to bring out the flavor. But Trapp liked his whisky how he liked it.

Which wasn't like this.

Tonight's commemoration honored the fifth year since Ryan had died, also serving as a pre-opening of Joshua's rebranded establishment. When Joshua had thanked Trapp earlier for making it all possible, Trapp had joked there were easier ways to launder his brother's money—accumulated as bug-out funds during Ryan's time in the CIA's covert action arm.

Now Joshua was waxing lyrical about the new wood he'd sourced for the bar itself, how the chairs were crafted locally— not in some sweatshop in a faraway land—and bragging that the only non-American products were the big screens angled so that you could see them from any seat in the place.

Trapp thought Ryan would have approved.

He was trying to kick back and enjoy himself tonight. Really. But there were too many strangers. Not that the bar was packed—just a few friends of Joshua's who had known Ryan as a civilian. Relaxed yet awkward, they were merry enough to join but not so far gone as to forget why they were here, their laughter coughed and swallowed as if this were a funeral.

Those patrons who had served were easy to differentiate, even the retired vets gone to seed. The difference was sometimes painted in the eyes, sometimes the shoulders, and almost always in the words they used. Trapp recognized most and could name a handful more, but he only counted two as friends: Lamar and Valerie Gilbaut, a husband and wife who'd met under less-than-romantic circumstances.

"Hey, you want another?" Lamar asked as he stood, scraping his $100 American-made chair back. "I'm liking this craft ale shit. Didn't think I would, but it ain't bad."

Trapp held his glass to the light, his mind swaying a fraction. "I'm good."

As Lamar departed, Valerie—who, like Joshua, didn't shorten her name—reached across and placed a hand on Trapp's wrist. "You don't *have* to drink it."

Trapp angled the glass. Joshua had assured him that the Edradour was the real deal, distilled in a peat-encased cask for that goddamn smoky finish. Trapp felt compelled to drink it with a smile and a grateful nod to the man who was, technically, his business partner. Even halfway through this double measure, his head thick with the effects of five prior smoke-free drinks, he was perusing the gleaming chrome bar for something less illustrious. A Macallan would satisfy him—expensive enough but smooth. Or maybe one of the Japanese brands—

A crash tensed Trapp's thigh muscles, ready to push him to his feet as he reached toward his jacket for a gun that wasn't there. A civilian friend of Joshua's had tripped and steadied himself on a table, sending several empty glasses to the floor.

Anyone watching Trapp would have seen a rugged, well-built man flinch at a loud noise, but in reality, he had already assessed the commotion as non-threatening. The spike of adrenaline that had activated his fight-or-flight response quickly dissipated, his heartrate never elevating more than a couple of beats past its resting state.

"Jumpy," Valerie commented.

"I didn't jump," Trapp said.

Valerie—herself a seasoned operator—nodded to his right hand, which had twitched to where a gun might have nestled on another night.

"I didn't jump," Trapp repeated.

"I've seen you watching," Valerie said with a wry smile.

"Calling me paranoid?"

"What would you call it?"

Trapp shrugged. "You're just jealous because you've lost your edge."

Valerie gasped in mock horror, one hand clutching imaginary pearls at her throat.

"What'd I miss?" Lamar asked as he returned with more ale for himself and Valerie.

Valerie gave a swoon and adopted an exaggerated Southern accent. "Why, this horrible man accused me of losing mah edge."

Lamar laughed. "We might've hung up a shingle back home, but we ain't chasing adulterers and insurance payouts, we're stopping white-hat cybercrime. Our shit is state of the art—"

"Honey," Valerie interrupted, back in her usual moderate Southern accent. "You've already made your sales pitch. I'm sure he's very proud. Aren't you, Jason?"

Trapp held his whisky up in a toast, said, "Absolutely," then tossed back the remainder, gulping it down like foul medicine.

He inched his chair out, checking for clear exits, for shifty movement, for eyes bearing down on him longer than a casual glance. It was only a second, probably less, but Lamar snagged on it.

"You're right, babe. Our edge is fine. But this guy, he's downright paranoid."

Trapp eased himself to his feet, returning Lamar's sass with a middle finger. "My paranoia saved my life more times than I can count. How many times did it save yours?"

Lamar rolled his eyes right back, fingers counting.

"Four," Trapp said. "It was four. In three missions. Don't—"

It wasn't clear to Trapp what drew his eye to the window, but it was enough to make him pause mid-sentence. Movement, or lack of it. There had been people passing to and fro all evening, this being a Saturday night in downtown Boston. There had even been folk trying the locked door, only to be turned away either by the handwritten sign that said *Private Function* or, if they were bloody-minded enough, by Joshua.

But this one was different. A man in a half-buttoned coat, face angled down under a baseball cap, his head turning as he walked. And it remained turned. Watching, not glancing.

Lamar said, "Hey, Earth to Trapp, where'd you go?"

Trapp willed his shoulders to relax and lifted his chin toward the pedestrian, who had almost completely passed by. Both Lamar and Valerie checked him out as he disappeared into the night.

"That guy?" Lamar asked. He'd had a half-second longer to see him than Valerie.

"I'm not sure he was drunk," Trapp said. "Gait was wobbly, but in a uniform manner, not a random stumble. Like bad acting."

"Gonna go interrogate him?" Valerie said.

Lamar laughed. "This ain't Fallujah, Jason, it's Boston. You're jittery, man." His amusement eased into a firm smile. "This is where you got involved in that terrorist shit, right? You maybe think *that's* got you chasing shadows?"

Trapp scanned the room again. Lamar was probably right.

Although neither he nor Valerie had gotten as good a look as Trapp had.

"Sure," Trapp said. "I'm just being paranoid."

He shifted to the bar, where it would be easier to watch passersby without being obvious. Joshua made a beeline for him in a true drunken stumble, rosy-faced glee, open arms as if greeting Trapp for the first time. He stopped short of embracing Trapp, reverting to a slap on the bicep.

"Ah, that Edradour's something else, right?"

"It's definitely something else," Trapp conceded.

"Want another? It's on the house. All on the house tonight!"

"A little rich. Too many'll spoil it for me."

Joshua nodded along, squinting. He came in close as if about to confide a secret. "This place... Ryan always made fun of me because I couldn't always afford a cleaner. Had to sometimes clean my own toilets. Like he never cleaned a toilet."

"Believe me," Trapp snorted. "We both did."

"Do you..." Joshua swallowed. "Do you think he would love this place? Or hate it? I mean... it's his money that paid for the renovation. It's like... his legacy..."

Trapp mirrored the bicep slap and was about to reassure Joshua that his brother would be proud of this bar when the doors rattled loud enough to hear over the music. Trapp tried to hold back his alert response, managed to keep his turn slow. No visible tension.

Joshua said, "Not another one" and hiked over, pointing at the sign.

"Closed," he said loudly enough to be heard through the glass. "We're closed for the night!"

It was him. The man who had passed by moments ago was back, gripping the handle and yanking at the door. The drunk man—or the man pretending to be drunk.

Coming up beside Joshua, Trapp hoped Lamar and Valerie were right.

The man at the door either hadn't heard Joshua or was ignoring him. Head down, fingers curled, he rocked the doors loudly enough to draw everyone's attention and quiet the conversations around the bar. Only the soft rock playlist strummed from the sound system.

Joshua rapped on the glass and the rattling halted. The man froze. Looked up slowly.

He might have been mid-twenties or early-thirties, looked Chinese or Korean. His face was thin, eyes dark, with a wispy moustache and goatee that didn't quite join up and an oddly-square forehead that left a gap between his skin and the white baseball cap. He took a half-step back, eyes roving the interior. They fell on Trapp and lingered, the man's body stiffening momentarily.

"Hey, asshole!" Joshua called, rapping on the glass again and pointing at the *Private Function* sign. "Can't you read?"

The slightly too-loud music sounded even louder without the cushion of human voices. So when one male voice piped up, it was even harsher. "Hey, he probably don't read English. Got lost. Give him directions to Chinatown, he'll be fine."

Trapp didn't know the man who'd spoken, one of the civilian friends-and-family. Fat, boisterous, with a girlfriend punching a few shades of beautiful above his fighting weight. She seemed to be squirming a bit. Trapp figured that what the man said might be considered racist, although no one was calling him on it. Perhaps the tension Trapp was feeling had spread.

The man on the other side of the door swayed, squinted at the sign, and made an 'Oh' face before straightening his back, pulling the top part of his coat across himself, and turning around. He hunched his neck down as if bracing against rain and stepped out into the street, checking both ways before trotting away.

"Asshole," Joshua said again.

Trapp watched the last part of the street that the man had occupied before vanishing. He had eyeballed Joshua as he'd checked the room. But he'd definitely stalled on Trapp.

It was true what Lamar had said about the proximity of the terror attacks almost five years earlier. This place was ground zero for Trapp. Months after Ryan had been killed, after Trapp faked his own death and went into hiding, an attempted coup had started with attacks across the continental United States, including a mass shooting right here in Boston. Trapp had run the two blocks to the TD Garden Stadium and taken out the perpetrators himself. Too late for too many, but he had saved lives.

That day was fresh in his mind. As fresh as yesterday. As fresh as his best friend dying because he and Trapp had gotten too close to those responsible...

"Hey, man." Lamar slipped an arm over Trapp's shoulder and squeezed. "That your buddy again?"

"Yeah," Trapp said.

"Seemed weird. Bad vibes."

Trapp stepped away, fully turned his back to the door for the first time that night, and looked at his former comrade. He tried to shake off the tension and raised an eyebrow. "Since when do you use words like 'vibes'?"

"We ain't in the field."

"It's a party," Valerie finished for her husband, presenting Trapp with a fresh whisky.

"Damn straight," Joshua said, his alcohol-flushed cheeks rising. "Let me grab one of those, and I'll be right back."

He headed for the bar, reaching up to one of the high bottles.

Trapp sniffed his whisky. Fragrant, pure, none of the peat or smoke that he just couldn't get his palate to warm to. Maybe he should try diluting the smoky malt with a few drops of water, see if it changed his mind.

"What do you think Ryan would make of this?" Trapp asked, gesturing toward the largest cluster of celebrants.

"He'd be embarrassed," Lamar answered. "But he'd do the same for us."

"Too right," Valerie said. "You'd do this for me, wouldn't you, babe?"

"Of course." Lamar pulled his wife to him and kissed her full on the lips. "I'd fill this place to the roof, and the music'd be better, and... don't hate me, but it probably wouldn't be a free bar."

"I don't want you spending all that money I left you on strangers anyway." Valerie returned the kiss with interest.

"Jesus," Trapp muttered, hoping they would hear.

They broke the embrace and faced him.

"Now who's jealous?" Valerie asked.

"More like nauseous," Trapp joked.

"Fuck you." Lamar clinked his glass off Trapp's, and both drank.

As Joshua returned, Trapp took a breath. "Listen, I know Ryan would be laughing his ass off, seeing us all being emotional about losing him and me drinking way more than usual..."

"Because you're soooo emotional," Valerie said with a smirk.

"If something happens to me," Trapp continued, "just don't make a big deal, okay? Raise a glass, if you want. I'll have my name on a wall, and that's enough."

Joshua blinked as if bewildered. "Hell, no, Jason, you're getting the full treatment!"

"Big ol' party," Lamar said.

"Gonna need a goddamn stadium for the memorial we're gonna throw your dead ass," Valerie added.

The laughs died suddenly. Trapp read their looks as curious

rather than worried, but then Lamar's brow furrowed, quickly followed by Valerie's.

"Not this asshole again," Joshua said. "I'm getting my bat."

As Trapp pivoted, Lamar took a huge step to the right, the sort of dodge that a football player makes when dummying a run. Only this step threw his wife to the side before he lurched back in to shove Trapp. But Trapp's instinct was to fend off any sort of assault, from friend or foe, so he resisted the push, turning 180 degrees and coming face to face with the man who'd tried to gain entry moments ago.

All pretense of inebriation or dumb confusion was gone as the man strode toward the door, a gun in his raised hand. Trapp had just enough time to register it as a Glock before the man opened fire one-handed.

3

A lightning strike of lead discharged into the bar, shattering the glass in the door before thumping into the flesh and wood behind without distinction.

Even as Trapp ducked aside, Valerie scrambled up off the floor and barreled into him and Lamar, tackling both men to the ground like a linebacker's riposte to her husband's quarterback move. They landed in a heap on shattered shards as the crowd around them took a further second to register what was happening. More glass rained down under the barrage, and the bar's occupants surged backward as one, flinching away from the incoming fire.

Six shots fired.

Trapp squirmed free from the weight of his two friends. He rolled backward first, kicking over a table more to obstruct the gunman's vision than for cover, then saw that Lamar had done the same.

Trapp crawled to peek out as shots seven, eight, and nine cracked from a weapon that bucked and flailed with each one-handed shot. The man's arm swung side to side with the recoil, spraying the bar with bullets in the least efficient way possible.

It was difficult enough to aim a .22 with one hand, let alone a .40 caliber piece of hardware like that. Too many movies or rap videos, perhaps, certainly no formal training.

After another two shots, the man paused.

Eleven bullets down.

There was blood on the floor, screaming and crying from those who couldn't flee, and the music was still playing—Whitesnake, Trapp thought.

Joshua lay splayed on the ground and made no attempt to hide, meaning he'd been hit. How badly, Trapp couldn't see, just the creeping inkblot of blood on his back.

First Ryan, and now he'd failed to see the threat to his brother in time.

No. He couldn't think about that right now. He couldn't reach Joshua to assess the damage. Had no idea if he was out from the shock or dying.

Get your head in the game. Do some good.

One shooter. Ill-disciplined, but ready to kill. A jihadi, or some other warped piece of shit who hated America enough to target service personnel or a bar full of flags and Army memorabilia.

Not an organized attack. But driven. A need to kill.

Trapp looked to Lamar and Valerie for backup, but they were wounded too—Lamar clutched his upper arm with one palm while the other pressed down on his wife's thigh. Valerie grunted and pushed hard with both hands on a hole in her abdomen. Blood sluiced over her fingers faster than she could stem it.

Trapp was unhurt. And since he was unhurt, he could deal out plenty of pain in return.

About ten feet between him and the shooter.

He just needed to close the gap without getting shot.

Another shot, and a former soldier who'd tried to rush the gunman fell—diving for cover or hit, Trapp couldn't tell.

He'd run into gunfire with a singlemindedness that few possessed.

Trapp understood it because he'd lived it more times than he could count. And now a bar full of people he barely knew were relying on his ability to do what most men could not.

Trapp positioned one foot square on the floor.

Valerie saw what he was planning and minutely shook her head. But Trapp couldn't stand by and wait for the cops to arrive or for the shooter's magazine to run empty. He still wasn't sure which model of Glock it was. Twelve bullets down, he might be out or he might be—

Bam!

Thirteen bullets down, meaning the magazine was either fifteen, seventeen, or twenty-two strong. Even if it were fifteen, two more bullets might cost two more lives. Trapp couldn't wait.

He lifted the heavy table like a shield and sprinted two steps before flinging it to where he'd last seen the gunman. A fourteenth shot rang out, splintering a hole through the tabletop to Trapp's left.

The furniture hit the doorframe, dropping to the ground as Trapp darted right. He gambled that the guy would need an extra split-second to readjust.

The shooter snapped his face toward him, about to swing the gun around when Trapp grabbed a chair and threw it. Ducking, the man stumbled backward, glanced up and down the street, then ran.

Fifteen bullets, Trapp guessed.

He looked back at his friends right as Lamar cried out, "Go get that fucker."

The shooter had less than five seconds' head start, and he was no professional operator.

Trapp took off after him, confident he'd catch up in no time. What he'd do to him when he got hold of him was something he hadn't decided yet.

But it wasn't going to be pleasant.

4

Trapp's head swam as his feet pounded the sidewalk, the cool night air pushing back the booze and shocking him into clarity.

He angled his weight forward, arms pumping, focused only on catching the man who had just turned a celebration into a bloodbath. He might have lost a yard of pace over the years, but he was still far superior to the average Joe, even when he had to squint through an alcoholic haze to zero in on his target.

The man's white baseball cap bobbed twenty yards ahead, weaving through the sparse late-night crowd—a couple of drunk soccer fans celebrating a win, several separate couples littering the escape route, a group of three suited bro-types who cried a macho "Hey, asshole!" as the gunman shouldered through them.

Startled pedestrians jumped out of the way as Trapp barreled past, his eyes locked on his target. The bro-types stepped sharply aside and swallowed their heckles.

The fleeing man darted into an alley, and Trapp paused at the edge, his senses on high alert. Vision clearing, he scanned the narrow channel, lit in brilliant white on the right, draped in darkness on the left. He noted potential cover and escape routes: dumpsters, shadowed doorways, a pile of plastic boxes.

The alley was open-ended, and the road beyond lay fifty yards away, but the shooter hadn't taken that option. He had hidden. Which meant he was planning to act against Trapp before fleeing into the night.

The distant wail of sirens reminded him that law enforcement would arrive soon. They'd want answers, too. But they'd be trigger-happy after seeing the carnage, full of adrenaline, eager to make a name for themselves as the hero cop who took down an active shooter. If they succeeded, they'd never need to buy another round in this town.

But Trapp needed the shooter alive.

He moved silently, listening for movement. The sprint had taken more out of him than it would have five years ago, but he wasn't yet sweating, let alone breathing hard.

Plenty left in the tank.

The scuff of a shoe on concrete.

There, behind that dumpster on the darker side of the alley.

Trapp's boots were not exactly combat grade, but they made no sound as he progressed. *Heel to toe... Heel to toe...* The harsh overhead lamp cast ice-white glare all around, spiking a throwing star of shadows in six different directions, longer on his left than on his right.

As he neared the dumpster, Trapp calculated that one of his shadows would signpost his arrival before he got close enough to grab the man hiding there.

He froze three feet from the dumpster. No bags piled outside it, so it probably wasn't full. Three wheels sat firmly on concrete, one at the front hovering a few inches over the uneven ground. And an armed man who wished Trapp harm lay in wait on the opposite side.

The sirens had stopped, but he could hear voices. Onlookers—confused, excited, probably TikToking the event live. The cops had sped to the bar in mere minutes. A few more seconds and witnesses would be waving them in this direction.

He thought about calling, "It's over" in his calmest, most authoritative voice, but if this was some gangbanger, high on drugs or angry at the world and determined to pass some initiation ritual, the guy might panic and rush out firing. And Trapp, drunk and a tad slower than optimal, might not evade death a second time that night.

But it was no choice at all, not really.

Trapp charged and shoved at the dumpster, which jumped thanks to that one off-kilter wheel. A thump told Trapp it had hit its target. Without breaking stride, he leapt around the side and yanked the shooter out with his right hand as he swept his left toward the man's trailing arm, which he'd expected to end with a gun.

His first mistake.

The hand was empty.

Instead, the Glock was firmly in the man's left. His eyes bugged wide, and he cried out in shock, but Trapp's attack hadn't disarmed him.

The man dropped sharply, weakening Trapp's grip on his coat, then drove hard knuckles into Trapp's wrist, breaking the hold entirely. The gunman dropped and rolled, sprang to his feet, and quickly found his bearings.

Too fast for Trapp to rush him.

Yet he didn't run. He just stood there—shoulders back, chin high, the Glock trembling in his outstretched hand.

Definitely a hired gun, way out of his depth.

"Stay back!" the guy shouted, his voice cracking. Little trace of a foreign influence, just a stilted non-specific American accent. "I'll shoot!"

Trapp held up his hands, keeping his tone even. "Think about this. You've fired, what, fourteen rounds? That Glock carries fifteen in the mag, and you didn't have time to reload.

The way your hand's shaking, are you sure you can make the shot? Because you better be. I won't give you a chance to reload."

The shooter's eyes flicked to his gun and back to Trapp. "Enough for one guy."

"Maybe. But then what? You're alone, no backup. The cops will be here any second." Trapp looked around as if the boys in blue might rappel from a nearby rooftop at any second. "I know you're willing to kill. Maybe you have already. But I'm guessing that someone else gave you that gun. You're not that familiar with it, or you'd have been more accurate in the attack on the bar. I just need to know one thing before you pull that trigger."

The gunman swallowed, his head moving in micro-twitches as he frantically checked for approaching cops.

From a couple feet away, even the most inept marksman couldn't fail to hit some part of Trapp. But this man continued holding the gun one-handed, like a rapper in a music video. His arm wavered, the hunk of metal tiring his muscles. That gave Trapp a fraction of a second advantage, perhaps as much as a half-second, the fatigue making it more difficult to apply the necessary 5.5 pounds of pressure needed to depress the Glock's trigger mechanism. Enough of the guy's arm was visible to reveal that the tendons in his forearm were not yet tensed for firing—he was fighting the gun's weight more than prepping to shoot. Additionally, he was aiming at Trapp's head, much smaller than his center mass, which made for a trickier target. Potentially another quarter-second advantage.

"You're clearly no jihadi," Trapp said. "It doesn't feel personal, either. So who hired you?"

The shooter's hand wavered again, three fingers and his thumb tightening on the grip, but the trigger finger remained looped in the guard.

"Who was the target?" Trapp pressed. "Was it me? Joshua?"

Trapp readied himself to move at the first change in the gun-hand's dynamic.

Duck, tackle him, knock him out, and drag him somewhere more private.

"I can't..." the man said. "They'll kill me..."

"I can protect you," Trapp said, inching closer. "Help you cut a deal. But you've got to put the gun down."

For a moment, it seemed like the shooter might comply. His arm began to lower, his grip on the Glock loosening.

Trapp transferred his weight to the balls of his feet, then twisted ever so slightly, ever so slowly, his toes pointed forward. If the arm lowered a few more degrees, he could attack the guy safely.

But then a police siren whooped.

The shooter's eyes snapped wide again, wild and desperate. He raised the gun, finger on the trigger.

Trapp launched down and to the side, swiping the gun-arm, expecting a discharge but hearing only the strangled mewling of a terrified kid. Instead of twisting for a shot at Trapp, the gunman pulled himself away. Trapp held on to his coat collar, revealing the tail of an intricate tattoo curling up from the man's back. As he reached for the throat, ready to apply a chokehold, Trapp's inebriation must have slowed his usual lightning-fast calculations. He got his forearm around the man's neck, but his enemy did something unexpected.

Perhaps sensing that Trapp's guard-hand would intercept the gun, the gunman pressed the barrel to his own chest, holding it in two hands for the first time with both thumbs on the trigger. No doubt about the direction of pressure, and way more than the required 5.5 pounds.

Trapp pushed him away a half-second before the gun went off. A chunk of flesh and bone and a spray of blood burst from the shooter's back, painting the alleyway—and Trapp—in red mist.

That half-second, the tiniest of margins, had saved him.

5

There was blood on his face, warm and tacky when his fingertips brushed it. His pulse hammered in his head. Trapp breathed in for six seconds and controlled the out-breath for ten more to regulate his pulse, then checked himself for damage. Finding none, he knelt beside the man and searched his pockets. A dead body was nothing new, and although he'd have preferred to question the guy, there might still be something useful on his corpse.

Sadly, he found nothing.

He pulled the man's collar wider to see his tattoo better. Not a snake but a dragon, a Chinese-style creature full of color and detail. Truly a work of art.

Triads?

Did Boston even *have* a Triad problem?

Trapp turned him over, saw that the gun had jammed open after firing the final round. Then he took in the man's face. Tried committing it to memory in case he needed it later.

Movement caught Trapp's eye and he raised his hands, anticipating the cops' arrival. Sure enough, the command "Freeze!" accompanied a clatter of approaching feet, and two uniformed officers dashed forward in standard shooting positions.

No point insisting, *It's not what it looks like.*

Trapp just said, "I'm unarmed. Give me instructions and I'll follow them."

Same as he had five years earlier, not two hundred yards from this spot on the devastating day that would become known as Black Monday, Trapp lay face down as a police officer cuffed his hands behind him. Now, like then, he offered no objection, only this time he knew he would have someone on his side to vouch for him.

The cops—one half his age who went by Morales, and his more experienced partner, Jameson—took no chances. Jameson covered Trapp while Morales cuffed him, planting a knee in his back as an added precaution. He couldn't blame them. They'd been called to a shooting, pursued a suspect, and found Trapp with a dead body, spattered with blood.

Once Trapp was secure, Jameson kept the gun trained on him from a sensible distance while Morales checked that the gunman was as dead as he looked, then called the body in. Within seconds, the alleyway was teeming with cops, at least six that Trapp could count from his face-down position. Three of them asked the same question: *Anyone else?*

"Wits said it was one guy," Jameson answered in a local Bostonian drawl. "Can't be sure if it's this guy or his dead buddy there."

"It wasn't me." Trapp figured he was no threat, so lifting his head from the damp concrete and speaking up should no longer spark automatic aggression from his captors. "I was a guest at the bar. I chased him."

"And shot him?"

"He shot himself."

"Yeah, GSR'll confirm. In the meantime, keep your hands where they are."

GSR. Gun shot residue. The pattern would expand over the victim's—no, not *victim*—*killer's* hands, a test that should exonerate Trapp in a matter of hours.

Killer.

"Can I ask you something, please?" Adding *please*, good manners, kept any sense of authority or command out of his voice.

"You can ask," Jameson said, waving a couple of the younger cops away to secure the scene.

"Is anyone dead? Back at the bar, I mean."

Dead people he didn't know were still dead people, innocents who hadn't deserved what happened. Dead people he *did* know—and Valerie's wound had looked pretty bad—always hit him in the chest like a concussion grenade. Should that make a difference in what happened next?

It shouldn't, but it probably would.

Jameson glanced at Morales, who'd rejoined him. The pair hoisted Trapp to his feet by hooking their arms under his shoulders.

"Two fatalities," Jameson said.

Morales nodded grimly. "Multiple GSWs, so it might go up."

"IDs on the dead yet?" Trapp asked.

Jameson led the way to their car, guiding Trapp on his right while Morales stayed on his left. "Let's get you processed, and we'll find out what we can. If you're on the up and up."

WHILE TRAPP FOUGHT the urge to pull at the cold, hard cuffs in the back of a cop car that smelled vaguely of vomit fighting valiantly against the odor of disinfectant, he steeled himself for the prospect of losing another friend. Valerie had lost a lot of blood, and Joshua hadn't been moving. Lamar's wound didn't look fatal, but if it had nicked an artery, he might not have made it.

At the station, they booked him quickly, and forensic technicians took his clothes and sequestered them in evidence bags, having furnished him with police training sweats. They swabbed his hand for GSR and samples of blood, then logged his fingerprints, which the CIA would ensure disappeared from the system before the sun came up. Finally, they transferred him to a cell populated with three meek, depressed-looking drunks and a tweaker coming down from his high. Trapp lay on a bench on his back and tried not to pre-empt his next move. Planning with an incomplete picture was a waste of time.

Hours passed, the fluorescent lights buzzing overhead. Adrenaline had long since faded, replaced by a dull ache in his head that he attributed to equal parts booze and regret at failing to capture the killer alive. Usually, he could block out the noise and fall into a deep sleep to replenish his mind and body. Tonight, he lay there reliving the shooting, the glass, the splinters, the bodies falling.

Joshua hit, not fatally but with a head injury from when he'd fallen. Which *could* be deadly too, of course. Valerie, Lamar, and the former soldier who had charged like a Lightning Brigade cavalryman. Had he been so drunk he'd miscalculated, or was he diverting the gunman's attention from a loved one?

The cell door clanged, and Trapp propped himself up on his elbows to see Officers Jameson and Morales.

"Mr. Trapp," Jameson said. "Ready for your phone call?"

"Great." Trapp swung his legs to the side to sit up, stretching his stiff limbs. "Long time coming."

"It's a big scene. Lots of resources. But it's clear you weren't the shooter. Detectives and science geeks say it *looks* like the guy killed himself. Had to confirm before cuttin' you loose, though."

They led Trapp to a small enclave with a phone on the wall. He dialed the personal number for Mike Mitchell. His superior at the CIA answered on the second ring.

"Jason," he said. "I heard what happened. Are you all right?"

"I'm fine. A little banged up. But no one's telling me anything. Valerie, Lamar, Joshua...."

"Alive. Lamar and Joshua are taken care of—minor surgery for them in the morning, like the other five shot in non-vital areas. Valerie's still in the OR, but prognosis is she'll live. Lost a lot of blood, but it was a through-and-through. Steel jackets."

A flood of relief passed through Trapp, like fluid draining from a pierced lung. Police normally used softer bullets that mushroomed for maximum stopping power, but steel jackets didn't deform as much, so at close range, they were less prone to spiral through flesh and tear up organs. "Still two dead?"

"Gordon Trent, a civilian near as I can tell. And Sam Carter, former Marine, served with Ryan briefly in—"

"Fallujah, yeah, I thought I knew the face. I was quarter-backing that one so never met the guy. I think he was a minor investor in the bar."

"And you caught up with the shooter? He say anything before you..." Mike let the implication trail off.

"I didn't. He did it himself. Said 'they' would kill him if he talked. I think he was part of some gang. He had this tat, real intricate, like a—"

"Listen, you're a witness at this stage, nothing more. Locals can handle it. Feds will send someone to mop up—active shooters are their wheelhouse. And if there's a terrorist link, Homeland will step in."

"This wasn't terrorism, Mike. I've dealt with enough true believers. This shooter was scared, like he was in over his head. And he had a plan, an escape route. This was no jihadi or what-ever. Too disorganized. I think it was a hit."

"If it was, shouldn't it have been more organized?"

Trapp saw the contradiction, but nothing was black and white here. "Gangs *can* be professional. Bigger, nastier ones like MS13 and Mexican cartels sometimes bring in pros to train their foot soldiers. This hitman, if that's what he was, he wasn't trained. If someone hired local assholes to do what they thought was an easy job and they sent some kid as his initiation..." Trapp's turn to let the sentence hang.

"Be that as it may, a mass shooting is a mass shooting. It's the FBI's jurisdiction and a local matter until they arrive. Throw a gang tat into the mix and it's doubly so."

"I need to make sure—"

"You need to rest up. You will take a step back and keep a low profile. The admin on getting you out of that place is a forest. Chopping it back gets expensive. Clear?"

Trapp's free hand clenched into a fist. He wanted to make Mike understand that something felt off, but he couldn't afford to alienate one of the few people who still had his back.

"Yeah, okay. Thanks, Mike."

"I know your friends were hurt, and I know how difficult it is to believe other people are good at their jobs too. But trust the system, just this once."

"I get it. I'll let the locals do their job."

Trapp hung up the phone, frustration coiling in his gut. He turned to find Officer Jameson a respectful distance away, nursing a coffee.

Trapp stepped forward. "Did you see the tattoo?"

Jameson raised an eyebrow. Sipped his coffee. "On the dead guy? Yeah, sure."

"It mean anything to you? A Chinese dragon? Intricate design?"

"Yeah, that's Triad ink, man. Guess the owners owed protection money."

"An hour's walk from Chinatown?"

Jameson shrugged. "Maybe they expanded. Or someone outsourced. Who knows?"

It made sense, in a way. The shooter's ethnicity, his youth, his inexperience with the gun, the way he seemed more scared than zealous.

Trapp thought again about the way the man had stilled when his gaze had stopped on him.

He didn't know what this was, but it wasn't about protection money.

Before he could ponder further, an overweight plainclothes detective came by and said, "Mr. Trapp, you're free to go."

"Already?" Jameson said.

"Friends in high places. Or low ones. Either way, we'll be in touch if we have more questions."

6

C hinese Embassy, Washington, DC

SOME MEN SHOULD BE AVOIDED *at all costs.* A mother's advice five short years and yet a lifetime ago.

Diplomatic attaché Fang Chen was not yet sure what type of man Li Chao was. As he worked through his forms in the Chinese embassy's smallest gymnasium, he moved with the precision of a machine. A flowing, double-handed blocking technique snapped into a sharp open-hand strike before he planted one foot behind the other and twisted in place to face the opposite direction. Sweeping both arms in an arc, he repeated the two-handed block in a mirror of the first, then jabbed forward with an open fist.

She recognized *Biu Jee,* a wing chun form, or a version of it. Her uncle, Ang-Lo, had been a well-regarded *sifu,* or teacher, back in her hometown, before he was arrested for hosting a class that did not adhere to the pandemic restrictions of the day. He was still in prison. Or dead. No one knew for sure. No one talked about him anymore.

Fingertips brushing her slender belt buckle—a gift from her mother, *for luck*—Fang tucked away thoughts of home, concentrating instead on the man before her, dressed in loose tracksuit bottoms and a white vest, his muscles tensing like steel cables powering a device designed for the most elegant violence a human could inflict. Violence was highlighted by the scars pocking his visible skin: a six-inch slash on his left bicep, a burn the size of a drink coaster on his shoulder that extended into his vest, two star-shaped blemishes marking his upper chest that could only have been bullet wounds, and a thin line of scar tissue slicing through his left eyebrow. He appeared to be in his early forties, perhaps a shade older, given the intensity of his eyes and graying at the temples, but the rest of him could have shamed an Olympic athlete.

Fang had accompanied her boss, Ambassador Wen Qiang, to greet Li Chao three days earlier on the tarmac as he stepped straight off a Gulfstream G550. Ambassador Wen and Li Chao had bowed to one another, an oddly formal gesture of respect between two men. They shook hands and spoke briefly out of Fang's earshot before Chao was whisked away in a diplomatic limousine.

She and Ambassador Wen had followed in their own limo, a silence filling the interior that carried an almost physical weight. Having closely assisted the ambassador for eighteen months, Fang knew when to inquire about Wen's pensive expressions and when to leave him be.

It seemed Li Chao had given the ambassador plenty to think about.

Now Fang hesitated at the gym's entrance, a sleek, soft-touch satellite phone clutched in her hand. Muted. It was her job to answer when it rang and to deliver it immediately upon utterance of the word *Chaffinch*. But now, seeing Mr. Li engrossed in his training, she felt like an intruder.

She wondered if he ever engaged in more mundane activities—reading a book, watching television, or taking a leisurely stroll while listening to music. But as she watched him, she realized that this was his life. His body was a finely-honed instrument, always ready to be called upon like a warrior monk, although she doubted this man ascribed to anything more holy than the Chinese Communist Party.

As if sensing her presence, Chao paused, one leg bent, his foot pressed against the opposite thigh. He lowered the foot and turned to face her. A flush crept up her neck, embarrassed at being caught staring.

"Miss Chen," Chao greeted her. "Is that for me?"

Fang stepped forward, holding out the device. "Your satellite phone, Mr. Li. I apologize for the interruption. It rang while I was eating breakfast, and you said to answer. The... person said it was urgent."

Only not a person. A robot. Or a person with a robotic voice, disguised via software.

"You like this form?" Chao asked.

"It is beautiful." His silence prompted her to articulate a more complete answer, and she wondered if perhaps he knew about her uncle's dishonor. She raised her chin and met his eye. "White Crane?"

"Very good. You train?"

"When I was a little girl, I trained in Wushu four times a week. Once my academic gifts became apparent, I was required to focus my study in other areas. I never learned White Crane or Wing Chun, but I recognize the..." She mimed the elaborate flowing arms that looked to untrained eyes like a wistful dance.

"The beauty of the form conceals its true purpose. Diplomacy?"

"I'm sorry?"

"Your studies," Chao said. "Diplomacy?"

"World politics, psychology, and secretarial skills."

"Impressive. Almost as if your life was mapped out for you."

Fang had nothing to say on that matter. She held out the phone, reverting to the role she was proud to play. "I didn't like to disturb you, Mr. Li. I know you value your privacy."

Chao accepted the device, his fingers brushing hers. Although not a sensual gesture, it sent a ripple up her arm. The man's fingertips felt tougher than they appeared, almost like animal hide.

"On the contrary, Miss Chen. I value your observational skills. I suspect you absorb a great deal more in your position here at the embassy than even the ambassador appreciates."

Fang's heart stuttered, or felt like it did. "I assure you, Mr. Li, I have the utmost respect for you and for Ambassador Wen. I would never—"

"Please." Chao held up a hand. "I meant it as a compliment. Hidden depths are an asset in our line of work."

Our line of work? Fang failed to see any similarity between her duties and... the things Li Chao was plainly capable of.

Before Fang could respond, Chao raised the phone to his ear, unmuted it, and said, "Bluebird."

He listened, his expression hardening. Fang strained to hear, chiding herself for even attempting to eavesdrop, but could only make out Chao's responses.

"And Trapp? Yes, I see. Perhaps it's for the best. I might still be able to use him. I will call on you again if required."

Chao ended the call and turned to Fang, his hard expression having turned thoughtful.

"It seems a person of interest to the state survived an unfortunate incident in Boston. No doubt he'll start digging. I need to accelerate my timeline."

Fang knew nothing of this man's business in the United States, although she could not help overhearing certain snippets. There were the news reports of a mass shooting in Boston, the chaos and bloodshed. But she had not connected the incident to their guest until now. The thought of being involved, even tangentially, made her look away.

Men to be avoided at all costs...

Chao seemed to sense her unease. "Don't worry, Miss Chen. Please, come with me."

He strode out of the gymnasium. Fang hurried to keep pace. This time, Chao didn't change out of his workout clothes, just donned his zip top as they wound their way through the wide corridors and up staircases to Ambassador Wen's office. More like a suite of workstations, really, ninety percent of them manned at any one time by people who knew better than to glance up in curiosity.

They found Wen deep in conversation with a handsome woman of about fifty in a plush, glass-walled office reserved for guests of a sensitive nature. The two shared tea at a low table covered with colored papers arranged in an ordered manner.

Chao knocked and entered without waiting. The woman looked affronted, her scowl aimed first at Chao, then Wen.

Chao said, "Ambassador Wen, I apologize for the intrusion." He addressed the woman. "I know the security of the staff residence is important, Ms. Liu, but this cannot wait."

"Then you know who I am." Shay Liu served as manager of security personnel at the Chinese Embassy's residential building. She made no move to leave, silently communicating her understanding of the room's status hierarchy.

Chao switched his attention to Ambassador Wen.

The ambassador sighed minutely. "I am sorry; this is a covert security matter of national importance."

Covert security matter.

It took a moment to register, but the ambiguous phrase burrowed into the woman and took root, sprouting understanding. She nodded sagely and said, "I will contact your assistant to rearrange."

"Respectfully," Chao said, "I need only two minutes."

Liu rose, gathered her bag, checked that something was still in there—cigarettes, probably; Fang knew she was a liberal smoker—then exited with a steely glance at Fang, as if this were her fault.

Wen stood after the door closed behind the woman. "Do you know what an awkward position this puts me in? I was promised your presence here would not impact my day-to-day business. Shay Liu—"

"Shay Liu will understand that certain matters are of more significance than delivering her reports on the inappropriate socializing of embassy staff."

Receiving only a faint nod in reply, Chao gestured to the glass wall. "If you would be so kind?"

Fang wondered if she should have left with Liu, but neither man had explicitly dismissed her.

Wen reached under the desk and pressed a button. All four glass walls frosted over so no one could see in and, like all windows facing the outside—where America and its agents lurked—the internal glass vibrated with white noise to prevent the use of radar mics or other bugs, even inside the building. Fang vaguely recalled learning in a security briefing that the noise was patterned on the background hum of the universe, making it impossible to defeat no matter the power of the NSA supercomputer dedicated to the task.

"Your business went well?" Wen asked.

"Not quite." Chao smiled. "It is almost as if the assassin they sent wasn't up to the job."

"Your... *sponsors*... specifically said that you might indulge a brief item of personal business before committing to matters of state. If you have failed in that, you must let it go."

"Those are my orders. But my business with Trapp will not

distract from my mission. It may even enhance it. Or are we to have a problem?"

The ambassador dropped his eyes to his desk. "There will be no problem as long as you do not act in a way that forces me to grovel to the president of this country. What do you need that is so urgent?"

"Might I borrow Miss Chen for a small errand?"

Wen frowned, clearly displeased. "She is just a secretary. I can have anyone—"

"I trust her. This is a minor task, but it is vital if we are to meet the deadline."

Fang's pulse sped up. She forced her breath to remain shallow. "Mr. Li, if this is in any way illegal, I must object. I can't risk deportation. There are people who would—"

Chao placed a reassuring hand on her shoulder. "Miss Chen, your actions will be entirely lawful. But the benefit to our nation will be immeasurable."

Ambassador Wen sighed, waving a hand in acquiescence. "Miss Chen, assist Mr. Li with whatever he requires."

Fang swallowed hard, her mouth suddenly dry. With the ambassador granting permission, she had no choice.

Chao smiled again, this time with what Fang perceived as a predatory glint. "Excellent. Let us get started."

As Fang followed him out, she wondered again about Li Chao, a man who flew on corporate jets, enjoyed diplomatic immunity, rated an elite-level security detail, and could order an ambassador to grant his assistant the night off.

She did not know who he was, and she wondered if she would regret learning more about him.

Some men should be avoided, after all.

7

The sterile hospital chemicals not only filled Trapp's nostrils but clung to him, clawing at his skin and scuttling their way down the back of his mouth. He'd been in plenty of buildings like this, in too many corners of the world to count, but he never got used to it. Having no desire to follow the blanket coverage of the shooting on the news channels and never one for entertaining himself with cellphone games or social media, he was alone with his thoughts as he paced outside Joshua's room.

Valerie was in recovery, and Lamar was being prepped for a minor procedure to clean out his through-and-through and stitch it properly. Still, Trapp needed to *do* something. Either sleep or start hitting things until the answers he sought spilled out.

Pulling out his phone, he called Nick Pope in the FBI's counterterrorism division, a solid operator he'd partnered with on several missions since re-emerging from his short-lived death. Nick was one of the few people Trapp counted as both friend and colleague.

Nick answered on the third ring. "Jason, I heard about the shooting. You okay?"

"I'm fine. Listen, I know this isn't your case, but tell me what you can."

There was a pause on the line. "You're aware it's being treated as a local crime, right?"

Trapp *hmm*'d in the affirmative.

"Then you know I can't share much without leaving a trail. The FBI's involvement is just standard procedure for any mass shooting, even with the suspect dead. But my involvement starts and ends with being cc'd on related emails. At the last update, Boston PD is proceeding as if it's a murder or gangland incident."

Trapp sighed, running a hand through his hair. He knew that already. "I get it, Nick. But it doesn't feel random, no matter how crappy the attempt looks."

"One thing I can tell you with confidence is that the agent they're sending is good. Paulo Drebin. You'll like him. Thorough, a straight shooter. Landed ninety minutes ago, and he's heading for the hospital as soon as BPD has debriefed him. Should be anytime now."

"Drebin? Feel like I know that name."

"Yeah, don't call him Shirley."

Trapp frowned. That sounded like a joke, but he didn't get it.

A female nurse emerged from Joshua's room, followed by a male doctor in green scrubs. The doctor blanked Trapp as he went about his day, but the nurse offered a kind smile, pointed to the room, and held up five fingers, mouthing, *Five minutes.*

Trapp nodded his thanks.

"*Naked Gun?*" Nick said, reading Trapp's silence correctly as confusion. "*Police Squad?* The cop spoofs. Paulo hates jokes about his name, so keep 'em to yourself."

"I hated those movies." Probably why he didn't remember fully. "And we're showing our age. You'd trust Drebin to run this if it *was* your case?"

Nick's tone turned serious. "Reputationally, yes. He takes no shit and can't be strong-armed. He'll do the right thing, wherever it leads."

Trapp appreciated the sentiment, but a nagging doubt lingered. There were career feds and there were feds who saw the job as a mission that defined their entire lives. A by-the-book, mission-driven agent like Drebin might freeze Trapp out of the investigation entirely.

After ending the call with a promise to stay out of it that he had no intention of keeping, and Pope knew better than to believe, Trapp slipped into Joshua's room.

His friend looked pale against the hospital sheets, his torso swathed in bandages.

"You awake?" Trapp asked.

"I'm high as a motherfucker and hurting at the same time," Joshua replied. "How does *that* work?"

"They say anything about the injury?"

"Hit my shoulder blade. Bullet nicked a lung, but only minor damage since it lodged in the bone."

Although far from fatal, this would be a painful one, and a long recovery. Difficult to anaesthetize that part of the body.

With a groggy voice, Joshua asked, "Did you get him? The guy who did this?"

"Yeah, got him."

"Questioned him?"

"Not exactly. But I didn't kill him. He did it himself."

Joshua turned his head at that, his good arm lifting to mime a gun, but didn't get it near his head before the pain made him wince.

"Right." Trapp was conspicuously aware of his own stiffness —upright, hands in his pockets. He wondered if he should do something more friendly, like sit closer, touch Joshua's hand, or give him a hug. No, definitely not a hug. "Guy was Chinese, or looked it. Said 'they' would kill him if he cut a deal. Any ideas who 'they' might be?"

Joshua shook his head slowly. "Why would I?"

Treating this like an interrogation, albeit a much gentler version, Trapp pulled up a chair, sat, and leaned toward Joshua. "Was anyone shaking down the bar?"

"Shaking down the— Why would you ask that?"

"It's fine if there's something going on. I just need the truth."

Joshua shook his head harder this time, wincing at the movement. "No, Jason. I would've told you if there was. I'd prefer *you* to handle it over the cops."

"No contact at all? Nothing from the Triads?"

"Nothing. I swear, Jason. The bar is solvent, and no one was shaking us down for protection."

Trapp leaned back, accepting the answer. Joshua might never know all the things he, or his brother, had done to keep this country safe—most of which would never be known by the public and some of which hadn't been sanctioned. But Trapp believed that Joshua would trust him to see off a few local hoodlums.

Still no connection to the victims, though. No clear motive. Maybe it *was* random after all.

A knock at the door interrupted his thoughts. A tall, wiry man with a shock of white in his dark hair stood in the doorway, his black suit and polished shoes impeccable.

"Jason Trapp? I'm Special Agent Paulo Drebin. I understand you're expecting me."

Trapp was about to pat Joshua's arm but thought better of it. He said, "I'll be back when I can," then followed Drebin into the hallway, conscious that they were on the same side. Manners and courtesy were the order of the day. "I guess we both got a heads-up from Nick. Good to meet you, Agent Drebin."

Drebin shook the hand Trapp offered, then took it back quickly, stuffing it in his pocket. Trapp wasn't sure, but it looked like he was wiping his palm on the material. He pretended not to notice as Drebin glanced down the hospital corridor toward two plainclothes detectives, one of whom was the tired-looking guy who had set Trapp loose, the other a younger woman with short curly hair. They both watched Drebin and Trapp but could hear nothing.

Drebin said, "Mr. Trapp, I appreciate your eagerness to help, but interviewing witnesses falls under my purview."

Trapp kept his reply as civil as he could. "Joshua is my friend. My business partner. Lamar and Valerie Gilbaut are my friends, too, and I'll be visiting them as soon as the docs let me. I won't step on your toes. But I won't let you hold me back, either. Can I go now? I need a nap."

Drebin studied him for a moment. "You think *you* were the target." It wasn't a question.

Trapp shrugged. "Just one possibility."

"All I know about you, Mr. Trapp, is that your file looks like the aftermath of giving a toddler a permanent marker. But not every assassin is out to get you. Sometimes, a criminal is just a criminal. Maybe they wanted your friend to sell up cheap, or maybe it was a tweaker, shooting at shadows. We just don't know yet. That's why I'm here."

Trapp nodded, feigning agreement. But the notion that he was the intended target had burrowed into his mind and nestled there, wouldn't move. *Paranoid*, Lamar had called him.

But someone had sent a Triad amateur after him.

"Where are you taking your nap?" Drebin asked.

"The bar has an apartment. Don't worry, I can get in from the yard out back. I won't go trampling over the crime scene."

"You got access? Keys?"

Trapp patted his pocket. "Partner. I won't be breaking in, if that's your concern."

"No, my concern is that the CCTV recording setup in the bar is a decoy, so we haven't been able to examine anything except street cams."

Right. Trapp had set that up. The cameras were no dummies, though. They fed to monitors behind the bar so that staff could keep an eye on things, but the hard-drive recordings were stored in a secure lockbox in Joshua's apartment upstairs. That way, if anyone robbed the place, the guilty party might swipe the dummy drives out front, but the real footage would remain safe.

"I'll get the drives over to BPD by lunchtime," Trapp said. "Good enough?"

"Good enough," Drebin said. "After you've made copies, I assume?"

"It's my property. No crime in that."

"A wise precaution."

"We good?"

Trapp again extended his hand. He was Mr. Courtesy. Mr. Cooperation.

Drebin shook the hand again, holding on to it this time. "We have the jurisdiction to go get those drives right now. But we'd rather not break in and cause a mess when we aren't on a clock. Please don't make me regret paying you a professional courtesy, Mr. Trapp."

"You won't."

"Take this." Drebin handed over his FBI business card. "Call me before you think about doing anything else."

Drebin turned to leave, again wiping his hand subtly inside his pocket, when Trapp caught a flicker of something in the agent's eyes.

A hint of... *satisfaction*. As if their meeting had been a success rather than the stonewalling exercise dressed up as conviviality that Trapp knew it to be. Drebin might be a straight-shooter, but sometimes straight-shooters were ordered to hold back.

And as Trapp folded the man's card in his fist, he resolved to step carefully until he worked out what Drebin was keeping from him.

8

F abian Pincher entered the Congressman's office in the US Capitol, the plush emerald carpet swallowing his footsteps as he passed a wall of historical memorabilia and political tokens. A chaos of papers crowded the expansive mahogany desk like fresh fallen leaves, unusual for a man so fastidiously organized that he barely poured himself a coffee unless it was scheduled in his planner.

Scheduled, usually, by Fabian.

An American flag stood proudly beside a wall of dark green, gold-leafed tomes dense with wisdom, which Fabian had occasionally browsed but found uninteresting. At the room's heart, Congressman Jake Redman sat behind his desk, almost silhouetted against the morning light from the window overlooking an innocuous stretch of DC park. His bearded features were set in a confident smile as he turned from the view to Fabian. Without a word, he slid an envelope across the polished desk, awaiting Fabian's acceptance.

They had made an excellent team over the past two and a half years, unspoken instructions like these as common as formal discussions on strategy, voting, and intelligence.

Fabian reached for the thick, brown envelope. The gravity of the room, the consequence of each action, was never lost on him, especially when his boss asked him to color outside the lines.

Today, though, Fabian paused.

"A simple exchange." Impatience enhanced Redman's Tennessee drawl. "You'll have a new contact this time. Girl. She'll approach you and say, 'Bald eagle.'"

"Bald eagle?" Fabian said.

"Other side's idea of a joke or somethin'. Maybe the guy's a twitcher. Just go with it. You gotta reply with 'Osprey.'"

Fabian hesitated to touch the papers, let alone pick them up. Maybe because his boss seldom gave in to impatience. Or maybe it was the idea of a new contact. "Sir, are you sure about this?"

Redman's tone was casual, bordering on dismissive. "We'll come out with the better part of this deal, I promise you that."

Fabian hated himself for hesitating, but he still didn't touch the envelope. If he didn't know what was in it, had never laid a finger on it, he remained uninvolved.

Redman sighed, a motion that inflated his chest and belly before the exhale turned his features to stone. "Do you want to put America back on top or not, son?"

"You know I do. But—"

"Either you retain faith in my ability to make decisions well over your pay grade or we're done here."

That was the rub. If Fabian engaged in activities that carried even the whiff of treason, he would never ascend beyond his current role as a senior aide, especially not to the chief of staff post he had been promised if the dominoes fell just right. Of course, if he failed to obey his boss's orders, that same ladder would be kicked from underneath him just as quickly.

"It's just the optics of cooperating with the Chinese, sir," Fabian said. "If it gets out, even though I'm sure this is all legal

... it could *end* you. You'd lose the chair of the HPSCI for sure, even if they didn't prove..."

Redman's gaze landed firmly on the envelope. Although some might call the man oafish or even fat, he was as powerful as Fabian, who worked out four times a week at five a.m. The strength behind this former boxer and football player was as impressive as his utter belief in his own choices.

Fabian flexed his fingers, then picked up the envelope.

Reading Fabian's lingering worry, Redman leaned back, interlocking his fingers over his stomach. "They're entrepreneurs, nothing more. Nigeria this time. Infrastructure. The specifics are all there." He nodded to the envelope. "In return, we get a chip I'm certain will help put President Nash back in his place. He needs to start toeing the party line, not..." Redman gestured angrily in the general direction of the White House. "Not bending the knee to North Korea."

Fabian understood Redman's objections regarding the upcoming summit at the UN. If it was *too* successful, it would cement Nash as a great diplomat, a peacemaker leading the world outside America's usual sphere of influence, which would drag the GOP away from Redman's vision for the party —and make it harder for Redman to beat Nash's hand-picked successor in the next presidential primary.

"This is *my* proposal," Redman said. "*I* instigated it. They ain't steering this boat. We hand over the US costings for the infrastructure project, they give me something I can use. Can I rely on you? Because if I can't, Natalie and Sonja are waitin' in line. Both would make excellent chiefs of staff if you're not up to it."

Some sensitive types might be offended or feel—*gasp!*— bullied. But Fabian saw assertiveness as one of Redman's better traits, which qualified him for office over so many others. That and his ability to get things done, to always—*always*—negotiate from a position of strength.

"I'll see to it," Fabian said. "You can rely on me, sir."

HOBART'S TOY Store was a multi-level outlet in the center of DC's shopping district. It reminded Fabian of FAO Schwarz in his native New York, where his mother had taken him twice a year as a child. Having arrived at Hobart's early with the envelope in a leather satchel, he browsed the boy-shelves, ruminating on how referring to them as *boys'* toys might get him cancelled in some states. Probably in DC, too, given the absence of gender-specific signage for the GI Joes and Transformers toys in the current aisle.

How would they refer to such toys in somewhere like California?

Them-toys?

Gender-neutral gratification instruments?

Fabian smiled to himself as he took the escalator up to two and commenced browsing the aisle towering high with Barbies and My Little Ponies. Although he believed himself completely at ease with both his heterosexuality and his status as a single man without offspring, he felt like an intruder. As if he might see some secret meant only for little girls. But he wasn't shopping. And he wasn't spying.

Or *hoped* he wasn't spying.

To appear natural, he called upon the six months of acting lessons he'd taken in the hope of boosting his grade point average at college. He was no longer Fabian Pincher, senior aide (and future chief of staff) to the next president of the United States but a doting uncle, invited out of state for a family weekend get-together, searching for the perfect gift for his fictional niece.

A young Chinese woman, pale and slim, caught his eye. She poked around the new batch of My Little Ponies at the opposite

end of the display table. Immediately, she looked furtively away
from him. She checked over one shoulder, saw there was no
one else around, and said, "Bald Eagle."

The young woman dipped her hand in her coat pocket and
kept it there. Fabian sensed she wanted this meeting over with
as quickly as he did.

Fabian nodded solemnly but flushed at the awkwardness of
actually saying, "Osprey."

The woman moved aside, eyes on the table of colorful toy
ponies, pretending to examine a glittery pink one as they
stopped within arm's length of each other. She was pretty,
smartly dressed, and carried herself well. He guessed she must
work out, maybe swim, given her posture.

"I guess this makes me a 'bronie,' huh?" he joked, trying to
ease the tension.

The woman stared at him blankly before taking her hand
out of her pocket and stuffing a small envelope between two
boxed Ponies.

Fabian cleared his throat, feeling foolish.

Why did I say that?

They browsed separately, gradually working their way
around, the woman never straying far from her package. Fabian
put his open satchel on the table and leaned over to pick up an
oversized version of the pink, glittery Pony, his trailing hand
sliding Redman's envelope out and mirroring what the Chinese
woman had done with hers.

They maneuvered closer until they were side by side, both
still browsing. As they crossed paths, Fabian could not resist
brushing one arm against hers, enjoying the softness of her
under the silk blouse while hoping she felt his firm muscles at
the point of contact. A fresh scent carried on her hair, making
him breathe a little deeper. He couldn't name the fragrance.
Something Asian, he expected.

He picked up the Pony box and the envelope she'd left,

replaced the toy which his fictional niece already owned on the shelf, and dropped the package into his satchel.

The woman scooped up the Nigerian costings and slipped away without a goodbye.

She wasn't as smooth or calm as the previous contact, a chap who had exuded hostility toward Fabian, but she was definitely easier on the eyes.

On his way out, Fabian imagined himself no longer the doting uncle but the protagonist in a spy movie, risking everything for the greater good of his country. And after all, exchanging confidential trade figures in exchange for pushing the right man another step closer to the White House was only a tiny, technical act of betrayal.

He pictured how a director might shoot the scene, perhaps in a dimly-lit coffee shop or on a sun-drenched park bench, where he would meet with shadowy figures, all in service of *President* Jake Redman.

Three short years. Two until primary season dawned.

The envelope in his pocket seemed to grow heavier with each step. But Fabian reassured himself that Redman would never endanger the United States. In fact, he was destined to save it. The future was bright, and Fabian was thrilled to be crafting a big part of it.

As THE DIPLOMATIC town car glided through the streets of Washington, DC toward the Chinese embassy, Fang Chen clutched the thick envelope in her lap.

If the exchange was above board, why the need for such secrecy? Why the covert handoff?

It all felt wrong. It certainly didn't fit with her role as an attaché to the ambassador.

Fang shuddered as she recalled Fabian's creepy demeanor,

the memory of his touch sending a new chill along her arm and down her spine.

Ugh.

As the powered gates opened and Chinese soldiers scanned the car with electronic wands, probing for bugs and explosives, Fang took the time to compose herself.

Waved through, the car rolled up to reception, and Fang stepped out, her head held high as she strode through security and down the halls to Ambassador Wen's private office, where Li Chao waited.

Alone.

Fang handed over the envelope.

"All went well?" Chao asked.

"As far as I could tell," Fang said. "No one arrested or shot me."

Chao chuckled, although Fang would never have addressed Ambassador Wen that way. Nor any of the diplomatic staff, for that matter.

But Chao appeared to take it in good humor. "No. And for that I am grateful."

To Fang's surprise, he fed the envelope into a shredder, the machine cross-cutting it into confetti.

He fixed her with an intense gaze. "Not a word of this to anyone."

Fang swallowed hard, her voice steady as she replied, "Of course, Mr. Li."

Chao gave another of his satisfied smiles. "This is just the first phase. It will neutralize a clear and present danger to China."

Fang wondered how many more phases he had planned.

9

With fatigue dragging him down, Trapp heaved himself out of the Uber that dropped him back at Joshua's Bar. Although the establishment and the street outside were still crime scenes, the buildings surrounding it were not, so Trapp trudged around the back and accessed the self-contained apartment from a door facing the yard. He could have insisted on a warrant for the CCTV footage, but he saw no reason to impede either BPD's or Drebin's investigations. Although that didn't mean he had to hand it over immediately.

Inside the small apartment, Trapp hung up his coat and treated the place like any other operations base, albeit one where the caretaker hadn't yet washed up from breakfast the previous morning. He headed straight for the closet that contained the water heater, a clothes rack, and an ironing board, where he pressed a false panel, let it float open, and input the eight-digit code for the safe-like box within. After it opened, Trapp disconnected the two hard drives inside and plugged in two spares, in case someone paid the bar a repeat visit.

Then he retreated to Joshua's living room, which wasn't exactly slovenly, but a single pizza box and empty beer can suggested that he had not been expecting company anytime soon.

The laptop Trapp pulled from his bag was brand new, sealed in a box, and was *Ideal for students, families, and photo & video enthusiasts*, according to the sign in Walmart. He'd paid cash. While he doubted the feds or CIA were actively monitoring him on his government-issue equipment, he would prefer to leave no trail on his or Joshua's devices should he need to take action that BPD wouldn't appreciate.

He made a coffee while it booted up, pushing aside any feeling of being a bad house guest as he settled in front of the monitor. He turned off the Wi-Fi and switched the laptop to airplane mode as an added precaution, then plugged in the first hard drive.

The last twenty-four hours were always recorded in full HD with no compression, but older than that, the security system would only retain a four-frames-per-second copy. Since only sixteen hours had passed, Trapp watched the scene shot from above the door in movie-like quality.

In frame was the front door, the sidewalk outside, and the first table on the left. Trapp fast-tracked to the time stamp of 9:51 p.m. and let it run.

The man in the white cap passed by at 9:52 and disappeared, coming back at 9:54 and trying the door for the first time, head down. No sound on the footage, but Trapp replayed the soundtrack himself as the man rattled the door.

Joshua getting riled.

A comment... speculation about the man's ability to read English.

Trapp offering to back Joshua up.

Joshua, announcing he was going for his bat.

The shooter retreating.

Four people strolled from the left, then three from the right, none of them looking in, until—and Trapp was seeing this part for the first time—the man in the cap strode from out of frame, the gun raised in one hand. The weapon bucked and flashed silently.

Gunfire... Glass... Screaming.

On screen, the shooter held the gun in his strange grip, no shooting squat or even squaring himself off for the recoil, which jerked the gun around as if an electrical current was being fed through the shooter's arm, the circuit forming each time he squeezed the trigger.

Trapp supposed the proximity of the victims offered some accuracy, but a true professional only fired one-handed when there was no other choice.

With his training and practice, Trapp could hold a Glock 17 steady one-handed and fire off a magazine with about 90 percent of the accuracy of a two-handed grip, which was pretty damn high, but that was in ideal conditions, without either adrenaline flowing through his system or lead flying through the air.

The next camera angle was taken from a less-conspicuous position, only slightly elevated for line of sight over customers' heads but directly ahead of the door, so that even someone wearing a hat to evade the visible door camera could likely be ID'd. This angle also took in more of the interior.

9:52 p.m.

This time, Trapp saw the shooter as he remembered him— a shuffling drunk-acting pedestrian who was gone as soon as he appeared. Trapp took in other faces, too, some of whom he'd later witnessed lying wounded on the ground. Gordon Trent threw his head back and laughed with his three companions, spilling a splash of white wine down his shirt. Trapp had paid little attention to those people last night, losing himself in conversation with Lamar and Valerie, occasionally branching off to shake hands and briefly catch up with others. He spotted Sam Carter, the former Marine, at ease with other vets, happy to see Joshua.

Trapp sipped his coffee and watched the top of Lamar's head as he shifted to retrieve another round of drinks, then Joshua, drunk and happy and sad and thankful.

The man returned. Joshua shouted at him. Trapp wandered into view, reacting to Gordon Trent, the "he probably don't read English" guy. The shooter ceased rattling the door and departed once more.

As the footage played, Trapp detached himself from the horror to come. A wider angle meant some of the people in frame, including Lamar and Joshua, would soon be wounded, and Gordon Trent would be dead.

The gunman swept into view, weapon up, staring a moment before adjusting his one-armed aim and firing. Muzzle flash. Gordon Trent falling, his friends dispersing. Joshua going down as Trapp tipped over a table and dropped behind it. Trapp watched as Sam Carter's heroism played out, silently thanking the Marine for his sacrifice. It was clear his actions had distracted the shooter, sparing Lamar and Valerie from further harm.

Burning with rage at being unable to find the shooter again and beat him to within an inch of his life, Trapp rewound the tape, further than 9:52, all the way to 9:40, replaying it at 3x speed until one of his earlier suspicions was confirmed: the shooter had passed by the window not twice, but three times before he opened fire. Trapp had only noticed him twice on the night itself, perhaps subconsciously registering the repeated face on the second pass.

The shooter's gaze remained fixed on the interior of the bar. He was searching for something... or someone.

Trapp slowed the scene right down. Back a bit... zoomed in...

...and confirmed what he'd thought before. Before the man tried the door, he'd slowed, taken a longer pause before stepping forward.

He'd seen something.

His target?

Trapp set it to normal speed and kept his own version of events in mind as Joshua tried to see the man off, as Gordon cast aspersions on his reading comprehension, as Trapp offered to back Joshua up and—

And there it was.

Trapp replayed it twice, confirming the timing.

When the shooter returned for the final time, gun up in that gangster grip, Trapp slowed the visuals, mentally mapping everyone's locations. The minute adjustment of the shooter's arm.

Pause.

That was when the shooting began. Right after he'd seen Trapp.

"Maybe not so paranoid after all," Trapp muttered.

He finished his coffee and prowled the apartment to check for signs of a break-in or for weak points that might haunt him should someone take another shot, all while wracking his brain for any time he might have pissed off the Triads or anyone who might use them for something like this.

He came up blank.

Even a mission involving the North Koreans, a plot he'd smashed with the help of his former girlfriend and others—which had necessitated annoying the Chinese, too—wouldn't have drawn this degree of backlash almost five years later.

That left Boston PD and Drebin as his only go-to, but the margins on this were tiny. If BPD had already made up their minds and straight-shooter-Drebin knew more than he was willing to share, Trapp needed to step outside the lines for a short while longer. And he'd need help.

One person came to mind, someone he had worked with before but hadn't contacted in years. He wasn't even sure if this someone would have the same number, so he called up an old app on his phone. It worked like WhatsApp but was a program of his contact's own creation with encryption that would make the Pentagon jealous. The app contained two names. One was Mike Mitchell, deputy director of the CIA.

He dialed the other. After two rings, his contact picked up.

"Wow, Jason Trapp," drawled Dr. Timothy Greaves. "Are we in trouble or is this a social call?"

Prior to becoming a target of the Black Monday conspirators, Dr. Timothy Greaves had worked as the National Security Agency's most senior research scientist for over ten years, designing security measures that had protected America's leadership throughout his tenure and beyond. The last time Trapp had worked with him, he'd held the nebulous non-title of 'computer expert,' working directly for the CIA on Mike Mitchell's various special projects. That said, 'expert' felt like an understatement. *Genius*, maybe. *God* might be going too far.

But Virtuoso?

Maestro?

Trapp settled on something far less pompous.

"I need a tech wizard," Trapp replied. "Know anyone who can help?"

"I know someone who *can* help," Greaves said. "Not sure if he will. Activating an ancient piece of code that set off an alarm on my phone sent me into palpitations. I thought nukes were dropping on Wisconsin. But that's a different app."

"I think I pissed someone off," Trapp said. "Someone I need to pay a visit."

"To apologize?"

"Depends what I did, but probably not. I need facial rec that can't be traced."

"Have you tried a reverse Google image search?"

"Of course."

Greaves audibly bristled, probably guessing correctly that Trapp had done no such thing. His next question came across as pointed, as if designed to make Trapp feel dumb. "Can you upload the photo to a secure FTP server if I give you the address?"

"Can't I send an email?"

"No, you cannot send an email to my half-billion-dollar workstation in a location I can't tell you about. What's your IP address?"

"I don't know. I'm using an air-gapped laptop."

"You know you can't send me a photo without being online, right?"

"Just give me a minute." Trapp was happy to play the dumb ape. It annoyed Greaves but also fed his sense of intellectual superiority. Of course Trapp knew he'd need to go online and how to find an IP address. While he responded, "I'll owe you a Big Gulp after this," he toggled out of flight mode and connected to the bar's Wi-Fi router, then navigated to a DOS window, typing *ipconfig /all*.

"I know you're messing with me, Trapp," Greaves said. "And by the way, I swear by intermittent fasting now. I'm forty pounds lighter."

"Now *you're* messing with *me*."

"Nope. Totally new man."

"Totally? What color's your hair?"

"Okay, not totally. I'm still rocking the blue, I just had to go to a darker shade to cover the gray you gave me. But I joined a gym."

"You do know joining a gym doesn't do anything? You actually have to *go*."

"Shut up and read me the IP address."

Trapp read out the numbers.

"Okay, thanks." Greaves went silent for a beat, during which Trapp didn't utter a word. No point when the man was working. Approximately twenty seconds later, Greaves said, "Wow, you got old."

Trapp frowned.

"Stop frowning," Greaves said. "It'll add years to your face. Do you moisturize?"

Trapp looked at the integrated web cam. "Cute trick. You activated it without turning on the light."

"Why would I turn on the light when it's so easy to disable? First thing you should do with a new computer is cover that spying bitch with masking tape. Is it this Asian guy with the gun you need help with?"

"Yeah. ID'll be public soon enough. But I want deep background. If he's connected to an unfriendly government or terror group, it won't be something I can find browsing his Instagram."

There was no sign that someone had penetrated the cheap laptop, but Trapp pictured Greaves—a lighter, slimmer version of the man he'd known—strolling around the circuit boards like he owned the place.

"Asher Chan," Greaves said. "Twenty-two years old, deceased as of last night. Known affiliations via Boston PD's gang database, which is quite a hodgepodge of very poor algorithms and out of date facial rec software. I could download an update for them..."

"Just the facts, please, ma'am."

"You're no fun. Okay, I'll leave them to their Bronze Age

tech. Asher Chan was picked up and questioned on extortion charges at nineteen, but they didn't stick. Witnesses suffered memory loss. Did six months on a minor drug offense. He's still hanging out with the same people and is suspected of continuing as a minor player in Chinatown, but he's kept out of trouble and off the radar while they look at bigger fish."

"Who are the bigger fish?"

"The triads who run things in Boston are the Iron Lotus Guild."

"'Iron Lotus Guild?' Seriously? Did a nine-year-old think up that name?"

"You mock, but they've had very few arrests, so they can't be particularly active."

Trapp thought about that. "I'm no expert in gangland activity, but few arrests where a gang is well-known doesn't mean low activity. It usually means they keep to themselves. Aren't too visible and keep their business tight."

"So they don't venture out of their established territory to assassinate assassins enjoying a drink with fellow assassins."

"They weren't all assassins. And I do a lot more than that."

"Ohhh-kay, then. Will there be anything else, or can I pass you to a colleague to complete a customer service survey?"

"Send me everything you just stole from BPD, including the business Chan was 'wrongly arrested' for extorting. And anything you have on the leadership. I don't think he was acting on impulse. The order came from somewhere. I'm gonna find out who and why."

"Sounds violent."

"You're sure there's no other connection?" Trapp asked.

"I've already pummeled his social media, and that's given me his Gmail account, which is linked to his Chrome browser. His search history tells me he likes Caribbean food, high-end motorcycles, and regular porn—with a preference for white, blond women his own age. Quite vanilla for a hired gun."

"No hint of a foreign government connection? China or North Korea? Not teaming up with the cartels or jihadis?"

"No flags whatsoever. I'll run his comms through a deeper dive, and if I can find a snatch of his voice—"

Greaves stopped talking so suddenly Trapp would've thought someone had cut the line, except he could hear the background noise of air conditioning or computer fans.

"Jason?" Greaves said, his pitch having risen an octave.

"Yeah, what's wrong? Who is Asher Chan really?"

"Asher Chan is Asher Chan." But Greaves held that urgent tone, the one that meant his heart was racing, his thoughts on hold as he processed something only he could see. "I fed every keyword I could think of into the listening system, so the bots would head out into the ether and ping when they heard something relating to you or the late Mr. Chan."

"And...?"

"They lit up."

"Which one?"

"All of them, Jason. It's not historical, either, it's live. It hasn't hit the news outlets yet, but it's all over the wires. They're building up to release it. You need to see this."

A link popped up on Trapp's screen. He clicked it, leading to a bare-bones site formatted like a news website—no graphics, just words. But the advance warning of what was about to hit the airwaves was enough to show that Greaves' shock was not unwarranted. Trapp's blood ran cold as he read the name.

His own alias, his code name.

Hangman was about to become public.

11

I
f Trapp were to be drugged, kidnapped, and revived on a helicopter before being dropped without explanation into the middle of a jungle known to hide terrorist camps or major drug operations, he would be frightened and disoriented, sure, but only for a few seconds. He would swiftly gain his bearings, take in his environment, and immediately scan for danger before securing the basic fundamentals of human survival: shelter, water, and food. In that order. Should he be detected and attacked, he would similarly assess his options and select the one that boded best for his survival.

It was what he had trained for.

It was the life he'd lived.

He knew how to handle that.

But seeing the word *HANGMAN* ticker tape across the screen under a red *Breaking News* banner kept Trapp's eyes glued to the television, watching in disbelief as classified information about CIA operations spilled forth. It didn't matter which channel—CNN, MSNBC, Fox—all of them carried the same story, almost word for word.

His hand rose unconsciously to his neck, touching the ragged scar his violent father had bestowed by way of a length of barbed wire looped around his throat. The day Ryan Price had clocked it during basic training was the day he'd coined the nickname which had stuck with Trapp throughout his career.

"Press release?" Trapp said.

"Looks like it." Greaves had remained on the line. "Anonymous posting on an aggregator, so it went out to everyone at once."

"Any idea how much they've got?"

"They're looping around again, so looks like just details of two missions for the moment."

The talking head, a smooth yet somehow sleazy-looking younger man with stiff blond hair, was going over the classified operations again. The first was a job Trapp remained proud of to this day.

"Robert Kaliil, a campaigner for the rights of a marginalized tribe in Uganda, was the target of a CIA assassination plot, one carried out by the agent codenamed 'Hangman.' Kaliil's supporters and family maintain that the CIA had approached him to inform on the rights movement, but when he turned them down, he became a target. It is not yet known if the assassination was approved by the CIA or if this Hangman was operating autonomously."

Robert Kaliil was, in fact, one of the reasons Trapp kept going, no matter how much shit got flung his way, why he never slept badly after ridding the world of people like this. Tribal rights was Kaliil's public cause, but he'd earned most of his fortune by smuggling child sex slaves across Africa, and he'd started expanding worldwide. Two eight-year-old girls had been rescued on American soil, which meant there were probably many more that had gone undetected, but the activist had been deemed too difficult to extradite and prosecute. Satellite intercepts weren't admissible in court, and the intelligence court wouldn't have tipped off their enemies about ways and means even if it was. Trapp's primary objective had been rendition, but "neutralizing" the target would suffice if extracting him alive proved too dangerous.

It had not been a difficult choice.

"Also on Hangman's list of kills is Jawahar al-Faris, a suspected Islamist fixer who had *allegedly* arranged the logistics and materials for eight attacks on US troops in various parts of the world. There is no suggestion that a legal solution to the man's apprehension and trial was explored, let alone attempted."

The dossier that the press had obtained barely mentioned the dead men's crimes or how they threatened the US and its citizens. Trapp figured the information was purposely incomplete.

The stiff-haired man-child continued with a smooth, unruffled demeanor. "This asset operated with impunity in at least twelve countries over ten years with the blessing of the CIA. The dossier, which appears to be real—and so far none of our sources have denied its legitimacy—lists the man's deployments, and for four of them we have scant details of the mission involved. The latest was a mere six years ago, meaning he could still be active. Derek?"

The feed switched to an older man, perhaps sixty, with a stern, gritty look about him as he positioned himself before the Pentagon building. Trapp had never worked at the Pentagon, but as the symbol for everything secretive and military, it served as an imposing backdrop.

"Thank you, Steve," Derek said into a handheld microphone, the graphic at the bottom of the screen declaring him a *Defense Correspondent*. "Several operations are detailed, but none more disturbing than the killing in Yemen of an American agent."

He went on to describe not just any operation, but the one

involving Ryan Price, the man they'd been honoring last night. The man who'd died when Trapp had lived.

"Although details are sketchy and largely redacted, according to what we have read, Hangman and his as-yet-unnamed partner were investigating a smuggling operation sanctioned by the CIA, but only one of them emerged alive. The follow-up shows that Hangman was investigated, that several hundreds of thousands of dollars from an operational slush fund went missing, and six months later, Hangman was involved in the Black Monday massacres. The implication seems to be that Hangman killed his partner for reasons unknown, probably money, then re-emerged during America's blackest day. Since then, he has continued to participate in CIA operations that are redacted here."

"Is there any indication of Hangman's true identity?" the stiff-haired man-child asked.

"None, Steve. But I'm sure the public at large will be very interested in learning exactly what this taxpayer-funded killer has been doing in their name."

Trapp jabbed the remote's off button and sat back, blowing out his cheeks as he tried to analyze this development coldly, pretending that he was watching events from afar that were happening to someone else.

He *wished* he was being dropped into a jungle full of people looking to kill him.

"Jason?" Greaves said. "Are you okay?"

"The timing is too coincidental," Trapp said. "That report has twisted the truth."

"I'm looking at the documents that were released. Redacted, so these were available to someone lower down the food chain."

"A mole?"

"It's either from inside—someone with high access but lower than top secret—or it's a world-class hacker."

"Can you figure out how this shit leaked?"

"On it. What about you, Jason? What will you do?"

"I'm being hunted. I need to find out who's on my trail."

12

As he slipped out of the apartment, Trapp hesitated, weighed down by a handful of belongings and daunted at an unknown enemy lurking out of sight. He had gathered his already-packed bags and removed the Sig Sauer P229a and two spare magazines from the same lockbox as the hard drives. Then he'd shifted the bed in Joshua's room, lifted a fake floorboard, and pulled out a case containing several thousand dollars in cash.

This was Ryan's legacy. The stash he'd built up—as most operators in their line of work did—saved from wages, plundered funds, and spare expenses, ready to invest back into defending the US of A... or a compensation package for the loved ones of those who'd perished while serving. It wasn't an enterprise actively encouraged by the Agency but never investigated, either. When the reward for your service was that your country would deny it knew anything about you, it paid to have an insurance package.

Trapp took twenty thousand in various denominations, promising silently to pay Joshua back once he could access his own funds without fear of being targeted. Joshua would understand. *Ryan* would understand, too.

He stepped outside, locked up, and navigated the back alleyways surrounding the bar, heading through the city toward Chinatown. He'd memorized a route with minimal CCTV and kept his head down as he used his duffel bag to hide most of his face while lifting his cellphone on the other side to call Mike Mitchell on a conventional line.

A woman's voice answered, crisp and professional. "Director Mitchell's office."

He'd been redirected to a landline, meaning Mike's phone was off.

"This is Jason Trapp. I need to speak with Director Mitchell immediately. It's a matter of national security."

"I'm sorry, sir, but Director Mitchell is currently unavailable."

Trapp's grip tightened, but he kept his voice even. The woman he was speaking to was unlikely to know that Jason Trapp and Hangman were the same person. "Lives are at stake. Put me through to him now."

There was a pause, followed by a click. Hold music filled Trapp's ear, a grating melody that he hated at first—and hated even more when his fingers started tapping along to it.

The operator returned. "Sir, may I ask what this pertains to?"

Trapp hesitated, then sighed. "Just give him my name. He'll want to take this call."

Another spell of hold music. Trapp paced the room, replaying the defense correspondent's words over and over, bastardizing the final moments of the best man he'd ever known.

Finally, the operator spoke again. "Mr. Trapp, Director Mitchell authorized me to tell you he is currently reviewing security for the North and South Korean presidents ahead of the upcoming summit. He requests urgently that you come in for debriefing and assures you... he asked me to say this exactly... he won't hang you out to dry." She seemed to take Trapp's silence as acquiescence and added, "We'll send a car to your location."

He won't hang *you out to dry.*

Cute, Mike.

But Trapp's instincts screamed at him to run. It felt like a net closing, the walls of an institution he had once trusted crumbling around him.

Hacked or infiltrated, it didn't matter. Someone or something had failed. If the file was as thorough as it appeared, there might be even more lurid interpretations of the things he'd done.

"That won't be necessary," Trapp said. "Tell Mike to stand by. He'll know what that means."

"Mr. Trapp, I must insist—"

Trapp hung up the phone, his heart picking up the pace as if preparing for a fight.

As much as he believed Mike's intentions, the decision might be taken out of his hands. When resignations started flying, there'd be unfathomable pressure to serve up justice, and Trapp would be the main course.

No, Trapp was lost in the jungle now. And although he would not make himself available for debriefing, that didn't mean he was going to hide.

Time to take the offensive.

THE LOBBY SMELLED damp but was surprisingly clean, if worn out and in need of redecorating about fourteen years ago. One of the two elevators sported an aged and peeling *Out of Order* sign, but Trapp took the stairs anyway. Instead of damp, the stench of urine and marijuana circulated here. He held his breath most of the way.

His Boston safehouse was a nondescript fifth-floor apartment in a poorly-maintained building whose landlord had been willing to accept a year's rent in a cash-stuffed envelope from a person he'd never physically met. It nestled in a beltway of the city, midway between a gentrified district of juice bars, yoga studios, and piercing outlets and the sort of neighborhood where cops drew straws before entering.

Like Ryan, Trapp had accumulated a sizeable contingency fund, and since coming back into the fold, he'd set himself up in four US cities, securing cash leases on properties should he ever need to bug out and gather himself. He'd spaced them fairly evenly: one on the West Coast in an unfavorable neighborhood in Los Angeles, one halfway across the country in Dallas, Texas, and one a couple of hours north of Washington, DC, a bargain cash payment for a remote, rotting cabin in rural Maryland.

On floor five, Trapp released his breath and progressed down a corridor that was eerily quiet. The last time he'd been here to set up some necessary improvements, music thumped and pumped from three doors. This corridor also smelled cleaner than expected, although that might have been the absence of piss rather than the presence of anything wholesome.

He disengaged the deadlock on his unit, moved swiftly to the kitchen, and opened a cupboard, where he killed the silent alarm with his fingerprint. He then gave the one-bedroom apartment a manual sweep with his eyes, augmented by an RFID and digital signal scanner.

His stomach reminded him that he hadn't eaten since the buffet the previous evening, so he opened the kitchen cupboard and selected a packet from a month's supply of MREs—meals ready to eat, used by the military for their longevity and nutritional content, but not their taste. It was overkill, and he'd be blocked up for weeks if he had to go through his entire stash, but better safe than sorry.

He returned to the living room and opened the coffee table, which was actually a chest full of equipment past-Jason had stored for a scenario just like this one: guns and ammo, standard burner phones and an encrypted satellite phone, surveillance equipment, a strobing cylinder for disrupting cameras along with a white noise device, tracking pods, a dry bag, a little money.

Then he booted up his laptop, paired it to a burner phone's hotspot, and reviewed the data Timothy Greaves had sent him on Asher Chan's known associates.

13

As he allowed himself to be escorted toward the White House Situation Room, President Charles Nash dug deep into his tired body and summoned enough energy to project the strong image that he'd cultivated over his five years in office. Almost twelve hours in meetings had sapped his focus, and if it wasn't for a barrelful of coffee that he was sure to regret later, he might have dozed off during the last two.

Ironically, it was during one of those earlier meetings that Mike Mitchell had succumbed to the consensus that allowing a high-ranking member of North Korea's Supreme Guard Command to review the US plans for the summit would show trust to a nation known for its complete, unrestrained animosity of the United States. But at least this meeting was only scheduled to be fifteen minutes. The location was a courtesy, but every scrap of classified information was blocked out. Even so, his security people had screamed bloody murder.

The female agent opened the door, and Nash walked through, into the beating heart of America's security apparatus. Four men and two women stood as he entered, and he waved them off with his usual thanks. One of the men was their special guest, his attendance having been subject to much debate, vetting, and—eventually—pragmatism.

Mitchell made the introduction. "Mr. President, this is Hwa Yung-Gi, our liaison with the Ministry of State Security."

Hwa Yung-Gi was a sixtyish man with a craggy, lined face with high cheekbones, and although he was short, he had broad shoulders and hands like a construction worker's. Wearing a pristinely pressed but cheap suit, Yung-Gi gave a shallow bow and extended his hand to Nash, speaking in heavily-accented but fluent English. For a moment, Nash thought he caught a flash of pink poking out beneath his sleeve as they shook hands, but then it disappeared.

"Mr. President, thank you for inviting me into your operation."

It wasn't exactly an invitation. Serious pressure had descended from both the South Koreans and the apparatchiks at State on the Department of Homeland Security and the Secret Service to allow a full unit of North Korean agents to oversee the domestic security team, to ensure that their president and his family remained safe during the summit. After engaging Mitchell to vet and clear the North Korean contingent, the White House had agreed to allow one agent to be present during security briefings with others stationed along the route to shore up the plans being made.

"Welcome," Nash said. "I trust you have been looked after?"

"I have," was all Yung-Gi said. His face remained expressionless.

"We have a lot to discuss," Mitchell added at Nash's tired gesture. "Perhaps you would all introduce yourselves."

First to introduce herself was Nancy Carlisle, deputy director of the Secret Service, followed by Hasan Gul of the FBI's Counterterrorism Command, leading on threats within the New York area; then Breyann Anderson, director of operations for the Department of Homeland Security; and finally Anton Wilde, who would run logistics on the transport and housing of both North and South Korean presidential families.

"I am Hwa Yung-Gi," their guest said when it was his turn. "I am a commander in the Supreme Guard Command, charged with close protection for President Kuk Il-Song and his family."

He didn't mention that he'd saved the life of his president's daughter and possible heir.

Nash had received a bullet-pointed briefing of the incident. Myo Il-Song, the president's daughter, had made a personal inspection of a region that had remained relatively fertile despite the famine starving the rest of the country. By redistributing crops and other goods, the North Korean government had left the thousands of people who had produced the food in the same life-threatening poverty as those whose yields had dropped. The information in Nash's daily brief was that Myo had personally overseen the crushing of the rebellion and the relocation of the would-be assassins' neighbors and close family members to reeducation centers to ensure that allegiance and right-thinking remained intact. Perhaps it was true, more likely not. Even the intelligence community had little confidence in the intel product that emerged from the hermit kingdom.

"I served many tours in the army," Yung-Gi continued, "and with our state security. In my youth, I was honored to be the army's national taekwondo champion. Sadly, age catches up with us all." He ended with a self-deprecating smile, although Nash thought the man looked perfectly able-bodied, despite his advancing years and thinning hair.

"Thank you," Nash said. "We are all deeply invested in this summit, and we will do all we can to ensure it succeeds."

"No, thank *you*, Mr. President." Yung-Gi addressed the room. "In the past, we would have denied a problem exists, but President Kuk's daughter is a compassionate soul. She does not wish to see our people dying from hunger and malnutrition. But with China suffering the same famine, there is little spare to trade with us."

"Then let us hope we can ease the sanctions that keep you from trading with other countries."

Yung-Gi just blinked, his lips tight and thin.

"Is something wrong?" Nash inquired.

"You imposed those sanctions," Yung-Gi said. "Why not simply remove them and allow us to trade freely? Why must we go through... this?"

He waved his hand around, referring to the massive security op.

Breyann Anderson of the DHS took that one. "We cannot allow North Korea to continue in its current—"

"Cannot allow?" Yung-Gi said. "Because America is the world's policeman, and only your might is allowed to prevail?"

"Come, now," Nash interrupted. "This is neither the time nor the place for geopolitical arguments. If we can finalize the agreement between your President Kuk and President Son of South Korea to allow limited agricultural trade, we can save lives and, possibly, begin a new friendship."

Yung-Gi stared at Nash, lips pursed, as if wanting to argue but knowing it was useless. "Very well. Let us first review the accommodation for Myo Il-Song and her family."

That was Nancy Carlisle's cue. "The director of the Secret Service and I agree that a single hotel for each president's party —their families and entourages—is easier to administer and is simpler for security..."

COMMANDER HWA YUNG-GI listened to the detailed plans for his president's visit, missing a little of the dense English as it came out in a stream of official language but understanding its intent, thanks to the dossier he had reviewed before they had agreed to hold the meeting on foreign soil.

Especially here, on the land of the enemy.

Yung-Gi's father had served in the army during the US invasion of Korea, a war that slashed his country in two, impoverishing one half and rewarding the other for decades of political deadlock and behind-the-scenes hostility. But nature had achieved what no diplomat ever could: It forced everyone to the table to talk.

There were still rumors swirling that the Americans had somehow instigated the famine, but Yung-Gi didn't know what to believe. He was certain the imperialist US would do such a thing if it could, but he doubted the technology existed to manufacture a disaster of such proportions without being detected.

No, this was simply bad luck. America taking advantage of his country's temporary weakness.

So here he was, in the heart of their security operations, accepted into their circle. He had been expecting either resistance or hostility but found none here. Just cooperation, and what he read in the president's face as honest intent.

Perhaps this was not the swindle he'd been expecting. Perhaps President Kuk was not the naïve, ailing old man Yung-Gi had suspected him to be: a man whose daughter was stronger, more competent, more *able* than him.

While the meeting today offered some reassurance, that did not mean that Yung-Gi would rest easy. He'd taken control of deep-cover assets embedded in the area, established by his colleagues in the Reconnaissance General Bureau, to aid him in digging out dangers not obvious to the Americans, as well as to root out any subterfuge in their actions.

He hoped he would not need them, but Yung-Gi was not a man who placed trust in the whims of chance.

14

I t was a warm evening in Boston's Chinatown district, and fried aromas filled the air along with chatter and laughter as SUVs and sports cars mingled with scooters and delivery trucks on the roads. Trapp settled on a restaurant with street seating, where he ordered shrimp fried rice and a soda.

He was hunting Jian Wu and Bolin Zhu, the two contacts that Chan had texted the most often. Their GPS data showed that they walked the same route every Sunday, entering the same several establishments on this busy street at the end of the cash-rich weekend. Collecting protection money, Trapp had guessed.

Right on time, the pair came into view, entering a grocery store that displayed fruit and vegetables in wooden crates both along the sidewalk and inside. Trapp had a decent view of an elderly couple behind the counter as they handed an envelope to Zhu, the older of the two gangsters. The younger Wu selected an apple on the way out, took one bite, then tossed it into the road. Insecure, Trapp thought.

Both men sported tattoos that sprouted from their loose clothing—they made no attempt to hide their identities or their guns. Wu's revolver stuck out the front of his waistband, while Zhu's auto rested in a shoulder holster under an open shirt.

They approached the next store, a clothing boutique, which was the main reason Trapp had chosen this spot.

The boutique's owner, Victor Lau, was an American-born entrepreneur who had sold some tech startup and, according to his socials, wanted a simpler life trading in real products made by hand. In his first month since opening the boutique, he'd been treated for broken fingers and a head injury, and the cops had visited him twice. Clearly, he was resisting paying these thugs for protection.

Wu entered the boutique first, shoving the door open with a bang that Trapp heard across the street. The young girl in attendance looked up sharply, then a man came hurrying from the back of the shop, ushering her away.

According to the same BPD database that had furnished Trapp with Asher Chan's profile, Jian Wu was in his twenties and had thirteen arrests for assault, often with a slew of witnesses. But the charges hadn't stuck, thanks to witnesses either retracting statements or simply disappearing. Even his mugshot had looked cocky, like the arrest had bothered him about as much as a parking ticket.

Zhu followed Wu, placing a hand on the younger man's shoulder and smiling widely enough for Trapp to see from the restaurant as he lifted his shirt to show the gun. Clichés became clichés because there was an element of truth to them, Trapp supposed, and this pair were playing their roles right down to the bargain basement B-movie script.

In his mid-thirties, Zhu had inexplicably adopted a mullet. He had never served time, despite featuring prominently in the BPD deck aimed at the Iron Lotus Guild. It was noted that he was brighter than average and had connections within the Triad hierarchy back in Hong Kong.

There was little on the gang leadership itself, though, just a series of loose connections to older businessmen in the community who had sketchy links to what were known as "Dragon Heads" in Hong Kong. Like something from a graphic novel, the Triads' naming conventions—*Dragon Heads* and the *Iron Lotus Guild*—would've amused Trapp if it wasn't for how serious their business was.

As Trapp crossed the street, finishing his Coke, he wondered why Asher Chan had been chosen instead of these two. Wu carried the swagger of someone who didn't give a shit about being caught, while Zhu was clearly the calm, measured brains of the operation. Pausing briefly outside the boutique, Trapp adjusted his cap, glanced both ways to confirm that every pedestrian and worker nearby was minding their own business, and pushed open the door.

Everyone inside ignored him as he drifted to a display of overpriced sweatshirts.

"I told you, I won't pay," Victor Lau said in quiet, strained English. Californian, educated. "This is *my* store. I don't buy into that tradition shit. I don't need your protection."

Trapp observed from under his cap, chin low.

Wu smiled. Cold. Predatory.

"You really don't understand, do you?" Wu said. Accented but fluent, a man who spoke a different language most of the time. "You pay, or we make an example."

"I get it," Zhu interjected, his accent less pronounced than Wu's, more of an actual Bostonian twang with a Chinese inflection. "You're American, you love America but wanted to explore your roots here. I understand. I applaud it." He clapped his hands three times. "But *we* are your roots. Tradition, Victor. *We* take care of the neighborhood. Keep out the *really* bad fuckers who'll ruin it. And all we ask is a little something to repay us for our efforts."

"Hello." Trapp stepped forward, placing himself between Wu and the owner.

Wu's eyes widened in anger. "Who the fuck are you?"

"A really bad fucker," Trapp said.

Wu's eyes bulged even wider as his chest puffed up and his jaw jutted forward.

Trapp was aching to break it. But he might be able to front his way through this. He had forty pounds and six inches on both of them. And he was carrying cash.

"I just want to talk," Trapp said. "You have information, and I can pay this gentleman's donations for the week." Trapp flashed them a wad of hundreds from his jacket pocket, then put it back. "How does that sound?"

Wu and Zhu exchanged glances, then burst out laughing.

Zhu clapped Trapp on the shoulder. "Boy, you're a big guy. Not a cop. Not a fed. Did we take something from you? Because there aren't any Good Samaritans around here."

"Give me the names of your leadership and where I can find them," Trapp said, "and the money's yours."

"The money isn't the point." Zhu backed up a couple of steps, keeping his tone friendly, only not friendly at all. "The point is, *he* pays. We need *him* to pay."

"You don't want my money?"

Victor edged away, as if sensing something terrible was about to happen.

"Oh, we're taking your money," Zhu said. "It just isn't suitable to pay off Mr. Lau's debt."

"Give me a name," Trapp replied. "Who gives you orders? Who sent Asher Chan to—"

"How do you know Asher?" Zhu asked.

"I watched him die. Give me a name."

"Fuck this." Wu reached for the gun in his waistband.

Trapp's hand shot out faster and closed around the revolver's grip, pulled back the hammer, and kept it there. "Dare me to pull the trigger."

Wu froze.

Zhu said, "Do you know who the fuck we are?"

Trapp shifted closer to Wu, who remained completely still. "Looking at the tats, poor fashion choices, and bad boy threats, you're low-level Triad assholes shaking down old people for cash you didn't earn. A name."

"What name?" Wu asked, his voice a higher pitch now.

"Leadership." Trapp pressed the gun's barrel against Wu's skin and faced Zhu. "Who sent Asher Chan into Boston to shoot up that bar?"

Zhu's mouth turned up at the corners. "You think I value this guy's balls over my honor?"

Wu spoke in quick-fire Chinese with a whining, pleading note. Funny how macho masks were as delicate as eggshells as soon as genitals got involved.

Zhu checked over his shoulder toward the door, presumably for witnesses. Back to Trapp. "I think I'll risk it."

Damn. Trapp wasn't going to front this out after all.

Zhu reached under his shirt, so Trapp whipped Wu's gun out of his pants, launched his foot into the man to send him hurtling backwards, and pointed the weapon at the other thug. Zhu had jerked to Trapp's right, parried the gun, and brought out his own. But Trapp was already moving again, pivoting to redirect Zhu's armed hand, so both were holding the other's wrist, guns pointing away.

Zhu was stronger than he looked. Or Trapp had lost a few yards of pace.

"Call it a draw?" Zhu said.

"Nah."

Trapp yanked him forward, tripping Zhu over his thigh and landing him face down. He stood on the Triad's hand to force him to release the gun, but Wu rushed forward, now leading with a knife. Still hoping to avoid a gunshot, Trapp heaved Zhu to his feet and shoved him into Wu. He safetied the gun and tossed it to the surprised Victor, then decided to finish things quickly.

He kicked Wu in his precious balls, doubling him over, then plucked the knife from his hand and grabbed Zhu as he tried to untangle himself from his friend. Zhu spun with an elbow that Trapp dodged before he punched Zhu in the stomach about half a second before driving his knee up into the man's face. As Zhu staggered, Trapp shuffled forward and landed an elbow of his own, sending Zhu's eyes back in his head. The gangster was unconscious before he hit the ground.

Then Trapp maneuvered Wu into an arm lock and frog-marched him toward the back, retrieving the gun from Victor along the way. Trapp booted the exit open, flinging Wu into the alley ahead of him.

In the cool evening, he pointed the gun at Wu's groin. As a negotiating tactic, it seemed a good starting point.

"A name."

"I can't," Wu said.

Trapp took in the narrow alleyway. "This is kind of similar to the place where your buddy Asher killed himself. Nice symmetry."

"Ask Zhu."

"Your pal back there? If he wakes up anytime soon, he'll have a serious concussion. Might not know his own name for a while. Besides, he'll take too long to persuade. You're the weak link. You're gonna tell me inside a minute."

"I won't."

Trapp stepped closer. Not within arm's length, just enough to emphasize his point. "A name."

Wu looked frozen. If this went on much longer, he might soil his pants.

"Xiao Guanyu," he said, his voice a nasal whisper. "She's our head."

"She? Very progressive. Where do I find her?"

"Her son, Zhen. She has dinner with him on Sunday while we do our rounds."

Wu spilled the name of the restaurant that Xiao owned, then Trapp pocketed the gun, and he was away, the assholes all but forgotten as he considered the best approach.

The jungle awaited.

15

Trapp snagged the window seat of a busy bar across from the upscale restaurant that Triad head Xiao Guanyu and her son Zhen were known to frequent. Routine was the enemy of good security, but it was also the preserve of the untouchable. Even the cops didn't suspect who she really was, at least not enough to profile her in their official database. The restaurant was busy, yet three smartly-dressed waitstaff stood to attention by the entrance.

By the time Trapp had downed two club sodas with lime, a black SUV pulled up. The driver, a muscular man with short-cropped hair and a low brow, climbed out and surveyed the area before opening the rear passenger door. A woman in a white pantsuit emerged: petite, late fifties, carrying a quiet air of authority—Xiao Guanyu, Trapp assumed. She wore too much jewelry, including a necklace too chunky for someone of her physical stature, and her jet-black hair was pulled back into a tight bun.

A younger man followed, hair in a GI fade, his eyes glazed in boredom. His suit was black, his tie a metallic blue.

But it was the driver that caught Trapp's attention. The tall, broad-shouldered man had a military bearing, and he constantly scanned his surroundings. Trapp recognized the signs of close protection training, the way he positioned himself between Xiao and any potential threats as the trio entered the restaurant, his bulk weightless as he practically floated on the balls of his feet, ready to move at the slightest hint of danger.

Trapp needed more information before making his move. He'd googled all he could, and Greaves couldn't keep quarterbacking him without leaving a trail. If the people targeting Trapp succeeded, anyone who helped him could face treason charges. So he had to be very careful who he approached.

He pulled out his burner and dialed a number he knew by heart. A familiar female voice answered.

"Number withheld, intelligence community's anxiety skyrocketing, and a bar all shot up in Boston. Hello, Jason."

"It's an open line," Trapp said. "Minimal encryption."

"I'm not worried about that. Are you? Why might that be?"

"I can contain it. Are you tracing this?"

"I'm at home with my feet up and a glass of wine. So no, I'm not. But since they want to debrief you about this news item, and the House Intelligence Committee is demanding answers, it isn't beyond the realms of possibility that they'll stake out your former girlfriend as someone you might reach out to. Thanks for that, by the way."

Trapp had dated Eliza Ikeda for far longer than his relationships usually lasted, but nothing good lasted forever. Ikeda couldn't cope with constantly worrying that his laser-focused drive to do what he believed to be right might one day result in a knock at her door by an anonymous high-ranking official offering condolences for her loss. For his part, Trapp had worried entangling himself emotionally would lead to him losing his edge, fulfilling the exact prophecy that she feared.

"Why take the risk of reaching out to me?" Ikeda asked.

"Google only got me so far, and I don't have access to anything meatier."

"I can't be helping a wanted man, Jason. I've got agents to run and a boss up my ass about the Korean summit, so—"

"I'm not wanted yet. They just asked me to come in. I politely declined."

"Semantics."

"I'm not asking you to do anything illegal," Trapp said firmly. "I wouldn't do that."

Ikeda's silence, followed by a subtle *hmm*, said she believed him, which gave him a small ping of satisfaction. Their time together was the happiest he'd been in years, and in his quieter moments, he still hoped for a second chance. *If* he ever arrived in a place where he did not see the necessity to acquire safe houses unknown to anyone, including his own government.

"Nothing confidential," he said. "Just what you already know. If you aren't comfortable giving me what I ask for, I won't push."

"Fine. If they're tracking you right now, I don't know how long you'll have, so make it quick."

"When I met you, you worked in Hong Kong," he said. "You must have had contact with the Triads and Chinese intelligence."

"Of course. I mean, they never identified themselves as MSS, but—"

"I need background on Triads. How they work. What the US side is like."

"Why the Triads?" Ikeda's voice was sharp.

He explained quickly about Asher Chan and the intel he'd forced out of Wu. No mention of Timothy Greaves.

"They don't play by normal rules, even in the big bad world of mafia or street gangs. This is their entire life, their identity, and the positions they hold within that organization are never questioned. Think seventies Cosa Nostra. That power, it's something they see as their *right*, as ingrained in them as free speech and gun ownership are in us. They will not hesitate to kill you if they think you're a threat."

"I know." Trapp watched as Xiao and her entourage were seated at a private table, the expert bodyguard standing nearby. "What can you tell me about their hierarchy? I know some have connections to the Chinese government, but do they cooperate with others?"

Ikeda was silent for a moment. Trapp could hear the faint sound of tapping as she drummed her finger against the phone. Calculating what it might cost if she gave him what he wanted.

"You probably know already about the roles of the Dragon Head, the 426s, which is a nod to the numerology superstitions they have."

"Yes, Wikipedia gave me the basics. Do they really call the bosses 'Dragon Heads'?"

"Are you mocking another culture's traditions, Jason?"

"Have you been promoted to HR or something?"

"The formal designations are more ominous in Chinese. Dragon Head in English sounds silly, but only because we're used to military-type ranks, even in organized crime. Commander, lieutenants, et cetera."

"Does the name Xiao Guanyu ring a bell?"

"Guanyu does. Not Xiao."

"She's in charge here."

"A woman?" Ikeda sounded shocked.

"Problem with that?"

She hesitated, and he wasn't sure if she was thinking or bracing Trapp for bad news. "Jason, if the Triads have appointed a woman in charge of the... what are they called in Boston?"

"For some reason, they call themselves the Iron Lotus Guild."

"Right. If she is their head, she must have inherited it from a husband or father with no other heir."

"She has a son."

"How old?"

Trapp watched them for a beat. "About twenty, twenty-one."

"Possibly he was very young when his father passed. Usually, he would take over when he came of age. Meaning Xiao only hung on to the position because she was impeccable."

"Isn't that the same for all gang leaders?"

"I mean *impeccable*. Not competent. But perfect. Women are still not viewed as equals in Chinese institutions like this. Subservient, at best. If she has survived in her position, especially with a son in his twenties, she'll also be ruthless. So ruthless that no one will mess with her, not even people who think they have the right to take it off her."

Trapp let it sink in. Watching, he saw that Xiao had appointed her security well and that there were others nearby posing as diners but whose attention was on everything except their meals. He couldn't just march in, shoot the bodyguard, and cart Xiao and her boy out. There'd be others. Maybe some he hadn't spotted.

"And their ties to the government?" Trapp asked. "All I found were rumors and gossip online."

"Rumors and gossip that are both accurate and don't go deep enough. The Triads have *always* been useful tools for the Chinese state, going back to the 1800s. They were used to strong-arm trading partners and keep opium suppliers in line. Nowadays, they intimidate political opponents and business rivals in countries where Chinese agents would cause diplomatic complications. They threaten dissidents abroad and carry out the occasional bit of hands-on dirty work if the threats don't take. In return, they're given a certain amount of breathing room by the authorities. Illegal activity mostly, but they do have a lot of legitimate income, too. Often seeded with criminal gains, but it all adds up to a very intricate business model that is almost impossible to crack."

Trapp frowned. "So it *is* feasible that someone in the Chinese government could use the Triads to target me?"

"It's possible," Ikeda agreed. "If that's the case, you're dealing with some very powerful players."

"Or someone I overlooked. And the Hangman stuff. Anything like that come up?"

"No, that's a little beyond even the highest-level Triad. Or if it *is* the Chinese, I guess they're up to something more than just pissing you off."

"Yeah, the thought has occurred to me. See why I can't come in yet?"

"Because you don't like being pushed around the board without knowing who the finger belongs to?"

"Because I'm a nobody. The hack to get that intel, or to compromise someone to carry it out of a government building... it's small change. There has to be more to it. Combine it with an attempt on my life, which the cops and feds aren't convinced was targeted..."

"It's the start of something we need to get on top of?" Ikeda said softly, coming around to Trapp's thought process.

"Exactly. What are they going to pull while everyone is distracted by me and that summit?"

"What if they're using *you* as the distraction in order to *hit* the summit?"

Both good points.

"Tell someone," Trapp said. "Someone who'll listen."

"I understand," Ikeda said. "If you need anything else, Jason... anything that won't get me rendered to a black site, that is... just ask."

"I will. Thanks."

Trapp settled in to continue his surveillance, signaling for another club soda and lime, his eyes never leaving the restaurant across the street.

Xiao or Zhen might have given Chan the instruction to kill him, but someone was operating them from up on high. He just needed to work out what to do next.

He pulled out his phone and started digging.

16

I ron Lotus head Xiao Guanyu seethed as she rode in the back of her bodyguard Dennis Rhee's preferred SUV along with her son. It was a cushioned ride with soft-touch leather seats that still smelled new, a retractable privacy screen, and the expensive system that maintained the interior at the exact temperature that Xiao favored but Zhen complained was too warm. Tonight, it felt entirely too warm for her, too.

The news that two of her men had been roughed up by an American was troubling, hence her detail's insistence on the most heavily-armored of their vehicles on a social evening. Not that it had been particularly social tonight, as much of Zhen's conversation centered around how violently he would eviscerate the American intruder.

Sometimes she thought Zhen would make an excellent leader. He demonstrated strategic planning and a clarity of thought under pressure that would make his late father's spirit soar. Yet she was not blind to the cruelty that too often clouded that clarity. It seemed that the violent side of their world was what he lived for, and Zhen's strategizing was usually directed at deflecting Xiao's threats to send him to Hong Kong—her version of an American parent threatening a wayward teen with boot camp.

She had eventually turned dinner conversation to domestic matters, but she decided against discussing the medical appointment she'd attended. Like many young people, Zhen had learned to behave like an adult outwardly yet retained the immaturity of a teenager. She was ashamed to realize that it would be many years before she could think of him as a man, which posed a massive problem for her. A problem that she had to put to the back of her mind for now.

"Speak freely, Zhen," Xiao said. "I didn't raise you to hold your opinions inside."

Zhen sighed. "I told you we should have sent more men. Asher was untested. For a job like that—"

"Our client insisted."

"On Asher?"

"On someone low-level. Isn't that right, Dennis?"

Dennis hesitated before answering. "I believe the word he used was 'disposable,' someone who would not be missed if he came up empty. He said it was an easy job—aim and spray. Maybe we went *too* low with Asher."

"You see, Zhen, if you hadn't been gallivanting with your thug friends and whores, you might have attended the meeting and offered some input. A single gunman that the Americans will write off as another crazed killer. Would you have chosen Asher?"

"Maybe," Zhen said. "Or Jian Wu. He likes the rough stuff, even if he's a fucking idiot."

"Quite. And if this man is our target or is acting on his behalf, we must act swiftly. We cannot draw attention to ourselves."

"We will be subtle," Dennis assured her. "Boston PD should have no reason to raid anything important."

"A sacrifice might be needed," Zhen said. "Give them Asher's friends if you have to. They can be replaced."

Xiao nodded, weighing whether this was her son's calm mind or his cruel one doing the talking.

The SUV pulled to the curb, and Xiao bade her son goodnight.

"Please go straight home with Qui-lan and Cho. I will join you in an hour."

Zhen opened the door. "Why are *you* not going straight home?"

"I have an unavoidable appointment. Mr. Vaughn has a unit that he can't keep for long and is contemplating investing in our portfolio."

"Force him to hold it for you. Surely—"

"Not everything is a battle, Zhen. Sometimes we need to act civilly. Good night."

Zhen exited without comment, straightening his jacket and falling into step with Qui-lan and Cho, who would drive him back to the duplex penthouse Xiao shared with him.

Once they were alone, Dennis drove in silence. Two motorbikes followed, as arranged.

"My results came back," Xiao said suddenly, surprising herself.

"Your appointment?"

Xiao closed her eyes, choosing her next words carefully. "Dennis, what would happen if I were to step down?"

"Zhen would take over, of course."

"And you'd be fine with that?"

Dennis's momentary stutter was enough to make a lie of his response. "It is his birthright."

Dennis had been with the outfit since Xiao's husband had been gunned down while leaving a theater. Xiao had shielded little Zhen, but not fast enough to prevent him from seeing the bloody mess his father became before he even hit the sidewalk.

She had acted swiftly, bringing in outside contractors from a private security firm—*mercenaries*—and hunted down the Chechens who had tried to move in by cutting the head from the snake. Her bloody revenge and successful counter-takeover had persuaded the heads in Hong Kong that she should keep the leadership seat warm in Boston, and she had made wise decisions ever since. Including poaching one of the mercs' most able men to head up her security and train new recruits. But Dennis was American born—white mother, Chinese father—so was never truly accepted by the Triads.

"Dennis," she said, "I worry that Zhen might lead the Guild down a dark path. If I were to... pass."

Again, Dennis's initial lack of words spoke louder than his reply. "You're not thinking of... stepping aside?"

"I need a capable leader of men. I will be informing the heads of my decision."

"Wait, what?" Dennis twisted to look at her for a second before turning back to the road, a glance in the mirror apparently not significant enough.

"You know what I am suggesting," Xiao said. "Please do not insult me by pretending you do not agree. Our Triad exists to keep order, to benefit our community. If we are not calm and measured, we are no better than American thugs. And if I do not trust my son to be calm and measured, I must recommend someone who is."

"Madam, I am honored, but—"

"But the pureblood Chinese won't follow you? It will take some persuasion. If I get Hong Kong on board, the rest will fall in line."

"But Zhen—"

"Yes, he has his supporters here. People like him who enjoy the violence too much. I will have Zhen sent to Hong Kong for a year to learn under one of our senior leaders, keep him out of the way while you put your stamp on things here."

It was hard to read Dennis's reaction in the rearview mirror, but he blinked a couple of times, and she could tell he was considering the proposal. Not that she saw it as a proposal. It was a bequeathment, and soon it would be an order.

"Your results," Dennis said. "They were not good?"

"No. They were not good."

"I'm sorry. I really am."

Xiao smiled, but the sadness of unfinished business filled her. Was life ever long enough?

She said, "We have a few months. I will be sure to send Zhen on his secondment before I pass and hand over to you before joining him at his new home."

"If that is what you think is best. It's an honor."

"You said that already."

"I mean it. And I'm sorry, I really—"

"Enough," Xiao said. "We will discuss this later. Right now, we have business to attend to."

They pulled up in a loading zone outside a nondescript, six-story office building. No fear of a ticket here. Dennis exited the vehicle, scanning the street. The two motorcyclist outriders were armed with MP5 submachineguns, and they also spread out—two of Dennis's best recruits.

Satisfied that all was clear, Dennis opened the door for Xiao.

As they made their way inside the polished lobby, Xiao struggled to put their conversation in the SUV behind her. This meeting with a new investor would help to solidify their legitimate business interests and conceal an importing enterprise that had proven a fraction too successful and had attracted the attention of the IRS. But her cancer had returned, and she refused to be poisoned by chemotherapy, which would render her weak and frail. She had weeks, months at the most, to persuade the heads that her plans were sound.

Then, another complication.

"Zhen," she said, not bothering to disguise her frustration. "I made it clear that you were to return home. What are you doing here?"

Her son shrugged. "I wanted to learn instead of *gallivanting*. Isn't that what you wanted?"

While frustration welled inside her, Xiao was faintly pleased. Zhen was usually impulsive, headstrong. Now he was almost humble.

Almost.

She sensed something bubbling under his calm exterior, as if he was trying to prove a point rather than ingratiate himself.

"Very well," she said. "But no threats. No violence. Understood?"

Zhen promised he'd behave, so they waited in the elevator lobby for the two guards to race up the stairs to the fourth floor. Receiving the all-clear, Dennis gave a nod and called the elevator, moving them aside while the door opened.

Empty.

All three ascended to the fourth floor, which was undecorated and littered with building equipment. They marched through the under-renovation corridors to the office where the meeting was to take place.

Dennis slipped inside, returning just over a minute later and holding the door for them. "All clear. Mr. Vaughn is alone and unarmed. The exits are locked from the inside."

Xiao led Zhen into the office, allowing a tiny shiver at the dip in temperature thanks to the powerful AC. The suited man who stood waiting for them was good-looking for a Caucasian, in a rugged sort of way. Middle-aged, with a solemn air about him. Did he know the true nature of Xiao Guanyu's business?

Undoubtedly. But does he care?

"Madam Xiao." He bowed his head respectfully. "It's an honor to finally meet you in person."

Xiao inclined her head, fighting to withhold a small smile. "The honor is mine, Mr. Vaughn."

But before the man could respond, a wave of dizziness washed over Xiao. Zhen swayed on his feet, his eyes glazing over. The Caucasian man lifted a mask to his mouth and nose, like the ones that drop from the overhead space on planes.

"What... What's happening?" Xiao managed to say, her tongue thick and heavy.

The investor smiled through his mask. "Don't fight it."

Zhen dropped to one knee, teeth bared, eyes flaring. "I will *kill* you."

"No, you won't. Halothane vapor has that effect on people."

As darkness closed in around her, Xiao noted the cheapness of the man's suit—ill-fitting around the shoulders, short at the ankle. She should have picked up on that.

Who *was* this man? And what did he want with her and her son?

As she sent a silent prayer to her late husband to watch over Zhen, everything went black.

17

Trapp hefted the unconscious Xiao over one shoulder, her weight nothing compared to the wounded comrades he'd pulled from battlefields around the world. Then he bent at the knees and grasped Zhen by the belt, carrying him to the back wall like a suitcase. He lay them both down and peeled back a corner of carpet before taking out his gun and a screwdriver. With the building undergoing renovation, there had been plenty of materials on this floor, including a sheet of particle board, which he'd slapped over a door that even the studious Dennis Rhee hadn't thought to check.

Xiao's dinner with Zhen had lasted over two hours, during which Trapp had conducted some press and social media research linking Xiao to several seemingly respectable people in the business community, a simple PR exercise that kept her appearance intact. Although Trapp hated himself for it, he couldn't help thinking the phrase *legitimate businessmen* in a mock-Sicilian accent.

It only took two levels of digging to see that she was interested in this property, which was owned by a guy called Mark Vaughn, who specialized in flipping stalled projects for profit.

Vaughn moonlighted as an angel investor, and he was not shy in bragging to his friends that he had a "BIG meeting with the BIGGEST playa in Chinatown on Sunday. Watch this space for GREAT news!" From there, Trapp just needed to correlate the Triads' movements with Vaughn's.

After knocking Vaughn out and stashing him safely in a closet, he'd concealed the second door of this office with the board so it looked like a hastily-repaired broken window and set the halothane canisters to remote-release over the doors via a button he kept in his pocket.

Trapp now pried the panel aside using the screwdriver and propped open the door with a fire extinguisher. He then carried mother and son down the dark, incomplete corridor beyond to a stairwell that was marked as an internal fire sanctuary. He opened the door and held still to listen, his hand close to his gun. No one came running. No one came shooting.

He descended swiftly with muted, echoing footfalls, and when he arrived at ground level, Trapp placed both his prisoners on the floor and searched them, removing an assortment of tracking devices using a handheld scanner—Apple Tags, a bespoke bug hidden on Xiao's pearl necklace, and their phones. He pushed open the external door and propped it ajar with a brick, speed-walked into the back alley, and scattered the items on the ground, giving the impression that he had tossed them before spiriting the pair away in a vehicle. Then he returned inside and carried his prisoners down two more floors to a sub-basement.

A long, wide warehouse-like setup, it was mostly empty except for rows of bare industrial shelving running the length of the building, some containing lockboxes and office equipment and a few appliances and electronics awaiting reclamation. Other shelves stored only a layer of dust. He'd checked that there were two exits, no occupants immediately above, and no street access.

He set the pair down on a blanket six feet from a chair, a table with a bottle of water on it, and some frightening-looking instruments that he might as well have borrowed from a demon dentist. Zhen was already stirring, so Trapp handcuffed them both to a shelving unit that was as solid as a scaffolder's pole. He locked the entry door, donned a pair of surgical gloves, and broke out a tiny bottle. The smelling salts revived Xiao first, then Zhen, the pair rising back to life, blinking, clearly trying to focus.

Xiao released a deep sigh at the handcuffs but little more. She sat up, crossed her legs, and stared at Trapp. Zhen, on the other hand, howled in anger and started yanking at the bindings, clanking and shouting until Trapp pulled the gun and aimed it directly at his face.

Zhen shut up, but his face was a mask of barely contained rage.

"This place isn't soundproof," Trapp said, "but there's no one to hear you unless they're standing right outside. I removed everything with a GPS before transporting you, so I have plenty of time."

Zhen yanked so hard at his bonds it had to have left a mark. "This is *bullshit!*"

Xiao, by comparison, remained stoic and silent.

"You can't do this," Zhen went on with a twist to his mouth. "You can't just snatch us off the street."

Trapp smiled coldly. "I think I just did."

Zhen spat in Trapp's direction. "When my people find us—"

"They won't."

Xiao spoke for the first time. "And what is it that you want, Mr....?"

"Answers. Starting with who ordered the hit on me."

Xiao bristled and turned her head away, lips pressed tight.

Zhen scoffed, eyes skimming off the strategically-placed tools. "You're even dumber than you look."

Trapp selected a two-pronged rake the size of a trowel. He had no intention of torturing this pair, but starting with a bluff was a decent gambit. He set the rake down and appraised Zhen. "Your mother is content to sit in silence, but you don't strike me as the quiet type."

Zhen glanced at his mother. Xiao remained impassive, her gaze fixed on a point under the empty shelving unit.

"Fuck this woo-woo meditation shit," Zhen said. "You're not going to sit here and go along with this, are you?"

"Zhen," Xiao said. "Be quiet."

Zhen looked scolded, a reprimanded child. But the child quickly grew a spine, the way teenagers do when they decide now is the time to stand up to their parents. "Fuck this. Mom, this is just *laowai* bullshit."

"No, Zhen." She checked her watch, an elegant Philippe Patek. "Say nothing. Dennis will find us."

Trapp returned to the table for a couple of gulps of water, then selected what looked like a rusty ice pick but which he knew had something to do with horses.

"*Zhen*," Xiao said with a deeper intonation. "Do not let him fool you. If he was going to hurt us, he would have started with that. Hold your tongue, and all will be fine."

Trapp met her eye. She hadn't wavered an inch. He admired that she'd read his intentions. But that was useful; she'd know he was telling the truth next.

Trapp replaced the implement and paced slowly. "Okay, fine. In that case, I'm simply going to keep you here..." He crouched on his haunches a couple of feet from Xiao. "And while you're begging me for bathroom breaks and water, I am going to wreck your thugs. One at a time, however many there are. You won't know where, and you won't be able to stop me. I'll take them down, just like your goons earlier tonight."

"What good will that do?" Zhen said.

"Well, with your foot soldiers turning up broken and

useless in the hospital and the leadership missing, how long until others move in? The Russians? Mexicans? How many of your boys will I burn through before they start quietly slinking away with their tails between their legs?"

Zhen was about to speak, some threat, probably, but he caught himself, gears turning.

"What's more important?" Trapp pressed. "Burning this one contact or destroying your whole business model?"

Trapp could practically see the calculations running through his mind, weighing the pros and cons of cooperation. Xiao stared at her son, but he avoided her gaze.

"The hit," Zhen said at last. "It was ordered by..."

Trapp watched him.

"It was ordered by... *fuck your momma*." Zhen extended his middle finger, grinning.

"My son knows nothing," Xiao said.

"Then why worry about him speaking?" Trapp asked.

"Because he does not understand the need for discretion."

"How discreet do you think *I'm* gonna be?"

"Very." Xiao looked impassive, immovable. "If you create too much trouble, perhaps the next person who comes looking for you will not be an amateur."

Trapp considered that. "I'm hoping so. When I've burned through your chaff and you're hemorrhaging money, it might be enough to get them to say hi in person."

Xiao again fell silent, her eyes returning to the spot under the shelves.

"Fine." Trapp stowed his gun in his belt. "Twenty-three, Wohan Way, off 14th Street. I'm going to shoot your security up. Should panic the gamblers enough to shut you down for the night."

"You wouldn't dare," Zhen said.

"Quiet," Xiao snapped.

The suspected casino had featured in the BPD database, a

collection of three converted apartments over an antiques store and a microbrewery. Triads used similar venues all across the US.

Trapp said, "How much would you lose in a night? Add to that what I'm gonna do tomorrow..."

"This *laowai*," Zhen said. "He's none of our fucking business. We did what that foreign asshole asked—"

"Zhen!" Xiao interrupted.

"I don't give two shits about some prick from Washington."

Trapp leaned in. "A foreigner? Who?"

"I don't know his name."

"Zhen, you do not understand," Xiao said.

"I understand plenty, *Mother*. You freeze me out because you think I'll ruin your image. All your decorum and tradition. Where has that got us? Tied up in some shitty basement with a psycho."

"Tell me," Trapp said. "Russia? Middle East?"

"No," Xiao said.

Zhen glared at her. Thinking. For a long moment, no one spoke. Trapp could hear the hum of fluorescent lights overhead. The distant *skritch-skritch-tap* of something tiny and sharp on metal. Rats, or air in the pipes. Trapp's skin prickled with anticipation that he was about to learn something useful, one way or another.

"Zhen, no," Xiao warned. "*Dennis will find us.*"

Zhen's grin had not faded, and he hadn't so much as glanced at his mother while she spoke. "China."

"You said foreigner," Trapp reminded him.

"I'm American," Zhen said with a hint of offense, then resumed his growly tough-guy independence. "He was Chinese. I know the difference."

"Of course. Please continue."

"*Zhen*," Xiao said. Again the hiss, the warning. "If you do this, you will never lead our guild. I will see to it."

Zhen smirked through his nose. "You don't have a say in it, Mother. I am old enough to take over now. If I chose, I could—"

"Let's continue with what you know," Trapp said. "Why one guy? Why someone so crappy with a gun? No professional hitters available?"

"We have plenty. Including me."

Another *skritch-skritch-tap* made the hairs on the back of Trapp's neck stand on end—a primordial reaction to vermin, to something that had leveled great harm on his evolutionary ancestors.

"Why?" Trapp pressed, pushing the sensation aside. "Why target me?"

Zhen shrugged. "How should I know? Laowai shit pissing off Chinese shit. I don't care."

Trapp's gaze drifted back to Xiao. Her expression remained unreadable.

"All right," Trapp said. "Here's what's going to happen. You're going to give me everything you have on this guy. Names, dates, locations. I'll let you both go, and I'll be out of China-town before sunrise."

Then, as it seemed Xiao was about to open her mouth to deliver words other than a warning to her son, Trapp's instincts screamed at him too loudly to keep ignoring. Xiao's demeanor had shifted. A glint of something in the corner of her upturned mouth.

Satisfaction?

Triumph?

That *skritch-skritch-tapping* of tiny claws... her eyes flickered to the door.

Not claws.

Not rodents.

A different kind of vermin.

"You were stalling," Trapp said, checking his gun.

"Of course," Xiao said. "And if my son had any balls, he would have too."

"Fuck you," Zhen said, then yelled, "Help!" His voice echoed off the walls. "We're here! Help us!"

A crash sounded, wood and metal breaking as the door caved in. Footsteps outside. Voices.

As the first Triad enforcers burst through the door, weapons drawn, Trapp was already in motion.

18

The gavel struck with a sharp crack, ending the late-night session of the House Permanent Select Committee on Intelligence and flooding Jake Redman with equal parts relief that no one had identified the source of the Hangman leaks and pride in his daring risk, a gamble that would surely pay dividends within the coming days and weeks.

Redman had convened the HPSCI as soon as the files exploded onto the airwaves. They had emerged faster than he'd expected, and although all the committee had resolved was to call key personnel, the twenty members out of twenty-four who'd attended the meeting had departed with a sense of bipartisan accomplishment.

Bipartisanship.

Something President Nash had inspired in his first term and was dangerously, in Redman's opinion, doubling down on in his second. Sometimes unity was needed, but to run a strong country, you needed to impose your will, not dilute it with platitudes to people who would never vote for you anyway.

Redman stood waiting for the chamber to empty, his habit

ever since ascending to the chairmanship. He relished these moments, watching their backs as they exited, the sheep from both parties alongside the wolves he had strategically placed to keep himself informed of any scuttlebutt that might threaten his position. Or maybe he should call them rats. It didn't matter. Ears like theirs were essential in the current climate with Redman's party creeping ever closer to the center, as if a country could be run on compromise.

On *friendship*.

As the other members filed out, Redman noticed the committee's ranking member, Rita Tarragona, hovering nearby, watching him with her notebook pressed to her chest like a sophomore hoping to catch a lecturer's eye. Effectively his second and a sop to the Democrat minority, take-no-shit leftie Rita had often been cited as a future presidential nominee before Nash had started doling out scraps of liberal meat to bring the Democrats on-side. More recently, she'd offered a voice for centrism and cooperation, but she didn't fool Redman. She was as much a wolf as those he had dressed in wool and set among the herd; she was just a different breed than his people.

"Comfortable, Jake?" she asked, her chin high.

The chairman started gathering his notes, his iPad, his two phones. "With state secrets dribblin' out of the Pentagon like a sieve? Not really."

Tarragona flashed the expression that meant she had something to say but was afraid it might draw conflict. "Weird timing, don't you think?"

"How so?" Redman adopted his pleasant face and crossed to the door.

Rita kept pace as they exited into one of the many corridors. "The president is on the verge of a historic peace summit, and now *this* is the story dominating the news cycle."

"Don't worry, it'll be gone by the time the Koreans sign. You know what news cycles are like. Some Russian hack won't keep the ad revenue flowing for long."

"A hack? That's a little presumptuous, Jake. And Russia? We only mentioned them in passing. Why not the hardline North Koreans? Why not China? You think Beijing wants us to make nice with their sphere of influence?"

Redman sped up to resist slapping the bitch, sinking deeper into the jovial good-ol'-boy manner that kept getting him re-elected. "Gut feeling. I spent years cultivating it..." He patted his ample stomach. "Learned to listen to it more than I listen to doom-mongering."

Rita bristled but led with a smile. "Pride goeth before the fall, Congressman. Remember that."

He halted outside his office, where they paused for a long, drawn-out moment as he tried to work out if she was delivering a threat or genuine concern.

She turned on her heel and strode on, leaving him alone with his thoughts as he entered his office to grab his jacket before heading home.

There would be no fall. When the end of President Nash's second term approached, Redman would seek his party's nomination, and perhaps one day he would meet Rita at the debate podium. Weirdly, he liked the woman, a... What did the young people call a relationship like theirs? A frenemy? She was an entertaining sparring partner, but he would annihilate her if he needed to. Just as he would not shy away from bringing Nash's second term to a premature end via impeachment, should the Hangman scandal expand to encompass him.

But what if that was what the Chinese wanted? Nash out of the way? Might Redman accidentally do their job for them?

No. President Redman would be far harder on the Chinese than Nash. And he sure as hell wouldn't offer to weaken America's military strength in the region simply to convince the North Koreans that they could all be friends.

A knock at the door jolted him. Fabian Pincher poked his prematurely-balding head in. "Congressman, your next appointment has been brought forward."

Redman frowned. "Appointment? It's almost midnight."

Fabian stepped fully into the room, checking over his shoulder that no one was listening. He had the manner of a nervous weasel, but he was loyal, easily manipulated, and worked like a shire horse. Would do anything for a morsel of power discarded from the congressman's plate.

Pincher by name, Pincher by nature.

He said, "It's the one that's not on the official schedule, sir."

Redman needed to force the unease out of his voice. "Oh, that one. Where?"

THIRTY MINUTES LATER, Redman tentatively approached a secluded corner of the Smithsonian's Air and Space Museum. Closed to the public at this time of night, it had been opened to host elementary-age kids from three different nations: North Korea, South Korea, and China. Local and foreign politicians had spent hours glad-handing with diplomats, teachers, and kids, milking photo ops to show their multi-culti credentials and oh-so-sincere yearning for world peace. The kids were currently secluded amid the Destination Moon exhibit and should all be asleep on their camp beds and roll mats by now. There were several adults milling around the building, too. Strangely, the North Korean elementary school teachers were all men, with hard, dead eyes and decidedly callused hands. This area, though—a section dedicated to World War II in the air—was off-limits for the next twenty minutes.

"Congressman Redman," the Asian man said, his voice smooth and even, like any political hanger-on. "Thank you for coming on such short notice. I thought it would be good to meet in person tonight, as tomorrow may be too busy for you."

Redman forced a smile as he shook the man's hand beside two mannequins dressed in ancient brown flight suits. Above them, a gray airplane hung at an angle to give the appearance of flight. "Always happy to strengthen the ties between our two great nations."

The 'consultant' mirrored Redman's false smile, his eyes as dead as coal. "The information you provided has been useful. We just need you to—"

Redman kept his volume to a harsh whisper. "I'm not some patsy you can shake down. If you want more from me, you'd better give me something in return, Mister... what do I call you?"

The man moved his hands behind his back. He was a foot shorter than Redman and about a third as heavy, but he exuded the same don't-give-a-crap attitude as Rita Tarragona.

"Call me Li."

"Like Bruce Lee?"

"If you like, yes."

"Okay, *Lee*," Redman said. "What do you have for me?"

This time, Lee's smile spread to his eyes, satisfaction oozing from him. He took out his phone, tapped the screen twice, and held it up.

Redman's breath caught. There, on the screen, was a photo of him shaking Lee's hand moments earlier in the shadow of the iconic Mustang. The congressman snapped his attention to the other side of the room but couldn't spot the hidden cameraman.

"Let me explain." Lee slid the phone back into his pocket. "We have a lot of incriminating evidence against you. Between this meeting and the papers your lapdog smuggled out, it would not bode well for your promise to be 'strong on China,' would it?"

Redman swallowed hard, his earlier bravado gone. He cursed himself for being so foolish. So arrogant. "What do you want?"

"Use your position to push for a full inquiry into the CIA's use of targeted assassination. Your president must have known something about the Hangman. About others, too. Sow discord. Cast doubt. Say you are doing it for your people. For your precious *democracy*."

Redman's mouth was dry. "And?"

"And," Lee said, "keep us informed on the investigation into the bar shooting in Boston."

"That'll be FBI," Redman said. "I don't know if—"

"Find a way. Find a connection."

Redman saw where this was heading. This Lee—or whatever his real name was—had engineered the Hangman business and likely wanted it linked to the shooting in Boston, which was stirring yet another debate on Second Amendment rights.

"That shooter died on the scene," Redman said. "He wasn't the man you're looking for."

"No, but I understand a witness has gone missing. We'd be interested in his whereabouts."

That made little sense, but Redman forced himself to focus. If he were to regain the upper hand, he needed to roll over and let them scratch his belly for a while. His pride could come after they fell.

"I'll do what I can," he said. "But I'll need something in return."

Lee raised an eyebrow. "This is not a negotiation. You will do as we ask, or you will be outed as a Chinese asset."

Redman steadied himself, his fists balled, ready to pound this little asshole into the floor and keep pounding. But someone else had sent the photo to his phone, someone who might still be nearby. Killing a foreigner in one of the country's finest museums would cause more problems than it solved.

"That will be all," Lee said.

Redman muttered, "We'll see" and barged past Lee, shoulder-checking him as he went.

Without looking back, Redman slammed out of the exhibit and stormed through the high, echoing passages to where Fabian was waiting. He didn't slow, forcing Fabian to scurry after him.

"That bastard," Redman said. "He thinks he can play me? *Me?*"

"Sir, what happened?"

Redman shook his head, his pace quickening, pleased that Fabian looked so frantic alongside him. "It doesn't matter. Let's just say he's playin' dirty. And we're gonna fight back. Are you with me?"

Fabian nodded, pulling back his shoulders as if that made him look more manly. "Of course, sir."

"You'll do what I ask? Whatever that might be?"

"If it means we come out on top."

Redman allowed himself a small, grim smile. "We always come out on top."

19

After Madam Xiao had placed such faith in him, Dennis Rhee could not fail her a second time tonight. With the stench of spent explosives stinging his nostrils and his ears pounding despite the plugs, he breached the basement with his handgun drawn and an MP5 submachine gun strapped to his back. It was a terrible offensive position, and he didn't have the basement's blueprints, so speed was key. Speed and efficiency.

Dennis's two leather-clad operators fanned out with MP5 stocks pressed to their shoulders. They'd spotted the stranger who'd been posing as Mark Vaughn drifting left. Dennis trusted his guys would have inferred the same as he had: that their target had military training, most likely American, given his stance and movement. That was okay; Dennis and his close-protection team were former military, too. Might even make this an interesting search-and-destroy exercise.

He had planned to wait until the target was clear of Xiao and Zhen, signaling Xiao to be patient via a coded tapping they had devised for just such an occasion. Zhen had clearly forgotten his hostage drills or hadn't paid attention in the first place. His panic had forced their hand.

They stalked among the shelving units in two-by-one formation, one of them penetrating forward to clear each blind spot while the other two backed him up, switching the lead each time with a tap on the shoulder. On the fourth cycle, Dennis was leading when he caught a glimpse of movement to his right.

He fired, the shots echoing painfully in the confined space. The target returned fire, three close-pattern rounds sparking off metal shelves, forcing Dennis back. He signaled his guys to hold position.

"He's boxed in," Dennis said. "We cut off his exit strategy. Pincer movement. Shoot on sight."

Nods in reply.

"Good. I'll secure the principals and get them out. If we're split up, rendezvous at the Gau-long warehouse."

More nods.

Dennis dismissed them with a silent OK gesture, then took off back the way he'd come, zipping through the maze of shelves until he located Xiao and Zhen—right where the stranger had run from.

"Where the hell have you been?" Zhen demanded, rattling the cuff.

Xiao gave Dennis a grateful nod. "Thank you for the hairpin," she said, referencing the bug hidden within that emitted a three-second radio pulse every ten minutes, making it difficult for an abductor to detect during a search.

Dennis carried handcuffs at all times and therefore a handcuff key, which he used to free Xiao, then Zhen.

"Give me that," Zhen said, gesturing to the submachine gun on Dennis's back.

"I'm getting you both to safety," Dennis answered. "Leave this troublemaker to my men."

"No!" Zhen grabbed Dennis by the lapels of his suit, eyes blazing. "I'm going after him."

Although Dennis could have taken the impetuous, over-confident kid down in six different ways, Zhen was still Madam Xiao's son. No matter her misgivings or views on succession, he was still bound by the hierarchy. For now. A glance at Xiao earned an affirmative dip of the chin, so Dennis handed over the weapon.

Zhen checked it hastily, flicked off the safety, and disappeared after the stranger.

SACRIFICING SPEED FOR STEALTH, Trapp wove through the shelving units. The basement felt like a small desert town with tightly packed rat runs down which insurgents would flee after shooting at troops. Different environment, but same nerves firing, synapses alive.

He ducked behind a shelf packed with filing cabinets still in their plastic wrap, listening intently for the scuff of a foot, a whisper, a breath.

His hunters moved at jogging pace, slowing every few steps, sweeping their weapons side to side. Thorough. Efficient.

Timing their approaches, Trapp sank under the eyeline of the guy to his right, closing the gap just as the enforcer rounded the corner. Trapp lunged, grabbed the MP5's barrel, and yanked it upward. The gunman's finger tightened on the trigger, sending a burst of three into the ceiling as Trapp brought his own gun up and pumped three bullets into the man's torso, spraying out the other side.

The second enforcer appeared almost immediately, weapon raised. Trapp used the first man's body as a shield, the rounds slamming into the standing corpse giving him the split-second he needed to evade the line of fire.

Trapp gambled that the other man was expecting him to bolt like a frightened rabbit. Instead, he dodged back and let off two shots, quick and precise. The first took the man in the chest, the second in the throat, a spray of blood splattering the shelves behind as he flopped to the ground.

Trapp paused for a moment, his heart rate elevated but steady. The gunfire would have alerted Rhee.

Trapp stepped over the bodies and ran silently toward where he'd left Xiao and Zhen. Keeping low, watching for movement, then—

A muted padding alerted him to someone incoming. He froze, listening. Tilted his head one way, then the other, like radar pinpointing an aircraft.

Trapp guessed it wasn't Dennis. It was either another enforcer that Trapp had not spotted up top, or...

Trapp scaled one of the shelving units, three levels up, almost twelve feet above the floor, and rolled carefully to the opposite side. There, stalking in an approximation of someone who'd only seen soldiers on TV, was Zhen. Two aisles away, plainly closing in on Trapp's last position.

The young man held the gun competently, and with so many units and struts in the way, Trapp couldn't get a clear shot.

He crawled onward, the opposite direction from Zhen, reaching the end of the basement and shimmying down the final upright. He was twenty yards from where he'd interrogated the pair.

The grid-like layout allowed Trapp an easy route back, slow and methodical as if sneaking up on a deer. He spotted Xiao's white suit through a tangle of chairs stacked two units away. No sign of Dennis or Zhen.

Trapp hesitated, listening, looking, all but reaching out with some latent psychic ability that he wished were real.

Nothing.

He glided around the corner, gun down but ready, and closed the distance in seconds. He must have gotten clumsy, though. Xiao turned suddenly toward him, crying out in alarm.

Dennis came running, just feet away, suggesting he was covering both his boss and the more obvious point of egress.

Trapp grabbed Xiao and pulled her close.

"Easy now," Dennis said.

"I'm leaving." Trapp pressed his gun into her side. "You shoot, I have enough time to pull the trigger."

"No need for that." Dennis held his hand out, gun to the side. "I just want her unharmed. You can go on your way."

"I'll release her when I'm clear." Trapp backed toward the door through which Dennis had attacked. It led to a freight lobby that would give Trapp access to the yard, where he'd parked a stolen van.

"I'm coming with you," Dennis said.

"Nope." Trapp strengthened his grip on Xiao. She was about half his size. Dennis could probably have made a shot to his head if he'd acted sooner. Now Trapp could finish her before Dennis even drew a bead. "I won't murder her for the sake of it."

"Who do you work for?" Dennis followed as Trapp hustled Xiao onward.

"No one," Trapp said, waiting for the slightest twitch of his gun hand. "Drop the weapon and stay where you are. I'm more than willing to shoot you."

Dennis ran his options and halted, placing the weapon on a shelf next to an empty box that had once contained a shredder. Trapp stopped, too. Dennis sidestepped away, showing Trapp both palms. "Okay, this is what we'll do. I'll be your hostage. We swap, and—"

Before he could make the offer that Trapp would reject out of hand, Zhen tore into view to Rhee's right, the MP5 up at his shoulder. Consumed by rage, yelling in Chinese, he opened fire.

"Shit." Trapp ducked away for cover, the bullets whizzing past him, forcing him to release Xiao.

As he readied to crouch at a new angle and return fire, he heard Xiao grunt. Everyone had stopped moving, even Zhen. Trapp was still close enough to Xiao to touch her, but he couldn't risk it.

She stepped to the left, twisting ninety degrees, revealing that her white suit was peppered with holes, blood blooming from the wounds to her torso, stomach, and legs.

Zhen's bullets had torn through his own mother.

She folded to the floor to cries of shock as Trapp made a break for the exit, firing blindly at the two men to cover his escape.

20

Trapp burst out of the door at the top of the basement's stairwell into a light drizzle, pausing to listen for pursuit but hearing nothing.

With no one behind him, he speed-walked through the alleyway to the street, pressing his back against the wall before peeking out.

He couldn't shake the thought of whether Zhen had *intended* to kill his own mother?

"Hey! Is that him?"

A group of jittery young men were waiting a couple of buildings down, massed together near the front door rather than spaced out like sentries. Whatever their positional short-comings, they had spotted him.

Rhee's backup muscle strutted out, pulling an assortment of cheap, street-thug weapons—pistols, knives, and even a couple of metal pipes. Although they weren't trained operatives like the ones in the basement, they had numbers on their side. Eight of them, all fit-looking young men. Trapp had maybe four bullets left.

Not good enough.

They charged toward him, shouting in Chinese.

Trapp cursed under his breath and sprinted away, driving hard around the nearest corner as a small-caliber bullet cracked off the wall beside him.

He wove through the narrow street, dodging startled pedestrians who scrambled for cover at the sight of the armed men. More gunshots cracked behind him, bullets ricocheting off walls and shattering the glass of a nearby storefront. Screams filled the air as bystanders fled the prospect of violence, sheltering in doorways, behind cars, in the maze of alleyways and side streets.

Trapp's heart pounded as adrenaline coursed through him. The Triads' shouts and curses followed behind, mingling with the panicked cries of innocent bystanders. He pushed forward, dodging at random, weaving around the street-sellers, unwilling to give the Triads a straight shot at him. These alleys were blind shooting galleries where even a poor shot, as the two with pistols seemed to be, should be able to hit him.

Not that these were conscious thoughts. They were pure instinct, his training and experience taking over as he navigated the unfamiliar terrain.

Emerging from the street of traders toward an even busier thoroughfare, the roar of motorcycle engines suddenly filled the air. Two bikes with helmet-free riders, their bare arms adorned with tattoos, screamed in from a side street ahead, their headlights a dazzling reflection off wet asphalt. They revved their engines, accelerating toward Trapp, intent on cutting off his escape.

Still acting on pure instinct, Trapp veered sharply to the right, his shoes skidding on the slick sidewalk as he hurled himself into a bustling night market.

The narrow space was packed with vendors hawking their wares and shoppers browsing colorful stalls, the air thick with the scent of sizzling meats and fragrant spices, cooking oil, and cigarette smoke.

Trapp barreled through the crowd, his arms pumping as he dodged and weaved between startled pedestrians, his senses heightened to a razor's edge.

Behind him, the motorcycles plowed into the market, engines snarling. Trapp heard the crunch of metal on wood as the bikes slammed into stalls, sending merchandise and debris flying. People cried out and scattered like birds, arms flailing as they tried to avoid the rampaging vehicles.

Trapp hated that innocent lives were in danger, but he couldn't risk being caught, not with the Hangman in the news. His mission was over, his key source of intel dead. His only hope was to get to safety and regroup.

They were not going to make it easy for him.

As Trapp burst out of the night market, he found himself in an open area with little cover, making him an easier target. And although the market had slowed them, the motorcycles were streaking in fast, their riders leaning forward as they hurtled closer. One of them unhooked a chain from his handlebars and wrapped one end around his hand.

Trapp scanned his surroundings, desperately searching for an escape route.

The thugs on foot had taken a shortcut that Trapp hadn't dared attempt and now were not far behind the bikes either, their shouts growing louder with each second.

Trapp spotted a young couple getting into a ten-year-old sports car, a high-end Audi. Time seemed to freeze as he ran a split-second scenario through his mind.

Then the bikes were upon him.

The guy with the chain pulled into the lead, jerking toward him faster than expected. When the chain swung his way, Trapp ducked, rolled, and sprang back to his feet, facing the oncoming gang ten feet away. He sprinted toward the sports car, jerking left to let one motorcycle shoot past, then lunging the last few feet when he heard the pop-pop of gunshots.

Trapp wrenched open the driver's side door, his fingers closing around the startled man's arm.

"I'm real sorry, buddy, but I'll make it right."

He dragged the squirming driver out. He didn't need to tell the woman in the passenger seat to exit. She scrambled out, falling on the ground with a yelp of panic as he slid behind the wheel, the leather seat still warm from its previous occupant.

The engine was already running. Now it growled to life under Trapp's heavy foot, slamming down on the accelerator and sending the tires screeching against the road as it lurched into motion.

In the rearview mirror, pressed back into his seat as he accelerated, he could see the motorcycles closing in, the second rider brandishing a chain of his own.

Must be a trend.

With the stolen Audi's engine howling its revs into the red, the motorcycles quickly caught up, the riders flanking him on either side. The one on the left, still gripping the chain, pulled up alongside Trapp's window and swung the weapon, aiming for the glass by his head.

Trapp swerved just in time; the chain clanged against the door. The motorcycle wobbled as the chain bounced back, but the rider regained control, revving his engine for another attempt.

On the right, the second rider had wrapped the chain around his torso and pulled out a gun, the sleek black metal dull under the streetlights. Trapp watched the man take aim, his finger tightening on the trigger, waiting for the telltale adjustment as he prepared for recoil.

Trapp slammed on the brakes, the Audi's tires screeching. The motorcycle continued forward, the shot going wild, the rider's aim thrown off as he struggled to slow down.

Trapp shifted gears and accelerated forward, ramming the back of the motorcycle with a crunch. The bike flipped, metal scraping against asphalt, sparks flying in its wake. The rider hit the ground hard, rolling several times before coming to a stop, motionless. No helmet, no leathers. Idiot.

Still, that's one down.

The remaining motorcycle rider's face twisted in determination. He was coming after Trapp, no matter what had happened to his pal. Or maybe because of it.

Didn't matter. All Trapp needed to do as the guy came up on him again was clip him to one side and he'd be toast. And he was only five or six feet away.

Suddenly, the squeal of tires and engines surrounded him as two more cars emerged from the light throng behind, their headlights blinding in Trapp's rearview mirror.

Must've been waiting for him.

The Triad reinforcements drove sleek sedans that quickly boxed him in from behind. Bullets pinged off the Audi's trunk, the rear window shattering in a spray of glass.

Trapp gritted his teeth, his knuckles white on the steering wheel. He scanned the road, jerking the wheel in small increments to keep them from pushing him into a skid and to throw their aim off as he nudged their front fenders. The Audi kept threatening to fishtail, its automatic anti-lock brakes proving difficult to control.

Up ahead, a left turn beckoned, a sign toward a Boston suburb outside of Chinatown. Trapp yanked the wheel to the left, the Audi's tires smoking as he bit into the turn. The motorcycle and one of the cars overshot the corner as the other car was pushed to the side, locking its wheels. It bought Trapp precious seconds as they scrambled to correct their course. Hope dawned that if he got free of their territory, they might give up the chase.

But Trapp's relief was short-lived. As he sped down the

narrow street, a large delivery truck emerged from a parking lot, its brakes screeching as the driver tried to avoid the stolen car. Trapp swerved, the Audi's bumper missing the truck by inches.

The Triads were relentless now, like starving dogs unwilling to give up their prey.

It was another risky proposition, but he locked on to a dilapidated warehouse up ahead, its windows boarded up. With a sharp twist of the wheel, Trapp aimed the car at the warehouse's flimsy wooden gate.

The Audi smashed through the posts, splinters flying as the car burst into the warehouse's cavernous interior. The Triad vehicles followed, their headlights cutting through the darkness like blades. Trapp took in the towering shelves, the scattered crates, and the rusting machinery and fittings that littered the place. It reminded him of the basement he'd escaped from moments earlier.

He screeched around a stack of pallets, tires barely gripping the dusty concrete. The pursuing cars split up, trying to box him in in the makeshift labyrinth. Trapp kept going, controlling his breathing. The Audi's bumper scraped against the shelves as he squeezed through narrow gaps.

As he'd hoped, the sound of crunching metal trailed behind as one of the Triad cars misjudged a turn, slamming into a stone column. The other car swerved to avoid the wreck, losing ground as it skidded on the debris-strewn floor.

Trapp made a sharp left and accelerated down a long aisle flanked by towering shelves. The remaining Triad car gave chase, its engine straining as it closed the gap. Bullets pinged off the shelves, sparks flying in Trapp's peripheral vision. He wanted to shoot back but couldn't risk splitting his attention when he was so tightly hemmed in.

Up ahead, a stack of oil drums loomed like a barricade. Full or empty? Trapp gritted his teeth, his foot never easing off the accelerator. At the last second, he jerked the wheel to the right, sending the Audi into a controlled skid. The car swung sideways, narrowly missing the drums as it careened around the corner.

The Triad car, caught off guard by the sudden maneuver, plowed straight into the barrels. The drums exploded, plumes of water erupting from the impact, giving little cushioning to the car as it flipped, landing on its roof and skidding to a stop.

Trapp raced toward the warehouse's far wall, a loading bay his only escape. He slammed through the flimsy metal door, the Audi's front end crumpling, but the car burst out into the night air.

Now he just had to dump the car and work out how he was going to get back to the safe house. There was no way Trapp could come in from the cold now.

IN THE BASEMENT, still reeking of gunsmoke and the coppery tang of blood, Dennis Rhee cradled Xiao's body, but the woman was already dead. Even if she had still been breathing, there were six holes in her, groups of three, blasted by her idiot son. He looked up at Zhen. The boy's eyes were filled more with anger than grief.

"We will hunt him down," Zhen said, his voice cold, hardened. "We need everyone."

"And what?" Dennis said. "Go out in a posse? Like cowboys? We don't even know where he's going."

"I don't care. We'll make him pay for killing my mother."

"He—" Dennis cut himself off. He was slick with the blood of the woman who'd wanted him to succeed her in place of a son who was unstable and impetuous, unable to see anything past his own wants and needs. "Someone has to pay."

But who?

The stranger? Or could Dennis get away with blaming Zhen?

Until he heard otherwise, Dennis remained bound by his oath. If Xiao had not conveyed her order to name him as her successor instead, he'd have to stand by Zhen.

Dennis laid Xiao's body on the ground and gently closed her eyes. Then he stood. He would honor his commitments, but he would also watch, and wait.

"Where would you like me to start?" Dennis asked.

"Washington," Zhen said. "I think he will go to Washington."

21

P resident Nash had learned to get by on very little sleep, peppering his day with brief catnaps that re-energized him whenever his schedule allowed. Despite only achieving four hours the previous night, he doubted there'd be room for even a five-minute doze today. It was only 7:30 a.m., but he'd already finished one meeting with his security advisors and was hopeful his second was about to conclude. The topic was the leak of classified information regarding the CIA operative designated "Hangman" and, more pertinent, whether it had any connection to the upcoming summit. He didn't sit behind the Resolute Desk for meetings often, but he'd favored it this morning.

"As of now, we have no direct link," Breyann Anderson finished after a long, thorough rundown of their shadow investigation. Shadow because the FBI and CIA were taking the lead on the leak while the Department of Homeland Security and Secret Service were heading up the summit alongside NYPD's finest. But if there was a connection, Anderson and his special DHS unit needed to be aware. "However, we agree that the timing is suspicious. We can't rule out the possibility entirely."

"Just no direct evidence." Robert Hawkins, the Deputy Director of the CIA, nodded in agreement. "Our top priority should be bringing in Trapp, even if that means alerting the public. We need to know what he knows. I expect he'll be active, given his history."

"It'd be weird if he wasn't," Mike Mitchell agreed. As deputy director of the CIA's Special Activities Division, Mitchell was the most familiar with Trapp's abilities and history—with Nash a close second. Not that anyone was allowed to know that. "Mr. President, I agree with Robert that we need Jason to come in, but to declassify Hangman's identity could be very damaging."

Nash leaned back in his chair. He saw in Mitchell's expression that the man was tightly controlling his personal feelings. As was he. "We already have an agent on Trapp, don't we?"

"Paulo Drebin, yes."

Hawkins' face tightened. "The FBI knows Hangman's identity, don't they?"

"Yes," Mitchell said. "And it will stay confidential."

"So Drebin is essentially looking for a missing witness to a shooting, who just happens to be a highly-trained Spec Ops soldier and assassin?"

"Trapp is a specialist in tracking down and extracting high-value targets in dangerous places. He can hide or he can fight." Mitchell tilted toward Nash. "Nick Pope tells me Drebin is a bloodhound."

Nash hoped so. He had been privy to more of Trapp's missions than a president should. There were plenty of people both in and out of government who wouldn't have to dig too deeply to connect them.

"What about security for the summit itself?" Nash asked. "If this is some ploy to distract us or to give foreign actors a free pass, I want to see every contingency covered."

"Foreign actors, sir?" Anderson asked.

Nash sighed, concerned he had come up with a scenario

that had not yet been discussed. "What happens if our visitors see an assassin on the loose in the United States and know that we can't find him? Isn't that the perfect excuse for them to step up their own security?"

After exchanging a cautious glance with Hawkins, Anderson said, "The protection for both Korean presidents is even more intense than your own, sir. We've secured two entire hotels—one for each party. Our security personnel and NYPD will be present throughout the premises and on the streets, which will be closed off for four city blocks around the UN."

Hawkins added, "We can slip Trapp's picture into existing photo decks under a pseudonym, and he'll show on any facial recognition tech. We're also coordinating closely with the UN's security team."

Nash nodded, but he remained troubled. "And the Chinese hardliners who oppose this deal? They've gone quiet in the last week or so. Another coincidence?"

"The president of China isn't happy with the summit," Hawkins said. "But he has muzzled his more excitable generals."

Anderson acknowledged the concern. "We're double-vetting every employee, every cop on duty, every caterer, driver, and masseuse. The nut jobs will not get this summit canceled."

"Writing them off as nut jobs is dangerous," Mitchell said. "Even the calmer heads in China fear a united Korea. And a united Korea allied with the United States? Well, that would blow the balance of power in East Asia out of the water. They already think we want to invade, to eradicate communism, like we tried in Vietnam and, well, Korea."

"Our job on that front is to help the Chinese see we mean them no harm." Nash gave the room his best *get it done* face. "Phase one is getting this deal over the line and honoring our promises."

Then he dismissed them, asking Mitchell to remain as his next appointment was shown in without preamble.

Agent Paulo Drebin had returned to Washington after a suspected sighting of Trapp on a freeway camera ten miles from DC in a car with false plates, and Nash had wanted to be briefed in person—in part to get a read on the man tasked with bringing Trapp in. Drebin showed no nerves, just a formal and professional stiffness that was rare in a law enforcement officer who was briefing the president for the first time.

Nash took to the couch. "Agent Drebin, I understand your 'lone shooter' case has evolved into something more complex."

Drebin nodded, his expression serious as he mirrored Nash on the opposite couch. "Yes, Mr. President. BPD has reported an uptick in violence involving Triads, including the assassination of the head of Boston's Iron Lotus Guild and several civilians injured during a serious motor vehicle incident."

"You said assassination?" Nash had never been comfortable with the word. "Doesn't sound like Jason."

"No," Mitchell agreed. "Even a powerful organized crime group wouldn't pose much of a threat to you or to the security of the United States. And blind revenge isn't in his psych makeup."

He prefers to get it done with both eyes wide open, Nash thought.

"So if he was involved, there'd have to be good reason. Your opinion?"

Drebin had a sheaf of notes with him but did not need to consult them.

"We only know about Xiao Guanyu's death because of informants. We didn't even know she was the head of this Triad until last night. According to BPD, the son, Zhen, is an unstable psychopath, which fits with the activity going on now. They recovered the bodies of two former US Army personnel, known to work for Xiao Guanyu, both shot at close range. They also found blood where a body was removed."

Mitchell shook his head firmly. "Trapp would take out hitters, yes. But I can't see him killing the woman. Tactically, he knows you don't finish off an organization like that simply by taking out the boss. And if he was worried about his skin, he'd have come in. It's something else. He's likely connected the shooting to the Hangman leak and come up with a mission of his own."

Nash reclined so he could keep both men in view. "*Is* there a link?"

"Other than the timing? Not yet."

"First the Hangman leak so close to the summit, now Jason Trapp is involved in a shooting twenty-four hours before his CIA codename leaks?"

"If he *is* assassinating members from the same gang who gunned down his friends," Drebin said, "finding him and bringing him in has to be my main focus."

"Good luck with that," Mitchell muttered.

"He can't evade every camera in the city."

Nash frowned. "What are our options?"

Mitchell blew out heavily, more than a sigh. "We may have to disavow Trapp to protect you and the CIA. The FBI would be clear to apprehend him. We still have the evidence of his staged death in Yemen five years ago. It provides plausible deniability for the administration."

Nash considered this, hating the thought of condemning someone like Trapp. "And what about Jason? Any idea what he's doing back in DC?"

Drebin shifted the paper and files to his other hand but did not look at them. "We're not entirely certain, sir. Hopefully... and I never stake an investigation on hope, sir, but it pays to remain open-minded..."

Drebin seemed to be waiting for permission to speculate, which Nash granted with a nod.

"Sir, he could just be coming here because there are people he trusts. Or he might be coming in on his own terms."

"Mike?" Nash said.

"Knowing Trapp, I highly doubt it." Mitchell fixed on Drebin. "And don't put too much faith in your cameras. Trapp could be in the next room listening to us right now, and we'd only know if he told us." Back to Nash. "He'll surface. When he does, Agent Drebin will need all the resources available to move in quickly."

Nash agreed, and they spent the next ten minutes thrashing out what task force might be necessary, contingencies in case Trapp stepped too far over the line on US soil, and a phone call to the director of the FBI to confirm everything they'd decided. Drebin would continue running point but might need to step aside if deeper political considerations came into play.

As Drebin and Mitchell left the Oval Office, Nash turned to gaze out the window. God help him if this summit didn't come off. God help the people of North Korea, currently starving in the tens of thousands.

And God help Jason Trapp if he endangered the tightrope walk that Nash was about to perform.

22

The street down which Hwa Yung-Gi walked was one of the most dilapidated he'd ever seen. Yes, there was poverty and starvation back home in DPRK, but this type of rot came from the culture of this failing nation. This was, his assistant had promised him, one of Washington DC's most notorious areas, packed with one- and two-story clapboard homes surrounded by chain-link fences. In the dawn hours, the air hung heavy with the stench of desperation, litter was scattered throughout, and feces that were as likely to be human as canine dotted the sidewalks every few feet. It was a far cry from the gleaming façades of the city's political heart.

Yung-Gi's senses were as piqued as if he were protecting Myo Il-Song or her children. He was less concerned about the prospect of a mugging and more about any sign of a tail, the prospect of which had required a surveillance detection routine that had taken him the better part of three hours to shake off. As part of the deal to allow him here, the proxy ambassador had negotiated the same diplomatic immunity enjoyed by the president's party, which allowed Yung-Gi to be armed at all times. He was doing nothing wrong in strolling through enemy territory, but his intent this morning demanded secrecy.

What had been deemed a "base of operations" was a decrepit two-story building, its windows veiled in wire mesh and its walls daubed with graffiti. Yung-Gi doublechecked the address, sighed, and wrinkled his nose as he approached the door. He knocked twice, paused, then knocked three more times—the prearranged signal.

The door creaked open, revealing a gaunt face with blood-shot eyes.

"Who're you?" the man mumbled in English.

Although Yung-Gi had turned sixty earlier this year, the young man looked so brittle he could have snapped the boy in two. He pulled his suit jacket straight and declared, "I have an appointment with Charlie Hu. Is that you?"

"Nah, but he said someone was stopping by. Thought he meant a customer."

The gaunt man stepped aside to let Yung-Gi enter.

Inside was a wide-open space, what would be a living room in a normal house, but here the bare floor still bore the remnants of a carpet underlay long removed, and the air thickened with the stench of drugs and a sour undercurrent of human sweat. Bodies were everywhere, some curled up and twitching on threadbare furniture, others sprawled in unconscious heaps on the floor. Yung-Gi picked his way through, making no effort to hide his disgust at the human detritus.

His contact, Charlie Hu, lounged on a tattered sofa in the back room with his girlfriend, Lana Po-Lin, draped over his lap. Both gave Yung-Gi a smirking nod in greeting. They were as greasy and vapid as anyone in the previous room, the only difference being they were awake. The gaunt man who'd answered the door, Yung-Gi now realized, was Charlie's deputy, Joe Min-Wai, although he looked positively ill. Compared to

Charlie Hu's more muscled frame, it was plain that Joe had fallen far short of the standards expected of a DPRK citizen. Joe stood by the window, scanning the street out back, shaking as if in need of a fix.

"You're early," Charlie drawled. His eyes were glazed, his words a little slurred—a man who indulged too much, though judging by his physique he at least avoided the harder drugs that would surely take the life of his deputy.

Yung-Gi paced the room, his gaze taking in piles of cash and scattered packets of white powder and dried flakes of what he assumed was marijuana. If this was the best support his people could offer, he would need to have a stern word with Myo Il-Song once she ascended to the presidency. The DPRK's foreign intelligence arms had long been tasked with generating revenue for the homeland. In recent years, the hunger for hard cash had grown insatiable.

But looking around, Yung-Gi saw the cost.

"We have a problem," he said, his voice neutral, professional. "The Americans have leaked information which seems to have impacted Triad activity."

Charlie shrugged, his fingers running through Lana's hair. "Not our business. As long as we stay out of Triad territory, they keep off our backs."

Like the others, Charlie Hu had been smuggled into the country posing as a Hong Kong exile, someone who could not go home due to Chinese crackdowns on dissidents. His English was very good, but the tone he used with Yung-Gi lacked respect. Possibly a result of almost a decade of exposure to this country.

In Korean, Yung-Gi explained, "It is our business when it threatens our country. If the Americans cannot control their citizens or their press, we must do it for them. I need to know what's happening."

Charlie's eyes narrowed as he replied in Korean. "You want

us to stick our noses into Triad business? No way, that's suicide."

Yung-Gi leaned forward, his voice dropping an octave, knowing he communicated a sense of menace to underlings and peers alike.

"Do you not understand? China refuses to help us with the famine ravaging our country. They want to bring us to heel. As much as I hate to admit it, our only choice is between accepting help from our worst enemy or allowing the starvation of millions. We could lose over *thirty percent* of our population. You might be here to make money for the Party and weaken the enemy, but now you have the opportunity to be part of something greater. A part of history."

Charlie sighed, looking around at the scruffy piles of money, the drugs, and the scantily clad woman draped over him.

"Nah, pass," he said in English, the disrespectful tone dripping with pure American malaise. "I'm good with the money and cheap thrills, thanks."

"You think you have *power* here?" Yung-Gi inhaled one last calming breath, giving the young man a final chance. "You exist because the Party allows it. You send money, but you are also obligated to do as I say."

Charlie sat up, Lana squirming down to his lap with a dazed giggle. "Nobody fucks with us here. No one dares. Even the Triads and Blacks don't bother us. You come over on some vacation because Big Kahuna Il-Song wants to play nice with—"

Yung-Gi drew his pistol and shot Joe Min-Wai in the head. His face caved in, and a spray of red burst out the back. The .44 caliber bullet left a small, dripping hole in the window.

"What the fuck, man!" Charlie scrambled away, as if trying to hide in the cheap sofa cushions.

Lana curled into a trembling ball, and Yung-Gi turned the

gun on her, although his eyes remained on Charlie. No one had stirred in the next room, despite the gunshot.

"I could kill her right now," Yung-Gi said. "Or I could take her back to Korea. How long do you think she will last in a prison camp? During a famine? And there is your mother, your father, your sister... Mae I think is her name. You will know their fate before you die like your junkie friend."

Charlie's jaw worked as he reacquainted himself with the conditions of his so-called freedom.

"Okay, man, okay. Chill the fuck out. What do you need?"

Yung-Gi slipped the gun back in its holster. "I need to know if you have competent people at your disposal, or if they are all fallen citizens like you."

"I have people, yeah."

"Find out what really happened in Boston. And keep an eye on the Triads here. If events spill over, if contact is made, or if you hear anything related to our leader or our country, I need to know immediately." He took an untraceable, unbranded cellphone from his pocket and tossed it to the terrified drug dealer. "But take no action without my approval. Mine is the only number in that phone, and the only number you will call. Am I clear?"

Charlie nodded rapidly, his arm around Lana, who had buried her face in his shoulder.

"Good," Yung-Gi said, turning to leave. "I will arrange for an audit of your operation here after the New York summit. I advise you to clean yourself up before that happens."

He stepped out into what felt like a marginally fresher morning than the one he'd left and pulled out his encrypted phone. He dialed a number and spoke with his diplomatic contact.

"I need to be included in the next security briefing," Yung-Gi told the former colonel tasked with coordinating his reconnaissance. "If they refuse, insist that to exclude me would be a grave breach of trust."

"Is there a problem?" the man asked.

"Not yet."

He ended the call and returned the phone to his pocket. While he didn't trust Charlie Hu entirely, he trusted him far more than he did the president of the United States.

23

Trapp crouched behind the dense shrubbery, unconvinced this was the right move or even that it would give him the slightest advantage. "Goddamn guesswork" were his words to himself, not for the first time that morning. Yet guesswork—albeit educated—was all he had at this stage. He needed more intel, so patience was going to have to be key.

While most embassies in Washington were either housed in existing grand old architecture or were built to project affluence and gravitas, China's concrete design was more like a fortified prison. Trapp had chosen what was technically a national park opposite China's only territory in the US, but this "park" was more of a landscaped lawn with bushes, trees, and a variety of shrubs. It boasted the added honor of housing a descendant of the apple tree whose fruit had swatted Sir Isaac Newton on the head.

Trapp was nowhere near the auspicious tree.

If anyone questioned his presence, his dark green overalls made him look like a city worker, albeit one with an aversion to sunlight, hence the low cap. He carried two concealed firearms, had three escape routes memorized, and had prepped a beast of a motorcycle should he need to retreat.

Relying on electronic surveillance would be futile; the Chinese security measures were far too advanced for anything but the newest tech to penetrate, and while Trapp's Boston safehouse contained a treasure trove of gear, "new" was not a word he'd have chosen to describe any of it. But he did have a remote DSLR camera the size of a rifle scope, which he'd positioned opposite the embassy gate with a half-decent view of the front lobby. The pictures fed back to a phone connected via a long cable, so no digital signals passed through the air.

While it was a long shot, Trapp needed to know more. He had an excuse to be here all day if needed, and he doubted that his occasional screen time would raise the hackles of a security guard.

His instincts told him it all led here. Not direct evidence that would hold up in court, not yet, but the "goon from Washington," the use of Triads on foreign soil, and the exposure of his Hangman nom de plume... it all pointed to Chinese government involvement. But who would go to this much trouble?

Had he really acquired so many enemies that he'd lost count?

Live long enough on Trapp's chosen path and he supposed it was inevitable.

As the morning ticked by, he slowly trimmed and tended the outer edges and, since hanging out only on the Chinese Embassy side would be deeply suspicious, he often retreated to the inner sections where he couldn't be seen, listening for vehicles or the gates moving. Over the course of four hours, he observed the embassy staff and photographed thirteen personnel entering or leaving, mostly casual or manual laborers like cleaners and security.

He could be here for days before he got a bite.

When he was out of sight of the walls, Trapp dropped his

city worker act, allowing his mind to wander between wracking his brain for any time he might have stepped on Chinese toes powerful enough to bring him to their attention and wondering if he should consider what both Ikeda and Mike had asked of him.

He trusted them. But could he trust someone else? Someone he'd never met?

He couldn't keep monitoring the embassy in person, not alone. If the person he was looking for was working inside or holed up at the embassy staff residence a short distance away, this was his only shot. If they were not here at all, he was wasting his time.

He took out a burner phone and a sandwich, then sat on the ground beside the screen focused on the Chinese Embassy's gate. The second burner could be easily traced, but only to his Boston safe house, which he was willing to ditch right now. It would tie up anyone looking for him for several hours, if not days. He still had Drebin's card, folded in half, which he now opened, and dialed the agent's cellphone.

The call connected after two rings. "Drebin."

Trapp allowed two seconds of silence before speaking. "If you know who this is, do not say my name or I will hang up immediately."

Drebin's tone was cautious. "I'm listening." The agent would be furiously swiping on the cell's screen, activating a recording app or a trace.

"I know you won't believe me on face value, but I need you to consider the way they've come after me."

"*After* you? Not everything is personal."

"Nick Pope will have been briefed on this. Speak to him."

"You mean the Hangman business? Don't worry, they're keeping it tight. But since I'm looking for you, I've been given clearance."

"In that case, you really need to believe me."

"I believe in the *possibility*. But then, I don't write off anything until I see proof." Drebin sounded exasperated, as if dealing with a particularly dim yet persistent underling. "What I don't see is conclusive evidence. Or even solid circumstantials. You need to come in and tell us what you did to bring this down on you."

"Nothing," Trapp said. "I've never gone up against the Chinese in any significant capacity."

Drebin said nothing for a few seconds, perhaps pushing the trace, perhaps processing what Trapp said. Back on the line, he asked, "What about *in*significant ways?"

"I don't know."

"The boss can't risk this interfering with the summit."

"Like you said, Agent Drebin, without even circumstantial evidence linking Hangman to the summit, there's little point acting on..." He paused, realizing his hypocrisy. "No point acting on guesswork with something of historical importance."

"You won't come in yet? Then give me something to work with."

Trapp watched the embassy, dredging through as many missions as he could, watching, remembering, thinking...

He said, "There was the Rwanda bribery job. But that was more human trafficking and industrial espionage, using thugs to intimidate American aid workers and executives. We ended up in a firefight with some locals and the Chinese bagman who paid them off, but..." Trapp trailed off, reluctant to say more. It might have been a corporate job with violent elements, but it was still classified. Unless he got permission from Mitchell or higher, he couldn't go into much detail here. "We tied up all the loose ends there."

"Unless you missed someone."

"I don't miss," Trapp said, regretting his arrogant tone but not enough to correct himself. Especially as he watched a black sedan with diplomatic plates pulling into the embassy. Not a limo, but it sat heavily on its axels, the tires making more noise than the purring engine. Armored for sure, much heavier than a normal vehicle.

He'd taken photos of the plates and the blacked-out windows when it left earlier but hadn't seen who'd gotten in.

"Tr—" Drebin cut off, remembering not to use names. "You still there?"

"Yeah, sorry. One second."

Trapp heard breathing. A patter of activity. They were definitely trying to trace him while he zoomed in on the car that waited for the gate to open.

It drove inside.

Trapp wedged the phone under one ear. He ate his sandwich with his left hand, his right controlling the hidden DSLR camera.

The car pulled up, the rear doors in view before the gate closed. A tall, suited guard hurried to the back door and opened it, allowing a slender Chinese woman to climb out. Mid-twenties, possibly younger. She kept her head bowed, hands before her.

"Where are you?" Drebin asked.

"Boston," Trapp said.

"I don't believe you."

Trapp said nothing. The second person to emerge from the car was male, sharply dressed in a suit and tie. He directed his gaze toward the gates as they came together.

Waiting for them to close.

A man who wanted security confirmed. A man who stirred a long-extinguished memory in Trapp, but not for any personal reasons. Nothing he'd expected.

"I'll... call you back," Trapp said.

"No, talk to me," Drebin said. "I can't let you walk away. The bodies you've left, the intel leak—"

"I just saw someone I recognize. He might be the key."

"Who do you see?"

"A shark. Maybe."

Drebin's tone shifted. Urgent, less controlled. "Trapp, where *are* you? You better not be conducting an illegal operation on US soil. Because that—"

"I said no names."

Trapp hung up and continued snapping photos of the man and woman, although the woman appeared too cowed by the man's presence to be of any significance.

Drebin was right; he was risking his freedom by pursuing this. But if he was right about the man entering the embassy two hundred yards over his right shoulder, events might be building to more than a personal vendetta. He'd glimpsed the man only briefly and hadn't managed a clear picture. But it *could* have been him.

Trapp had never directly encountered the MSS agent known as "the Shark," but like all field operatives, he'd been briefed. An elite assassin loyal to the People's Communist Party, Li Chao had supposedly retired from his nation's service to pursue opportunities in the private sector. That briefing was years ago, though, long before Trapp's staged death in Yemen.

Over the past two decades, the Chinese had expanded into Africa like a juggernaut, the money to be made from the continent incalculable.

Could the Shark have had a hand in Rwanda?

Had Trapp missed him?

Back then, Li Chao was still on the MSS payroll, so why on earth would he be instigating this action against Trapp now?

Could he be the one who'd exposed his Hangman alias?

Trapp slowly packed up his surveillance gear and gardening tools. He needed to analyze the images on the SD card that he zipped into a secure pocket.

Movement caught his attention. A Chinese guard from the embassy was approaching, headed right for Trapp's position.

The wiry man's holster was empty, his firearm presumably not permitted to be worn outside the embassy grounds, but regardless, Trapp couldn't risk a confrontation here, not with the limited cover and the possibility of arrest.

"Hey, you!" the guard called out in English. "What are you doing here?"

Trapp stood to his full height, chin low to hide his face from cameras under the cap, and prepared for the worst.

24

As the guard scrutinized Trapp's city-worker ID, the plastic card felt flimsy and inadequate under the man's obvious suspicion. A bead of sweat trickled down Trapp's back. He lacked access to professional counterfeits, so had mocked up the ID himself using graphics copied from image searches online. It might pass muster with the average civilian but wouldn't fool a cop, so if the guard knew anything about American ID, he was toast.

"This does not explain what you are doing here," the guard said, handing back the laminated counterfeit. "I need to see inside that bag."

Trapp's grip tightened on the duffel. "I'm just doing my job. You don't need to search my tools."

"The area is restricted." The guard glanced back at the embassy where a colleague—no firearm that Trapp could see—stood at a pedestrian gate, his boots in the other side of the frame, as if stepping onto American land might set him aflame. This guy had no such qualms. "I must insist."

Trapp rubbed the back of his neck, careful not to raise his face to an angle where cameras might capture it. He chose to play the role he'd been projecting all along —the intimidated but standing-his-ground working Joe. "Buddy, I'm not on embassy property. I don't think you have any authority here."

The guard's stance shifted, like an asshole in a bar with one too many inside him. "I am authorized to protect the embassy and its personnel. No one sent advance warning of work being carried out, so if you have nothing to hide, open your bag."

Damn, Trapp should have thought of that. A restricted area like this, the park closed to the public... the city would warn a paranoid embassy like this if works were scheduled.

The guard reached for his radio.

Trapp couldn't let that happen, but a physical confrontation could expose him to the very people who were attacking him for reasons so far unknown.

Choices: fight and risk everything or run and hope they bought that he was a nobody troublemaker.

The guard's fingers closed around the radio, thumb shifting to the transmit button. Trapp could hear the crackle of static.

Ensuring that his cap remained in place, Trapp raised a fist to the sky and yelled, "Free Tibet!" Then he shoved the guard hard in the chest, making him stumble backward over a rock and onto his butt as Trapp bolted into the shrubs.

He heard the guard scramble to his feet, cursing in Chinese, followed by the commotion of at least two bodies fighting through the bushes to reach the park where Trapp sprinted over untended lawns. The two-foot-high grass and weeds slowed his usual pace, as did the heavy duffel that he could not allow to fall into Chinese hands. He lifted his feet higher and doubled down as a brief check over his shoulder confirmed two men pursuing him.

Trapp made it to a path. He sped up, racing toward the edge of the square where he'd parked the motorcycle he'd bought for cash on Craigslist last night. Behind him, he could hear the first guard shouting.

As he came to the spot where the path emerged onto the road, he caught movement off to his left in the trees that lined the park's border. The second guard, faster than the first, racing out to cut Trapp off.

"Shit!"

The guard—a bulky guy easily as heavy as Trapp—was six feet away, adjusting his run, framing to tackle. No time to calculate angles of evasion, Trapp dropped the bag, lowered his shoulder beneath the guard's incoming head, and drove upward at the moment of impact. Like two cars colliding head-on, they canceled out one another's momentum, but Trapp's upward motion gave him the advantage of a mid-air spin, while the Chinese guard thumped backward in place. He hit the ground with a winded yelp. Trapp staggered and lost his footing, rolled, then used the motion to flip back onto his feet and diverted to retrieve his duffel bag.

But the original guard was almost upon him, and two more were sprinting from the direction of the embassy to back him up. The two newcomers had neglected to stow their sidearms before rushing out into America.

Trapp could overpower the closest guard and retrieve the bag, but would he have time to get to his vehicle? How hopped up on adrenaline were those armed guards closing in fast?

"Shit!" He raced empty-handed toward the street.

Once on the road, he put distance between himself and the trailing pack and made it to his motorcycle, a 2007 Honda 800cc sport tourer that had cost him a mere $3000, thanks to its dented body work and a mutual acceptance that a cash payment didn't have to be reported to the IRS so long as nobody came asking. He kickstarted the bike and revved the engine. The machine wasn't the most powerful he could have chosen, but it still throbbed to life beneath him.

He spun the wheels to create a sheen of smoke, squealing the tires as he sped away, leaving his pursuers behind.

Watching for tailing vehicles, he turned out into morning traffic, wending his way through the sluggish cars, and slapped a handlebar in frustration.

He'd lost the duffel, but he'd pocketed the SD card containing the images, so all wasn't exactly lost. Still, he couldn't be sure about prints or DNA. He'd wiped it all down as he packed it, then handled it only with gloves during the op. But even a partial print on the surveillance gear could get him locked up.

As for the appearance of the man he believed was the Shark within days of both the Korean summit and an attempt on Trapp's life? Coincidences happened, sure, but not like this.

Not with Trapp.

IN AMBASSADOR WEN'S whited-out cubicle, Li Chao had his hands on his hips as he stared at the open duffel bag before him. Gardening tools, firearms, and a sleek remotely operated camera setup. All available on the civilian market, none of it military grade, and certainly not CIA. He could not decide between fear and elation at the discovery.

When Chao had spotted a figure lurking in the closed-off parkland, he hadn't expected it to yield a bounty like this but had alerted security anyway. It was only after the man had neutralized an experienced soldier that Chao grew certain it was the man he had come here to destroy.

"I will take this up immediately with the White House," Wen said, standing side by side with Chao. "I will demand a groveling apology and action taken against those responsible."

While that would be the correct thing to do for an ambassador, Chao was no diplomat, and there was an inkling of an advantage worming its way through his mind. "Wait."

Wen looked at him sharply.

Chao said, "I want this all tested for evidence that Jason Trapp was the man conducting this illegal surveillance. Any scrap of DNA or fingerprint will do."

"What will that accomplish?"

"If Trapp is acting on his own, we can use it as proof of the CIA's illegal acts. And when we expose the files, their summit is finished."

25

Agent Paulo Drebin had always liked the FBI's J. Edgar Hoover Building on Pennsylvania Avenue. It was utilitarian and efficient, more formal than its sister buildings in New York and LA—and better not get him started on North Dakota. Plus the recent lobby reconstruction had it looking better than it ever had.

He sat across from Special Agent in Charge Debra Munitz, with Nick Pope from counterterrorism beside him. The CIA had suggested Pope sit in, a suggestion backed by President Nash. Drebin was uncomfortable with this, not least because there were no grounds for suspecting that terrorism was a factor. If the CIA recommended someone "sit in," they were here to cover someone else's ass.

"Trapp hinted at what my research suggests is a Chinese codename," Drebin said, for an asset known as "the Shark. I strongly believe Trapp is in DC and he thinks this Shark operative is here too. That might be the lead he's following."

"Why would he be interested in this Shark?" Pope asked.

"Trapp also said something about Rwanda. That was the only exchange of fire with the Chinese he could recall."

Pope glanced over at SAC Munitz, who gave him a nod.

Pope said, "There was a classified operation about four years ago. Although it was confirmed to involve a rogue Chinese faction, rather than the MSS. I don't know anything else about it."

"Then I need everything we have on this," Drebin said. "Along with potential links between Trapp and the Triads and anything that might tie the Shark to Rwanda."

Pope gave little away, just a hop in his eyebrows. "That's a tall order, Agent Drebin."

"Maybe," Drebin conceded. "But it's the closest thing to a solid lead we have." Drebin addressed Munitz. "Ma'am, I know this is going to be difficult, but with Agent Pope here, from *counterterrorism* no less, we can call it national security. With a fugitive loose and a foreign operative potentially operating in DC, an attack may be imminent."

Munitz remained a statue, backlit by the glare-resistant window behind her. Without moving an inch, she said, "I'll approve the request and expedite it. Nick, you'll back it? See it goes to a friendly supervisor?"

Pope sighed. "I'll see what I can do."

ANOTHER HOUSE PERMANENT SELECT COMMITTEE ON INTELLIGENCE meeting, another morning of chin-flapping and accomplishing not very much. Usually, this would spike Redman's blood pressure, but he needed to manage today's session with care and precision—not easy for a man who preferred a sledgehammer over a chisel. And nowadays, desperate-for-controversy news shows did things like hire shrinks and body language experts to analyze every word, every gesture and microexpression.

"The recent leak of classified information relating to the

CIA operative codenamed 'Hangman' demands immediate attention," he intoned. "A full-scale inquiry is required, but as we all know, that would take some time. Still, the public scrutiny gives us an urgency to uncover the truth, if only in preliminary findings."

Redman pushed the lingering anxiety aside, focusing on the task at hand. The intel he'd handed over to his press contact was exactly the leak he needed to both expose and cover up, while steering the investigation on the right course to ensure he came away clean.

"Congressman Redman," Rita Tarragona interjected, her voice carrying a note of skepticism, "I agree this leak is deeply concerning. But starting a full-scale inquiry without all the facts might be a waste of taxpayer money and could involve innocent patriots in a witch-hunt."

Redman fixed her with a gaze of steel, softened at the edges. "Then we treat this as evidence gathering to present to Congress. An inquiry would be the House's decision. But this is our *duty*. The American people deserve answers. It is our *duty* to provide them."

The word *duty* tasted funny. Speaking it that way, with emphasis, with repetition, carried the ring of falsehood. Real duty had nothing to do with this.

Thomas Decker spoke up. "I concur. It's a matter of national security. We should act swiftly to contain the fallout. In fact, I have already filed a request to declassify Hangman for this committee..."

Swiftly. Another word that sounded false with its added emphasis. But as one of Redman's wolves, Decker was doing his job as well as could be expected.

"And if it goes wrong?" Tarragona countered. "If we rush in without a clear strategy, we could compromise current operations. And lives."

The debate continued. Redman navigated the next hour

with practiced ease, imposing authority while mediating the narrative, steering it with unusual grace and subtlety.

Focus on the leak first. Make others probe Hangman's actions.

It was only half an hour into the session when Fabian entered with the sheepish hunch of a dog about to be struck for peeing on the carpet. The aide scuttled around the periphery, made for Redman, and whispered in his ear, "A bunch of lawyers are here."

"Lawyers," Redman drawled, elongating the word with utter disdain. Fabian was also a lawyer, but Redman proudly had no such qualification. "CIA by any chance?"

"Yes. They want us to cease this probe into—"

Before anyone announced them or bade them enter, four grim-faced men of indeterminate late-middle-age strode in. Apparently a CIA badge and an attitude was enough to bypass the Capitol police—something Redman would be chewing a supervisor's ass about very shortly.

The committee fell silent as the thicker-haired of the men approached the chair.

"I apologize for the interruption. But this matter requires the committee's full and immediate attention."

"This isn't an interruption," Redman said. "It's the Central Intelligence Agency overreaching yet again. You cannot dictate the actions of this committee."

The lawyer nodded, his expression anything but apologetic. "I understand your frustration, sir. But under the Classified Information Procedures Act this committee is required to consult with agency officials before continuing. Failure to do so would be a breach of national security procedure, which could result in—"

Redman held up a hand to cut the man off. Hs mind whirred. He couldn't simply ignore the injunction, but he couldn't let them shut him down, either. If the Chinese weren't satisfied, they would ruin him. Not to mention, this was the ideal bludgeon with which to attack President Nash. He needed time to think.

"In the interests of our relationship with CIA," he said, his tone intentionally resigned, "we will recess for one hour. The committee will confer with legal counsel. But this is not the end of the matter."

No, Redman thought, that first Hangman file was just the beginning.

BY NOON, Paulo Drebin's desk held a small city of files and documents. He'd been expecting a digital transfer in about forty-eight hours' time, but Pope had alerted him that since the original file might have been leaked electronically, comms had to go old school until the NSA plugged that leak. Receiving the two boxes via courier far quicker than any government department had any right to expect, Drebin considered that having a counterterrorism bigwig clinging on might not be such a terrible thing after all. He had loaded up his office with coffee and protein snacks and prepared for a marathon research session, but as he pored over the pages, his frustration grew.

"This is ridiculous," he muttered barely thirty seconds in.

There was so much black blocking on the Hangman papers that he could barely get through one intact sentence. The only unredacted document was related to "the Shark," an assassin and spy, now managing director of an "intelligence consultancy." His real name was Li Chao.

The most informative passage concerned an operation in Germany where the Shark was rumored to have been dispatched to silence a defector eight years ago. Four German police officers were found with their throats cut, the dissident's wife shot in the head, his infant daughter suffocated, and the target himself beaten to death. Drebin glossed over the order in which his bones were broken, not needing the detail to understand the Shark's deadliness.

But nothing tied him directly to Trapp, Hangman, or Rwanda.

Drebin went online to request removal of the redactions, citing that fuller detail might give some clue as to where Trapp had hunkered down. As soon as he logged on, he noticed a flag on the electronic register.

The HPSCI, through Congressman Jake Redman, had requested the same files for review—everything but the Shark intel.

"Damn it."

That was why everything was so heavily redacted. Letting a public committee get ahold of it would risk Trapp's identity getting out, along with whatever dark secrets he was hiding.

Then another message chimed. A news alert. He only had three set up today, having silenced all others, so if something new had hit the networks, it couldn't be good.

Drebin clicked on the link and read the headline. A breaking news video clip autoplayed.

The commentor's voice seemed to fill the room, building a narrative that was going to make Drebin's job a lot harder.

26

T rapp had made the best of his workspace, a stained and battered dressing table with a mirror that had misted over long ago. There were arguments rumbling through the walls and floor, the sound of sexual gymnastics bleeding through the ceiling, and even breathing through his mouth, he couldn't escape the musty smell that permeated every inch of the apartment. But his laptop, phone, and the surveillance photos from the Chinese Embassy were his sole focus.

With the help of Timothy Greaves' facial recognition access via an encrypted corner of the dark web, Trapp could put names to faces without worrying about Greaves getting in trouble. Having spread the photos out on the bed, Trapp had scanned several personnel using his phone camera and uploaded them to the laptop to mine databases from CBP, Homeland Security, and all the three-letter agencies linked to the Pentagon.

Two security guards were identified as Chinese soldiers, while three of the cleaners were flagged as suspected illegal immigrants, but there were no other criminal or terror flags.

Since he'd been so hasty with the camera, he'd only managed a slightly-blurred snapshot of the man he thought could be Li Chao, *the Shark*. But it was a young woman, Fang Chen, who caught Trapp's attention.

He selected her clearest photograph last, laid it flat on the desk across three interlinked circular stains, and framed the picture in the scanner function's viewfinder. A quick drag-and-drop into the necessary box generated minimal information but enough for Trapp to work with.

Listed as an attaché but appearing to be more of a personal assistant to Ambassador Wen, Ms. Chen represented a potential weak link. No military background and no political affiliation were listed, just her visa details and current address in Washington which was, unsurprisingly, in the Chinese Embassy's residential quarters—a short walk from the embassy itself, where the majority of staffers lived.

Trapp considered his options. Smuggling himself into the embassy somehow— disguised as a cleaner or with fake diplomatic credentials—could be seen as an act of war, especially with the missing duffel that might be linked to him. He had to be smart about this. Either lure his targets out or wait for their next move and counter swiftly.

More background had filtered through: Fang Chen's immediate family set off no sirens, but the note about an uncle who'd been arrested and subsequently disappeared piqued Trapp's attention. If he was a dissident, someone abused by the state, Ms. Chen could be amenable to temptation. Although she could just as easily have been the one to report her uncle— brainwashing ran deep in the People's Republic.

It was a gamble. Fifty-fifty at best, but probably far less favorable than that.

An alert bonged on the laptop and phone almost simultaneously. He'd set both to flash a notification on certain keywords in the news, as the Hangman story was not going away. Pundits and politicians alike had begun weighing in, although the available facts were mostly recycled. Expecting some Hollywood name or political hopeful to appear as a talking head, Trapp clicked the link.

A video player sprang to life, which annoyed him—he preferred to read, not to be assaulted by mindless talking heads. But this wasn't the crisp, high-definition footage of TV cameras or even the average smartphone. Its contents were grainy, low-resolution, ill-defined due to the poor optical zoom.

As the scene unfolded, Trapp's blood ran cold.

The news anchor, in a small box at the bottom right of the screen, narrated. "We have received shocking evidence that the CIA operative known only as 'Hangman' may have been involved in the extrajudicial killing of a foreign national. The images we are about to show you are graphic in nature..."

The visual was unmistakable. Jason Trapp—*Hangman*—holding a gun on a man with hands raised at shoulder level. The target's face was as pixelated as Trapp's, but there seemed little danger from the man lying on a pile of boxed bread in the warehouse just outside Kigali as he pushed himself to his feet, shaking. The screen was swaying, partly obscured, the camera operator hiding, filming from afar.

Without hesitation, Trapp's past self pulled the trigger, and his target crumpled to the ground in a lifeless heap. The blood spatter had been further blurred for the tender viewing public, but Trapp remembered the incident with complete clarity.

To the untrained eye, it appeared to be a cold-blooded murder. A ruthless execution by a rogue operative. Such poor-quality evidence might not hold up in court, but it could still sway public opinion, despite this being a sanctioned hit carried out under orders.

The dead man was no innocent, but a trafficker of women, children, weapons, drugs—anything that lined his pockets. He'd been paid to provide slave labor for Chinese infrastructure and mining projects, and his militiamen had raided a village in neighboring Uganda to fulfill a work order. They'd abducted fifteen teenage boys, thirty-two men, and eight able-bodied women, killing three US aid workers in the process. Trapp and Ryan had been dispatched to take out the militia's leadership, locate the kidnap victims, and eradicate those wishing to procure human beings for free labor. The point wasn't to make the news. The right people would find out. And sometimes a superpower needed to remind the rest of the world that its reach was long and its determination unwavering, even if its attention often wandered.

The unlucky moneyman had been Chinese. As had been his security detail.

The Shark had not been part of that operation, though. There had been no military or MSS involvement. They'd have heard about it at the time or shortly after, not ten years later.

As much as he wanted to delve deeper, none of that mattered now. As the video ended and the commentary took over, it was clear the court of public opinion was in session, and Trapp could feel that the jury had turned.

His gaze fell again on Fang Chen, the young attaché. If he could bribe her, entice her, or—if he could find leverage—threaten her sufficiently, she could be the key to exposing those behind this. Because it wasn't solely a Chinese operation. There had to be more.

A Chinese national. With diplomatic immunity.

He had two choices: Risk prison for doing going off grid; or accept the outcome of the Hangman leaks.

It wasn't really any choice at all. Fang Chen would be his primary target.

27

F ang Chen stepped into Heroes' Lair, a sprawling cavern of a comic book store where Li Chao had arranged for her to arrive at this precise time. Although air-conditioned, a heavy heat hung over the place, the scent of plastic and paper warmed through large skylights amplifying the morning rays. The vibrant chaos of colors enveloped her, a weirdly pleasing transformation from the fake grandeur of Washington, DC outside.

Rows upon rows of what appeared to be thematically-organized aisles, troughs filled with plastic-wrapped comics, their covers emblazoned with heroes; some familiar Marvel icons that she'd seen in movies, while posters of lesser-known vigilantes dangled: demonic, saintly, dynamic, sexy, fat, white, Black, Asian... so many variations.

So many patrons for a weekday morning, too. Grownups young and old, debating and exclaiming—enthusiasm that was both intimidating and inviting. And so totally foreign.

Fang almost turned around, ready to return to the embassy and tell Li Chao she wished to return to her regular duties after thanking him for the opportunity.

But was it an opportunity? He'd made it seem that way, though the more she thought about it, the more it felt like an order. Besides, it was too late to change her mind.

Fabian approached—from the front or the side, she couldn't tell. It was contrary to Li Chao's brief sessions with her, drumming skills into her regarding situational awareness and anticipating what a man like Fabian might say to corrupt her over to his own side. She hoped Chao was not watching her somehow.

"Hey there." Fabian had a different buzz of nervous energy about him, eyes darting around the store while he maintained a rigor mortis grin. "Nice to see you again."

Was his manner for the benefit of witnesses? Old friends meeting up? They had not planned this. She'd expected a rerun of the toy store scenario, strangers brushing by, exchanging information without attracting attention.

"Yes," Fang said. "Nice to see you, too."

Fabian's stiff grin softened into a nervous smile as he slipped a file into the comic book bin beside them, which was filled with some evil-looking heroes in capes, characters she did not know.

"The Hangman file," he said. "But there's little in there that isn't already out in public. They redacted a ton of stuff. You won't get his real name or any personal info."

He leaned closer, and for a brief moment, Fang mentally located the pepper spray in her clutch handbag as her hand brushed her lucky belt buckle. His lips passed her cheek, and his breath fell hot on her neck. She fought the urge to recoil.

"Government lawyers are all over it," Fabian continued. "Only releasing what they're legally obliged to. Sorry, I can't get you much more than this. What do you have for me?"

"Keep the file," Fang replied, as she had been instructed to.

Chao did not want her wandering around DC with state secrets, regardless of how little they gave away. Something had

happened, but they hadn't told her what. Must have been to do
with the alert that sounded earlier that morning and the bag
Chao and Ambassador Wen had inspected in private.

Besides, they knew more than Fabian already—the Hangman's real name was Jason Trapp. They also knew details about
several of his missions. She just didn't know why they were
playing this game. Until three days ago, she'd been a glorified
PA with a neat job title; now she was...what? A spy?

She said, "I have another request."

Fabian shifted his weight, retrieving the envelope from the
comic book bin. "Hey, I was thinking. We're nearly done here,
right?"

"My request will benefit your boss. And probably you, too."

"Sure, no problem. Maybe we could discuss this request
over a coffee?" He stared at her, his eyes somehow both wide
and dopey. "We could talk more about what we're doing here.
Two people running messages back and forth."

He gave a small chuckle. No, not really a chuckle. More of a
titter.

What man *tittered*?

But she couldn't alienate him. That had been made very
clear. Equally, she was ordered not to engage socially with him.

Another man to be avoided.

"I'm sorry," she said. "It may look bad for you to be seen
with me... in a place like that. Maybe another time? When all
this is resolved?"

Fabian glanced away, his jaw tight, cheeks tinged with red.
When he faced her, he was all fake smiles again, rejected but
hiding his disappointment. "Of course. That's... sensible. Rain
check, then."

Fang finger-walked through a box of comics before steering
the conversation back where she needed it to go. "You work for
a man with big ambitions. That means *you* have big ambitions."

Massage his ego, Chao had told her. *Make him feel important.*

"Yeah, sure," Fabian said.

Reassure him.

"Even if it seems we are being very demanding, this will help you. *Both* of you. I promise."

Fabian shrugged, his expression turning serious. "Okay, cool. What do you have for me?"

As Fabian had done with her earlier, Fang leaned in close, her fingertips brushing a tightly packed line of comic books. When she selected one to lift out, her voice barely rose above a whisper.

"Project TIPTOE."

Fabian lowered his head, his breath once again on her skin. "What is that? Tiptoeing?"

"It is a codename. Mr. Redman must get it on the public record. Project TIPTOE."

Fabian frowned. "Yeah, but *what* is it?"

Fang shook her head.

Do not engage. Do not negotiate. Instruct him.

"Say it back to me," she said.

Fabian hesitated, then nodded. "Project TIPTOE."

"Mr. Redman can call intelligence chiefs to testify, and he will." Fang was supposed to use the full name of Redman's committee, but she'd forgotten it. "Am I correct?"

"Yes, but—"

"Please, Fabian." She looked up at him, desperate to pull away.

If he is reluctant, threaten him.

"Please," she said. "Do not make me tell my boss that you can't do this. It will end badly. For both of us."

Fabian took a deep breath and stepped back, creating distance between them.

"It is hard now," Fang added, her rehearsed lines now

exhausted. "But when this is over... perhaps we can have cake with our coffees."

Do not engage.

Again, Fang worried that Chao could be watching, listening to her improvising as she used something new she'd learned about Fabian—that he liked her, and that he was annoyed at her rebuffing him.

Reassure him—one of Li Chao's instructions, twisted into something else. Would he be mad at her for this?

"Okay, fine," Fabian said, a bounce to his knees, another shift in his smile. "I'll tell him to get it on the record. You're sure this will help him?"

"Of course. We all want the same thing." Fang hadn't noticed how fast her heart had been thrumming. Only now that Fabian had agreed did it slow, and she breathed easy. "I will leave first. Please give me five minutes."

Once out on the street, busy with foot traffic in this cosmopolitan district, Fang had all but forgotten Fabian, concentrating instead on Chao's crash course in counter-surveillance.

Focus on your surroundings.

He'd said Americans watched all Chinese diplomats, assumed the worst in them. If they suspected China's involvement in the leaks, everyone needed to be on high alert. It had left her seeing shadows where none should be.

If any sort of surveillance tied her to Fabian Pincher, she must not risk leading them back to a diplomatic vehicle. Hence, she had to perform two maneuvers before returning.

Nothing else matters. Observe, remember, process.

Fang stepped into the first coffee shop she came to, stared at the chalkboard menu over the array of gleaming chrome coffee machines, then pretended to have forgotten something. She marched out of the door and strode purposefully back the way she had come.

Eyes up, watch all the faces. A bad tail will avert their gaze. When you turn around a second time and return the original way, watch for repeat faces; that's how you spot a tail.

The sidewalk was a dense stream of bodies dodging through one another, a pre-lunchtime rush as office workers and DC staffers hurried to an early meal. No one stood out; no one seemed concerned about her. She drew a couple of appraising male looks that quickly averted when she caught them, but she didn't think that was anything to do with surveillance.

Then her heart almost stopped. It made one huge thud in her chest, then fluttered, and only Chao's briefing kept her feet moving.

Give nothing away. They cannot kidnap you off the street. Keep walking. Call when you can.

Just a few feet away, hands in his pockets and eyes hidden behind sunglasses, was—*maybe*—the man whose face had been presented to her several times, in many different AI-augmented forms: clean-shaven, bearded, older, younger, hat, no-hat, and... glasses and sunglasses.

Was it Jason Trapp? The Hangman himself. Walking toward her. She was walking toward him.

But she could not look at him, not directly. The guy hadn't stuttered in his walk, hadn't deviated or turned away. He was just another face in the crowd.

Was it actually him? Or was she imagining his face on a stranger because Chao had made her stare at so many variations of it just this morning?

She wanted to stare at him, to summon the pictures Chao showed her and put herself at ease. It couldn't be Trapp, surely.

No matter how much she tried to hold herself together, every fiber inside her urged her to run, to scream for help. But Chao's calm urgency lingered, his manner, his faith in her ability to succeed today... it kept her panic from rising and over-whelming her.

As she lost sight of the man, Fang fought the urge to stop dead in her tracks. Instead, she continued onward, slipping her hand into her clutch handbag, fingers closing around her pepper spray, ready to fight for her life.

28

In his bedroom within the White House Residence, Charles Nash buttoned up his fresh shirt, his thoughts conflicted as he pulled a slackened tie tight around his neck. Not satisfied with how it nestled in his collar, he started over and tied a new Windsor knot, fielding imaginary press conference questions about the intelligence leak in his head while a second pocket of his brain recited a victorious speech as he stood alongside the presidents of both Korean nations.

He messed up the knot. Started over.

As a boy, and even as a young man, he'd looked up to older people in powerful positions and assumed they had their shit together. When he finally reached that station in life, he learned it had nothing to do with having their shit together and everything to do with having learned from their many, many mistakes.

As a freshman president, juggling the multitude of balls thrown at him daily, he'd assumed that by his second term, he would navigate the position with far more finesse than in his early days. That, too, was a fallacy. He knew the intricacies of the Washington landscape better, sure, and he had a handle on who he could and could not trust, but that didn't mean a new crisis or international tangle was a piece of cake, even if he appeared calm and collected.

There—his tie looked good. His shirt was crisp. He would look as presidential as a man could for the Oval Office meeting.

He made his way to the drawing room, where FBI agents Mitchell and Drebin rose from their chairs as people always did when he walked through the door, no matter how many times he waved them off. Nash greeted them in turn, saw that a coffee pot had been delivered, and helped himself.

"What can I do, gentlemen?" Nash asked as he took a seat before them. "I don't want to shy away from this. If I can speed up the investigation or provide more manpower, I'll give you what you need."

"Mr. President," Mitchell said. "I strongly advise against you getting directly involved. Law enforcement can handle Trapp. And if you hobble the intelligence inquiry, you risk implicating yourself."

Nash sighed. "I understand that, Mike. But I can't just sit back. It looks like I'm doing nothing. Feels like it, too, quite frankly. Do we even know if it's a traitor removing files or an aggressive nation hacking us?"

"We don't know yet. The systems have been shut down since the file came out. We don't know if the footage was ours or from an independent source."

"And it's definitely real?"

"We think so."

At first, Nash had been appalled at the execution, but he'd been filled in on the so-called victim and the reason that the world was better off without him. Strange how a man pointing a gun and firing a bullet through the head was somehow less palatable than a drone strike. This was one area where the experienced President Nash differed from the freshman Nash —he saw far more solidity in the black-and-white world of good guys versus bad guys, the block of gray in between narrowing with every order.

"And Trapp?" Nash asked. "Where are we with locating him?"

Drebin's posture was rigid, and his gaze hadn't wavered an inch. "Sir, we have Trapp's prints and DNA at the scene in Boston. If the press link Hangman to Trapp, there's no doubt they will jump on it. Especially after his alleged involvement in Black Monday and his partner's killing."

Nash saw what he was hinting at. "They're trying to paint him as a traitor."

Mitchell shook his head. "Which is patently absurd."

Drebin barely moved. Just a half-glance at Mitchell. "With all due respect, I can't rule anything out." He started ticking off points on his hand. "The Triads, who we know the Chinese government uses as independent muscle." Then his first finger popped up. "Trapp is on the run instead of coming in for a debriefing, current location suspected to be Washington, DC or the immediate area." The middle finger joined his other two. "Trapp contacted me to explain himself, but used an encrypted device and told me nothing, except giving away a possible Chinese spy's codename." A fourth finger rose. "If he is spying on Chinese nationals, then he is committing federal crimes. Regardless of his status in the CIA, if he is engaged in an unsanctioned mission, he must be held accountable." His hand folded back into his lap. "I'm sure you would agree, sir."

Although Nash knew Drebin was right, he also knew Trapp. As bloody-minded and stubborn as he could be, Trapp never acted against the United States. But as President, Nash was expected to uphold the law, was judged by a higher standard, and would have to set an example—even if there were extenuating circumstances.

"We will follow the law where it needs to go," Nash said.

"No matter how uncomfortable that might be for me personally."

Drebin nodded grimly, neither annoyed nor happy.

"Thank you for your insights, Agent Drebin," Nash said.

Drebin stood. Nash shook his hand, and the FBI agent exited, met by a Secret Service agent who would show him out.

Once Drebin was gone, Nash turned to Mitchell, whose expression remained grave. "Sir, if Trapp's full identity is exposed, we will have to distance you from him. He knows the drill. He *will* be burned and buried."

"I understand, Mike. And I understand that Trapp knew this was always a risk when he signed up."

The words tasted bitter, but Nash had to prioritize the bigger picture, the nation's interests.

"What is the status on our other problem? The timing?"

"Of the Korea summit? Other than the proximity of China geographically, we still can't find a direct link. And we can't work out how Trapp might be involved."

"Coincidence, then?"

"How many operations of this nature coincide with international politics?" Mike paused in case Nash wanted to interject, but the president held his tongue. "Our DPRK liaison is concerned about the issue of an assassin—Trapp—on the loose so close to his president's visit. He wants a meeting."

"Anything from the South Koreans? Are they worried?"

"Less than Mr. Yung-Gi. I'll meet and reassure him that it's all in hand," Mike said. "But we need all the security providers on alert, and we'll keep the relevant agencies updated. Any hint that this crosses over, we'll stomp on it right away."

Nash finished his coffee and placed the cup on the tray to one side. He needed to be specific without actively ordering Mike to break any laws. "If we can help Jason, if it can be done without blowback or implications..."

"I'll get to work on possible contingencies."

Nash's watch chimed with a reminder: he had seven minutes until his next meeting in the Oval Office. "Time's up. Keep me informed."

As Mike left the room, Nash allowed himself thirty seconds' reprieve to sink into his chair. Sacrificing Trapp might be necessary, might be the right call for the country. But that didn't make it any easier to tolerate.

29

Although Le-Carré-esque spycraft wasn't Trapp's usual modus operandi, he had honed the skills over the years. He was more accustomed to approaching directly, favoring threats and self-preservation over bribes and gentle persuasion. But he thought Fang Chen, a low-level employee with access to those up the chain, required a more nuanced touch.

She had suddenly turned around on the bustling Washington street and was heading toward him instead of away. The heightened pulse and urge to do something—anything—raced through him. But the young woman passed by without a glance, her strides long and urgent but not panicked.

He didn't think he'd been made; she was no spy, after all. Unless she had the most rock-solid cover of any Chinese spy working under the ambassador... But Trapp did the same as he would've if she were a skilled operative.

He didn't risk turning around immediately. Even the least experienced civilian possessed a degree of instinct, regardless of formal training; unnatural movements or a sudden change in direction from a stranger sent warning signals to the brain.

Trapp slowed to look in a window, planning to alter course after a few seconds of browsing. But then he saw a patrol car.

Two cops, rolling by at a snail's pace, the woman in the passenger seat scanning the sidewalk, the male driver attentive to the road but also checking oncoming cars.

He had taken every precaution he could think of to avoid being recognized. A cap sporting the Ferrari brand, evading most elevated CCTV cameras, and a realistic fake beard augmented with additional bumps to imitate an alternative facial structure. High-end computer programs could identify people from the way they walked, so he'd placed a ball bearing in each shoe to alter his gait.

Both cops looked in his direction.

Instinct screamed at him to run. Or hide. Or fight. The human need to find safety was as ingrained in him as anyone. The only difference was that Trapp controlled it better than most.

He kept his pace even and didn't look up, but neither did he hunker lower, no change in his demeanor. He'd give it five more seconds.

1...

The left ball bearing shifted awkwardly and dug into the soft spot between his instep and heel. He pushed on with only a slight stutter in his step, reluctant to add the limp that the pain demanded.

2...

Trapp slowed, giving his left foot a shake, but the ball bearing remained stuck. It was like stepping on a Lego barefoot, which he'd only done once, but it convinced him that replacing waterboarding with crossing a room full of tiny plastic bricks blindfolded would speed up the enhanced interrogation process.

3...

The cop car passed by him, no change in speed, no lights. Neither officer reached for a radio or phone.

Trapp slowed, exhaled the deep breath that had nestled in his lungs, and found himself staring at a display of lingerie. Hoping he didn't look like the sort of sleaze ball who deserved 911 treatment, he knelt to adjust his shoe and ball bearing, then set off back the way he'd come.

The Ferrari hat had been intentional—it was red, noticeable. He now swapped it for a plain, dark green one, took off his jacket, and slung it over his shoulder. Not the greatest disguise, but on the slim chance that he'd misread Fang and the about-turn was a counter-surveillance move, she'd have been focused on the red hat and would likely recognize it if she changed direction again.

There was nothing in her profile to suggest she had those skills, though, and she was awfully young to have attained that level.

No, Trapp would play the odds—she was an excellent way in.

He caught sight of her and resumed his pace, holding back, watching other faces coming his way. Fang re-entered the comic book store.

Had she forgotten something or was she really into superheroes?

Trapp found himself a movie poster to investigate, looking past it to Fang, who lingered at the checkout, her back to the door. No fear indicators, no furtive double-checking over her shoulder.

Trapp hadn't been able to see inside the store earlier, as he'd been hanging back to surveil the area for security, hoping to see where the town car that dropped her off had parked. But there was something here. Something he hadn't expected.

A long-lingering look from a man who seemed surprised as he passed Fang. He was slim and balding, early thirties, with the sharp dress sense of someone important offset by the mannerisms of a nervous college kid. He said nothing to her, just paused long enough for Trapp to be sure he recognized her.

Another operative?

When the man paused near her, Fang's shoulders tensed. She held her neck stiffly, still waiting her turn to speak with the cashier. She *knew* this man as he knew her, knew he was watching her, if only for a few seconds.

Trapp committed the man's face to memory, then refocused on Fang. Out of one corner of his eye, he watched the man exit the store, look both ways up and down the sidewalk, then hurry away with his shoulders hunched, eyes down.

Instinct didn't just catch cues that saved his skin; it also bore down on him when he needed an edge, and now it raised the question again: was Fang really the mousy, terrified assistant that she appeared to be, or something more?

ON HIS WAY back to his hotel, Trapp took a different route, conducting countersurveillance maneuvers at random— random, because if he didn't predict his movements himself, no one who'd picked him up would, either.

The Hangman leaks dominated headlines, but they would only connect to him if Drebin and Mitchell chose, and whether that happened would depend on public perception. So far, the loudest voices in the news were debating America's role as the world's policeman. But Trapp saw far more: an assassination attempt, his codename and his partner's smeared with the stench of treason, and a foreign operator working in an untouchable capacity in the heart of the nation's capital. It was all connected. He just wasn't sure how.

He wanted to call Ikeda again, but he wasn't sure if she

would even answer. Besides, it wasn't fair to drop that on her, to force her to choose between the Agency and him.

Another woman came to mind, someone he hadn't spoken to in weeks. He'd kept in touch sporadically since they had thwarted an attempt on the president's life earlier that year, and she was currently riding a desk as she recovered from her injuries and trauma. She was pending evaluation before reassignment abroad, and he guessed it would be driving her nuts.

Madison Grubbs picked up after three rings. "Hello?"

"You know who this is?" Trapp asked.

She was cautious in her reply. "I can guess."

"I don't want to get you in trouble. I just need to know the gossip. How bad do they want me?"

A deceptively trivial question that could cost her job, depending on how many layers deep her answer went. If the CIA or FBI had linked the Hangman leak with China, there could be more eyes on the senior embassy staff, which meant low level staffers like Fang Chen would also be observed, alerting more dangerous eyes and ears. Even scuttlebutt could be invaluable, especially given the plan he was considering.

"You know I can't tell you anything," Madison said. "Come in. Stop running around Washington while your dirty past gets broadcast. The Agency will look after you."

Trapp sighed, knowing she'd had to say that, just as Ikeda had, in case they were being recorded. It also told him more than the words themselves let on.

They know for certain I'm in Washington. They know I'm not just hiding out. They'll be nervous.

"I understand," Trapp said. "Can you at least tell me what sort of priority this is? Anything that won't get you fired."

Madison's end went silent. Thinking it through or initiating a trace?

She and Trapp had been friendly. Trapp had nothing but respect for her, and he'd gotten the impression it was reciprocated. But it was just one mission they'd shared, not the intensity of repeated combat that bonded brothers and sisters for life. The main thing that prompted him to call her was that she would do the right thing, even if her superiors expected her to do the opposite.

She said, "They want you to come in, but their main focus is on plugging the leak and appearing strong and stable to the Koreans. If anything, they'll play it down in public."

It sounded like she was being prompted. But it also sounded plausible.

The Koreans...

Both Mike and Drebin had spoken of that, and Trapp agreed about the Hangman timing.

"Thanks, Madison. I appreciate it."

"The only thing you might have to worry about is Jake Redman's intelligence oversight committee."

"House Permanent Select Committee on Intelligence. Yeah, they'd be all over a leak like this. Don't worry about it."

"Jason, please, come in," she said. "I promise, we'll—"

Trapp hung up, his fingers moving right back to the encrypted phone. There was a patching delay before Mitchell's phone started ringing.

"Where are you, Jason?"

"Washington," Trapp said. "How about you?"

"Don't be smart with me. No, actually, *do* be smart. Why are you out there alone?"

"You know why."

Mitchell gave a *hmmm* and said, "The Shark, though? Seriously?"

"I know what I saw."

"What does he want?"

"I don't know. The Hangman release—have you traced it to China yet?"

"I can't say."

"Is the Shark the connection here? Can't be coincidence, surely?"

"I *can't say*. I'm more concerned about him being in the country—*if* it's him—at the same time as the New York summit. As is everyone else."

"I don't see it, Mike," Trapp said. "North Korea and China are allies. He wouldn't go against Beijing, would he?"

"It's not that simple. Closer ties between North and South Korea will not sit well with the real hardliners. Which side do you think Chao fell in with before going private?"

If Li Chao wanted to disrupt the summit, why go after Trapp, who had nothing to do with it? No matter how many ways he looked at it, he kept coming back to the conclusion that Li had something personal against him.

"Jason," Mitchell intoned. "You know what happens if this goes bad."

"I'm burned," Trapp said flatly, draining all emotion from his voice. "I get that."

"Are you running an op?"

"Not yet."

"Why take the risk? Because they targeted you personally? Or because Ryan's brother was caught in the crossfire?"

Trapp had more reasons than he could list, chief amongst them being *instinct*. If he let them tie his hands, lock him up for his own protection, he'd be paralyzed. Neutered. Unable to fight back.

"I don't care what you say about me," Trapp said. "Traitor, rogue officer, whatever language you use to disavow me. But I can't let people think Ryan is a traitor."

"I'll quash that," Mike assured him. "No matter what happens with you."

"Thank you." Trapp believed him.

"I can't speak long," Mike said. "I'm heading to a briefing

with a North Korean security guy, then into a hearing with an asshole named Jake Redman."

"Redman?" Trapp said. "Why is that the second time I've heard his name in as many minutes?"

Mike explained about the subpoena, playing it down as a nuisance fishing expedition. While he talked, Trapp used the unencrypted civilian laptop to google Jake Redman. The top searches were Wikipedia, Congress's official website, C-Span, some Fox News videos, and the man's own web page.

"Jason?" Mitchell said. "You still there?"

"Yeah, just checking something out."

Trapp scrolled through Redman's official website, a sprawling, bombastic self-promotional article showing the two sides any politician needed to woo voters: a man of the people chowing down on a huge plate of chicken wings in a small-town diner, and an autoplay video of him striding the halls of Congress, shot from a low angle to heighten his gravitas.

"Holy shit." Trapp hit pause.

Congressman Redman greeted the Democrat ranking member, whom Trapp recognized as Rita Tarragona, a pally handshake demonstrating their willingness to cross the aisle for the good of the American people. But it was another man alongside Redman that had grabbed his attention, a balding hawk standing to one side. The same guy he had seen in the comic book store. The one who clearly knew Fang, and who Fang didn't want to speak with.

There he was; some sort of aide to the congressman in charge of an intelligence oversight committee.

"You need to tell me something, Jason?" Mike asked.

"Not yet."

30

Hwa Yung-Gi stared at the glass-fronted portrait of a US president he had never heard of: Chester Arthur, a man with an impressive mustache. Having perused the small plaque declaring Arthur as presiding over the United States between 1881 and 1885, Yung-Gi refocused his gaze to take in his own reflection—an old man he barely recognized. But what he'd lost in physical prowess, he had gained in experience. And experience was telling him he was being shielded from what the Americans knew.

His turned as his contact entered the room, a man he'd met in the Situation Room on his first visit to the White House.

"Sorry for keeping you waiting," Mike Mitchell said, shaking Yung-Gi's hand. "I've just come from a briefing with the president and the FBI. I understand you're concerned about a few unfortunate developments."

Yung-Gi sat at the small table opposite Mike amid a gathering of comfortable chairs more suited to an American coffee house than a serious meeting space. *This is how it is done here,* he told himself. It might not be the snub that it felt like.

But it wouldn't hurt to let the Americans worry that they'd

offended him, so he sat stiffly, refusing to relax into the deca-
dently-comfortable chair.

"Hangman," Yung-Gi said. "He is loose in the city?"

Mike opened his mouth in a half-smile, as if he'd been
about to deliver bad news but changed his mind before speaking. "We do not believe he is currently active. And even if he
were, he is on our side. Absolutely nothing to concern your
summit security."

"And the Triads?"

"We see no connection between the incident in Boston and
the accusations currently circulating in the press."

Yung-Gi recognized it for the non-answer that it was. At
home, he would have responded with a direct accusation of
lying, but that was not the way of things here. Even when they
truly were lying, Americans could get highly offended when
called on it.

"Mr. Mitchell, I must insist on regular updates, along with
official investigative documents. Although we are some
distance from New York, I am sure you agree the timing is
extremely suspicious."

"We do," Mike conceded. "That's why I want to assure you
that there is *no* evidence of a link between the Hangman situation and the upcoming summit. *But* while Hangman is a separate domestic matter that is being handled by our best people,
we are treating the issue as if they *are* connected. Should
anything hint at danger to your president's safety, we will alert
you immediately."

Yung-Gi nodded, keeping his expression neutral. "I appreciate your reassurance, Mr. Mitchell. But I will need to see all
you are doing in that regard, or my superiors might be even
more suspicious than I am."

Mitchell leaned forward, his hands clasped on his knees. "I
completely understand. We will ensure the summit proceeds as
planned, and we guarantee the utmost security for all parties

involved."

While the man seemed sincere, Yung-Gi's experience nagged at him. Something was being withheld. However, he could not openly accuse the CIA deputy director of lying.

"Very well, Mr. Mitchell," Yung-Gi said, rising from his seat. "I will accept this for now. But please keep me informed."

Mitchell stood as well, extending his hand. "You have my word."

After a firm goodbye handshake, Yung-Gi left the meeting room and was escorted back through the White House security checkpoints. Waiting for his car to be brought around, his burner phone buzzed. He answered right away.

"What do you have for me?" Yung-Gi asked in Korean.

"Triads," Charlie Hu reported, his Korean tainted with an American accent. "Acting strange. My guy in the area says there are new players in town, staying as guests at one of their casinos."

"From the Boston chapter?"

"I don't know for sure, but no one is smiling. Isn't a social call."

Yung-Gi frowned, processing. Nothing confirmed but more activity he didn't like.

"Keep your distance," Yung-Gi ordered. "Don't engage directly. But be prepared for further instructions."

"Got it. We'll be ready."

As Yung-Gi's car arrived, driven by a young-looking athletic man in a suit, he wondered if he needed to bring in more people. He could not risk an open street war. But at neither could he contemplate failure, not when millions would starve.

He would do whatever it took, no matter what it cost him.

∾

As Mike Mitchell took the oath before this closed session of the Intelligence Committee, Jake Redman kept his arms by his side, hoping his suit jacket hid the disco-rings of sweat forming under his armpits. He'd mopped his brow twice and smiled bravely at Rita Tarragona, assuring her he'd been fighting a cold for a couple of days.

This wasn't like him. Even when he was skirting the boundaries of acceptable behavior for a congressman, he was usually cool and in control.

A bead of sweat trickled down Redman's left temple into his beard. He took his handkerchief from the desk—no point returning it to his pocket—and dabbed at the errant moisture. He no longer had any doubt he was being used by the Chinese to further their own agenda.

Sure, it might help him gain traction, but it was still...

He could not bear to think the word.

"Congressman?" came Rita's voice. When he didn't answer, she hissed, "*Jake.* Are you okay?"

That snapped him out of his trance. "A reminder, ladies and gentlemen, that although we are minuting this, unless the president declassifies today's session, Mr. Mitchell's testimony is classified. The purpose of calling him is twofold: to establish the legitimacy of the Hangman stories currently in circulation, and—if true—the source of the leak and what the CIA can do to prevent further such breaches."

Nods all around, including Mitchell.

Rita invited Mitchell to explain his position and what the Office of Special Operations entailed, to which Mitchell gave a frank reply: he oversaw small, under-the-radar missions essential to the safety of the United States and her allies. He added that his people had seen off sizeable threats, from terror cells to assassination attempts, and that they were instrumental in dismantling the network that had facilitated the Black Monday attacks, which still loomed heavily over the American psyche.

There were other questions, the answers to which were mostly officialese that Redman zoned out. His mouth was dry and his armpits slicker than ever as he rehearsed his own lines in his head. He dabbed at his forehead twice.

God above, maybe he *had* been poisoned. Not with any chemical, though. The poison infecting Redman was far worse.

It was Thomas Decker who uttered the word plaguing the media first. "Mr. Mitchell, what can you tell us about the operative codenamed 'Hangman' and whether his missions were fully sanctioned by either current or previous administrations?"

Mitchell leaned into the microphone fractionally, as those reluctantly testifying often did—he needed to emphasize a point, or he was lying. "The codename Hangman is defunct, and that individual no longer works for the CIA or—to my knowledge—any government agency. In addition, their identity is protected by law. So even if it were revealed, no media outlet can release that information. We have conveyed that to every media organization in the country."

"But the rest of the world is not bound by our laws," Rita pointed out. "What is to stop, say, a French newspaper from spreading more revealing details?"

"They are our allies. We have reached out to all our friends, requesting the same restraint."

"But they don't have to obey. Do they?"

Mitchell cast his eyes over Rita and Jake before leaning in again. "They do not."

The committee members shuffled, waiting for Rita to signal that she was done, then Decker asked, "Mr. Mitchell, can you confirm that the footage released of what appears to be an execution does depict the individual known as Hangman?"

Mitchell considered it carefully, and this time when he leaned in, his tone was softer. "I cannot confirm or deny it. The footage is low resolution, the lighting is poor. We cannot geolocate it to Rwanda without landmarks. For all we know, it was faked yesterday on a cellphone and run through a filter. If and when we locate the original file, we will examine it properly."

Decker pressed him, "Can you confirm Hangman did, in fact, execute a foreign national in the sovereign country of Rwanda sometime in the last twenty years?"

Again, Mitchell's voice was softer than when they started the session. "I do not recall that specifically. With the files locked down, we are working to pull that information."

"But it's possible?"

Mitchell deepened his tone. "I cannot speculate."

Despite what amounted to a mealy-mouthed delaying tactic, Redman was satisfied he had identified the tells in what he had expected would be a practiced liar. Spies were supposed to be good at that. Mitchell seemed to be altering his pitch between answers he wanted to give and the one he was dressing up as firm but casual. Redman had only learned his teenaged self's tell when he was thirty and his momma revealed that she was not, in fact, blessed with a supernatural gift to sniff out untruths, but that young Jake's sentences rose an octave on the final word of each sentence whenever he lied. Perhaps this was why Mike Mitchell had never made it as a field operative. Or at least, so Redman figured.

The only thing that kept him together as the session wore on was picturing the potential fallout for President Nash. Mitchell had testified that Nash knew nothing about Hangman's activities, so if the committee could prove this to be a lie, it might well sink Nash and his centrist agenda. Possibly even risk the drawing up of articles of impeachment.

But the session was drawing to a scheduled break, and Mitchell didn't appear fazed at all. He was as forthright and direct as anyone in his position could be.

Redman was about to change that. He hoped.

"We're coming up to lunch," Rita stated. "If no one has

anything further to add, can we release Mr. Mitchell for an hour?"

All concurred except one.

Redman steadied the tremble in one hand by gripping his damp handkerchief in his fist and gave a gentle cough to one side before speaking. "Director Mitchell. I do not like to bring up gossip and rumor. But one document, or file, or... or, maybe an operation... has come to my attention. I don't know what it is, but confidential sources have been whispering."

Everyone was looking at Redman, some on tenterhooks, others annoyed, as they'd been expecting to tuck into their lunches in a few minutes.

Redman hadn't gone all the way yet. He could still withdraw. Make something up. But if the threats from the Chinese were true, he really had no choice. And it might as easily be an opportunity for him.

"These whispers, Mr. Mitchell, concern something called 'Project TIPTOE.' Is that some sort of codeword? Can you tell the committee what that might be?"

Mitchell's brow furrowed. His confusion appeared genuine. He spoke in his low, gravelly voice. "I'm afraid I have no knowledge of that name. But I will look into it and report back to the committee."

Redman nodded. "Thank you, Mr. Mitchell. Reconvene in one hour."

Satisfied that he had done as instructed, and that Mitchell didn't seem to know about the operation or whatever it was, Redman's discomfort eased. He would change his shirt and return fresh, ready for the director of the NSA, who was scheduled next.

Then Rita approached him. "What's Project TIPTOE?"

He shrugged. "Just something I heard. Might be related to this Hangman traitor."

"We don't know if he's a traitor yet, Jake. And if you're

coming down with a bug that might impair your impartiality, maybe consider taking the rest of the day off."

As she walked away, he smiled to himself, but the word he didn't want to face sat heavily in his stomach as he tried to envision the positives. He had planted the seeds given to him by the Chinese, and maybe set himself on the path to replace President Nash, but he had also, possibly, maybe... hopefully not, committed the one crime he'd sworn he would never touch.

Treason.

MIKE MITCHELL STOPPED before the Oval Office's gatekeeper, Helen Borstal.

"Mike, there are to be no interruptions unless a nuke is about to go off," Helen insisted.

"There is," Mike said. "Potentially as bad, anyway."

Helen wavered a second before stepping aside.

Breaking all protocol, both written and implied, Mike opened the Oval Office door and hurried in. President Nash was deep in conversation with three women and two men near a whiteboard which held a top-down photo of a section of New York City, marked with overlays and symbols that showed the streets to be closed off around the UN Building. All looked up sharply, Nash brimming with annoyance.

"We're in the middle of—"

"Mr. President," Mike said, acutely aware that he was somewhat short of breath. "I'm sorry, but this can't wait."

31

U nder cover of dusk, Trapp monitored his target from an elevated knoll in a public park, concealed by a copse of trees and thick shrubs. It was chilly, and there was a dampness to the air, and his knees and neck ached from remaining in one position so long. He could not lie flat, or he'd lose sight of where he needed to watch, thanks to his best equipment being seized by the Chinese Embassy guards. His only kit this evening was a small set of binoculars and a messenger bag of useful items stashed nearby that he'd brought from his Boston apartment.

The embassy staff's residential building was promoted as a home away from home for diplomatic and security personnel serving their country on foreign soil but unable to afford a secure brownstone in Washington, DC. Trapp saw it differently, as a bastion of control.

Designed to ensure that residents adhered to strict government protocols, the building was an extension of the state, a testament to the extent of Beijing's power. It was as much Chinese territory as the embassy itself, the least likely place for an American operative to attempt recruitment.

But with strong circumstantial evidence that the Chinese had compromised a powerful member of Congress, Trapp had to accelerate his plans. A high-risk, high-reward strategy seemed like his best choice.

The digital sweep that had given him Fang Chen's name had also tapped her diplomatic visa records, which gave him her address: fourth floor, apartment number two.

The rear of the residence was more aesthetically pleasing than he had expected with a flower garden designed to keep staffers content and less likely to venture into the capitalist nightmare of the city. Razor wire atop the wall was cleverly hidden by bushy trees with narrow trunks.

Trapp had considered using fake documents to get in the front door, but posing as a plumbing inspector would likely draw suspicion now that Li Chao knew that someone had been surveilling the embassy.

From his vantage point, Trapp couldn't determine the apartment numbering. Fang's could be second from the left or the right, or it might face the other street. So he was forced to watch until she appeared briefly in the apartment second from the left, closing her curtains and turning out the lights earlier than most. She seemed to be alone.

Trapp waited as evening melted to night and the gardens emptied. When the area had been deserted for nearly an hour, he pulled a ski mask over his face—to buy a few spare minutes if discovered during this next phase—and moved forward.

He retrieved the unassuming pouch he had concealed in the roots of a tree and the telescopic ladder he had stashed earlier. It wasn't quite as tall as the wall, but that was fine. At the top, Trapp sorted through the bag and pulled out a cylinder the size of a soda can, which he placed on the razor wire-topped wall, hitting the timer before releasing it.

He counted down in his head, then pulled himself over, lying flat on the wire as the cylinder strobed like an insane disco light. His overalls, made of a thick, Kevlar-like material, protected him from the barbs at this deliberate angle, allowing him to swing his legs over, push off from the wall, and shimmy down one of the ornamental trees into the shadows.

The cylinder ceased strobing.

It was a gimmicky device, confusing cameras with night vision capability, making it look like they'd glitched out for a few seconds.

Now Trapp just had to map a route to the building itself.

He swapped his ski mask for a cap to appear like a manual worker and buy himself a few seconds if challenged. Trapp flicked a switch at the back of the cap, activating dull, red LED lights in the peak that strobed like the cylinder. The effect was too dim and too fast for human eyes to see but served to obscure his face from cameras.

Sticking to the outer edges where surveillance was less effective, Trapp reached the main building, where he waited. No guards rushed him. The cameras he could see remained still, pointing out from the façade.

This side of the residence had crenelated angles for privacy with balconies just large enough for two chairs, a drinks table, and maybe a potted plant or two. The whole arrangement made scaling the exterior wall easier.

He silently rose onto one balustrade, reached for the next balcony, then hoisted himself up with catlike grace. He repeated this three times to reach Fang's balcony.

Voices below. Footsteps. At least four people, probably men, based on the footfalls.

Trapp held himself still. Waiting. Watching.

Two men in Chinese military uniforms marched below, eyes roving. Trapp craned his neck, locating the other two in the opposite direction. None appeared tense, and their head movements looked practiced, as if they'd done this a thousand times before.

Standard patrol.

They aren't looking for you...

Trapp pressed himself against the wall, trying to melt into the shadows. The patrols moved slowly, like they were killing time, their gaits formal but sluggish. They carried automatic weapons slung over their shoulders, covering every path around the flowers and lawns. Trapp controlled his breathing —six seconds in, ten out—as he held his position.

Their circuit took fifteen minutes, during which Trapp realized he had no way of knowing when they might reappear. They hadn't seen him, but if they did, all he had was a solitary 9mm handgun.

He edged out of the shadow and rose to Fang's window. Using a specialized glass cutter, he scored a circle near the handle, then reached through and disabled the alarm sensor with magnetic contact plates before turning the handle to open the window and slipping inside. Fang's bedroom was empty, the scent of flowery cosmetics in the air. The bed was unmade, a closet door open, and a mug sat on the bedside table.

Although he had no intel on whether the embassy residences were outfitted with listening devices, he used the audible equivalent of a strobe effect to pump barely-discernible white noise out of a thumb-sized speaker that would mask conversations without alerting anyone who might be monitoring live. A whispered hiss would be the most they'd pick up.

Better paranoid than dead.

His footfalls remained silent as he prowled toward the door. He gripped the handle, ear to the jamb. A TV was all he could hear.

If there were cameras, he would be visible to anyone watching. But he was betting there would be too many residents to monitor constantly. Assuming the Chinese government would even go that far.

Trapp depressed the handle and pulled. The door opened

smoothly but dragged on the carpet, emitting what felt like the loudest scraping noise ever. He waited for a sign that Fang had heard him.

Nothing.

He bladed his body and glided into the passageway, stepping gradually toward the living room—hating that he was a prowler, the worst kind of man, about to frighten a young woman half to death.

But it was what he had to do.

He stepped out, gun in one hand, a finger to his lips, and entered Fang's field of view.

She jumped, startled by Trapp's appearance, but her eyes were glued to the gun as she pushed herself back into her couch, shrinking away as if she hoped she could disappear.

Trapp raised his hands, keeping hold of the gun, and made his voice low and urgent. "I'm not here to hurt you, Fang. But I need your help."

Fang's eyes switched to the door. Back to Trapp. "What do you want?"

"I want the people who've been passing you US secrets. Fabian Pincher. Jake Redman."

"I do not know who they are. I have never heard of them. Go, or I will scream."

"We can offer you money, amnesty, a place to live," Trapp said, glancing down to check that his white noise speaker was transmitting. "You just need to cooperate."

"I will not betray my country."

"I know what you've been doing," Trapp said. "You'll be declared persona non grata when Jake Redman goes down. He's an inveterate coward. I guarantee he won't stay quiet."

Fang's eyes flickered with panic.

"If you help me, I can make sure you won't be deported. I promise. But if you don't, you're gone. Done. You and your spy buddy, your immunity won't matter."

Fang's gaze hardened. "I won't betray my country."

"I don't want you to betray China. I want you to betray an American traitor."

Fang stared back, still terrified but defiant. "The creepy man I met with?"

Trapp frowned fractionally as he pictured Pincher's face. It wasn't the worst description he'd ever heard. "Yeah. Creepy guy."

Fang looked to the door, to the window, to Trapp. "OK... I might be able to do that. But you must agree... it will not implicate anyone from China. You are the oppressors. You are the colonizers. Not us."

It went unsaid, but Trapp read a silent addition to her words: *China has a right to spy on other countries, while America does not.* "Where will you meet him next?"

Fang opened her mouth to speak when there was a knock at the door. A man spoke Chinese outside, authoritative but tense.

"Hide this." Trapp pulled out a spare burner phone and tossed it to her. "Tonight was an attempted burglary."

Fang collected the phone and stared at it.

A key slid into the outer lock.

Trapp ducked out of the room as the door opened. He must have been a fraction too late, as one of the men bellowed, "Tsíng!" which Trapp took to mean "Stop!" But he barreled back through the bedroom and out the open window.

Maybe their audio bugs were wired for any sudden change in pitch. Or maybe their tech had just gotten better since he'd equipped his Boston safe house with the white noise device. If they found him, he'd be mown down by automatic gunfire. This was Chinese territory, after all. They wouldn't even have to explain themselves.

He hopped over the handrail and dropped to the next balustrade. Two male voices railed overhead as the window clattered open.

Trapp dropped two more stories and hit the ground running, sticking to the outer edge of the flower garden, partially concealed by the foliage. But floodlights burst on, illuminating the area like a football stadium as an alarm wailed to life.

He pulled his ski mask down, visual interference from his cap's rim useless against the glare. His arms and legs pumped, heavier than they would've been a mere five years ago, but he maintained a fierce sprint. His endurance hadn't waned, even if he'd lost half a yard of pace.

He was almost back at his ingress point when the first gunshots clattered into the night.

With slugs ricocheting against the wall, shredding bushes and tree branches, he could tell they didn't have an exact bead on him.

Yet.

Trapp sidestepped ten yards left, then pulled his gun and fired three shots into the dirt. Enough to make any incoming operators pause, enough to give them a location, which he vacated fast, crouch-running to his planned escape point.

Trapp had used a tree to shimmy down like a rough fireman's pole, but he'd located a sturdier one to ascend. He was sure-footed and pulled himself up, discovering too late that the tree shook the higher he climbed.

That was the bead the guards needed.

Trapp leapt from the branch, a volley of gunfire splintering wood and perforating leaves behind him as he landed chest-first on the razor-wire-topped wall. He slipped but tensed so that his arms and torso held firm. But he'd hit at the wrong angle, and half a dozen tiny blades sliced through his overalls and cut into his skin.

Teeth gritted against the pain, he levered one leg up, found the summit, and pushed upward as bursts of three from semi-auto rifles pounded closer.

Movement inside the grounds.

Only seconds until they were upon him.

Trapp wrenched free of the razor wire, tearing his skin in bloody, ragged cuts, then rolled onto his back and dropped over the other side.

Back in the US of A.

He clutched his torn skin, hoping to hold it together so he wasn't bleeding out on the streets as he ran, and collected everything he could carry—the retracted ladder, the messenger bag, anything that might be used to implicate the US in a mission against sovereign Chinese territory.

Trapp fled through the park, located his motorbike, and discarded the ladder in a dumpster, then pulled on a tight leather jacket, keeping his other gear with him this time. It wouldn't stop the bleeding but would slow it until he could gather his wits, patch himself back up, and consider just how likely it was that they would find the blood, collect his DNA, and use it as evidence against him.

32

The following morning, Trapp was nursing a burrito, watching Fang from a covered booth. He winced as another sharp throb flared on his chest. The cuts from the razor wire had not been particularly deep, thanks to the overalls, but the way he'd ripped himself free had torn his skin and lengthened the wounds. He'd treated them with antiseptic that stung like hell, applied Steri-Strips to close them, and secured gauze with strong adhesive tape to keep it all together. After dozing off with the help of a handful of Advil, Trapp had been woken by his phone ringing. At first confused, he could not understand who might have that number, and then it dawned on him—he had programmed it into the burner he'd given Fang.

He wasted no time or resources on surveillance gear, employing only the beard with additional prosthetics and the ball bearing-in-his-shoes trick that had served him well so far. There would be cameras everywhere in this obscenely gentrified stretch of DC, currently cordoned off for a food fair showing off the vast array of ethnic dining available in the city. Each stall handed out free samples, discount coupons, and shots of whatever drink they felt best represented their restaurant—both alcoholic and non.

Fifty yards away, Fang Chen took up a position near a waffle van.

A waffle van. At a food fair.

Right.

Other than advertising their wares as "Belgian," Trapp couldn't see the ethnicity.

If this really was her meeting point and not a sting to lure him out, Fabian Pincher was late.

Fang sat at a picnic table and arranged her coffee, napkin, and waffle into a spread perpendicular to the table's edge. The waffle was a monstrosity smothered in chocolate sauce and whipped cream which she daintily prepared to tuck into with a fork. It was the first time Trapp had seen her smile.

"How do you feel about such a decadent treat?" Trapp asked.

Fang and Trapp were wearing simple EarPods, not some smart bone-conducting satellite-enabled tech, and their line had remained open since she'd arrived at the fair.

She said, "My superiors do not want their representatives getting fat. Like Americans."

Trapp touched his stomach. It wasn't the generalized insult about his fellow countrymen that gave his gut a sinking sensation, though. Nor was it the two cops making a purchase from a nearby churro bar, a twist on the donut stereotype.

Fang's cooperation had come too easily. He'd hoped to talk her around, to apply solid leverage, but the interruption had cut them short. Yet here she was, chowing down a calorie-laden waffle, frosty-cool under pressure.

Perhaps she saw this as her best chance at ending a situation she hadn't asked for. Or, after last night, he was finding it more believable that her job as an ambassador's assistant might be a cover.

The cops paid for their churros.

Fabian Pincher emerged from within the breakfast crowd and approached the waffle van, pausing before Fang saw him. He checked his breath in a cupped hand, then proceeded to her table, armed with a thermal coffee mug.

The ease with which Fang had been able to set up this meeting stank of an ambush. He'd broken into a protected site, after all. And Trapp knew backing off at the right time was just as crucial as knowing when to press on, to persevere. When suspecting a trap, no matter how desperate the mission, there were two choices: counter with a better plan or walk away.

The two cops were eating their churros from paper bags, chatting, eyes on everything except each other. They were good officers, neither of rookie age, and they moved with confidence and caution. Trapp expected they were a visual deterrent to would-be petty thieves, eyes for possible terrorist actions, and —maybe, possibly—on the lookout for a man they'd been alerted to on a BOLO at their morning briefing.

It was now too risky to record Fabian and Fang's chat, then simply walk up behind Fabian and march him off with a gun in his side. Thankfully, Fang still came across clear and crisp, Fabian somewhat faint. But the recording could be enhanced.

"Thank you for yesterday," Fang said. "Our sources say you achieved what was asked of you."

Good. Nothing specific. No "as you know" line that would raise Fabian's hackles.

"Yeah," Fabian said. "He wasn't happy about it. From what I hear, the witness went straight to the president. What is that, anyway? What did you get him to ask about?"

"Nothing to concern you. No one will be hurt, I promise."

Again, no specifics. Fabian was undeniably an amateur, but Trapp was having doubts about Fang. And the more doubt he had, the less he watched her.

"Hey," Fabian said, almost stammering. "About that rain check. Coffee? Me and you?"

Trapp wanted to slap Fabian around the back of the head. In Trapp's experience, when an attractive woman from a hostile country shows interest in an unremarkable man in a privileged position, the unremarkable man should run a mile in the opposite direction, preferably in the direction of the FBI.

"I have a coffee," Fang said, lifting her cup. "Why don't you grab one? I can recommend the waffles, too."

Not quite flirting, but not batting him away. Keeping him on the hook, talking.

Fabian jumped up like he'd been electrocuted and rushed to the van, unscrewing the lid on his empty thermos as he waited behind a couple considering their choice with the studied manner of picking a mortgage.

Trapp needed to shift his focus wider. He stood slowly, looking in the opposite direction from Fang, hoping the cops didn't decide to mosey on over as he circled past them for a new angle. Around the perimeter, trees lining the street cast shadows and buildings occupied by local businesses complemented the fair as much as they competed. No vehicles. Perhaps that was why one of the cyclists caught his eye.

The man was on an e-bike, leaning against a tree some thirty yards away, flicking through his phone. His helmet was larger than the average commuter, closer to those favored by couriers or food-delivery riders, and his fanny pack was large enough to conceal a gun.

It took Trapp nearly a whole minute to spot the man's twin, the other half of the pincer—also with a bike, full pads, an ostentatious helmet that would hide his face, and a large fanny pack hanging heavy on his hip.

Searching around more carefully, Trapp spotted a figure in the window of the near-empty coffee shop directly behind Fang and the returning Fabian. He could not be sure with reflections playing on the glass, but the man in the suit sipping his drink looked a lot like Li Chao—if not his face, which was obscured, then in his manner: slow, languid, methodical. A predator lying in wait.

Trapp almost told Fang it was a nice try and considered abandoning his plan entirely and circling round to go after Chao directly. While it would be satisfying, he quickly dismissed the idea. If the Chairman of the HPSCI was compromised by the Chinese, that had to be Trapp's priority. Fabian was the link between the leaks and the summit.

"This is nice," Fabian said.

"It is," Fang agreed, then said nothing more.

It was painful to listen to. Trapp was tempted to cut it short. Fang had set him up, although she probably hadn't had much choice.

Trapp set out at a stroll on the tree-lined sidewalk, emerging a hundred yards farther along, where the scent of sizzling meat and spices filled his nostrils. He listened as Fang made only token gestures to bring Fabian around to business matters, again indicating either a lack of professional experience or an abundance of it. Only one rider remained in view, his back to Trapp, who scanned the area while pretending to look at his phone.

Trapp took out his encrypted device and dialed 911, activating a distortion function for his voice as he muted his channel to Fang.

"911, what's your emergency?"

"There's a bomb at the food fair on Northampton and Rowe," Trapp said. "You need to evacuate the area."

Before the operator could respond, Trapp ended the call and edged back toward the main thoroughfare, where he sought out the police officers. It took a minute before they abruptly huddled together, earpieces feeding the report to them. They replied into radios clipped to their shoulders, their expressions growing more grave by the second.

But they weren't evacuating.

Trapp's hand slipped into his pocket and closed around the items he'd bought as he'd circled around the fair: firecrackers and a lighter. Since police officers were trained to know the difference between the snap-snap-crack of a firecracker and a gunshot, Trapp positioned himself near a cluster of metal trash cans behind a shawarma van. When he was sure no one was watching, he lit the fuse and tossed the firecrackers into the metal can.

Then he crossed the street to an eight-foot billboard, leaning there with a view of his quarry.

The cracks and pops erupted from the trash can, which became an echo chamber and enhanced the racket, launching the two cops into action.

One shouted, "Shots fired," and civilian cries of confusion and fear filled the air. Fairgoers ducked and covered their heads. Confusion and panic spread like fire across a puddle of gasoline.

Trapp felt a twinge of guilt, hoping no one got hurt in the melee, but it wasn't a concert hall full of bottlenecks; there were plenty of places to run without it becoming a stampede.

"Evac! This way!" The second cop was trying to direct folk away from the bangs, gun drawn, dodging bodies to get eyes on whoever was shooting.

The Chinese agents' attention was torn between the chaos and the still-seated Fang. Fabian was on his feet, a human meerkat searching for danger. As several dozen fairgoers funneled around the seating area, zigging and zagging, Trapp seized the opening he needed.

He surged forward alongside a woman and two kids, hoping he looked like a harried dad, closing the distance to Fabian and Fang's table amid the frightened bystanders.

The rider he approached was still trying to keep Fang and Fabian in view and failed to notice Trapp looming behind him. In another second, Trapp had secured him in a chokehold and was squeezing him into unconsciousness as he pulled the man into a doorway.

No one stopped. No one even slowed.

Trapp stepped out in the flow again, branching off into the seating area, and in one swift motion, he grabbed Fabian by the arm and hauled him aside, pressing the muzzle of his gun against the man's spine.

No turning back now.

33

Commander Hwa Yung-Gi stepped out of his car, holding his jacket over his gun. The multi-story parking lot's concrete walls and low ceilings echoed his footsteps back at him as he approached the group of four men and two women scattered around a cluster of parked cars. There were no cameras here, not even license plate checks going in and out—one of the few lots that still had humans patrolling and issuing tickets.

A sober-looking Charlie Hu stood on the edge of the group, his posture tense and eyes sharp as he glanced from Yung-Gi to the people around him. Yung-Gi noted that Charlie's girlfriend Lana was not present. Two of Charlie's gang were white, the rest Korean. They all looked like street-level gang members with their tattoos, piercings, and visible weapons. Yung-Gi doubted that anyone would realize they were unwittingly acting as colleagues of an embedded foreign agent.

All shifted uneasily as Yung-Gi's inspection of them lingered.

"They do not look like professionals," Yung-Gi said to Charlie Hu in Korean.

One of the Korean women answered, "We got the job done. You gonna pay us or what?"

Yung-Gi sighed at the insolence—a woman speaking back at him like that, and a youngster at that. He wasn't sure if she was born in the homeland like Charlie or recruited from the American gutter, so he ignored her and addressed Charlie, reverting to English for the benefit of the Caucasians: "Report."

Charlie said, "We've been taking turns hanging out in Chinatown. Talking to locals, watching that casino where the new guys are staying. We're certain the Triad newcomers brought muscle with them, but they're also working with local assholes. The weird thing is, they've been leaving Chinatown a lot. Usually they stick around."

Yung-Gi nodded. "You said your people were listening for rumors."

One of the white guys with a shaved head and a tattoo on his neck spoke up. "Yeah, Pops. I hear the new guys are here on some kinda revenge kick. Looking for someone who stirred up trouble in Boston. Thing is, we don't have a man inside."

"So details are scarce." Yung-Gi considered the information. If this person they were looking for was this "Hangman," then he had to speak with them personally. Nothing could derail the summit, especially not a rogue spy.

And who knew if the spy was a rogue? The CIA was not beyond disavowing an agent after the dirty work was done.

Charlie nodded, turned to his gang. "We can take out the Triads if necessary."

They exchanged nervous glances, and the Korean woman who'd spoken earlier stepped forward. "That's heavy shit. We're gonna need cash up front."

Yung-Gi faced the young woman, his eyes hard. "Your payment is set. Your duty is not negotiable."

The woman opened her mouth to protest, but Charlie

stepped in front of her and said, "I'll take care of that, don't sweat it."

"You better," the annoying woman replied.

"Do you know where they are now?" Yung-Gi asked. "These newcomers?"

"Roughly, yeah," Charlie said. "Seems like they're gearing up for something."

"Then move in. But wait for my instructions. No cowboy mistakes."

Charlie and the others nodded, expressions swinging from afraid to insulted at this old man ordering them around.

As they dispersed, Yung-Gi turned and marched back to his vehicle.

If the Triads were indeed searching for Hangman and the American authorities knew this, then the situation must be even more complex than he realized.

If he needed to sacrifice these thugs to expose it into the light, then he would.

34

"One word and I'll shoot out three vertebrae before the cops even know you're in trouble."

Trapp met Fang's gaze, firing her a silent warning. Her only reply was an expression of fear and resignation.

Trapp pulled Fabian into the throng, and they moved with the flow. As they broke free of the main thoroughfare to enter a series of side streets and alleys, the shrieks and grumbles of the fair were replaced by the distant wail of sirens. Every time Fabian tried to speak, Trapp shushed him with a hiss and a shove. The buildings around them swiftly grew more dilapidated, a vibrant, prosperous neighborhood giving way to abandoned storefronts and crumbling façades.

Trapp scanned the area, searching for tails or nearby law enforcement, then made a beeline for the location he'd scouted hours ago.

The windows of the dark brown building were boarded up, the exterior paint peeling, its neighbors on either side in a similar state of disrepair and abandonment. The faded sign over the door said *MacMillan Tool & Die*. Trapp hauled Fabian toward the former workshop, booting open the rusted metal door that he'd forced open earlier.

The air inside the defunct metalworks was thick with dust and old oil amid the corpses of decaying machinery. Shafts of sunlight filtered through gaps in the windows' boards, casting an eerie glow and illuminating particles floating in disturbed eddies.

Trapp shoved Fabian into a sturdy metal chair, its legs scraping against concrete. He selected zip ties from the pile he'd prepared and secured Fabian's wrists and ankles while the aide watched, boggle-eyed and whimpering like a dog denied its dinner.

As he stepped back, Trapp allowed himself a small smile. "Okay, that was more difficult than I'd hoped. But now we can have a nice chat. Aren't you glad I made the effort?"

Unwilling to torture an American who was clearly caught up in something he didn't understand, Trapp said nothing for the next ten minutes, instead pacing and laying out an array of rusty, menacing-looking tools, then peeling off the prosthetic beard with its additional contours. They would source a copy of this version of him from the cameras today, so it was dead to him now.

Occasionally Fabian found his voice with questions like "Who are you?" and "What do you want from me?" but Trapp remained silent at the nearby workbench as the pitch of the man's voice grew ever higher. Each piece he moved clanged against the surface, reverberating off the walls and making Fabian flinch.

"Listen, man," Fabian tried again. "I'm no one of importance. I don't have money. My family isn't rich."

Trapp selected a particularly nasty-looking implement, remembering he'd used the same technique with Madame Guanyu, although he'd had decidedly less success in intimidating her than he was having now. The double-pronged fork with long shaft was a device for digging out weeds by their roots, but the metal had lost all its gleam.

Trapp turned to face Fabian, his eyes hard.

"You've been passing intel to the Chinese. *What*, exactly?"

Fabian's face drained of color. "I don't know what you're talking about. I haven't passed anything to anyone."

Trapp leaned in close, aiming his breath against Fabian's face. "Lying to me is pointless. I know about Fang Chen. I know about the congressman." He passed the weed-tool in front of Fabian's eyes, inches from his nose. "You'll tell me eventually, Fabian. And when I prove you're a treasonous snake, you'll never see daylight again."

"Shit." Fabian screwed up his eyes and pulled his face away. "Shit, shit, fucking shit." He was sobbing now. "I'm sorry, I'm sorry, I didn't know." He swallowed hard, his Adam's apple bobbing. "It was nothing. Business stuff."

Trapp folded his arms across his chest. "Go on."

The confession poured out of Fabian like a burst dam: the intel on a Nigerian construction project which he'd passed to Fang, assurances that it was all for the greater good of the country, receiving a thumb drive in return, then passing a redacted file regarding some "washed-up spy that went rogue or something." His next statement made Trapp perk up.

"Fang told me to get some document on the record." Fabian's voice shook. "It wasn't a public section of the hearing, not yet, but it will be eventually. I don't know what that is, I swear."

Trapp's brow furrowed before he quickly masked it. A document the Chinese wanted on the record? Didn't sound good.

"Which document?" Trapp asked.

"Who are you?" Fabian asked again. "Why are you doing this?"

Trapp reached to his T-shirt collar and pulled down to show Fabian the old, jagged scar that encircled his throat, the skin puckered and discolored.

"My father did this when I was a kid," Trapp said, his voice flat, emotionless. "Got me a nickname. One that stuck."

Recognition dawned, Fabian's mouth falling open. "You're... Hangman? The operative from the leaks who—"

Trapp cut him off with a sharp look. "The one who's been screwed over. Just like your boss, Congressman Redman. He's being used, Fabian. But I'm guessing he knows what he's doing, while you're just a weaselly little asshole trying impress a traitor."

Fabian shook his head. "Jake is a *patriot*. He would never betray America."

"Wake up," Trapp snapped. "Redman's a pawn. And the Chinese already own the fucking board."

Trapp could see the conflict playing out in Fabian's eyes.

"What do you want from me?" Fabian asked, his voice barely above a whisper.

"Help me bring Redman in," Trapp said. "If we prove he's been compromised, you get to make a deal, and we use the evidence to ship out the Chinese diplomats running you. It's the only way you don't go to prison."

Fabian hesitated for a long moment. "Okay. I'll do it." His chest jerked, another sob breaking forth. "God help me, I'm so fucking sorry..."

"Good. Now which document did they want on the record?"

Fabian was about to reply when a series of crashes and bangs resonated from the outer wall. The main door to the workshop burst open, and six armed men stormed in—all Asian, wielding a variety of firearms. Bringing up the rear was Dennis Rhee, his waistcoat and trousers making him look like a stockbroker after work. Zhen Guanyu followed close behind, a sadistic grin plastered in place.

The first gunshot was deafening in the confined space, and Fabian's head snapped back, a spray of blood and brain splattering the floor behind.

Somehow, the Triads had found Trapp.

B ullets chewed through wood and ricocheted off metal all around, showering Trapp in splinters and forcing him to dive for cover. They had split into two groups, cutting off his main escape routes. Trapp rolled behind a heavy-duty bench stocked with scrap, then crawled toward the next aisle. He felt a couple of cuts on his torso reopen, ignoring the tearing pain as he angled his body to be harder to hit.

The front exit was no-go, barred with sheet metal. The back passage to the steelworks yard was secure, with three Triads covering. The other three, plus Dennis and Zhen, had dug in between Trapp and the side entrance he'd broken in through, although they had spread out somewhat.

In the echoing, smoke-and-sawdust-filled air, the attackers preserved ammo as boots thudded on the hard floor, surrounding Trapp, ready to move in. All he had was a Glock and a couple of magazines, but having glimpsed their approach, he'd assessed them as gang-types rather than professionally trained.

Dangerous, but he'd survived worse odds. He just needed to test their resolve, probe for the weak spot, and act.

At the closest sound, too close for comfort, Trapp sprang to his feet and leapt out from behind the workbench, gun blazing in the direction of the footfalls. The three gunmen parted, surprised by his sudden attack, but he'd had no time to aim properly, and the shots went wild.

He weaved through the maze of metalworking stations with the kind of speed and agility that comes only with a lifetime of practice. Orders barked in Chinese, then the Triad hit squad spread out farther, widening their perimeter.

Good.

As they fanned out, it became clear they weren't complete amateurs. But neither were they experts. Trapp's gaze flicked up to the metal mezzanine level. No sign of a spotter.

The floor above was Trapp's alternative egress point, giving him access to the neighboring building and the street outside where his bike was parked.

He rounded a slab of a workstation that was topped with a broken lathe and took out the first gunman with a shot to the head. A second followed the sound of Trapp's gunshot and fell to a double-tap to the chest.

Trapp moved immediately, relocating away from anyone with half-decent hearing, and set himself up alongside a bank of lockers with most of the doors missing.

The third Triad caught up and found his dead comrades. He must have seen a shadow shift or heard a sound Trapp didn't realize he'd made. Number Three swung the gun Trapp's way, firing as if he knew his target was there.

Trapp dropped to one knee as slugs tore through the thin metal above him. Then he rolled out and lay flat, squeezing off two shots as he went. Both slammed home into the man's chest, dropping him without ceremony. He fell with

Couldn't assume it was three down, three to go, plus Dennis and Zhen, but that was all he'd seen breaching. Thanks to the ringing in his ears from so much ordnance in a tight space, he couldn't hear if anybody had joined the party late.

There were two ways out, three if he included the door through which the men had entered, and he wasn't about to dash headlong into their backup. Others could be stationed at the mezzanine exit, but wouldn't they have joined from the bird's nest position if they had?

He couldn't assume that his planned escape route would remain clear.

That left the back, which Trapp had reconnoitered and knew passed through a storage yard. All he needed to do was cross twenty feet of open concrete to reach the doors, which he'd seen occupied during the original breach.

Yeah. It's just that easy...

"Jason!" came Zhen's voice. It was muffled, a faint echo; could be the other side of the massive space, or a few yards away. "Jay-son! *Jayyyyy-soooonnnn*." Like a playground taunt. "There's nowhere to run."

A boot crunched on debris nearby, but Trapp couldn't see past the cover keeping him safe. Closer than Zhen's voice, it was either Rhee or another gunman.

Trapp pushed up off the hard, dusty floor and ran, firing blind, three shots in either direction. He was met with wild gunfire in reply, floor and walls pluming dust as chips of concrete peppered his skin.

They'd been waiting, but he'd been fast enough to surprise them.

He burst through the yard door into a passageway. Bullets whizzed past his head, raking the wall as he ducked through, finally beyond their field of fire.

The hallway didn't have direct access to the yard but twisted and turned, the walls closing in on either side as shouting and gunfire followed Trapp. He felt as if he was being herded, pushed toward a bottleneck.

As he rounded the final corner, Trapp slammed out through a still-functioning fire door. No alarm sounded.

The yard was a weed-strangled graveyard of dismantled vehicles, like an illegal chop-shop catering to the farming industry: tractor chassis, doors leaning in domino rows, stacks of wheels, tires, axels.

"Stop!"

Dennis Rhee stepped out from behind a tower of sheet metal, a gun on Trapp. Of all his pursuers, Rhee was the last one Trapp would have picked to face off with.

Trapp obeyed, sucking in deep lungfuls of air to subdue his raging adrenaline. His eyes darted, searching for a gap or a weakness. If he could get close enough to Rhee, he might stand a chance, but the man's unwavering grip and aim confirmed what Trapp had suspected when he first laid eyes on him: professional to the core.

Rhee said, "The gun."

Trapp made his weapon safe and tossed it aside, watching Rhee, who watched him right back—and didn't follow the gun's flight.

Yep, professional.

Trapp awaited the inevitable. A squeeze of the trigger, a deafening bang, then... whatever came next.

No gunshot sounded. No one spoke, either. Rhee was waiting.

Zhen and the remaining men caught up, spilling from the building, weapons rising. Zhen's face, as ever, was twisted in a sneer.

"Look at you. The great Jason Trapp. The CIA's top dog!"

So the kid knew about him. The posturing, the taunting... was that the only reason Rhee hadn't shot him in the head already?

"You killed my mother. Took her from me. From our community."

"Your mother's death was an accident," Trapp said. "One that you caused."

Zhen's face contorted in rage, his finger on the trigger of his oversized six-shooter, a beast of a .44 Magnum, made famous by the Dirty Harry movies decades earlier. He pointed it with real venom. "Liar! You *murdered* her. And you're going to die for it."

"Zhen..." Rhee's tone carried enough of a warning to give Zhen pause. "We wait. You know we wait."

But the kid was hurting, his jaw working, shoulders twitchy, both hands tensing on an off.

"You're just a pussy," Trapp said, aiming to rile him up. "Besides, what are you even going to kill me with?"

"With this, motherfucker!" And Zhen strode forward, the Magnum outstretched for emphasis.

Before Rhee could warn him, Trapp lunged to the side and forward, batting the gun from Zhen's hand and throwing him toward Rhee. Before the two nearest Triads could raise their guns, Trapp barreled into them and sent them sprawling into the third. He drove an elbow into one as he fell, the unexpected pain causing the pistol to slip from the man's hands before Trapp grabbed and lifted him to use as a human shield as he pulled back toward the building. He loosed several shots, killing the tangled pair before Zhen came around, blasting.

The man in Trapp's grip danced and howled as the huge slugs tore into him. Trapp returned fire to pin Zhen back. As his shield became dead weight, he let go. Speed was better, and he was almost back at the building.

Then a voice cut through the tension, calm and measured. "That's enough."

Li Chao himself—the Shark—stepped out of the same door Trapp had come through, his hands clasped behind his back, his expensive suit and tie spotless. He surveyed the scene with a cool gaze.

Trapp whipped the gun around, but Dennis Rhee rushed out too, taking the opportunity to gain an angle on Trapp.

Then Zhen stepped out, his huge gun wavering. "But... he *killed* my mother."

"Your mother's death was regrettable," Chao said, his voice cold and emotionless as he paced, unbothered by Trapp's gun. "But your patience is necessary. Just as it is necessary for our American friend here to drop his weapon before Mr. Rhee executes him."

"I could end you," Trapp said.

"Then you end, too." Chao turned to face Trapp. "Hello, Jason."

"Li Chao. The Shark, huh? Hell of a name. You think it up yourself? Thought you'd be bigger."

Despite the name, Li Chao didn't bite. "And I thought you'd be harder to capture."

Trapp took the barb on the chin and shifted the topic in a more relevant direction. "You did all this to meet me? Shooting up the bar? The Hangman leaks? I'd have responded better to a greeting card."

"It is not all about you."

"For an assassin, you talk a lot."

"If I were ordered to kill you, you'd be dead now. But a bullet to the head feels anti-climactic after all this time. Drop the gun and take a chance. Or shoot me and die for certain."

The two men stared each other down. Trapp had to admit it felt like the final reel of a western, a standoff about to descend into violence.

He tossed the gun. "Fine. Let's get it done."

36

Hwa Yung-Gi stepped out of his car two blocks from the meeting point that Charlie Hu had suggested. He watched for other eyes scanning his way, prepared to open fire if one of the Americans sizing him up came anywhere near him. In his suit, regardless of the cheapness of the fabric, he must have made an inviting target.

Turning onto a deserted street, he passed the abandoned building with the sign *MacMillan Tool & Die*. The standalone construction was hewn from large brown blocks and a sheet of graffiti-smeared metal secured the front door and windows. There was a wide alley down one side, presumably for access to the rear, and a burned-out repair shop connected to the other.

Yung-Gi continued on, barely glancing that way, then took a left along a narrow road to a dusty, makeshift parking lot where Charlie Hu's gang of scumbags waited.

"Well?" Yung-Gi asked as he approached.

"Benny followed a couple of Triad soldiers here," Charlie said. "Figured they were doing a deal. But they started hanging around that old metalworks. We held back as ordered, but then a bunch more showed, and we heard gunshots."

"An execution?"

"Way more. Unless they're executing a football team."

"Police?" Yung-Gi asked.

"Not in this neighborhood. Besides, there's some sorta emergency in the nice district a half-mile that way. Dunno if it's anything to do with this."

Yung-Gi nodded, but he was acutely aware that causing trouble could jeopardize his position here.

"Stay sharp and keep watch," Yung-Gi instructed. "I need to make a call."

He stepped out of earshot and dialed a number. After a moment, the line connected.

"Mike Mitchell."

"Mr. Mitchell, this is Hwa Yung-Gi. I have been made aware of an incident involving gunfire in DC, and my sources tell me Triad activity may be to blame. I require an immediate update."

There was a brief pause before Mike replied, "Once again, I assure you, the situation is being handled. You would have been briefed in due course."

"That seems to be all I hear, but never any details. Is Hangman involved? Are you apprehending these criminals?"

"We have no intelligence relating to Triad activity. The incident you're referring to looks like a hoax, but it *is* being investigated thoroughly. Now *please...*" Mitchell's patience seemed to be wearing thin. "I understand your concerns, but I must ask you to focus on your own responsibilities. Perhaps now is the time for you to head to New York. Your presence there will be crucial."

Yung-Gi closed his eyes, recognizing the polite words as a dismissal. "Very well. Thank you for your candor."

He ended the call and returned to Charlie.

"If the Triads leave, follow them," Yung-Gi said. "If any other players show up, alert me immediately. We may need to escalate matters our own way."

Charlie nodded. "Understood."

As Yung-Gi returned to his car, he told himself that he was prepared to sacrifice his liberty should it be necessary, and he would absolutely sacrifice Charlie and his friends. It was a dangerous line to cross, but if the Americans wouldn't share critical information, he had no choice but to act accordingly.

37

L i Chao unbuttoned one shirt sleeve and began rolling it up into a tight cuff. It struck Trapp as an oddly gentlemanly gesture, like an English duke inviting a rival outside for fisticuffs. But there would be no Queensbury rules involved.

The yard now felt less like a machine graveyard and more like an underground boxing ring from a seedy exploitation movie. If it had been nighttime and raining, the effect would be complete.

"What *is* this?" Trapp asked, watching Chao's methodical tucking of his cuffs into the material. "You release hacked information, employed Triads to kill me. You're compromising members of the US Congress, murdering their aides. This can't be personal. We've never fucking met."

No reply. Trapp pressed on. Not because he thought he could ruffle the guy, but because his tactical position was shit. He needed information, however he could get it. Any edge would do.

"I do not believe that everything was to manipulate me into fighting the great Li Chao hand to hand. There's no way on earth I'd stoop to something like this, no matter how much I hated the target. And someone as professional as *the Shark* wouldn't."

Which was true. The man ultimately responsible for Ryan Price's murder had met a swift, brutal end. No cat-and-mouse games. No toying with his prey. Just justice, of the Old Testament kind, delivered at the first opportunity Trapp had found.

"First of all," Li Chao said, having completed one sleeve perfectly and started on the other, "you have no proof of our involvement. And *you* are not the reason for my being here. You are an indulgence. A hobby authorized by my superiors. Providing that how I choose to dispose of you does not interfere with their orders, I have a certain level of freedom." He finished with his second cuff, tucked neatly above the elbow like the first. "My life has been one of discipline. Duty. Dedication to what is right. This is the first time I have chosen my personal desires over professional instinct. I must admit, I find it... freeing."

"What the hell did I do to you?"

"It is enough for you to know that it will not go unanswered."

"Rwanda?"

Chao's jaw tensed, and he swallowed hard. "How well do you remember the murders you committed there?"

Trapp had no way out, too many guns on him, not enough room to maneuver. "My target was trafficked in children. Child slave labor, including sex slaves. He was bribing officials as a middleman for some Chinese project too. If you got burned on that, lost money, I'm sorry. But the guy was evil, pure and simple. On another day, if it had been Chinese children, you might have been the one pulling the trigger."

Chao paused in his preparation, his body tense, breathing hard and slow. Then he seemed to snap. "You think this is about *money*? My superiors would never have condoned my plans here if it were."

"Who are your superiors?"

Chao regained his composure, removed his tie, rolled it up, and set it aside on the hood of a rusting tractor. "You know I will not tell you that."

Chao paced slowly aside. Trapp pivoted to track him ninety degrees left, six feet away, leaving Zhen and Rhee at Trapp's back. Chao sank into a low stance that reminded Trapp of some martial arts demonstration, most of his weight on his back leg, hands crossed at the wrists, fingers splayed. An elegant pose.

"Are we fighting for a trophy?" Trapp asked, shucking off his jacket and tossing it aside.

His simple white T-shirt had no sleeves to roll up. He settled for pumping his arms, fists clenched, feeding a fraction more blood to the muscles.

"No trophies," Chao said. "Just an ending."

"If I win, these guys will kill me, right?"

"They will not. Dennis, ensure your ward is under control."

Still six feet apart, it felt like a sparring session, unreal, as if an instructor might step in if they got too rough. Rarely did he have time to warm up, to scope out an enemy and prepare for an attack. In truth, it was kind of unsettling.

Chao shuffled forward suddenly, an insect's pounce, stopping after two-foot lengths as Trapp held his ground.

Testing him.

Trapp jigged forward, a straight jab that fell intentionally short.

Chao didn't flinch.

"Okay, that's where we are, then." Trapp had fought counterattackers and bulldozers alike, and both were beatable, as long as he didn't rush in. "An ending."

Trapp feinted with another jab, a reverse from his rear fist that launched with his bodyweight behind it. As he expected,

Chao slipped the punch easily, and Trapp had his knee up to unleash a straight kick. But Chao's foot met his ankle. A flick made Trapp wobble, then the underside of Chao's fist cracked into his cheek.

Trapp dropped back, shocked by the man's speed. They were around the same age, and Trapp was no slouch, fitter than most younger men, stronger, more skilled. Chao was plainly faster, though, and now Trapp needed a second to clear his vision.

"Disappointing," Chao said. "A child would do better."

Trapp extended one hand as a guard, then blinked and set himself. Chao kept smiling, set in that backward-leaning stance.

Trapp had little faith in ceremonial martial arts. There were plenty of techniques in his quiver of hand-to-hand training, from Krav Maga to karate to ju-jitsu, and many moves he'd worked out for himself. But nothing was set. His goal was first to survive, then to subdue the enemy, and kill if needed.

Chao came at him, a shuffle, then a switch of feet, a kick aimed at Trapp's knee, which he stepped over, just as a lancing pain fired through his midriff. Somehow, Chao had dropped lower and thrust a straight hand into the soft spot at the bottom of Trapp's ribcage. His fingers felt like iron rods. As Trapp reeled from that, the kick that had missed swept around again, and Chao's heel crashed into his head.

He stumbled, fell, and rolled. Dirt clouded around him. He rolled again for distance, brought his legs across in an arc, and used the momentum to regain his feet. Although he didn't know which way was up, he struck out forward and connected with Chao's incoming body. Not quite luck, just a calculation of where he found himself most vulnerable.

By the time Trapp managed to orient himself, Chao had taken a cautionary step back, and although his nose was bleed-

ing, Trapp didn't think it was broken. A quick nod of appreciation from the MSS agent, then they were into it again.

Chao opened with a kick, easily blocked, but it was only a
ruse to get inside Trapp's reach. The fists were a blur, "rail-
punching" as Trapp had heard it called. Chao connected with
nearly every blow, none of them knockouts, but Trapp felt more
wounds on his chest reopen; his head rocked back as pain
speared his kidney, doubling him over. It was all happening at
once, to fast to react to, let alone counter. He blocked the knee
that rose at his chin, covered his head with both forearms, and
as soon as the punches rained in again, he unleashed a fierce
upper cut.

Trapp's knuckles glanced off Chao's forehead, then the
Chinese agent twisted and threw a side-kick into his knee. If
Trapp hadn't pivoted at the last second, the joint would have
shattered, leaving his lower leg hanging on by the tendons. It
still hurt like hell and collapsed under his weight, but he was
mostly intact.

Landing hard, he rolled again, expecting to leap up, but
Chao was upon him, a kick in his back, knuckles in the head, a
knee pinning him as a succession of punches rained down.

Trapp rarely lost a fight. He could count his defeats on the
left hand he held out to try to push Chao off him. Chao trapped
his hand in a locked grip and twisted; a wet snap and burst of
pain heralded two broken fingers. Trapp cried out, and a fist
landed in his mouth, silencing him. Then a larger, harder limb
—an elbow or knee—slammed into the back of his head,
rattling his teeth and his brain.

Then the assault ended. Or paused.

Trapp was dizzy, nauseous, possibly even concussed. He lay
there on his back, gathering his breath. He'd been tired and
injured, unduly focused on Fabian, on Fang. He was unprepared for Li Chao.

The assassin held out a hand toward Zhen and nodded

toward the Magnum. Zhen reluctantly handed it over, and Chao turned to face Trapp.

"I had a container prepared," Chao said. "I thought about beating you slowly to death over many days."

Trapp lay there, trying to figure out how to push himself upright.

"I *want* to make this last," Chao went on, now circling around toward Trapp's feet. "But the longer I wait, the more nervous our people get."

Sirens wailed in the distance, coming closer.

"Cops," Zhen said.

"They are not here for us," Chao replied.

Backup for the food fair incident. Trapp doubted anyone had heard the gunshots from the metalworks. If they had, it was unlikely they would report them.

Trapp rolled onto his side, groaning with the wave of nausea that swam up his gullet. He lay still, one arm under his body.

"The gut is a painful place to get shot," Chao said. "No vital organs. You bleed out so very slowly, so very painfully."

Trapp could see properly again, although the scene swam with worms of light, and Chao stood at an angle that didn't seem possible. He slipped the fingers of his floor-side arm into one of his pockets.

"Turn him over," Chao said. "Hold him still."

The sirens were closer now, almost upon them when they abruptly shut off. Must have been trying to get through a snarl-up of traffic a block over.

Someone grabbed Trapp's shoulder to pull him onto his back, but he resisted, positioning his leg to stop from rolling. A fist in his spine made him arch painfully, leaving him staring up at the sky again. One hand in his pocket.

"Stop playing," Chao said, hefting the .44 caliber weapon. "You cannot win."

"I don't have to win," Trapp said. "I just have to survive."

He had found the lighter and the remaining bunch of fire-crackers. He'd thumbed the flint just as Rhee had tried to roll him, and by the time he'd been punched and landed on his back, the fuse was lit in his pocket.

With the sparks burning his skin, Trapp whipped the stack of linked firecrackers out, making all step back. He propped himself on one elbow and hurled the explosives into the air, angling on Chao. They went off, cracking and popping, airborne under their own force. Chao flinched and backed off —the bright flashes would have part-blinded him, while the noise was disorienting. Not quite a flashbang, but a diversion nonetheless, allowing him to kick the gun from Chao's grasp.

With an almighty effort, teeth gritted against multiple pain points, Trapp scrambled to his feet and launched away from Chao, barging into an equally-surprised Dennis Rhee, who pitched to the side. Trapp then sucker-punched Zhen in the stomach, doubling him over.

He'd be a great human shield but an even better battering ram.

Trapp dragged him to one side, kicked his ankle to lift him off the ground, and threw him into the pair of Triads trying to bring their guns around. All three went over, and Trapp sprinted back into the building.

Inside, he noted a blue flashing light through one of the gaps in the boards on the front of the building. The cops were here.

No running back. No going forward. He could only head upward.

38

Trapp's body screamed in pain as he raced down the way he'd come moments ago. He rounded the corner just as a placing of three rounds burrowed into the wall where he'd veered past. His knee and broken fingers throbbed, and his head pounded from the blow. Blood seeped from his reopened wounds, sticking his shirt to his skin, but he pushed through, focused on nothing more than escape.

Plenty of time to feel dumb about his mistakes later.

In the cavernous workshop, he couldn't see if the blue flashes had been stationary or moving, but they were gone now. He snatched up a rusted metal pipe, testing its weight in his uninjured hand without stopping.

Not a gun, but it'd have to do.

Fleeing the racket of three armed men crashing out behind him, Trapp burst up the metal stairs onto the mezzanine level, the clanging of his footsteps giving him no stealth at all. Since he could hear the Triads closing in, he figured it'd be useless anyway.

He raced along the narrow walkway, searching the way out

he was sure lay in this direction. At the end, he spotted a ladder leading to a hatch in the roof.

A gamble, but his only chance.

He scaled the ladder, his shattered hand flaring pain with every half-grip. As the three thugs taking point in the pursuit reached the walkway, he threw open the hatch and clambered onto the roof, a volley of incoming slugs battering the ladder and tiles.

The rooftop was a maze of vents and air conditioning units, allowing him a quick, lurching sprint to the adjoining building with—thank God—a degree of cover. He was slowing, energy sapped.

Running out of time, Jason...

Gunshots rang out behind, tearing up the aluminum units as he ducked behind a large inspection hut for a freight elevator.

He peered around the edge and spotted one gunman—open shirt, long hair, tattoos exposed—emerging from the hatch, the stock of an MP5 to his shoulder. Trapp ducked back, shifted around the far side slowly so his boots didn't crunch on the gravely surface.

The man stalked along, his footfalls quiet but not silent. Trapp waited.

Waited.

The guy was fully exposed, inexperienced in clearing his blind spots despite his proficiency in holding the firearm, allowing Trapp to charge out, his knee giving him a faint limp as he swung the metal pipe. It connected with the Triad's skull with a crunch, and Trapp grabbed the gun, liberating it as the man crumpled to the ground.

He jogged to the edge of the roof, where he found the adjoining building—a burned-out repair shop that hadn't offered as much convenience for interrogating Fabian. Its roof was nearly eight feet below. There was a ladder twenty yards to his left, but he could already hear the remaining pair closing in. And he had no idea about the trio from the main yard.

Probably spooked by the cops stopping by.

He could only hope they'd rabbited.

Trapp strapped the MP5 to his back and lowered himself over the wall so he dangled there like a puppet, his broken fingers screaming with pain. With only a couple of feet to drop, he let go and landed in a practiced but messy roll, jarring his knee once again.

With a more pronounced limp, Trapp set off to the left, keeping close to the wall, aiming for the roof access door of the repair shop.

The remaining Triads on the metalworks roof called to each other as they searched—amateurs revealing their position. If Trapp wasn't running on fumes, he'd have taken them out with relative ease. But since he didn't know the location of Li Chao or Dennis Rhee, fleeing was his best option.

The door was locked, but Trapp used the butt of the MP5 to smash the handle, breaking it open.

Too loud. They'd be on him any moment.

He slipped inside a dark, debris-filled stairwell. The air was stale and thick with the scent of damp, burnt wood. Trapp descended cautiously, alert for any sound of pursuit.

The repair shop was a maze of charred walls and collapsed beams, the smell of burnt rubber and oil now overpowering the charcoal odor. He picked his way through the rubble, his feet crunching on broken glass and fast-food containers left behind by homeless people or partying kids.

A floorboard creaked behind him.

Trapp whirled around, bringing up the submachine-gun just as one of the Triads braced to shoot. Trapp squeezed the trigger first, blowing three clustered rounds through the thug's center mass.

But the man Trapp shot had been a distraction so the other

could get close. This guy, a muscular bald man with tats climbing the sides of his head, swung a knife—either he was out of bullets or he figured he had an advantage using a blade this close.

Trapp sidestepped, the blade slicing inches from his face. He brought the MP5's stock down hard on the Triad's wrist, sending the knife clattering to the floor, then pulled the gun around, but the gangster was too close. The two men grappled, trading short, sharp blows and crashing into the walls as Trapp fought for the strength to pry himself loose.

Squirming his good hand free, Trapp reached around and manipulated the man's arm the wrong way to tear his rotator cuff, then slammed his head into a metal beam. The man went limp, and Trapp let go, dropping him to the floor.

Breathing hard, limping and cradling his fingers, Trapp first spat blood, then scanned the room for any sign of backup. He spotted a doorway leading to the outside and staggered down the final stairs toward it, his knee forcing him to go one step at a time. The door was half off its hinges, so all he needed to do was shove it open with his shoulder. The rusted hinges made a grinding sound rather than squealing.

Trapp emerged into a narrow side street and assessed his surroundings.

He could hear sirens approaching, growing louder.

His clothes clung to him, soaked with sweat and blood. His muscles ached with every movement.

He limped to the secluded spot where his motorcycle waited with new plates, hidden under a tarp behind a dumpster.

Checking the street, he saw nothing but a beat-up dark green Mustang idling, a car he'd seen earlier when he entered the metalworks with Fabian. It had been empty then, and Trapp had registered nothing out of the ordinary about it.

Trapp whipped off the tarp and swung his leg over the seat with a grunt, his knee again reminding him of the injury.

He took up the helmet and pulled it on, wincing at the contusion on the back of his head. Then he turned the ignition over, and the machine purred to life. He set his fingers in the least painful position he could, kicked the bike's shifter into gear, and twisted back on the throttle.

The engine vibrated through his bruised body as he sped away. His broken fingers ached with every twist of the throttle, but he had no choice. If he was lucky, he might have time to clear out his hotel room, then secure a new bolthole before Li Chao or the guys on his own side found him.

Regroup. Then go on the offensive.

That was the plan.

Vague, but it was all he had.

He glanced in the side mirror and cursed under his breath.

The old Mustang he'd seen on the street earlier was behind him. First empty, then idling, now tailing. Not a subtle vehicle for a stakeout or rolling surveillance.

Not law enforcement.

He took an easy right, keeping to the speed limit, and sure enough, the car followed.

What *now*?

Around the bend, he slowed suddenly—not stopping, but it was enough for the Mustang to catch up and for the faces inside to register shock at Trapp's proximity.

One Asian and one white dude in the front, an indistinguishable person in the rear.

As Trapp sped up again, going a couple of miles an hour over the speed limit, two motorcycles joined behind the car from a street Trapp hadn't seen, a pair of dirt bikes ridden by an Asian guy and a Black guy, both forgoing helmets in favor of scarves pulled up over their mouths and noses. Trapp couldn't see tattoos, but they didn't feel like the Triads. There was something raw about them, something menacing.

Hired muscle?

As the bikes pulled level with the Mustang, Trapp slowed again and caught snatches of Korean being shouted by one of the bikers—a language he recognized but didn't speak. Discussion over, the bikes fanned out, drawing a huge honk from an oncoming Mazda. The two riders reached down and drew handguns, then accelerated toward Trapp.

Why the hell did they have to make everything so damn hard?

39

G unshots cracked through the air, one bullet shattering a car window as Trapp roared by. He ducked instinctively and swerved around a delivery truck, narrowly avoiding a shopping cart full of empty cans as he sped into a loading bay, then back out.

His bike could outmuscle the dirt bikes in sheer power, but now traffic was picking up, and the car mounted the sidewalk to gain on him. The few pedestrians leapt out of the way, but Trapp realized he had to draw his pursuers away from populated areas.

There was a freeway sign up ahead, combined with a *Road Closed* warning. Perfect. He'd jam the car up on the on-ramp, then lose the others through speed alone as they wound through the construction equipment.

Trapp leaned into the sharp turn, his knee flaring with pain once again as unfamiliar city streets blurred around him. He was nowhere near the areas he'd reviewed this morning, but he just needed to hold them off a little longer.

Trapp blew through a red light, threading between cars that screeched to a halt and swerved, swearing at him via blaring horns in his wake. He accelerated, gunning the bike toward the overpass looming ahead, preparing to maneuver around machinery, over uneven concrete and asphalt.

As he neared, Trapp's stomach sank.

The overpass itself was under construction, sawhorse barriers and lights and equipment blocking the way—a gaping segment was yet to be positioned, leaving nothing but a fifty-foot drop. Construction workers dropped their tools and scattered for cover as the chasing vehicles gained on Trapp. Trapp skidded to a halt, fishtailing on the loose surface to turn around and barrel back toward the men chasing him.

His pursuers, who Trapp was convinced were street-level gangbangers, came at him head-on, the car in the middle, the bikes either side. Weapons drawn.

Not a game of chicken I can win.

Trapp again pumped the brakes, dipped the handlebars, and this time he spun the wheels so hard that smoke billowed before he took off to the right at a 45-degree angle, front wheel rising up, then thumping back down to grab the pavement. The bike to his right veered to avoid being rammed like Trapp had expected, and as he reached the next sawhorse, Trapp screeched to a halt, dived off the bike, and rolled forward, snatching a screwdriver from a scattering of assorted tools.

The rider had no time to aim as Trapp ducked aside and thrust the screwdriver into the speeding bike's front spokes, jerking his hand away to avoid losing it. The sturdy tool held as it whipped into the forks, slamming the vehicle to a stop and catapulting the rider twenty feet, over the edge of the unfinished road and down to his death.

Trapp picked up a hammer and closed the gap on the car, which had now halted. The white guy got out, a handgun held high. Trapp swung the hammer at his head, connecting with a crack as loud as a gunshot. The man crumpled, but the rider from the second bike took his place, a knife in his hand.

Trapp hopped aside and parried the knife, but there wasn't room for a full swing of the hammer as the biker closed in to punch him in the gut. Still wearing the crash helmet, he head-butted the attacker's face, demolishing his nose, then followed up with a thunderous elbow to the jaw, dropping the guy.

Another thug emerged from the car's rear, trying to blind-side him, but even with his injuries, Trapp moved with lethal efficiency, fending him off with an open hand to the jaw, then raising the hammer to finish him. Where the hell this fresh wave of energy was coming from, he had no idea.

He'd pay for it later.

The ominous rev of a sleek engine gave him pause—the new arrival was a black car with tinted windows. Trapp wasn't afraid of more attackers; he was so hopped up on anger and blind rage by now that he'd have taken on an army. But the gangbangers stopped fighting, the one that was still conscious crawling away from him.

Trapp grabbed the thug by the back of his jacket and raised him up, holding him between himself and the newcomer.

The car door opened, and a man of around sixty or seventy stepped out, a gun by his side. Asian, but not anyone Trapp had seen before. No one he'd photographed at the embassy, and he didn't strike Trapp as Triad stock. His presence commanded immediate attention from those he was fighting. Given that they'd been shouting in Korean earlier, he made a calculated guess.

"Why are the Koreans stepping in here?" Trapp asked. "What is going on?"

The man's eyes locked on to Trapp as he raised his gun, pointing it unerringly at the human shield's chest and there-fore, at this range, Trapp's chest, too. "Who are you?"

Trapp wiped sweat from his brow. "You should know. Your boys here are trying to kill me."

"Not my orders."

Through the open window, the driver said, "Hey, it wasn't my fault. He attacked us. We had to improvise."

The older man held the gun held with a precision and familiarity that the street thugs lacked and kept his tone almost conversational. "Why are you at war with the Triads? On the eve of our summit?"

"You're North Korean," Trapp stated as the gears clicked into place. "Facing some dissent around the visit? I'm guessing that's why the Shark is active."

The man's eyes narrowed, his gun as firm as ever. "The what is active?"

"Li Chao," Trapp said. "The Shark."

For a moment, the Korean agent's composure faltered. The name Li Chao clearly meant something to him.

"He's the one using the Triads. But that seems to be news to you."

The man's eyes flickered with uncertainty.

"I'm still playing catch-up," Trapp admitted. "But if you're worried about Li Chao, then you don't need to worry about me. We might even be on the same side."

The man's grip tightened as he neared, but his eyes gave nothing away. He might leave things as they were and go about his day. Or he might shoot Trapp dead and go after Chao himself. Or shoot Trapp dead and go join Chao.

Too many variables.

Trapp still had the gangbanger he'd headbutted in his grasp, so he dropped his bodyweight and swung the guy at the same time, causing the older man to stumble. Trapp gained ground, gripping the man's wrist and turning the gun around to force it free of his fingers.

Now Trapp pointed the weapon at the man in charge. Yet another thug, the Asian kid who'd been driving the Mustang, now emerged with a gun in his hand.

Trapp put the old man between himself and the latest gang-banger. "Drop it, or he dies."

At a nod from the old man, the gangbanger followed instructions, setting his gun on the ground and stepping away from it.

The old man sighed and looked ashamed. "You are the Hangman, yes?"

Trapp allowed the jab to wash through him. Very little of his face was visible, and his scar was completely covered. If the North Koreans had concluded that he was trying to interfere with their summit...

Police sirens were closing in once again.

Keeping his gun trained on the old man, Trapp edged toward his motorcycle. His body ached and throbbed in protest, and he could feel the ooze of blood congealing under his clothes.

The old man watched, seemingly unafraid, as Trapp mounted his bike.

"What's your name?" Trapp asked.

"Hwa Yung-Gi, of the Supreme Guard Command. Yours?"

Trapp flipped the visor of his helmet down and stuffed the safetied gun in the front of his pants. "Don't follow me. I'll take care of the Shark. You deal with... whatever you're here to deal with. I promise you, it isn't me."

40

"I reiterate, Mr. President, it is completely unacceptable." It was not the first time Ambassador Wen had stated this almost verbatim as he tried to force Nash to admit responsibility for, or knowledge of, the incursion at the Chinese diplomatic residence. "I still have not heard a satisfactory explanation, nor have you described any actions taken to address this violation of the CIA's protocols *and* US federal law, not to mention Article 30 of the 1961 Vienna Convention on Diplomatic Relations."

Nash had chosen a private office for the meeting, situated close to the security desk through which his visitors would have to pass. He'd asked Mitchell to accompany him but to remain silent unless called upon. He had never met the young woman who accompanied the ambassador, although she'd cleared their security checks as Fang Chen. Apparently, her instructions were also to remain silent.

Nash had only met the ambassador in person a couple of times, both occasions where it had been Nash's job to complain about the actions of the Chinese government. Unfortunately, he was on the receiving end of the tongue-lashing today. Nash was never going to accept responsibility for a possible rogue agent, but he had to cover his backside should any new information become public. He was uncomfortably entangled with Jason Trapp. The man had saved his president's life almost as many times as he'd risked his own to protect his country.

At least, it feels that way.

Nash pushed the emotion aside. "Ambassador, we take this accusation very seriously, but so far you have offered no evidence that the intruder was a US government agent. In fact, you have no clear footage of this person, and you have no proof of his nationality. I can assure you that a full investigation will take place, and if there is even a hint that this is some rogue agent operating with or without the knowledge of any federal agency, severe repercussions will be forthcoming. But if I may be honest with you, I doubt it."

"Your agent did not just break in on a whim. He made inappropriate suggestions to this young lady."

Wen gestured toward the woman who, in Nash's mind, appeared far too young to be an attaché. Those plum positions were normally achieved through years of experience and loyalty or were inherited from a family member high up in the Communist Party. Ms. Chen had kept her eyes firmly on the carpet beside Nash's feet so far. Now her eyes flickered up to meet Nash's briefly before returning to the carpet again.

Ambassador Wen said, "And can we expect an apology today for the victim who was violated by your agent?"

"As we have established," Nash replied kindly, "we do not know for certain who made the approach. It might be helpful if you elaborated on what these 'inappropriate suggestions' involved."

It was clear Ambassador Wen was steering clear of anything involving espionage, for that might attract questions about what Miss Chen might have to offer. The innuendo of *inappropriate suggestions* gave a flavor of sexual advances. Jason

Trapp was many things—impulsive, insubordinate even—but he was not a traitor, nor was he a predator out for his own gratification.

Wen scowled. "You must direct your FBI and your police to find the culprit responsible quickly. If you do not, then what use are you as president?"

"If, as the president, I could direct investigations wherever I wish, then there would be no point in democracy."

Wen cupped one hand over the other and let it rest on his trim stomach, puckered his lips momentarily, and narrowed his eyes, which added up to an incredibly satisfied, almost smug air. As if to say, "*That* is why we discarded democracy."

"Thank you for your understanding," Nash said, gesturing to the door. "We will be in touch as soon as we hear anything of note."

"And the coming summit?" Wen made no attempt to move. "Our people are understandably disappointed to be shut out of negotiations."

"The final negotiations are between Presidents Son and Kuk, while I am merely mediating. Nothing more."

Wen's smile was patently false. "We will not accept anything that intrudes on either our sovereignty or our security. I hope you understand that."

Again, Nash forced himself to remember he was judged by a higher standard than most humans. "Thank you for reminding me. I hope you will understand that I have another appointment, for which I am running late."

Ambassador Wen bristled but turned his back and headed for the door.

Nash was not going to say anything else, but Mitchell stepped forward. He had been asked only to observe and offer an opinion once the meeting was over, but he apparently could not remain silent.

"Ambassador, please wait."

Wen paused, turning his head. His attaché mirrored the action.

"This is the *president of the United States*," Mitchell said. "You do not simply turn your back and leave the room."

Wen turned fully to the two men, his hands returning to their cupped position before him. He sucked in a breath, and Nash got the impression the ambassador was considering harsh words.

"Mr. President, I apologize for my bad manners. It has been a trying night and morning, and perhaps my emotions got the better of me. Please accept my sincere apologies, it won't happen again."

Nash extended a hand, and Wen shook it firmly. Nash gave a nod of appreciation, then Wen left the room with his assistant.

"I'm sorry, Mr. President," Mitchell said. "I hope I didn't overstep."

"No, Mike, it's fine. Are we sure that it was Jason?"

"Not yet. But Nick Pope has an update, along with Agent Drebin."

THEY GAVE Ambassador Wen a few minutes to vacate the corridor outside before exiting the room and walking toward the West Wing, past on-duty Marines and other staffers who politely acknowledged Nash in various ways, then into the Oval Office, where Nick Pope and Agent Drebin were waiting. Nash made his apologies for keeping them and got straight down to business, asking for updates relating to Jason Trapp and how the Hangman leaks were impacting the investigation.

"We issued a warrant along with his photograph," Drebin said. "DC Metro, federal agencies, all government buildings' security, and State Patrol. As requested, we issued several additional warrants and updated BOLOs too, mostly AWOL soldiers and a couple from the back end of the FBI's most-wanted list."

"The press shouldn't pick up on Trapp specifically," Nick Pope added, "but it gives us the legal framework to bring him in and, if necessary, treat him as hostile to national security."

Pope and Jason were friends, and Nash picked up on the awkwardness in the counterterrorism agent's demeanor.

Drebin clasped his hands behind his back, his chin up, like a soldier standing easy. "It will be less efficient this way, sir, I hope you understand this."

"I do," Nash said. "And I can't order you to keep an identity secret when the person might be guilty of federal crimes."

"But Agent Pope can. And has. And my SAC agreed. So that's the route we're taking. Sir."

"Very well." Nash faced Mitchell. "You know him better than anyone. If it *was* him, what is he up to?"

Mitchell assessed Drebin and Pope before answering. "It's hard to say. From a top-level perspective, he identified a threat either to himself or the United States and has decided that whatever actions he's taking are worth the risk to his own liberty. He'd know the risk."

"*If* it was him," Pope added, the *if* in case of a future review.

"If," Drebin said. "We know he killed a bunch of suspected gang members in Boston before coming to DC. We know he believes he has circumstantial evidence of the presence of a Chinese assassin and sometimes spy on US soil. And moments before this meeting, I received a report of more Triad killings."

"In Boston?" Mike said.

Drebin pointed at the floor. "Right here in DC."

"You're sure they were Triads?" Nash asked.

"As sure as we can be," Pope replied. "The tattoos, ethnicity, weapons. One unidentified civilian executed, six dead Triads, all in a derelict block. No incidental wounds on those who were shot."

"Incidental wounds?"

"Meaning," Drebin said, "that it didn't take a lot of bullets to kill them. Center mass or headshots."

"A professional," Pope clarified.

"And a further incident a couple of miles away, but they don't look like Triads. Gang bangers, we think, but reports are a single individual took them out then fled on a motorcycle."

"ID?" Pope asked, somewhat surprised at the news.

"He wore a helmet. We have people working on dash cam and street footage to work something definite. One oddity, though."

"Only one?" Nash couldn't resist a touch of sarcasm.

"I got the report just before we came in here, sir." Drebin barely altered his tone, keeping it low and factual with no apologies or hesitation.

"Fine," Nick said. "The oddity?"

"A witness. His name sounded familiar, so I checked. Hwa Yung-Gi, the DPRK security liaison. He was present for the violence. Made a report to Metro PD."

All were silent for a beat.

Then Mitchell said, "He's been tapping me up for more intel than he needs. Trying to, anyway. Looks like he's doing more than advance supervision of our security protocols. He's cleaning *our* house before *his* guests arrive."

Nash held fast. Didn't want to push anything. They were here to advise him; he'd decide based on what they could offer.

"So facts..." Pope listed them off. "A dead civilian, who we can be reasonably sure was the one abducted from the fair with the active shooter scare; six Triads killed professionally; a Chinese spy—"

"Potentially," Drebin corrected.

Pope bristled and continued. "*Potentially*, a renowned Chinese spy running around; a second gang, possibly connected, and a DPRK agent taking on his own projects. And that's before we get to the leaked Hangman business." Pope shook his head. "It's a mess. We need to be the ones who catch Trapp, and we need him soon."

"So can we confirm that he's no threat to security?" Nash asked. "Or is he prying something loose that we can use?"

"We'll find out, sir." Pope received a text message but didn't take out his phone.

"You can get that, Nick." Nash headed for his desk. "The Chinese want Trapp's head on a stick, and they would love to embarrass us while the eyes of the world are pointed this way. Speaking of which, let's urge Mr. Yung-Gi to get himself to New York and out of our hair. Sort it out, gents. Quickly."

"Yes, Mr. President," Drebin said.

Nash dismissed them, leaving him alone with Mitchell, who said nothing, waiting for the president's orders.

"Should we tell them about TIPTOE?" Nash asked.

"Not yet," Mike said. "I just hope Trapp knows to keep quiet about it.

41

The street was eerily quiet.

Instead of turning in, Trapp chose to play it safe and continued past the junction, abandoning his hotel room. There would be a plethora of evidence left behind but no data; he had been careful to only use the burner laptop for mundane searches. The device he had used for facial recognition and other more compromising research was still with him in the backpack that he'd kept in the compartment under the bike's seat.

As he rode away at a steady one mile per hour under the speed limit, he inventoried everything else he carried with him: a few hundred bucks in a clip, one untraceable satellite phone, two fresh burners acquired that morning, and the Smith & Wesson that he'd liberated from Hwa Yung-Gi. Plus, one motorcycle, a helmet, and a first aid kit. Which he definitely needed to use soon.

Roadblocks were springing up, but they hadn't caught up to him yet, and by the middle of the afternoon, Trapp had left the city. He found a picnic area off the highway where he used a public restroom to clean the blood from his face. He didn't dare unzip the jacket. All he could do with his fingers was bind them and let his body stitch itself back together.

Other than his fingers, he decided nothing was broken, although the knee could do with about a week of rest and a bucket of Advil. His ribs would heal, but for now, he'd have to do his best to ignore the bruises and swelling. Thankfully, the blow to his head had not ended in a concussion.

Using one of the burner phones, he logged on to a news site and read the headlines, shocked to find that his face was one of half a dozen put out by the federal government as a "person of interest."

They had to, he supposed. If he had been linked to any of the incidents, be it the Triads in Boston, the food fair bomb threat, or the new pile of bodies he'd left behind along with, more pertinently, the corpse of a congressional aide, they would have to speak with him. And since his role in national security was so heavily classified, the brass would need deniability.

Other news outlets featured debates raging about Hangman, supporters and detractors arguing their cases. A modern virus of black-and-white views battled it out in a chaos of futility. Some commenters were grateful to have someone like him out there protecting the country, others insisting that murderers like Hangman made the US and the world *less* safe. Hell, maybe the latter group was right. Maybe it really would be better if everybody laid down their arms, linked arms and sang kumbaya.

There's only one problem: who jumps first?

Trapp snorted. He browsed social media using keywords that often sprang up during these times, finding more attitudes that made him feel like a man out of time.

Were assassinations like this truly necessary in the modern world? Was *Trapp* necessary in the modern world?

Whatever the answer, he was relevant right now, so he set back out toward his destination.

The motorcycle ran out of gas ten miles from where he intended to stop, but he hadn't risked filling up due to camera coverage in gas stations, one of the first resources tapped when the FBI went searching for a wanted man.

Unwilling to risk hitchhiking or stealing another vehicle, Trapp trekked off-road. By now, the city was far behind, and while this might not have been a rainforest or jungle, the rural terrain was still rough going—his knee and his ribs hurt with every step, slowing him down. He crossed the boundaries of farmers' fields and pressed onward into the forest in the northern part of the state. People who lived in Washington, DC often forgot that so much nature awaited them less than two hours from their brownstones and the majesty of the capital.

Several times, as the pain of his injuries flared into agony, he considered giving up and throwing himself on the mercy of the law. But the legal process often depended on public perception rather than facts or ethics, and given the shitstorm raging across both the news and social media, Mitchell and the others above him might have no choice but to sacrifice him.

Besides, he'd never given up before. He didn't plan on breaking that streak today.

Sweat drenched his face and dribbled down his back to mingle with dirt and blood, stinging the cuts that littered his body. His fingers ached with a deep and pulsating pain, and he winced every time he steadied himself against a tree or pushed underbrush aside. It required every ounce of strength to plant one foot in front of the other.

But the air tasted of earth and leaves, the scent of pine needles reminding him of long-forgotten camping trips, drawing a smile even as his vision swam. Every time his steps slowed, he pressed on harder, recalling how he'd been dismantled as a much younger man, pushed to the brink alongside

Ryan Price, then reassembled into a machine that served his country without once complaining.

And he would not complain now.

Once he found the trail, he knew he would make it. Knew he would rest soon. He lumbered like a wounded bear, pushing aside tree branches, his feet sore but firm on the soft forest floor.

Always pushing on.

The prepper hut that he'd bought for cash some years earlier from the daughter of a paranoid old man was not in the best of shape, but it was watertight, tapped into a well with a manual pump, and there were enough canned goods and military-style MREs to sustain him for years. He had hoped he'd never use this place, expected he'd only occupy if the shit ever really did hit the fan. But for now, it was a suitable fallback, the existence of which he'd shared only with Ryan Price and one other person.

As he approached the stoop, overgrown and draped in the encroaching forest, the hammer of a gun cocking made him freeze.

Trapp raised his hands, his head low. Just as Yung-Gi had appeared more embarrassed than concerned to lose the upper hand to Trapp, now Trapp was just annoyed that someone had gotten the drop on him.

"You took your time," Lamar Gilbaut said, stepping out from the trees and lowering his gun.

Lamar favored his left side, moving gingerly but unaided. The bullet wounds from several nights ago must be taking their toll, but he was mobile. He'd signed himself out of the hospital and somehow made it all the way out here.

He hadn't been sure that Lamar would come but had suspected he would once he saw the news and made the connection that Trapp had gone dark on his own mission.

He was glad to have a friendly face nearby at last.

"I've been busy," Trapp said.

"Yeah? Well, you look great."

"I *feel* great." Trapp coughed, constricting too many muscles and flaring pain once again.

"Let's get inside. I've been investigatin' this shit. We got work to do."

TRAPP FOUND it easier to cut his T-shirt off his body than to peel it off over his head. Most of the blood had come from the razor wire cuts, which had reopened then begun to scab over again; removing the shirt felt like ripping off a body-sized Band Aid. He showered under the manual-pumped cold waterspout while standing in a tub to catch the dirty water, assessing all his damage as non-permanent and redressing the cuts after he'd dabbed himself dry. He stepped out of the bathroom strapped up, stiff, and in need of a vacation. Preferably six weeks in Tahiti.

But all he had was this fine country retreat.

The inside of the prepper hut was every bit as decrepit as Trapp remembered. He had never maintained it to the degree that he'd maintained his safehouses in the built-up areas, and the reason was twofold: It was a long way from a Costco or Walmart, and he didn't need to. All he required from it was to provide the three basics of human survival: shelter, water, and food.

Lamar had clearly been here for a day at least, and he had come as well-equipped as anyone would who had just discharged themselves from a hospital and relocated to the Maryland wilderness. Trapp had half-expected a board set up like on a detective show, with red string connecting different photos and maps. Instead, Lamar had spread out several prints on the floor beside sheafs of paper discarded in a pile—since there was no trash can—and placed one thin stack on the rickety table.

"These are all offline musings," Lamar said in his New Orleans drawl. "Everything I could either pull from my personal files or remember that might have involved the Chinese or someone with serious Chinese investments."

"I don't think this is about money," Trapp said, lowering himself into a chair where he could view the final stack.

"Agreed. What does that leave?"

The final paper on the floor had one word written on the front in thick black marker. *RWANDA.*

"It was definitely Rwanda. Li Chao reacted to it." Trapp had spoken of this to Mike: the footage released to the world, and subsequently pored over by multiple talking heads and commentators ever since. "I guess some Chinese businessmen were involved."

"I remember," Lamar said. "It was one of those shit-shows that turned out okay. Not as intended, but okay."

"Are we assuming Li Chao is upset at us for offing someone of importance?"

"That was my thought at first." Lamar shifted the stack marked *RWANDA* with his foot. "I think it has to do with this man, Jia Ru."

The first sheet of paper featured a man in his late fifties or early sixties—difficult to tell given the poor-quality black-and-white photocopy—but Trapp recognized the receding hair and well-worn face.

"Head of security," Trapp said. "He tried to surrender."

"Like your child smuggler."

"Right, but what's his connection to Li Chao?"

"This." Lamar sifted through the papers and produced what appeared to be a heavily redacted military record from the

People's Republic. It featured a nineteen-year-old recruit, and according to the note with Lamar's jottings, this was someone touted with great potential and some of the highest scores possible. Even that young, the Shark's blank eyes stared Trapp down.

Lamar said, "Jia Ru was Li Chao's mentor."

42

Li Chao was not a man accustomed to begging, nor could he recall apologizing to anyone since his very earliest days in basic training—except to his mother, father, or wife. Since all three were deceased, he'd never expected he'd have to say sorry again, primarily because he had never failed before.

Ambassador Wen's office was one of the most secure locations in either China or the United States. Although, he supposed, he was technically in China right now. He frosted the glass to the cube, blocking out Fang Chen, who had accompanied him back to the embassy after his poorly executed mission and was out there awaiting instructions.

He had no excuse. No reason to stall any longer.

Chao called the number on his secure uplink phone and slotted a bone-conducting comm bud into his ear so no one could intercept what he had to say. As the line rang, Chao assessed himself and decided that although Trapp had surprised him with his speed and agility, it was still nothing more than a few lucky shots which any brawler could land, given enough latitude. His eyes might darken with bruises, but even the injury to his nose was superficial.

"Speak," said the voice in his ear.

"The operation is progressing as expected," Chao said.

"Good. And your man? Dead?"

"Not dead. No."

"Then captured, incapacitated. Prepared for shipment."

Li Chao bowed his head, ashamed even though there was no one to see him. "He got away. The police were nearby, and he created a distraction. They investigated. I could not risk being caught. Or identified on one of their body cameras."

There was a pause, then a muffled click, and Li Chao recognized that the person had muted him, presumably to discuss options.

The worst thing about Trapp escaping wasn't the fact that he remained free. It was the manner in which he had achieved it. If Chao had simply killed the man, it would all be over, and he would be free to focus on his primary objective. But he had fallen afoul of personal desire by indulging his baser instincts. He had killed people with his bare hands before, more than he could count, mostly forgettable traitors and agitators. But there was nothing quite like taking on a true enemy, eye to eye, making sure they knew it was you who drained them of their life, one blow at a time.

Only... Chao had gone further than that, hadn't he?

He'd wanted to beat Trapp to the point where it was clear he could have killed the American had he chosen. To ensure that he broke Trapp's psyche as much as his body. Jia Ru's widow and children deserved justice, an oath he'd made long ago which he still intended to keep, even if it took another twelve years.

Aside from Jia Ru's family, China had lost a great man the day Trapp stormed into Rwanda. And so had Li Chao.

"Your personal mission is over," said the voice, flicking back on the line. "You will ignore Jason Trapp and proceed as planned."

"I can handle both. You know I can."

"Because of your actions, the Americans have made Trapp's face public. He will be destroyed, but not by you. After what happened at the embassy residence, they will have no choice but to imprison him."

That wasn't enough.

Chao couldn't leave it to chance or trust the Americans to ensure justice. Especially when it came to someone whom many no doubt fêted as a hero.

"I can use him in the primary mission," Chao said. "He will not be a distraction but an asset."

Again the muting click. The wait was shorter this time.

"Will the objective be more likely to succeed if you involve Trapp? Or less likely to succeed?"

If Chao answered that it would be *more* likely, they would want details. If he said *less* likely, they would order him to desist. Immediately.

"The operation will be executed as planned no matter what," Chao said. "But if you allow me some breathing room, I can use him to deal a body blow to the CIA."

Again the click. Again the pause. Again the swift return.

"If Trapp's involvement is peripheral, you have our permission. But your personal agenda is over for now. Unless he comes for you directly, you must not engage with him. When matters reach their conclusion, providing the Americans have not gotten to him first, you may pursue whatever you wish afterwards."

Chao wanted to press his point, but they had compromised more than he'd expected.

"Thank you," Chao said. "I won't let you down."

They had already hung up.

43

There was nothing quite like a crisp, cool morning in the middle of nowhere. Trees, rocks, and dirt were lit by a low, intense sun burning through the mist of the valley, accompanied by the fresh scent of grass and leaves. He wished he was here for a leisurely hike.

After a fitful night's sleep, his tightly-strapped knee supported his weight with minimal discomfort. He had found the hiking trail on a tourist site and verified that there were no cameras whose footage could be examined by the FBI or CIA. The trail center was just a hut, reminiscent of the one where he and Lamar had strategized the Rwanda operation, though this one was bigger and cleaner.

Connected to Lamar through his earpiece, Trapp mingled with the other early risers—about twelve retirees—without looking directly at anyone. They didn't look the type to spend their days monitoring the airwaves for fugitives.

"I see him," Lamar said in Trapp's ear.

"Alone?" Trapp asked. He wasn't worried about being overheard as he had separated from the tourists and positioned himself on a bench as if to take in the stunning view.

"No one around. Clear line of sight for ten miles. They'd need a drone at 50,000 feet to watch you."

Trapp looked up. He wouldn't see a drone, even if it was there. "Send it."

Ten minutes passed in silence. Missions were mostly about waiting. In twenty-four hours, twenty-three and a half were spent in silence, followed by half an hour of chaos.

But hopefully not today.

The man he'd been expecting lowered himself onto one of the benches to Trapp's left, wearing jeans and hiking boots and a puffer vest over a plaid shirt. He really looked the part, as if he'd fallen right out of a Mountain Warehouse advertisement.

"You're a hard man to find," Nick Pope said.

Trapp had watched him approach, having instructed him to start on the northern route, the most open path. Lamar had kept him in sight, monitoring for tails or backup.

"Dr. Greaves came through," Trapp said.

"Bit of a weird one, but yes. Inviting me to go hiking on my day off. I didn't expect that from a guy I've only met a couple of times."

It was Nick's turn to look over the view. He'd been injured during an operation a few months back, and although he appeared to be on the mend, he was tenser than usual.

"What can you tell me about the leaks?" Trapp asked. "You must have analyzed the files by now."

"That's not how this is going to work." Nick kept his eyes on the view. "If you give me something, I might—*might*—reciprocate."

"If you tell me about the files, how they leaked, it will help me connect the dots. I'll give you what I have, and if you can deal with it, I'll back off and lay low until it's over."

"Seriously? You?"

"I'm mellowing. Talk to me."

"Okay, I'll bite." Nick leaned forward, elbows on his knees.

"The investigation first focused on *who* leaked it, but they found nothing. I sent it up the chain, and it somehow found its way to none other than Dr. Greaves. You have anything to do with that?"

"Maybe he had a flag on anything relating to it. He's got pull now."

"Yeah, he does. He personally examined the files and found them linked to a previously known hack—mostly unimportant stuff like supplier details, so it didn't create a big hoo-hah, but Greaves thinks it was a smokescreen to sneak out other documents. He found markers of Chinese MSS subcontractors. *But...* as soon as he told me that yesterday, I got in touch with several of my Chinese contacts. Back channels that I trust implicitly. They know nothing about it, Jason."

Trapp thought about that. "If they aren't playing you, it just confirms that Chao isn't operating under orders from Beijing. Which means someone else is paying his check for this visit."

"He's still a state-approved business consultant."

"Yeah, which gives us another problem."

Nick nodded. "Protected by diplomatic immunity. And his cover is solid. We can't prove that he is the Shark any more than you could prove *I* am. The worst we could do is deport him. And only then if we got definitive evidence of wrongdoing." He sighed and sat back. "Your turn. Give me something I can use."

"Take a good hard look at Congressman Jake Redmond. Chair of the HSPCI. I think he's helping Li Chao. They had a tracker on Redman's PA, or whatever he was."

"That bloodbath you left us back in the city?" Nick swallowed, glanced at Trapp, then away. "They found Fabian Pincher dead. You have something to do with that?"

"I'm a witness. Does that count?"

"Don't be glib, Jason. This is fucking serious. A congressman's *aide*, the Chairman of the Intelligence Committee, no less? You're hinting that Redman's dirty?"

"Fabian was feeding intel to the Chinese. Or they were feeding it to him, I don't know which way the juice was flowing. But he was a whiny little bitch, had to be acting under orders. He all but confirmed it was Redman."

"Evidence?"

Trapp thought about what he had. "I'm working on it."

"I hope you're not relying on that young woman from the embassy. She spilled everything."

"Everything?"

"You tried to recruit her."

"Nothing about Fabian or Redman?" Trapp asked.

"She admits to meeting Fabian Pincher but claims she met him on a dating app. She didn't plan on seeing him again."

Trapp saw the breadcrumbs being vacuumed up as they spoke. "You know a guy called Hwa Yung-Gi?"

"DPRK liaison. Advance scouting party for the Il-Song family. Seems like he's been looking at some of the same things we have. Outside his remit. He'll be on his way soon. I assume you met him near some dead gang members?"

"Yeah, we had a nice chat. He knows who Li Chao is, but he wasn't aware he was in the country. Looked worried. His allies might have more than we do on Chao."

"Worth a try, but I doubt he'll give us anything. We're still the enemy until the ink's dry on that treaty."

"So we concentrate on Li Chao," Trapp said. "He wants me. But he has other business. I think that business will lead back to Redman eventually. I'm just a... side quest."

"Side quest?" Nick said. "You're playing Dungeons and Dragons now?"

Trapp said nothing. Bad choice of words.

"Tell me about Rwanda," Nick said. "That was you, right? On the film?"

Trap told Nick how CIA analysts had tracked money linked to terror groups and human traffickers on the African continent, bankrolling an operation which had directly affected US citizens. Trapp and Ryan were at the pointy end, Lamar and Valerie the backup. The analysts were pulled back, and Trapp was given the green light to execute both the money men and those physically committing the crimes.

Lamar, quarterbacking that mission, had spotted the additional unit rallying and managed to coordinate Trapp's and Price's escapes. But since a handful of security personnel had glimpsed the pair, Trapp had made the decision to cut off all loose ends. They circled back, killed the two units, including the head of security, before continuing their momentum and raiding the smugglers' HQ.

"That's where someone must have hidden with a decent phone—decent for back then—or a camcorder."

"So why exactly did you ask me here?" Nick asked.

"I just wanted to give you what I had," Trapp said.

"You could have done that over the phone or had Greaves slip me another note."

"Better in person. Shows you I'm not completely paranoid. I still trust *some* people. And I know you'll make sure this gets to the right ears."

Nick laughed. "It sounds kind of like you're just going to roll over and let the rest of us do the work."

"Maybe I am."

"Really?"

Nick stared at Trapp. Even from this distance, Trapp could see the incredulity.

"You're better resourced, and you're better placed," Trapp said. "If a rogue Chinese agent is operating here, what he's doing won't be small. And what's the big thing on the agenda right now?"

"The summit."

"The timing of the Korea summit and the revenge against me, there's no connection. It's just opportunistic."

"Side-quest?"

"Side-quest."

"And you just want us to run with it."

"Whatever 'it' is, yes. Chao is using Redman for something. He probably helped get the footage into the public domain without Chinese fingerprints, but that might be leverage. They make it look like Redman did that, they have him on the hook."

"Devious."

"It's what I would do. You too, Nick."

"When we do it, it's heroic."

They didn't speak for some time, and Trapp half-expected Lamar to butt in. He didn't, although he had listened throughout.

"Where are you going to be if I need you?" Nick asked.

"You won't need me. If Li Chao is looking to use the summit as a cover for something like, I don't know, assassinating Nash or one of the Korean presidents, you'll find it. And if some DPRK security liaison can track me down faster than you can, he might be worth bringing into the fold."

"Yes." Nick nodded but made no move to leave. "We'll think about it."

Trapp took his cue and stood, wandering toward the trail center, thinking he might buy himself a new hat. For the first time since the shooting in Boston, he was ready to kick back, heal, and let others do the hard work. He could surface once it was all over and his name was in the clear once again.

"Jason," Nick said.

Trapp paused, half-turning.

Nick asked, "Could this have anything to do with TIPTOE?"

Trapp turned fully toward Nick, the first time the pair had locked eyes since the counter-intelligence agent arrived. Trapp's throat was tight and dry.

"What did you say?"

"Project TIPTOE. It's not part of the public hearings, but it is on the record. Redmond brought it up. Have you heard anything about that? Anything that might connect to Li Chao?"

Trapp wasn't one for hyperbole. Nor was he one to overreact. But his mind lit up with confusion bordering on fear.

Nick took a couple of steps forward.

Trapp stopped him with a hard look. "I can't tell you what it is. It's just a rumor. Or it was. But if it exists, it's not something you want to be subpoenaed over. I promise."

"It's that secret?"

"If TIPTOE really is the end game, maybe they're using Redmond to see if they can get access. He wouldn't have the clearance, though."

"Jason, just tell me what it is."

"I can't, I'm sorry." Trapp set off toward the exit, calling back. "But what cannot happen, what must not happen, is for TIPTOE to ever see the light of day. That goatfuck will be a hell of a lot more painful than anything happening to me right now. I'll be in touch."

So much for healing while others took care of things.

44

J ake Redmond's first impression of the FBI agent was "geek." Despite the wide shoulders and chiseled jawline, there was just something about the man.

Washington Metro officers had informed Jake of Fabian's death the previous day. Jake had masked his fear with bluster, his shock transforming into grief. It was a natural reaction, and no one suspected what was truly going on behind Redmond's tearful eyes—no one except Redmond himself.

The obvious question was whether Fabian had been assassinated now that their Chinese "friends" were finished with him. Surely, if Jake's blackmailer intended to eliminate Redmond as well, there would have been no warning; they would have simply murdered them both.

In response, he had increased his personal security. His in-house team was fully aware of the elevated threat and had agreed to tighten ID checks and post additional guards, both on the floor where his office was located and around intelligence hearings.

Immediately after the Metro officers informed him of Fabian's murder, Jake was already calculating how to distance himself from the ambitious little weasel. He had insisted the threat couldn't be linked to him or his position on the HSPCI, as Fabian had very limited access to confidential intelligence matters.

The FBI agent, however, was showing every ounce of respect and courtesy one might expect from a young man meeting his girlfriend's father for the first time, which irritated him to no end.

Upon hearing the agent's name, Jake decided to put him at ease with a joke: "That's great. Just don't call you Shirley, eh?"

Drebin replaced his ID wallet in his suit pocket and gave a stiff smile. "Good one."

"How can I help the FBI?" Jake asked, leaning back in his chair and opening his arms. He'd spent twenty-five thousand dollars on consultancy fees to learn this pose. It conveyed openness, sincerity, and a down-to-earth attitude that voters liked, and he fully expected that an FBI agent would appreciate the same approach.

Drebin folded his empty hands in his lap and fixed Jake with a long, uncomfortable stare. He was about to speak when Drebin finally broke the silence. "Thank you for your time today, Congressman. I know this must be a difficult period. Were you close to Mr. Pincher?"

"We were colleagues." Jake lowered his chin and manufactured a semblance of emotional struggle, his eyes blinking slightly faster. "We occasionally had drinks and sometimes lunch. He was an aide looking to make a name for himself, but... and I hate to speak ill of the dead... I don't think he was up to it."

"He was incompetent?"

"I wouldn't say incompetent. But he'd reached his level."

"So no promotion anytime soon?"

"Exactly, Mr. Drebin." He resisted the urge to point a finger and smile, knowing it would be inappropriate. "Is that what this is about? Money?"

Drebin continued to scrutinize him, as if probing his soul, then asked just the right question. "Congressman, are you aware that Mr. Pincher was associating with a woman who works at the Chinese Embassy?"

He had prepared for this. He placed his hands on his desk as if to steady himself, his mouth dropping open a fraction as his brow furrowed. "The Chinese?"

"Yes, an attaché with the ambassador's office."

"I had no idea." Jake summoned a breathless gasp without overdoing it. He hoped. "Was he taking money from her?"

"Did he know of your dissatisfaction with his performance?"

"Well..." Jake sat back, finger on his chin. "We discussed his potential for advancement. I made it clear I was content with his current role, but when he took on extra responsibilities, I felt he was often... out of his depth."

"So definitely no chance of promotion in the near future?"

"None."

"Congressman." Drebin shifted for the first time since pocketing his ID. "This aide of yours, with whom you enjoyed drinks and meals occasionally, who had access to your schedule and presumably to this lovely office, was killed alongside several known Triad members who were linked to the Boston shooting a few days ago. Your aide was seeing a woman from the Chinese embassy, and he frequently brought you information and files related to recent intelligence leaks."

Your aide.

Jake had hoped that openness and cooperation would make this a box-ticking interview—condolences, assurances of swift justice—but it was turning into something more.

"Agent Drebin," Jake said. "Perhaps Mr. Pincher made an error in his dating life. He was a brave young man who clearly refused to cooperate with criminals. But he knew nothing that could compromise national security. Now." Jake stood, pushing his chair back with more force than he would normally. "If you will excuse me, I have meetings."

Drebin stood too and gave a curt nod. "I will have more questions shortly, sir. I'll speak with your assistant to schedule a better time."

The agent didn't offer his hand before departing, and Jake got the impression he rarely did.

When did the FBI start employing oddballs? Some new quota Jake hadn't heard of? Drebin certainly spoke with courtesy and respect, yet he seemed to see more than Jake would have liked.

He'd have to do something about that.

On Jake's way to meet with his allies on the HSCPI, to feed them questions he preferred not to ask himself, he was intercepted by Rita Tarragona, who fell into step alongside him.

"Rita, how lovely to see you."

"I was sorry to hear about your assistant," Rita said.

"He was a congressional aide. And no, he had no knowledge above his security clearance."

"Jake, I wouldn't use something like this to get one up on you. Surely you don't think that little of me."

Jake did indeed think that little of her. He wouldn't hesitate, if matters were reversed. In this town, the smallest hint of wrongdoing was an advantage to be exploited.

"So," Rita continued, "now that we're off the record with no hearing and no witnesses, why don't you tell me about Project TIPTOE?"

Jake frowned, looking bemused. "That thing from yesterday?"

"Yes, that thing from yesterday."

"Just a thing I heard about. Thought I'd mention it to the head of CIA Special Operations. It's nothing you need to worry about."

Rita pushed open a door to a passageway leading to a less frequented canteen, a good spot for discreet meetings. She seemed to know where she was going.

"You brought it up at the end of the session. A few softball questions, then that guy, Mitchell, was it? I saw he lied. I saw how much it meant to you. You wanted to see his reaction."

Despite the fact that they sat on opposite sides of the aisle and differed in opinion on almost every subject, Rita was one clever cookie. Cleverer and more alert than most of the ladies within these walls.

"Rita, if there was a threat to our country related to this... Project TIPTOE... I'd be clear with you. But you can't go accusing a respected member of the intelligence community of a federal crime on a gut feeling. If you think someone lied to Congress, you're welcome to present your evidence. I'll make time for it in committee myself."

They halted before the canteen doors, where no one could hear them.

"Even he can't lie," Rita said. "The only time it's permissible to mislead a hearing is due to a genuine error or when something is above top secret and endangers the United States."

"Or embarrasses the government," Jake added.

"That would still be a crime. Embarrassment isn't the same as security."

"No, my dear. That it isn't." Jake grinned, hoping to end the conversation.

"This is about you and your ambition, isn't it?"

"I don't know what you mean."

"If Project TIPTOE and the Hangman leaks become tied to Nash's term, maybe he vacates the presidency sooner. That would open the door for you." Rita playfully prodded Jake's chest. "You want your competition scurrying for cover. And frankly, I wouldn't mind that either."

"What are you proposing?"

Rita's smile brightened. "I'm happy to see President Nash go down. If it means someone like you gets the nomination in three years, debating blowhards like you is a damn sight easier than reasonable men like Charles Nash."

"Does that mean you won't object to certain details being made public, should a motion go forward? Perhaps even a subpoena?"

Rita didn't answer verbally. She widened her smile, resembling a snake about to strike, then walked back the way they had come. Jake watched her, contemplating potential trouble.

He could handle Rita Tarragona. He just hoped he could handle whatever came next.

45

Lamar Gilbaut wasn't a wanted man. He was a mass shooting victim.

Although listed somewhere as a "known associate" of Trapp, he had given no reason to be seen as an accomplice. Yes, he'd been out of contact for thirty-six hours, not visiting his stricken wife, but there was no other reason to suspect him of wrongdoing.

Even if the Boston PD or federal agent Paulo Drebin suspected him of aiding Trapp, Lamar had been evading tails and hiding in both concrete and actual jungles for thirty years. No proof, no arrest.

Still, he'd be no use to Trapp or the country if his head wasn't straight.

Massachusetts General Hospital had been a godsend. They'd treated Lamar and Valerie with respect and efficiency. Joshua was in good shape and expected to fully recover, and Lamar, who had been shot in the arm and grazed on his back, would mend without lasting trauma. Valerie, however, had a bullet lodged in her thigh and another that had torn through her body near a kidney, nicking a tube. She had been asleep for three days, stirring at roughly the same time that Jason Trapp's face was revealed to the world.

Although she had lapsed back into a deep sleep, she was no longer in a coma. Lamar believed she would understand if he left her bedside, discharged himself, and set about aiding their friend. It was a testament to their military bond that, despite not speaking with Trapp in person for nearly seven years, their kinship remained unbroken.

With a whisper in his wife's ear, he had departed and calculated the only backstop Trapp would use if he had no other choice. And it would be only if he had no other choice that Lamar would intervene.

Any muddying of the legal waters could see his PI license rescinded, and he was enjoying civilian life as much as Valerie. Another year of financial stability, and they would consider having children.

Trapp hadn't told him what Project TIPTOE was, but Lamar had rarely seen his old friend so spooked.

Not spooked. That was probably insufficient.

Rattled.

That's right. Jason Trapp was rattled.

If he was right about Li Chao's real objective, the former MSS agent needed to be stopped. Empowering Beijing would weaken Washington, threatening the free world.

The journey back to Boston wasn't quick. Lamar changed vehicles twice in camera dead spots and took a circular route to appear as if he'd returned from the south. Nobody stopped him at the hospital except to check his ID. The ICU receptionist recognized him, buzzed him through, and gave him a friendly smile.

Lamar made his way to Valerie's room. He expected to see her sitting up, reading a book or listening to one on her phone. Instead, the person in the bed was entirely covered with sheets, a bandage around their face, and numerous tubes intubating and feeding them.

That was not his wife.

Lamar jerked away from the room and strode purposely toward the first white-coated doctor he saw, a middle-aged woman with copper-bright hair whom he had seen around the place.

"Who is that?" he demanded, pointing back at the room.

The doctor stepped back and was joined by a male and female nurse who Lamar had enjoyed some brief conversations with.

The male, a mousy white man with round spectacles, said, "You're back. Does Dr. Rawlins need to see you?"

"Rawlins? He's *my* doctor. Why would he need to see me?"

"Because you're... here." He exchanged confused glances with the female nurse before the doctor came forward.

"Excuse me, sir. You are causing a disruption. Please, can you step outside? We will discuss this calmly."

"Calmly?" Lamar said. "Where's my wife?"

"She's at Pinkfields," the female nurse said.

"Pinkfields?" Lamar didn't know what they were talking about. "Is that a different ward? Did she improve?"

"No. *Pinkfields*. The private hospital in New England. You had her moved last night."

"*I* had her...?" His heart rate spiked, his thoughts narrowing to a fine point at the back of his eyes. "Please tell me you didn't discharge her to a bunch of strangers."

"They weren't strangers," the male nurse said. "They were two ambulance drivers with ID. Patient transport services. All the paperwork was there. Your signature was on it. A doctor at Pinkfields had witnessed it."

Lamar gripped his head with both hands, ran his fingers over his short hair, and swallowed hard. These people had let his wife out of their sight based on procedure. The fact that he had to show ID, even though the receptionist recognized him, spoke of the security in this hospital. You couldn't just remove someone. Except if you showed up with a clipboard, maybe you could.

"I need all your security footage right now."

IT TOOK Lamar nearly half an hour to speak with the hospital manager, who wanted to call the police immediately. Lamar resisted, threatening to sue the hospital if they didn't comply. Although they couldn't give him the security footage, they offered to view it themselves and look for inconsistencies.

They found that a sizeable panel van driven by a young Asian man in a baseball cap had blocked most of the camera's view at the entrance. The man made no attempt to deliver or to pick up goods or people, and he left soon after the ambulance into which legitimate paramedics had rolled Valerie's gurney.

Valerie had been semi-conscious, but they'd sedated her for the journey, as was procedure.

Upon checking with Pinkfields Private Hospital, known for its top-tier and expensive intensive care unit, they learned that the drivers who collected Valerie were on authorized leave and that Pinkfields had noticed that an ambulance had gone missing approximately an hour after Valerie was picked up. The doctor's name on the paperwork was real, and the signature looked legitimate on the photocopy that Massachusetts General made before releasing Valerie into their care. Unfortunately, Pinkfields' attempts to contact the doctor and the two drivers resulted in unanswered calls for two and a disconnected cell phone for the third.

After Lamar relayed all of this to Trapp over the sat phones they'd agreed to use only in emergencies, Trapp said, "They'll be found dead somewhere."

"Along with Valerie."

"No," Trapp said firmly. "If they wanted her dead, they could have injected her with something. These people have strong contacts. They probably blackmailed the drivers and made a doctor sign legit paperwork under duress."

"Who the hell are these people, Jason?"

"They'll make contact. They're using her to control you because they know you'll get to me. We'll get her back, Lamar."

"How will they contact us?"

"A message to the Chinese Embassy will find its way to the right people."

"Jason." Lamar gripped his skull with one hand and the phone with the other. "Listen to me very carefully. We are not going to mess around with these guys. We're not mounting some dumbass rescue. Valerie won't make it."

"This is your call."

"Then my call is..." He hated himself for capitulating, but losing Valerie would be far worse than some national security issue. "Unless we have clear evidence that Valerie is dead, we do whatever they tell us. Or, God help me, Jason, this is the end of me and you."

"Of course," Trapp said.

But Lamar wasn't sure he believed him.

46

As Marine One moaned to life on the White House lawn, Charles Nash marched along the corridor toward the patio with Mike Mitchell at his side, a growing sense of trepidation building like sea fog on a winter's night. Never had the United States held such a pivotal summit as the one scheduled for less than forty-eight hours from now. Even Middle Eastern peace negotiations felt tame by comparison. For all their fondness for slaughter, at least the jihadis didn't have nukes. Most of the objectives had been agreed in advance; it was merely the mechanism of delivery that Nash was to mediate.

And it *would* be Nash, not some proxy.

He could see out the front as the rotors of the copter turned in a lazy circle, the engines whining as power was brought up to speed and every diode tested prior to takeoff. He was reliably informed that his transport today would be the smaller of the models used, a VH-60N White Hawk. It didn't matter which helicopter transported him; it was always "Marine One." Although, as Nash learned in his first week as president, if that same helicopter were to land, disgorge Nash, and replace him with the vice president, as soon as that helicopter took off, it would be known as "Marine Two."

Emerging onto the deck, Nash held his ground as Marines lined up on the lawn, standing to attention. Focused on the helicopter, hands clasped behind his back and chest puffed out, it was as if he were posing for a publicity shot. There were no photographers here, though, only Mitchell. But the presidency was a role as much as a job. You had to live it every minute of every day.

"There's no way around this?" he asked.

Even though Mitchell was not the highest-ranking official in the CIA, he was certainly the person in whom Nash placed the most trust. Their relationship had been forged in fire, and Nash placed great value in a thing like that.

"I don't think so, sir," Mitchell said. "Both Jake Redmond and Rita Tarragona are stepping up the pressure. I assume it's for their own political ends. But we *have* to fight it. We cannot reveal the existence of this file in public, let alone its contents."

Nash turned his head toward Mitchell, as if expecting him to be brandishing a thick manila file with the words *PROJECT TIPTOE* stamped across the front, just above the red letters spelling out *TOP SECRET*, although he knew the file was above top secret and no paper copy had ever been printed. The fact that Redmond knew this assignation, along with the fact that he had now subpoenaed Mitchell and several other high-ranking CIA, NSA, and FBI officials, proved that another agenda was at work here.

Trapp's message to Nick Pope had made it to Mitchell, who had in turn reported to Nash that Trapp suspected Redmond of being a mole for the Chinese. At first Nash hadn't believed that Redmond was an out-and-out traitor, despite their political rivalry. But today's news of the subpoena regarding Project TIPTOE spoke otherwise.

"I assume we can't have him arrested," Nash said.

"It would be difficult without admitting we know what TIPTOE is," Mitchell replied.

The White Hawk was getting up to speed now, the noise and wash increasing by the moment. Nash didn't want to raise his voice, in case it carried.

"And the files?" Nash asked. "Can they be destroyed?"

"It's possible, sir." Mike glanced furtively at the helicopter and the two Marines jogging toward the president. "But it might raise red flags. Other branches will see it. Some of them with oversight duties. It could bring down hellfire on all of us."

"And presumably, even if there's nothing there, the fact of its absence will prove wrongdoing on our part."

"That's how I see it, sir."

The two clean-cut, perfectly pressed Marines arrived, and the taller of the two raised his voice over the noise of the White Hawk.

"Mr. President, your transport is ready. We'll have you in New York in no time."

Nash nodded and returned the man's salute, dismissing him as he turned back to Mitchell.

"Then the only tactic we have is to bury them in legalese and paperwork."

"Sir, bureaucratic delays only delay off the inevitable."

"Not if Trapp fixes whatever mess he's in. It all started with him. The shooting in Boston, the Hangman leaks, the assassination video. And now this. We know Jason wouldn't be playing this game if he didn't have a damn good reason. So let's try to give him time to sort things out. It might shunt something juicier into the news cycle, and all this will go away."

"And if he doesn't?" Mitchell asked.

Nash was already on his way to Marine One, calling back, "If he doesn't fix whatever this is, then we'll have to rely on Agent Drebin to bring him in."

lthough Trapp's whole body ached, an intense stretching session and a light bodyweight workout had banished the main kinks, leaving only the injuries to his fingers and knee truly hampering his movements. Everything else hurt but was background noise to his well-trained nervous system. He now stood by the old wood-fired stove, the rich aroma of roasted coffee underlying the scent of wood smoke. He poured himself a cup, then another for Lamar—both black—and headed out to the porch.

After learning of his wife's abduction, Lamar had returned to the off-grid safe house in record time, and Trapp had supplied contact details to the embassy for his sat phone, which was still untraceable, as far as he knew. His biggest concern now was whether Lamar had taken appropriate steps to avoid being followed in his distraught state. The former Ranger and CIA officer was a smart operator, had worked under fire many times and made some tough calls regarding friends who paid with their lives for the greater good.

The greater good.

What a facile phrase. A strange platitude hammered into

the skulls of people who might be forced to make the ultimate sacrifice. People like Trapp and Lamar. But it was more difficult to surrender those they cared for deeply. Especially when the greater good *was* their family.

Walking up onto the porch and greeting Trapp with a hug and a hard back-slap to break it, Lamar looked every inch the man that he had been when he ran with Trapp and Ryan.

"I was freaked out earlier, but I got it together now," Lamar said. "I wasn't followed. Any contact yet?"

"None." Trapp read his friend's face as he handed over a fresh coffee, and was comforted by what he saw. Lamar at least believed that he hadn't detected anyone following him.

"And you heard nothing else?" Lamar asked.

Trapp had spoken with no one since he'd left Nick at the trail center and returned here, where he'd been mentally playing out scenarios until he ran out of ideas. Trapp had identified the best course of action but would need Lamar to agree.

"Regardless of what he's doing with Valerie, I think we can draw him out."

"I won't risk her, Jason," Lamar said.

"I won't either. But you have to understand he *will* kill her, just as he'll kill us, once he gets what he wants."

"I ain't wet behind the ears."

"I know. I just need it out there."

"Then we fix it so he can't kill her. Or us."

If they were to exchange Valerie for Trapp, as seemed likely, it would be a simple case of insisting on somewhere public, although not so public that a civic-minded resident might recognize Trapp or be unduly concerned about an injured woman being traded between two groups of heavily-armed men.

The call came an hour later. Lamar answered the sat-phone on speaker.

"Mr. Gilbaut," said Chao's distorted voice. "I assume this is being recorded and you are attempting to trace my where-abouts. You can play this back later, I don't care. But let's not waste time."

Trapp did not wish to reveal that they were severely lacking in such resources, so he simply shrugged at Lamar.

"Do you have the..." Lamar started, playing the stricken husband as Trapp had advised, although he was much cooler than he had been on the phone at the hospital, despite the suffering carved into his face.

"She is well," Chao replied. "We just need one thing from you."

"You want me to bring you Jason Trapp."

"No, that would be a waste of a good hostage." A pause, then: "I assume he is listening."

"I'm here," Trapp said. "I'll cooperate with whatever you want, just let Valerie go."

"Your surrender alone is pointless." There was another pause, and Trapp wondered if Chao was about to allow Valerie on the line, but he did not. "We want a document that your government has buried. Project TIPTOE."

Trapp's intake of breath might have been audible, but he didn't care. Lamar held his expression grimly still, as if taking an exam that was not going well.

"You," Chao went on, "will paint yourself as a disaffected rogue agent with access to the CIA's dirty secrets. In exchange, I will not allow the young Triad idiot access to Valerie Gilbaut. I have fitted him with a leash, but there is no choke collar for this... *hún dàn*."

Trapp guessed *hún dàn* was a specific insult that didn't translate easily into English.

He said, "I don't have the files. I don't have clearance either."

"Then Valerie will die and you will continue to be painted as a traitor, as will your friend Ryan Price."

Trapp realized he had been clenching both fists for some

time, except for his broken digits sticking out in their splint, and his good fingers were starting to ache. He eased them out and stretched his hands, avoiding Lamar's eye.

"Why bring Ryan into it?" Trapp asked.

"Because we decided that you would respond well to that sort of pressure." Even with the voice changer, Chao's condescension dripped through the phone. "Let me be clear: Deliver the TIPTOE file to me and I will, in exchange, return Valerie Gilbaut to her husband and restore Ryan Price's good name. You, on the other hand, will remain a traitor, and you will surrender to me for transport back to China, to be put on trial for your crimes."

"Give me a second to think," Trapp said. He muted the phone and addressed Lamar, needing to understand. "So Chao did have a private agenda, but his main mission is to reveal Project TIPTOE on the eve of the Korea summit—"

Lamar finished the thought. "And it'll look like a burned, deranged operative has turned traitor. Revealing secrets that makes Edward Snowden look like the CIA's best friend in the process."

"Then he returns to his Chinese paymasters and disappears forever."

"Do we have a deal?" Chao asked.

Trapp unmuted the device. "I want proof of life first."

A series of clicks sounded, then Valerie said, "Lamar."

Lamar dropped his face toward the phone as if about to dive through and grab her. "Valerie, I'm coming for you babe. Hang in there."

"What day is it?" Trapp asked.

Lamar shot him a confused look.

Trapp repeated himself. "Valerie, what day is it? Date and month. Quickly."

Valerie replied accurately.

"What's Lamar's middle name?" Trapp asked.

"Pierre," Valerie replied. "After his grandfather."

"What was your zip code when you were in high school?"

"50236," Valerie said. "It's me, Jason, I swear."

Trapp would have preferred to interrogate her further; such was the ability of AI to mimic voices and tone. Quick-fire questions were a solid way to infer they weren't typing answers into a computer for a bot to mimic Valerie's voice.

"Satisfied?" Chao asked.

"I want to see her alive and well before we give you anything," Lamar answered for Trapp.

"Agreed," Trapp said. "We'll get you what you want and tell you when it's ready."

"You have until 9 a.m. tomorrow."

The line went dead. The look between the two men needed no words.

Less than 24 hours.

"Don't fuck this up, Trapp," Lamar said. "No tricks. No nonsense. We get what he asked for."

"Of course," Trapp said.

But allowing the truth about TIPTOE out into the open would do far more damage to the world than one more dead friend. The problem was, Trapp knew he could not live with himself in either scenario.

"You gonna tell me what this thing is, then?" Lamar asked.

"Yeah," Trapp said. "I suppose I have to."

48

"What you have to understand is that none of us wanted to be there," Trapp said, closing his eyes and replaying the scene in his mind. Many years ago, he had sat in a windowless room with three other men and two women. He had little in the way of expectations for the session, but he was pretty annoyed. He should have been out training, except for a strained rotator cuff that had grounded him for a few weeks. Not for the first time. "But we did as we were told."

Lamar seemed in no mood for chitchat as he set up the phone to use as a camcorder in the hut's small bathroom. They had erected a sheet behind Trapp, pure white, and covered the windows and hard surfaces with thick blankets and a comforter.

When they were as certain as they could be that no one examining the footage could identify the location, Lamar hit record, and Trapp stared straight down the lens. *Stay in the present.*

"There will be a lot of people out there with a lot of things to say about me. I hope reports remain accurate and do not reflect badly on my colleagues, either former or present. I am acting alone. I am acting under instruction, but alone.

"If this is ever made public, it is likely because I have been implicated in a crime against my country or because a document known as Project TIPTOE has been made public.

"'TIPTOE' was the codename for an exercise called the 'Covert Emergency Neutralization Protocols.' Although was only supposed to be a thought experiment, it seems someone in the deep state had the bright idea to expand it and keep it on file, in case it ever became useful.

"I know as much about this as I do because I unwittingly helped write some of it. Workshops, think pieces, hypothetical scenarios. Essentially, it is a dossier on every significant world leader, which the CIA keeps up to date in case of a crisis.

"More specifically, it is a plan for how to assassinate the leaders of every enemy and every ally that the USA interacts with.

"I was told that it was meant to be used to defend our allies —seeing their security weaknesses, especially while hosting dignitaries, and acting to cut off threats. But should a nation turn hostile, that same information could be used offensively.

"As far as I and other participants knew, Project TIPTOE was a paper exercise, and I sincerely believe there would be no attempt from the current administration to enact anything within those pages."

Now, the part that made him sick to his stomach. Trapp heeded Chao's instruction, the order to paint himself as a rogue agent working against the government.

"But I cannot stay silent. It is the right of every American to know what their government is doing with their tax dollars.

"You may judge me harshly. And I cannot blame you for that. But in time, you will understand that what I have done is right."

Lamar hit the stop button, and Trapp lowered his head. He

had rarely felt shame in his life. Guilt, yes. Regret, plenty. But shame never. *Hardly* ever. Even his mistakes were committed with the best of intentions.

Because even as he sat here, Trapp knew he could not go along with Lamar's plan. And that even Valerie herself would not expect him to. She would willingly make the ultimate sacrifice, as would Lamar, if her country came calling. But Lamar's wife was the only family he had left, and Trapp was seeing something in his old friend that he'd never seen before: panic. If Trapp couldn't temper Lamar's need to get his wife back, he would act on his own, and Trapp would have no way of containing it.

"I don't like it either, Jason," Lamar said.

"I mean it. TIPTOE was just scenario planning, in case a threat occurred. A thought exercise."

"I never would have had you down as that naïve, Jason. But you know what?"

"You don't care?"

"Exactly. Now that I understand what we're dealing with, fuck it. Let's get it done. Who do we have to screw over to get our hands on it?"

Contain it. Reassure Lamar that you're on the same side.

Trapp said, "You must use state of the art kit to go toe-to-toe with those cybercriminals, right?"

Lamar chewed over the words he'd spoken only days earlier when Trapp had jokingly suggested he was losing his edge. "You need some kit sourcing?"

Trapp exhaled, lowered his head again. "This could be the worst thing I've ever done."

49

Most of those who Trapp had trusted enough to reach out to since the shooting were people he had worked with for years, but one was relatively new—Madison Grubbs. When Trapp first met her, he saw a young, idealistic intelligence analyst; gutsy but naïve. In their one mission together, they'd been assigned to identify a prisoner in the Middle East and determine if he was a dangerous terrorist living under a false name. After he and a swarm of others escaped during a prison break, killing one of Madison's friends, she'd volunteered to help hunt the terrorist down.

During the mission, Madison held her own through ambushes, raids, and interrogations. She left clues for the authorities when abducted and resisted divulging information to her captors. Injured and despondent toward the mission's end, she selflessly insisted that Trapp leave her to pursue their target and thwart an attack on the president.

For a desk jockey, she had acquitted herself with distinction, but she'd since returned to Langley, Virginia.

They had stayed in touch, albeit sporadically, mostly Madison sending random pictures of food or selfies from locations she deemed "awesome." Trapp never reciprocated but always replied, although she suggested he cut back on thumbs-up emojis, which she said younger people found sarcastic.

Trapp had not cut back on his thumbs-up emojis.

Although not required to carry a firearm, she understandably favored maximizing her personal protection, so Madison attended the Harvey Winkel shooting range three times a week, or so Trapp had gleaned from scrolling through his WhatsApp messages. He was already in reception waiting for her when she arrived, and she was visibly pleased to see him, though she was smart enough to remain guarded.

"Jase—" She caught herself. "James! Great to see you."

Trapp wore a baseball cap and hoped his three-day beard masked him from any witnesses. It wouldn't fool government facial recognition, but he doubted this libertarian enclave would be connected to a network monitored by the FBI.

"Thought I'd take you up on your offer," Trapp said.

"I'll sign you in as a guest."

Madison, still in her pantsuit and carrying her gun in a locked case, had a word with the guy behind the caged reception desk, signed the book, and slapped a sticker on Trapp's chest. It read *VISITOR* with *James Harvey* scrawled underneath.

She purchased a box of ammo, then they were buzzed through to the range.

Gunsmoke hung heavy, and cordite made Trapp's nostrils flare. The racket was muffled by the ear protectors he selected from a peg by the door.

"To what do I owe this honor?" Madison asked as she took to the gallery at the far end. Three stations separated them from the nearest shooter, ensuring privacy—another reason Trapp had chosen this location.

Madison placed her bag on the shelf, setting her lockbox and ammo on the counter before her.

"Good to see you're keeping up the practice," Trapp said.

"Small talk?" Madison unlocked the box and began loading her Glock 17. "That's not like you, Jason. Why are you here?"

"Can't I just catch up?"

"You're not funny." Madison gave him a wry look before continuing to load cartridges. "Or are you here to turn yourself in? It'd be great for my career."

"I came because I thought I could trust you. Can I?"

"My earlier statement stands," Madison said, slapping home the magazine and taking aim at the paper target. "Nothing that will get me fired or prosecuted."

"I just need some of those whispers you might have heard. Anything with a Chinese or Korean connection."

"Literal Chinese whispers?" Madison squeezed off three rounds, then turned to Trapp, her gun pointed down. "Want a go?"

"Don't mind if I do."

Trapp had been waiting for an opportunity to remove his jacket, which he now folded and laid neatly on top of Madison's purse. He accepted her firearm, squinting through the goggles at her target. All three shots were center mass, about three inches apart.

"Not bad."

Trapp raised the weapon, set his stance, and fired three shots. The grouping was so tight it looked like one big hole obliterating the middle circle of the head.

"Show off," Madison said, taking the gun back. "What do you mean by whispers?"

"Your office is a clearing house for suspicious intelligence, right? Anything that isn't an actionable threat but might become one. Do I understand that correctly?"

"Pretty much. The big stuff goes through the NSA and Langley. If there's a suspicion they can't dig deep enough into, it comes to us. We're the detail guys." She spoke with a hint of disdain, despite this being her bread and butter.

"How are you otherwise? Still seeing the physical therapist?"

Madison fired four times, and Trapp saw one corner of the paper target flap, meaning at least one shot had gone awry.

"Sorry," Trapp said. "I don't mean to pry."

"It's fine. And yes, I'm there twice a week, but I feel like this does me more good." She fired more rounds until the gun racked empty.

"So what can you give me?" Trapp asked, eyeing his jacket.

"Nothing springs to mind. But with the president already on his way to the summit, it wouldn't be outside my remit to review certain data tags. Anything specific I should look for?"

"It'll look like money laundering or a shell business set up to donate to... maybe political campaigns? Where people shouldn't be accepting such donations?"

Trapp didn't want to point directly to bribery but allowed her to think along those lines.

She was already thumbing rounds into an empty magazine. "If I find anyone of interest or who might be in danger, I'll have to run it up the pole. You know that, right?"

"I do. And I wouldn't ask you not to."

Madison paused, facing Trapp with her magazine half-full. "You're not going to tell me the full story, are you?"

"Better you don't know all of it."

"Don't treat me like an asset, Trapp. I'm not some informant you can discard."

Trapp took a step back. "I wouldn't do that."

"I'd love to believe you." Her chin dipped, eyes rising. "Sorry, I just think I could do more if given the chance."

"If you can do this for me and keep your superiors in the loop, I'll see what I can do when it's over." He put his hands on her shoulders, encouraging her to meet his smile. "If I'm not in a federal penitentiary."

Madison finally smiled back, and Trapp felt a wave of guilt

and shame descend upon him. Letting go of her shoulders, he estimated that his jacket had been in place long enough.

"I'd better go," he said.

Madison, ready to fire again, didn't look at him. "That's cool, go. I'll sign you out. Don't want to risk anyone recognizing you."

Trapp picked up his jacket, shrugged it on, and put his hands in his pockets—one on his phone, the other on the device Lamar had sourced.

"Goodbye, Madison."

Trapp didn't look back as he left the range, wiping down the ear protectors and goggles as he went.

Was it the lack of personal history that had made him zero in on Madison? Or was she simply the shortest route to his goal? If Madison hadn't been an option, would he have betrayed Ikeda the same way? Or Nick? Or Mike?

He wasn't sure. And at the level of desperation he'd reached, there seemed little point in hypothesizing.

TRAPP DROVE to a diner north of Langley, one with no cameras attached to the network, much like the shooting range. Lamar waited in a booth beside a portly blue-haired man who was nursing the largest milkshake available on the menu.

"Intermittent fasting really paid off, huh?" Trapp said.

"Fifty pounds down, fifty to go," the blue-haired man said.

It was the first time Trapp had seen Dr. Timothy Greaves in years, but they greeted one another like regular friends, albeit without physical contact. Greaves wasn't keen on handshakes, and he would have rather eaten a live frog than hug. After another moment of pleasantries, Greaves snapped his fingers and held out a flat palm, onto which Trapp deposited a metal case the size of a large cell phone. It had two buttons and three lights, one of which was currently green.

"Any problems?" Greaves asked.

"Does my conscience count?" Trapp asked.

"Nope."

Greaves plugged the device into his laptop, which looked like a chunky relic from the 1990s but was more than likely one of the most powerful computers in the state.

"My current job is so boring," Greaves said. "You should have come back into my life sooner. I've been losing my mind with only the Russians to challenge me."

Greaves was a savant of the highest order. Once he learned something, he rarely forgot it and could always adapt or improve upon whatever had impressed him. The affinity he showed with computers and his almost symbiotic relationship with technology had made him a valuable asset to both the CIA —and Trapp personally.

"I'm sorry, Jason," Lamar said. "I know she's your friend."

"Not for much longer," Trapp said. "But a friendship... I'll give that to save a life. What I won't do is steal secrets that the Chinese can use to cripple our security networks worldwide. And kill possibly hundreds. If it gets out, the CIA will be kicked out of every country, including our closest allies, and the summit will be fucked." Before Lamar could begin what Trapp knew would be an emotional outburst, he asked Greaves, "Now you can secure this with a kill switch, right?"

"Of course." Greaves looked faintly offended as he continued to squint at the stolen phone data on his screen.

"So when they verify it at the exchange, it'll look legit. But when they try to release it, you'll scoop it up before it goes public." Trapp eyed Lamar. "Good enough?"

Lamar gave another of his grim nods, a gesture he seemed to have perfected over the past twenty-four hours.

"I thought you said she had some serious pull," Greaves said.

"No," Trapp replied. "I said she had network access and a

direct line to the mainframe. *You* said you just needed a way of bypassing the login security."

"Congratulations, Jason." Greaves closed his laptop lid and folded his arms like a sulky teenager told that he can't go to a party. "You have successfully cloned the phone of a low-level analyst. Yes, she has remote access, but there is no way we can use this alone."

"What do you need?"

"A hard line into the system. Or very close proximity. Only then can I use the cloned device to break through the firewalls."

Trapp's head dropped as the implication washed through him.

"Which means what?" Lamar asked.

"It means we have to break into an Agency facility," Trapp said.

50

The three men agreed there was to be no digital burglary that evening, which gave Lamar time to source vehicles, weapons, and comms that Trapp could not risk venturing out to obtain. Low-level hacking had furnished them with the name of the cleaning company used for the site, and it took little research to acquire a uniform suitable for Trapp. But a cloned cellphone, a pass, and a car key fob would not be enough. Trapp couldn't simply ride into the underground lot and start distributing viruses like candy.

They made their move at six a.m., three hours before Li Chao's deadline. Trap had attempted to make contact to request an extension, although the term *extension* felt glib. An extension was something you asked a professor for when you'd been out drinking instead of completing your physics paper. Unfortunately, the phone that had called them with the ransom demand did not even ring or go to voicemail. It was simply dead.

Either Chao would call them, or he only planned to activate the phone at the time of his choosing.

So Trapp had to make another small demand of Madison

Grubbs. He'd asked her for anything she could get first thing in the morning, before most of the other analysts would be at their desks, and she'd agreed to head in earlier than usual.

She would be devastated when she found out the truth. He didn't see how they could keep it from her for long.

Since Trapp knew Madison's routine well, he had hidden at five a.m. near the coffee shop with a drive-thru which she favored. The drive-thru was mysteriously out of commission, although not so mysterious to Trapp, Lamar, and Greaves. Madison parked and made her way inside for her fix.

While she was busy, Trapp used the clone of her key fob to unlock her trunk, sequester himself inside, then wrap himself in a thermal blanket to deflect the automatic heat scanners that some stations employed.

For the next thirty minutes of travel, Madison sang completely out of key to the *Mamma Mia* soundtrack, giving real gusto to the big notes. Trapp just had to remain still.

At a stop that he guessed was the barrier, the car idled for thirty seconds before Madison greeted someone by the name of Phil. She was chirpy and direct.

"Early start," said Phil's muffled voice.

"Yeah. Unfinished business," Madison replied. "You know how it is."

She was permitted through and parked in a space on the first go, then retrieved her bag from the back seat before locking up and walking away.

Trapp had hoped she would reverse into a spot, giving him more cover when he popped the trunk.

He waited a full five minutes, then used the emergency release to crack the hinge. Anyone standing right beside him couldn't help but notice the movement. But if they were farther away, it would go unnoticed.

Even the most adept guards watching the monitors were human. They had no choice but to take their eyes off screens for a few moments. All he could do was hope that they'd be looking somewhere else when he moved.

It was the kind of risk he would not take were time not drifting by so fast.

Trapp eased the trunk lid open just enough for him to slip out, down onto the concrete, and rolled under the car, pulling the trunk closed behind him.

Minutes ticked by, but no one came. Just him, his breathing, and a sheen of perspiration awaiting the all-clear.

When he emerged from under the car, he mooched along as if he was just another Joe starting a crappy shift. This was, admittedly, a CIA staff parking lot, so a cleaning subcontractor might have no business being here. But time was of the essence, and he could risk no more research.

Trapp activated the earbud connected to the phone Greaves had equipped him with and said, "I'm in."

"Good," Greaves said. "Head north until you hit the main elevators. Then track to the right."

"I'm underground. I don't know which way is north."

Greaves grumbled, and there was a beat of silence before he replied, "You're heading north now. I can see you. Keep going until you hit the bank of elevators."

Trapp didn't see another person, and although he was moving as if he belonged there, he was a big man. Broad and unshaven. He felt like someone in costume, not a genuine custodian or cleaner.

At the elevators, Trapp followed instructions and tracked along the wall. Taking out the scanner with its two buttons, he pressed the top one. It was a chrome box, much like a hard drive case. There were no flashing lights, no dials, nothing to draw suspicion should Trapp get stopped.

"That's it, keep going," Greaves said. "I'll tell you when to stop."

Trapp wished he had brought some sort of prop. A cloth or

a broom or something, although that could just look hokier than the uniform. He didn't have to penetrate the building, didn't have to impersonate an analyst or anybody's friend. And he hoped he would get out of here without encountering anyone at all.

"Okay, right there," Greaves said.

Trapp stopped where he was and pressed the device against the wall where Greaves expected phone and non-company Internet cables—for staff Wi-Fi, public facing screens, and contractor use—would be.

"Is this good enough?" Trapp asked.

"Yes. But I can't get a strong enough signal through the concrete. Get me in there, and I can piggyback onto the system using Madison's login details."

Get me in there...

Trapp had hoped it would not come to this.

"After I'm in," Greaves said, "I can deploy a package that will sniff out any common interaction points between the company lines and the less secure comms. Then it's just a simple brute-force ram raid that'll circle round to Langley's servers."

Trapp reached into his overalls and removed a flat plastic-wrapped putty-like square the size of a napkin. "Brute force?"

"It'll light up thousands of alerts like an overloaded Christmas tree. Too many to shut down before I get what we need."

Trapp took the small wad of explosive from its pack. "It'll look like Madison did something wrong."

"For a while, probably. They'll grill her, but then they'll see the signatures I'm leaving behind."

"Signatures?" Trapp stuck the explosive on the wall and inserted a pea-sized detonator. "Like, saying who made the hack?"

"Hackers love to have their work recognized. They leave

certain signatures behind in junk code. Nothing that back-tracks to the real world, just a little F-U, and they think they're creating legends for themselves. Right now, I am Piotr Grigorin from St. Petersburg. He'll take the heat and the credit. I doubt he will disabuse anyone of it within the community."

Then Trapp heard the first voice that didn't belong to himself or Greaves.

51

"Hey there! Morning!"

Trapp turned a little too sharply. His soldier's senses were tuned for danger rather than a commute to work. The man approaching wore a three-piece suit with a garish tie. He was carrying a satchel on a shoulder strap and some kind of iced coffee drink from Starbucks.

Trapp lifted his chin in greeting. "Morning. How are you?"

"Good, thanks. Did you get locked out again?" The man's tone was friendly and sincere. And he was referencing something a cleaner should probably know about if he'd worked here awhile.

"Yes. Well, not *again*. It's my first day."

"Ah, well, yeah. Lot of people end up down here. Take the wrong elevator, then they can't get back in. Their ID won't let them." The man coasted closer, a friendly smile on an unassuming face. "Let me see what you've got there. I'll call security and have them let you back up."

"What I've got here?" Trapp said.

"Yeah, the ID they gave you. It's got an R-FID chip that gets you in and out of places, but not the staff parking lot, unfortunately. I mean, it's silly. You can get in here somehow if you're with the right person, but the doors won't let you out." He gave a sorry sort of laugh. "I can't really scan you back in myself either. Not without permission. You understand, right?"

Trapp nodded. "Right."

Greaves said, "Get rid of him. I need access *soon*."

"They gave me the spiel at orientation." Trapp led on from the guy's assertions, a form of agreement that should put him at ease. "I was kind of intimidated by it, if I'm honest."

"Yeah, I was just like that, too. You get used to it. So..." The man was six feet away, his hand held out flat. "Let's see it then."

"See what?" Trapp was hoping to play the idiot for just a little while longer.

"Your ID? In fact..." The man's brow furrowed, and his head tilted to one side. "How come you don't have your lanyard on?"

"I..." Trapp, patted his chest as if the requested item was there mere moments earlier, and feigned deep confusion. Then, mortification. Panic. "I can't believe it. They're gonna fire me. My first day on the job and they're gonna fire me. Social services already wanna keep my kids away... if I miss another payment... Oh my God, I can't believe it."

"Calm down, buddy, calm down. Where did you last see it?"

Trapp's new friend extended his palms flat and started looking around on the floor as if divining for lost treasure. "*When* did you last see it? You must have had it in the elevator."

"The elevator, that was it," Trapp said. "I must have dropped it when I was helping Elsie with her buckets."

Buckets?

Trapp wanted to slap himself. Did they even *use* buckets around elevators where CIA analysts would be traveling?

"Don't worry, they'll be able to look you up and match your face. You just need to wait with me. I'll give security a call." The man took out a cell phone and started scrolling, as if looking up a contact. "We'll have you back inside in a jiffy."

But that was when Trapp noticed the cell phone was not displaying contacts. He caught a flash of the little green and red telephone buttons that said the line had been open already.

This was no hapless administrator. He had assessed Trapp as being out of place from the moment he laid eyes on him.

"How long?" Trapp asked.

"Oh, just a few minutes, they're not picking up right now," the pleasant man said.

"That's too long," Trapp said.

The analyst, or whoever he was, looked around sharply at Trapp. His body shape said he was about to bolt.

Trapp grabbed him by the shoulder, pulled him back, and maneuvered him into a sleeper hold as he dropped his cup, spilling cold coffee on the floor and on Trapp. The analyst was clever, but he was'nt a brawler. He fought, but as Trapp constricted his carotid, cutting off blood flow to his brain, the man passed out within seconds.

Then Greaves said, "Okay, you're all clear."

"You're in the camera systems as well?"

"I've been in there for the past three minutes. They're getting nothing but the same parking lot scene played on a loop. But there is some activity right now. You need to exfil ASAP."

Trapp was lowering the unconscious analyst gently to the floor when footsteps came rushing from somewhere Trapp couldn't see. The echoes were too much, too varied.

Definitely a trio, though.

Someone gave an order to "Check over there."

Another said, "I'll take everything from E3."

Sure, Trapp could take on the average rent-a-cop without breaking sweat, but CIA hubs typically employed security personnel with a military background. Trapp wouldn't beat them as easily as he had the analyst, and he'd probably have to inflict severe damage to subdue them. He didn't want to hurt guys simply doing their jobs, especially colleagues who were on the same side.

"Over here!" Trapp called.

He heard everyone stop. He checked on the plastic, and asked Greaves, "You ready?"

"I am."

Trapp stood to his full height and started waving. "Over here. Come on. He fainted."

The trio consisted of two uniformed security guards and a man in a suit carrying a bulky radio and a gun in a shoulder holster. The two uniforms unlatched the guns on their hips and flanked the suited man without drawing. All three approached.

Trapp maneuvered the stricken analyst into the recovery position and recycled the panicked expression and actions that he'd tried moments earlier. He may not have been the world's greatest actor, but was sure he could pull this off for a few seconds.

One of the uniforms crouched, two fingers to the unconscious man's neck.

The man in the suit said, "Who are you? What are you doing down here?"

Trapp opened his mouth, and an alarm wailed to life. It was no fire alarm, but a long, high-pitched siren.

"You're welcome," Greaves said. "That's the imminent-threat-to-life alarm. It means get the hell out."

The guards were wary now, the suit radioing for information.

"Get it done, Jason," Greaves said. "Hurry."

Trapp took in the men, two tending to the unconscious analyst who was coming around, the suit squinting at the radio as if that might improve the signal. A quick glance back at the square stuck to the wall, and one of the uniforms followed Trapp's eye.

"Now," Trapp said, covering his ears.

The explosive blew a manhole-sized breach in the concrete, exposing a void behind the wall through which phone lines and cables ran upwards. With the guards disoriented by the shockwave, Trapp reached into the hole with the chrome case, pulled back on one of the ends to expose a pair of snips, and jammed it into the wires. It didn't matter which ones, just so long as Greaves had a hotspot attached directly.

Trapp didn't wait for confirmation. He barged past the suited man, who still seemed stunned by the blast, pitching him back on his ass, then broke into a sprint as the other two rolled over onto their knees, blinking, shaking their heads.

He was back at Madison's car within seconds. He unlocked it, got in, and at that moment, the guards gave chase. A cry of, "Hey, freeze!" echoed too late.

"You can open those barriers, right?" Trapp asked.

Trapp reversed out, revved the car, and accelerated. The guards drew their weapons. Must have left the analyst to fend for himself.

Trapp spun the wheel, rounding a corner so he was hidden by pillars just as the first bullets were fired.

He floored the gas and said, "Greaves, did you get that? I need the barriers down now."

The rear window disintegrated under the barrage, and Trapp leaned on his side, his head down, only one eye popping up to see ahead. More bullets zinged through, spiderwebbing the windshield and pocking the dashboard. It was only a matter of minutes—maybe seconds—before he would be hit, and if he failed, Valerie would die.

Trapp drove hard toward the black-and-yellow arm barring the exit. There was an automatic ramp that rose and fell to prevent ram raiding—that ramp was now elevated to prevent him from escaping.

"*Greaves.*"

"Do you have to doubt me all the time?" Greaves asked.

The arm rose, and the ramp descended. Trapp hit the ramp when it was six inches from full retraction, bounced the car upward, and crashed it down hard on its suspension. Didn't stall it, thankfully. He gunned up toward the street, mapping his escape route and planning contingencies in his mind.

Then he braked hard.

A flow of people blocked the road; early risers and those pulling all-nighters evacuating the building, as they should, heading for an assembly point. One of them in particular stood out.

Madison.

She stared directly at Trapp. Her mouth fell open, her eyes squinting. Trapp recognized a look of dismay and disappointment.

He countered the guilt with the image of Valerie dead as Lamar grieved over her ruined body, then floored the accelerator, making the tires smoke and squeal. The flow of people parted, and he shot out into the road. A bullet came at him from below, but the gunfire ceased as he peeled away. The guards couldn't risk hitting civilians.

Speeding into the near-empty streets, Trapp saw that it was 6:30 a.m.

They had two and a half hours.

52

Trapp sped directly to the street where he'd agreed to meet Lamar, dumped Madison's car, and jumped into the brown panel van that Lamar had bought for cash, which required no false plates and attracted no stolen reports. The DMV would not register the change of ownership until Lamar initiated it—which he would not.

"You get hold of Chao?" Trapp asked.

Lamar shook his head. "Not yet."

"We need to get ahead of this."

"This isn't some squabble with the Triads or even an attempt to recruit a Chinese diplomat. It was a raid on the CIA. They'll take this city apart looking for you now."

"We've got two hours to stay out of their crosshairs, then it's over. They'll spend that long combing the scene and reviewing video. Once they figure out we jacked the files, they'll step it up, probably lock down the entire DC area."

"I'm looking at them now," Greaves said from the back of the van. "Some really worrying shit. A couple of things you should probably look at yourself, given current events."

"Later. Right now, we've got to do everything we can to make sure we take Valerie back."

"No," Greaves said. "This isn't just a hypothetical wishlist." He waited until Trapp and Lamar gave him their full attention. "There's also a list of assets in each country. People-assets. People they can call on to initiate these assassination plans, fixers to help agents get close or obtain weapons. It'll be a worldwide bloodbath."

Trapp imagined even friendly nations sending out para-military hit squads to arrest hundreds of people who probably didn't even realize that the CIA deemed them an asset.

He shook it off. "Doesn't change the situation. I just need a guarantee it won't get into the open."

Lamar exhaled sharply through his nose. "And I need a guarantee any extra shit you put on there won't get Valerie a bullet in the head."

"Lamar," Trapp said, pausing to ensure his friend was paying attention. "This is bigger than one life. Valerie would be pissed if we messed this up just to save her."

"*Just...*" Lamar frowned. "What do you mean 'just'? All I've given? All I've lost? You know I'm with you, but I won't kill her." He faced Greaves, his face blank—worse than a scowl. "Now, can you install the failsafe without them seeing it on verification? Yes or no?"

Greaves gave that slightly-theatrical offended look, but Trapp intervened; now wasn't the time for his brand of humor.

"Yes or no," Trapp pressed.

"Yes," Greaves answered simply.

"You know they need to get this out before the summit," Lamar said, turning back to Trapp. "And you know they'll execute her if they see we've fucked them."

"Yeah, I do know that," Trapp said. "That's why I want to get out ahead. It's risky, but I need to find a location as close to DC as possible."

"What sort of location?"

"Wherever the Boston Triads call home," Trapp stated.

Greaves sarcastically tapped the keys on his small mobile laptop. "Okay, I'll just plug in my Triad detector."

"Washington has a Chinatown district, doesn't it?" Lamar said.

"It's pretty big," Trapp replied. "And we can't just go around asking where the nearest Triad hideout is. But we might have someone who does know."

"Who?"

"The DPRK guy."

"And you've got his number?" Greaves said.

"No." Trapp thought about the last few days, replaying the incident near the overpass when the gangbangers had cornered him. He had injured a few, killed one, and Yung-Gi had been a witness.

"Check out law enforcement records for the incident at the overpass. Metro, FBI, whatever you got."

As Trapp spoke, Greaves had been operating his computer, nodding along.

"They weren't following *me*," Trapp added. "They were following the Triads. They'd somehow linked the Boston shooting and the additional Triad presence in Washington to the Hangman leak. Yung-Gi is a serious operator. But the people he was using aren't. Pull up all the suspects, check their phones, track their movements. If there's a cluster in Chinatown, we go from there."

～

THERE WAS no guarantee this would work, but like the break-in at the listening station, they had little choice. Time was pressing, and they needed an advantage.

The District of Columbia's Chinatown wasn't as sprawling

as Boston's, but still lively and colorful. As they pulled up to a storefront selling Chinese lanterns, dragon costumes, and silk clothing, Trapp and Lamar spotted a pair of bouncers down a side alley guarding an unmarked metal door.

Given his injuries, Lamar wasn't ready for serious rough stuff, but he insisted on serving as Trapp's backup anyway. Trapp himself was still smarting, his knee troublesome and fingers sparking agony at the wrong movement. But it wasn't like he had any other choice.

They had dropped Greaves at a safe location where he could return to work, avoiding association with the CIA incident. He'd supplied a thumb drive with the files and tracking virus, then destroyed the laptop to prevent recovery. Trapp and Lamar were now well-enough equipped with firearms to rob a bank if they chose.

The two bouncers were bald, with identical mustaches and shared maybe half a neck between them. They held out their hands with the certainty of people who were rarely questioned.

One said, "No."

Lamar shrugged. Trapp shrugged. Both slapped the hands aside, drew their handguns, and whipped the butts into the men's noses. Cartilage broke, and the men fell. Trapp and Lamar searched them—no firearms, just batons. They zip-tied the bouncers' hands behind their backs and pushed inside, guns up as they ascended the staircase to the main floor, then began clearing doors as if breaching a terrorist's den. Most doors led to closets and locked cabinets.

The first human they encountered was a terrified receptionist behind a grill who lifted her hands, closed her eyes, and screamed. She was alone.

"Buzz me through, will you?" Trapp asked, his gun visible but not pointed at her.

One of her eyes crept open, and a shaking hand pressed a button under the counter. The heavy door clicked open.

"Remember, I do the heavy work," Trapp said. "Backup only."

"You got it," Lamar replied.

Trapp pulled open the door and slid in, finding a room half the size of Joshua's bar, equipped with card tables, a roulette wheel, and a dozen slot machines. More than a dozen people were playing the slots, despite the hour. None had apparently heard the screams.

Trapp opened fire.

Slot machines erupted in showers of sparks, glass tinkling to the floor, and the patrons ran, shrieking, with their hands over their heads. Some older businessmen-types had younger, scantily-clad women on their arms and—to their credit—shielded the women as they ushered them away. Two suited men with tattoos snaking up their necks sprang into action, drawing guns.

Trapp pumped two rounds into the first man's chest as Lamar shot the second.

Unlike the listening station personnel, these were gangsters, likely killers. Trapp knew enough about the Triads for his conscience to remain clear.

On this, anyway.

"Is that all?" Lamar asked.

"Nope." Trapp ran to the doors that the dead men had been guarding and kicked them open, revealing a smaller room with one card table and eight men, guarded by a young man whose entire neck was sheathed in tattoos. As he reached for a weapon, Trapp raised his gun.

"Don't."

The man slowed, took his gun with two fingers, set it aside, and retreated with his hands on his head. The players, mostly elderly gentlemen, surrendered without a fuss as Lamar drew a bead on the guard.

"I'm looking for two men from Boston," Trapp said. "Zhen

Guanyu and Dennis Rhee. First one to talk doesn't get hit in the face."

Blank stares. The guard kept his hands up but his eyes moved.

"You, do you speak English?" Trapp asked.

"Yes," the man replied, heavily accented. "They take girls."

"They took girls? Where?"

"Upstairs, they stay in the suite."

"Upstairs," Lamar echoed, turning to cover his back.

But the guard indicated another door behind him.

"Go," Trapp ordered. "All of you, get out and take everyone else with you. Come back, you die. Clear?"

The guard nodded and translated. The exodus commenced, everyone hurrying out, giving Trapp and Lamar a wide berth. Once they were gone, Trapp gathered the guard's gun, secured it in his belt at the small of his back, and covered Lamar as he tried the door.

Locked.

The racket would have alerted anyone upstairs to their presence, so the element of surprise was gone. Speed would be their only advantage.

Trapp shot the knob off, and they infiltrated as they had before, clearing one door at a time.

Halfway up the next staircase, he could see that the upper floor resembled a home more than a hotel or casino, with a freshly-painted handrail and cheap carpet on stairs that ended at a landing with four branching doors. But there was no ambush.

While Zhen might be the type to incapacitate himself with drugs, Trapp doubted that Rhee indulged—which meant that he would be hiding up here, waiting for a chance to ambush the intruders. Each room was a landmine waiting to go off. Trapp and Lamar held their position at the halfway point.

Trapp looked at Lamar, who shook his head and pointed downward.

Trapp shouted, "Okay, you know we're here, and we know you're there. I only want to talk. We've got ordnance that could've blown this place to pieces if we wanted you dead. But we're here to make a deal that benefits us both. Forget any bad blood you have with me. This is about your survival. We'll be waiting downstairs."

Trapp and Lamar backed downward, out through the room into the casino, double-checking that the area was free of people before taking up positions by the doors that led into the private room. From here, they could watch both the grotty-looking suite and the exit via the reception corridor.

They waited about two minutes until first contact.

"I'm coming out," came an American voice.

"Is that you, Dennis?" Trapp called back.

"Yeah, it's me. You want to talk, I'm here to talk."

"Come on out, then. Let me see you."

"How do I know you won't just shoot me?"

"Because if I was going to shoot anyone, it wouldn't be you taking the bullet first. It would be your *hún dàn* friend," Trapp said, recalling Chao's insult.

"Fuck you!" Zhen shouted, followed by low tones of quick-fire conversation.

"Here," Dennis Rhee called. "I'll come out, you come out."

"Deal," Trapp answered. "I'll lower my gun, but I'm keeping it on me."

There was no response, except for a shadow elongating from within the private room. Then Rhee stepped out with his hands held to the side. He had put his weapon away but hadn't surrendered it, the clasp of his shoulder holster still closed.

"What do you want, Trapp?"

A roar of anger rose from behind him, and Zhen Guanyu ran out, using Rhee as a shield. Trapp did the same, pivoting to keep Rhee between him and Zhen, who was again waving his Magnum. Zhen adjusted and surged forward, so Trapp shimmied to one side and shoved Rhee in the shoulder, spinning the bodyguard into Zhen. The young Triad stumbled without dropping his gun.

Trapp pulled Rhee aside, who offered little resistance, and before Zhen could swing his gun up, Lamar was on him. He over-rotated Zhen's wrist, freeing the weapon, then kicked his knee out from under him. As Zhen fell face-first, Trapp backhanded him.

"No more of that," Lamar said, "or we'll take you out for real."

Trapp kept Rhee in his peripheral vision, impressed that the guy hadn't attempted to draw on them. "I want to make a deal. The sort of deal that gets you out from under Li Chao without any blowback. You do this, and you can return to your stomping ground in Boston."

Zhen got back to his feet, glaring at Rhee. "Why didn't you do something?"

"Because there's nothing to be done," Rhee replied.

"You fucking coward."

"I am not a coward. I'm employed to keep you and your hangers-on alive, and this, in my judgment, is the best way to keep the Guanyu legacy alive. If you wish to take a different approach, be my guest. You are, after all, the boss."

Zhen scowled. Trapp would have thought he was mulling things over, but if there was ever a poster boy for impulse-control issues, it was Zhen Guanyu.

The Triad boss lunged with a fast jab at Trapp.

He wasn't a weedy man by any stretch, but what muscles Zhen had were inflated in the gym, probably with steroid enhancement. They slowed him down. Trapp barely had to move four inches for the punch to miss, and he replied with a hefty slap to the face. He then slapped Zhen again on the back of the head, hard enough to make his brain rattle and his ears ring. It must have made him dizzy, too, because his knees buckled, dropping him to the carpet.

"Go sit in the corner," Lamar said. "Let the professionals talk."

Zhen made no move to retreat, but neither did he try to attack again. He stood, puffing up his chest, eyes watering, trying and failing to act like he wasn't particularly hurt.

"Madame Guanyu would not want this chaos." Rhee said. "The deal?"

"I will leave you alone if you leave me alone," Trapp said. "I will also rid you of Li Chao and whoever is bankrolling him, and you can just go back to running your gambling dens, selling your drugs, killing each other, whatever floats your boat."

"That's it?"

"No, there's a condition. We're due to make an exchange with Li Chao soon. Nine a.m. He's been using you as muscle all along, so I guess he's not planning on breaking the habit. Am I right?"

Rhee and Zhen exchanged looks, and Trapp didn't need them to answer.

"Tell me the meeting spot," Trapp said. "Send them whoever Chao wants, whether it's your guild or whoever owns this place. But you two stay away."

"And everything just goes back to normal?" Rhee asked. "You guarantee that?"

"We're in the end game now," Trapp said. "After today, yes. I guarantee it."

53

Hwa Yung-Gi had never felt more foolish than he did right now. He closed his suitcase lid and zipped it, then attached the buckles and pulled them tight. He wore a dress shirt and his best suit trousers, preparing for his flight to New York City.

"I have so little time to conclude matters," he said to his contact, ignoring the room's other occupant.

"We have analyzed the risks, and the reports you have sent us give enough assurances that the president will be in no danger from this 'Hangman' person."

"It would be better if I could eliminate the risk altogether. I do not like to play the odds."

"Yung-Gi, you have done a fine job and your commitment is noted. But President Il-Song will not tolerate further incidents that rile the Americans."

Yung-Gi hefted the suitcase so it stood on its wheels. "Am I to be in the main presidential detail?"

"Of course; you're the best we have."

Yung-Gi swallowed further arguments. He was under orders, and breaching those orders would be fatal not only to his career, but perhaps also those he cared for. He had little in the way of family back home for them to threaten, but there were nieces and nephews that could be used against him.

"Thank you for updating me," Yung-Gi said. "My flight leaves for New York in three hours. I will be on it."

His superior gave him some more flattering small talk, and Yung-Gi reciprocated with humble replies. After hanging up, Yung-Gi put on his tie without speaking. He slipped his jacket on and looked at himself in the mirror, inspecting the angles of his shoulders and the hang of the jacket. He looked impeccable. Or as impeccable as a tired old man could look.

"That's it, then?" Charlie Hu asked from the armchair at the side of the room.

"You heard the instructions," Yung-Gi replied without looking at the young man. "I am not permitted further incursions into this matter, as I expected. But I did not arrange for your release from custody because I have grown attached to your company."

"What do you want me to do?"

Yung-Gi turned toward Charlie. "Do I really need to spell things out? The asset who was watching that Triad casino reported a significant event."

"Big-ass shootout from what I hear, yeah."

"Then the Triads are still in play. Which means a former Chinese intelligence operative is still in play, and he just happens to have revered a man by the name of Jia Ru. You probably do not know who that is, but rest assured he was a militant isolationist who advocated only for China to grow mightier than her enemies. No negotiations, no compromise. How do you think a man like that feels about our people having friendlier relations with the United States? Because when our current leader passes, Myo Il-Sung wishes us to stand on our own, not propped up or controlled by a supposed ally. Even one as useful as China."

Charlie's eyes had practically glazed over. "Do I need to take a test after this, or do you have orders for me?"

Imbecile. But this was what he had to work with. "Get rid of everyone who seems to be *thinking* bad thoughts about this summit. Triads. Rogue Americans. Chinese agents. Use the slush fund I have left you under the bed and bring in whatever hands you need."

Charlie whipped the bag from under the bed and opened it. He whistled in appreciation at the thousands of dollars in loose bills which Yung-Gi had acquired. He didn't think it necessary to tell Charlie that much of the cash was liberated from the safe house in which the pair had first met.

"The Triads," Yung-Gi said. "Li Chao. The Hangman. Take them all out."

"All of them?"

"It is your duty. Do it today."

"I'll have to use our people if you want it that fast," Charlie said, as if he thought Yung-Gi might reconsider.

"Do what you must." Yung-Gi turned and opened the hotel room door, pulling his suitcase behind him. He paused in the doorway. "You have plenty to lose if you fail. And do not think that bag of money will get you far enough to be safe."

54

Trapp stood half-hidden by a dump truck's gigantic tire, its bay upright after emptying its load. The shadow was cool despite the increasingly oppressive morning heat. From this position, he had a clear view of the entrance and the two vehicles approaching his position, three minutes early.

The construction site had once been the forerunner of the current Chinese Embassy residence. Now it was dominated by a three-story skeleton of gray concrete, girders, and exposed rebar. Trenches dug into foundations beyond the structure hinted at future apartments, and possibly retail space, too. Bricks, cement, and construction vehicles were neatly arranged, though the mounds of earth and gravel created an alien landscape dotted with black-and-yellow backhoes and lifting gear.

Greaves had checked the place out for them: Owned by a Chinese private company, the Chinese state retained rights to access the site, but rebuilding seemed to have been interrupted by internal Party politics. As a result the site was deserted, without even security guards to witness those present.

Trapp and Lamar had fallen back into their old routine as

they'd set up for this meeting, covering ground and agreeing on contingencies. The pair skirted around the issue of Project TIPTOE's incendiary implications. Trapp would not let it out in the open. He hadn't lied to Lamar, not really; he was determined to keep Valerie alive, but not at the expense of releasing the TIPTOE files. And Valerie would expect the same of him.

The lead car coming toward them was a dark blue sedan, unremarkable in every way except for its diplomatic plates. The accompanying minivan was similarly untouchable, in theory at least. Both vehicles kicked up a lazy rooster tail of dust as they slowed.

Trapp stepped out and raised his hands to shoulder height, elbows bent, opening his jacket to show he had no weapons. He turned in a circle, revealing he'd hidden nothing at the back of his pants—an initial show of good faith.

"They're here," Trapp said.

"I can see," Lamar replied in his earbud.

"Keep an eye on that minivan. I bet Valerie is in there."

"Way ahead of you, pal—"

A wall of static hit Trapp's ear.

"Lamar?"

The static fizzled, then fell dead.

Shit.

It couldn't be a coincidence that the cars had stopped just as the signal died. They must have brought a jammer, which would also block the radar mic Trapp had installed to capture any incriminating words Chao might say.

No plan survives first contact with the enemy.

The sedan's front doors opened. A short, stocky man with a bulge at his armpit exited from the driver's side, and Li Chao emerged from the other. Impeccably dressed, as always, Chao wore an elegant vest over his dress shirt, his tie already removed.

Trapp envisaged a repeat of the fight at the metalworks,

which was fine with him. He was prepared this time, both mentally and physically. The cuts on his chest had healed to scabs, and his tightly strapped knee was back to around ninety percent—jarred, not sprained. He could cope with the pain in his fingers. He was also prepared for Chao's ostentatious fighting style.

Chao strolled forward. "You have my files?"

"They're safe," Trapp replied. "You have our human being?"

"Of course." Chao signaled to the vehicles. "But I relinquish nothing until we know what we're dealing with."

The stocky man went to the minivan and opened the trunk door on its top hinge, revealing Valerie on a secure gurney on the car's bed with the back seats down. She might not have been comfortable, but she was conscious and even offered a feeble wave toward Trapp.

"The files," Chao said.

"You're jamming the signals," Trapp replied. "I can't let my man know."

"Of course we are. I would be an idiot to allow you to coordinate against me."

Lamar should have been watching from a nest on a scaffold platform with a rifle. He could have taken out Chao, but with the minivan driver and any passengers still hiding inside, killing him was not an option. Not if they wanted to be sure that Valerie would live long enough to be rescued.

Plan A was toast.

Plan B was still in play.

Lamar remained concealed but shouted, "I'm here."

At the sound of his voice, Trapp snapped his head around.

This was not plan B.

"Good," Chao said. "Come out. Now."

Lamar traipsed around the side of the gravel pile, his hands in view. One held a thumb drive, the other a grenade. The pin was pulled, but he was holding the lever in place.

"What the hell, Lamar?" Trapp said.

"No wife, no files," Lamar said, inching his way along, keeping his distance not only from Chao and the stocky, armed man, but also from Trapp.

"There is no need for this," Chao said. "I am upholding my part."

Chao again signaled, and the rear door of the minivan slid open, disgorging Fang Chen with a chunky-looking e-tablet in her hands. Trapp didn't recognize the device, but then he supposed the MSS and its private contractors would be foolish to use American-designed kit. Fang kept her face down, hiding behind her long hair like a wallflower at a party as she advanced with quick steps, halting between Lamar and Chao.

Lamar glanced at Valerie, and she lifted her hand to wave at him.

"What's going on?" Trapp asked. "What are you doing?"

Lamar allowed his eyes to switch to Trapp briefly before holding on Chao and the stocky backup. There were undoubtedly more personnel in the minivan, the driver at least. There would be others nearby too.

Trapp had to find Chao's weak spot before Lamar did anything rash. He had planned alternatives. But Lamar waving a live grenade was not one of them.

"You're gonna kill him," Lamar said. "Whether we get Valerie back or not. I know you, Trapp. You'll let her die. Me too, and yourself, if that's what it takes to keep this from getting out."

"We have to," Trapp said. "No one person is worth the lives of everyone who'll be exposed. Not to mention whatever the Shark is planning next."

A thorny intake of breath betrayed Chao's annoyance. Trapp knew he detested the nickname, as did all the operators familiar with the man's work, which was the main reason the codename had stuck within US intelligence circles.

"I'm not losing her," Lamar said.

Trapp had been afraid Lamar might deviate from the plan, but he hadn't thought it would go down like this. "I don't believe you."

"Enough," Chao interrupted. "Give the files to *her*. Now. She will verify them, then we will exchange the prisoner." He inclined his head toward Trapp. "You, of course, will come with us."

Trapp might never have shared with Lamar the strength of bond he'd had with Ryan, but he had known Lamar as a loyal patriot. Valerie too. This wasn't him.

"Valerie would never forgive you," Trapp said. "Even if it saves her life."

Lamar pressed his eyes closed, gripping both the thumb drive and grenade tighter.

Trapp believed that Lamar had made his mind up already. Only his conscious brain now resisted what had to be done.

Fang took one step toward Lamar, hand out but eyes still down. She uttered, "Please give me the drive."

Chao watched, forming one point of a triangle between Lamar and Trapp.

Trapp watched as Lamar wrestled with the impossible choice.

Then Valerie shouted from the minivan, "Babe! You know what you gotta do. So do it!"

Lamar screwed his eyes shut again, hands to his temples, his mouth a grimace, crying out in frustration, but only for a second. His eyes snapped open, glaring at Li Chao.

"I do know, yeah," he said. "I think I always did."

Then he tossed the grenade at the Shark's feet.

55

As Trapp dove for cover behind the gravel pile, the stocky bodyguard bolted away from the grenade. Lamar took off toward the minivan, a pistol drawn from his belt while Li Chao raced toward Fang Chen. At first, Trapp thought he was maneuvering her out of the blast radius, but he swung her around to use like a shield.

"Fucking coward," Trapp spat as he hit the ground.

The explosion was loud and bright. It didn't pack the full force of a United States Army frag grenade but spewed white mist in an almost mushroom-shaped dispersal and kept on blowing, spinning to blast a miniature hurricane of confusion.

Lamar's gun fired four times and, as he peeked back out, Trapp saw the two men who'd jumped from the minivan fall to the ground with blood sluicing from their heads. The bodyguard aimed, but Lamar was faster, shooting him in the chest and neck.

As Lamar reached the back of the van, Trapp noted that he had engineered the best of both worlds: He refused to sacrifice Valerie, but despite his earlier wobbles, he could not betray his country.

Thanks for the heads up.

Trapp took off after Chao and Fang, tracking them into the half-constructed apartment block. But after only a few yards, three bullets slammed home six feet and eight feet beyond his position, forcing him to duck behind a backhoe.

Sniper.

Some distance away—one of the elevated buildings surrounding the site.

The obvious thought was that Chao had no intention of letting him walk out of here, but then Trapp caught sight of the Chinese agent. Still gripping Fang's wrist, hunkered behind a breezeblock wall, both pinned flat. Chao nipped his head out, his intense concentration easy to read.

As another two shots blew rock and dust over Trapp, Chao made a run for it with Fang. Bullets raked the wall where they'd been hiding, but they made it inside the project and out of range.

"Who the fuck is that?" Trapp asked himself.

Yung-Gi? Or some other player?

Or perhaps Dennis Rhee had decided to rid himself of two pains in the ass, instead of trusting Trapp's assurances.

Trapp noted that Lamar had vanished. Hopefully, he was on his way back to his nest to take out the sniper, who had to be shooting from a separate construction site two blocks away, a soon-to-be towering hotel.

He had to trust that his friend would make good.

Trapp raced out into the open, diving to retrieve the Sig Sauer P229 that he had stashed beneath a forklift in case they searched him. Securing his fingers in place was painful, but he could still fire the gun with his right hand. He ducked and bolted again as the sniper attempted to catch him through the smoke.

Inside the frame of a building, with multiple walls covering him for now, Trapp plowed ahead with his gun up, swinging it in wide arcs to cover every angle ahead. Driving deeper into the frame of concrete and metal, he covered both sides, wishing Chao had taken a more circuitous route so that he could have picked up the semi-automatic he'd liberated from the Triad casino.

Trapp kept low and kept moving, his mind flashing to how he'd counter the sniper now that he'd left the smoke cover far behind. He was exposed, even moving from pillar to stanchion to pile of sheet metal. With each new position, he paused to listen and to assess what he could do to lure Chao out.

Lamar had gone off-book and a sniper was ready to pick off any escapees, leaving Trapp as both the hunter and the hunted. With the change in plans, he predicted Lamar would secure Valerie and destroy the drive, then rejoin Trapp to pick up their original plan. He just needed to stay alive a little while longer.

He darted out from cover, angling for a pillar marked with a red painted diagram. Gunfire echoed through the empty space, and, for a moment he thought a round had nicked his leg. But no, it was just the exertion of a sudden change in direction that sent a spear of pain through his knee.

Safe behind the pillar, he leaned against it, working his knee joint, moving his leg back and forth. Satisfied it would hold up, he assessed the rest of him. Still intact.

Still in the game.

"Hey, Sharkie," Trapp called. "If it's a rematch you're looking for, I'm good to go."

"No more Hollywood bullshit," Chao replied, his voice bouncing off the metal and concrete all around.

It gave Trapp only a general idea of where he was, combined with the fact that he had ceased firing. There was still a hundred and eighty degrees of sight where Chao could be concealed and, more than likely, approaching.

Trapp called back, "You can't get away. And diplomatic immunity won't save you. This isn't Chinese soil anymore."

He followed his line of sight with the Sig. Checked one way around the pillar before swinging back the other way. He heard movement.

"A bit like Taiwan, eh, Sharkie?" Trapp called to Chao, a mocking lilt to his words.

"I do not have the ego that you are hoping for."

That was a lie. Ego had already driven the assassin to endanger his larger mission for revenge.

But more importantly, Trapp now had a general lead on his opponents. And his next move was a bit of a gamble.

He bolted from his pillar and sprinted hard toward the back end of the building. Sure enough, gunfire blasted his way. He dived behind the stack of sandbags he'd been aiming for, and chunks of metal that would have torn him apart impacted burlap with meaty thumps instead.

Righting himself, he looked up to see Chao emerging from cover with Fang, who still clutched the e-tablet like a precious purse that she was afraid could be stolen at any moment. Chao had one hand around her wrist and his gun hand pointing toward Trapp.

The V-shape between two sandbags gave Trapp a safe view. "What are you doing?" He checked his gun—ready to fire. "She's *your* agent."

"She's a nobody. But you tried to take her. I know how men like you operate. You will try to turn her again, demand she give evidence in exchange for immunity. She *was* tempted."

Fang let out a distraught sob. Trapp wondered if Chao really understood what sort of man he was. There were things that Trapp had done and would be willing to do again that made him anything but proud. If he thought Trapp would try to save Fang...

"I would rather have seen you kill my friend than give you the files that I'm carrying." He hoped this bluff would buy

Lamar some time to get back in position. "I don't care about the girl at all."

But Chao wasn't buying it. "I will search both your corpses and take what I wish. You can give yourself up now. Or there will be another death on your conscience."

"Like you said, she's a nobody. She's no use to me. So go for it. Shoot her."

The bluff almost worked. Chao dragged Fang to a sturdier location—another pillar, this one marked with a green symbol and stenciled numbers. Chao would know this impeded his line of sight, yet Trapp could not pass up the opportunity to spring his move.

He dug his toes into the ground and pushed off like a hundred-meter sprinter vying for the finish line. His angle took him to the left of the pillar where he spied Fang and Chao, Fang a clear hostage and human shield, her fingers curled around her belt buckle in what looked like a nervous tick. Chao was banking on Trapp wanting to save her. But Trapp saw only Chao's fingerprints on this: all that had happened, all that *would* happen, was on him.

Trapp made it to a pile of eight cement sacks before Chao got a shot off. Not a huge bunker, but it allowed Trapp to aim and fire.

The e-tablet in Fang's grasp split, the bullet passing to the side of her body without catching flesh. She dropped the device in shock and screamed. Even Chao seemed surprised.

Trapp pressed home the advantage and unloaded six more rounds into the pillar, spraying grit and dust across the pair.

Fang wrenched away, Chao's grip weakened by debris in his face, and ran perpendicular to Trapp's position. He tracked her momentarily, but it was clear she was unarmed. Nowhere to conceal a gun in an office dress.

Chao briefly aimed at her back, but Trapp reminded him

that he was here with two neatly placed rounds into the pillar. He was too well-hidden for a clear shot.

Trapp repeated his previous move, adopting a position like an Olympic athlete and pushing off from an imaginary starting pistol, firing twice as he sprinted the fifty yards back to the sandbags. It was on the third shot that his slide racked open. He held it out for a moment longer, as if he hadn't been counting the bullets he used, allowing Chao a glimpse of his now-empty weapon.

Chao came out shooting just as Trapp made it back to cover. Almost right away, Chao's gun also racked empty.

People like Trapp and Chao could reload a gun in a couple of seconds. Which Trapp did, but he was already on the move as he ejected the magazine. He mentally mapped his intended route, relying on Lamar to get there too.

56

Charlie Hu was afraid of heights, so he lay on his belly next to Samuel Jeffers, closer to the man's feet than to the high-powered rifle that had cost Charlie a quarter of the cash Yung-Gi had given him. The floor was filthy. Jeffers had a padded mat to lie on, but Charlie had spent enough time in crack houses and meth dens that the filth didn't bother him.

Samuel, a former Army Ranger who claimed to be in his forties but looked as old as Hwa Yung-Gi, had inspired little confidence in Charlie upon meeting him, stinking of decay and body odor worse than many of the homeless who bought from Charlie's people. But Samuel had a home, and he knew a thing or two about shooting people from a distance.

"As long as I got my painkillers, I'm as good as it gets," the sniper had boasted.

Since Samuel had been willing to take half his payment in Oxy, he'd been a bargain, and Charlie would bag the rest of the old man's money.

"You see him?" Charlie asked.

"If I did, I'd have shot him," Jeffers replied, his eye to the scope, still scanning for movement. "All I got's the lady in the car, but as we established, she looks like bait to me."

Charlie felt brave enough to inch closer to the edge, using binoculars to scan the area, the unreal sensation of looking through a lens easing his vertigo. A trio of men were waiting on the street, baggy tops concealing their guns. All three together had cost less than Samuel Jeffers.

"The others are in place," Charlie said.

"Won't need 'em," Jeffers said. "Lookie here, it's the pretty little China-girl."

Jeffers adjusted his position, made a tweak to his scope, and aimed. Pressure on the trigger.

"Wait," Charlie said. "Maybe she'll draw the others out. More bait?"

Jeffers exhaled slowly through his nose. "You're the boss, kiddo."

FANG CHEN HAD NEVER BEEN SO frightened. Over the past week, her new life had frayed her nerves to the breaking point. Even though exchanging intel with Fabian had initially given her a mild thrill, the anxiety when he'd shown interest in her had become overwhelming. And when Jason Trapp had broken into her apartment, she'd been terrified, but also weirdly proud that a US agent would target her. If she dug really deep into her soul, she could not deny being tempted to give up, because Li Chao frightened her far more than the Americans did.

And yet he intrigued her too.

She was surrounded by exactly the kind of men her mother had warned her to avoid.

Chao had insisted she be here today. He'd claimed he saw something in her that made him trust her implicitly, praising her instincts, especially when she confirmed that Jason Trapp was tailing her. Initially unsure if he was grooming her for a significant role, either as a companion in the bedroom or as a disposable asset, Fang was now certain it was the latter. Both Chao and Trapp treated her as a bargaining chip, her life worth only as much as they could use her to their advantage. All she wanted now was to end this phase of her life, the initial excitement tainted by her collision with reality.

Now that they had left her behind, she returned to the meeting point—the only way out she knew. The sedan and minivan were still there, but no one was left alive. Three men lay on the ground, taken out by Trapp's partner, who had the thumb drive.

If she could get to public roads in a vehicle with diplomatic plates, no cop or federal agent could even give her a speeding ticket.

She had to move now.

She ran for the sedan, reached the car unhindered, and opened the driver's door. Climbed in.

Yes!

The key fob was on the dashboard. She just needed to press the brake and hit the start button.

As she depressed the brake pedal, the door flew open, and Trapp's partner aimed a gun at her. Fang lifted her hands to the steering wheel, closed her eyes, and said goodbye to everyone she loved.

"Step out, slowly."

Fang pried one eye open, then the other, and regarded the man. All she wanted to do was fold herself into a ball and cry.

"Now. Don't make me drag you out."

Fang willed one leg to move and planted her foot outside, then did the same with the other, standing on ground that felt like sand. She removed her hands from the wheel, kept them out in front, and exited the vehicle fully. The man stepped back, gun trained on her.

"Turn around, hands behind your back. I'm gonna zip tie you."

Fang knew she'd be sent home in disgrace. No career, no honor for her family, and the Party might punish everyone she cared about because of her. Especially her incarcerated uncle. All because Li Chao and Jason Trapp had dragged her into their game. And now another man wanted to constrain her.

Fang sensed his approach, a heavy footfall close behind. She let out the biggest sob she could muster, then doubled over, holding her stomach, and shaped her mouth to vomit.

"Hey, okay, okay," the man said, coming closer.

Fang turned her head, confirming his gun was out to the side. He held two black zip ties in his other hand. Her damsel-in-distress act, that most American of tropes, worked surprisingly well on a man who had killed three Chinese security agents.

Her hand at her stomach found the object disguised as a belt buckle, the lucky gift from her mother. She slid it back, unsheathing the razor-sharp, six-inch-long stiletto blade concealed in the leather. Her assailant wasn't expecting her sudden thrust.

She surprised herself, feeling no disgust as the blade sliced into the man's stomach with little resistance. It felt like cutting chicken livers. Blood oozed over her hand, and the man's look of surprise was the only thing that made her feel remotely bad.

She twisted the hilt, deepening the wound, and shoved him away. Maybe men were to be avoided. But this one had paid the ultimate price.

∾

"THIS BABE'S DOING my job for me," Jeffers remarked.

"What happened?" Charlie asked, picking up the binoculars and shuffling to the edge on his belly.

"Gutted him. Want me to take her?"

Charlie had spotted the woman. He didn't recognize her, but as she got to work searching the guy she'd just stabbed, he weighed following direct orders against gearing up for a bonus.

"Let's see where she leads," Charlie said. "She might bring others in."

Jeffers angled his face toward Charlie, his scraggly facial hair and nasty, rotten teeth enough to put Charlie off his own product for life. "Whatever you say."

THE FRAMES of the partially-built apartment blocks loomed over Trapp, casting long, jagged shadows between the occasional slice of light. The scent of dusty cement filled the air, and the distant sounds of city life felt worlds away. Ahead, the second building site stretched out, where several foundations had been dug and poured. The one he was interested in still had a ramp for transporting equipment in and out. It looked like a dead end, and it was, but it also served another function.

The foundation was half-finished with a lattice of rebar poles forming the vertical supports. The ramp would be removed eventually, a fourth lattice installed, then the ramp section filled in with cement from the truck above. The L-shaped footprint allowed Trapp to conceal himself from his incoming enemy, and he made sure to disappear downward to leave a hint for his pursuer. There wasn't much tactical cover, but if things worked out, he wouldn't need it.

Keeping an eye on the ramp entrance, Trapp waited for the first sign of pursuit. He was surprised there weren't more operators swarming the area, but then realized every agent Chao activated was a potential liability. If they were already under counter-intelligence surveillance, then they would act as a flashing sign pointing to their boss. Same for the Triads, who held no loyalty to Chao.

Trapp glanced down into the hole. So what if an accident meant it got partially filled a little early? Anyone stuck down here would never be found.

A figure scuttled into view, then quickly ducked away.

"Hey, Sharkie," Trapp called, hoping to rile him up. "Hoping for that rematch?"

Chao slipped into view just long enough for Trapp to pinpoint him.

"This is not a cowboy standoff," Chao called back. "I can retreat, regroup, and come at you again any time."

"This is about more than me. That's why you tried to capture me when you could've just burned that metalworks to the ground. And why you spent so long setting things up with the congressman. You want me? I'm here."

Trapp was relying on Chao's ego and desire for personal revenge. A man like Chao would usually be far more disciplined, but there seemed to be a deeper hurt driving him toward Trapp.

"It's the last chance you'll get," Trapp pressed. "I have the files you want. We have our hostage back. And there's enough evidence to send you and your diplomatic friends packing. You'll be done."

Silence.

"Time's ticking," Trapp said. "As soon as my friend's got his wife out safely, he's coming back for you."

Sooner than that, actually.

But Chao needed another push.

"Jia Ru," Trapp called, the name of Chao's mentor who'd died in Rwanda. "I remember him, you know?"

"He was a great man," Chao called back. "Do not speak his name."

Trapp was getting somewhere, so he pushed it. "Jia Ru. A

decorated former colonel. Working security to a pedophile slavemaster caught bribing government officials in a failed state. A real hero."

"That is a *lie*." Chao was closer, an edge to his voice, anger bubbling. "He was attending on state business. The official your slaver was trying to bribe was one of our collaborators. Jia Ru was there to ensure his safety until a contract was signed."

Trapp frowned. It could have gone down that way. If Jia Ru had been trying to protect the government official, not the asshole Trapp had targeted, then killing him had been a tragic mistake. But it was the Chinese who'd attacked them after they'd extracted the real slavemaster. Trapp would have been an idiot not to protect himself by killing every person who'd been aiming to kill him.

Wars were messy, even covert ones.

Especially covert ones.

"Great man or not, he died screaming," Trapp added.

"Do you think I'm going to just walk in there?" Chao scoffed. "When I am so close to proving to the world what the Chinese and Koreans have always known?"

What the Chinese and Koreans have always known?

No time to unpack that, but it had tripped a trigger in Trapp's head. It pointed to something bigger that he hadn't seen yet.

"How about a show of good faith?"

Trapp held both his hands out in the open, the Sig in one. He ejected the magazine, racked the slide to pop out the round, then dropped the gun at his feet.

"Your turn."

Hesitation.

Then the figure emerged from the lip of the ramp. Trapp kept ducking his head back and forth, his hands still in the open. He didn't want to risk Chao coming to his senses and whipping out a surprise attack.

In truth, Trapp had no interest in ending this with some mano-a-mano nonsense, what Chao had labeled "decadent Hollywood bullshit." At least they agreed on that.

Chao approached, sticking close to the side, working the angle, gun outstretched in case Trapp sprang out to surprise him. Which was tempting. But he and Lamar had a plan, and they needed this part to play out.

"That's far enough," Trapp said.

Chao held the gun upward and turned around so Trapp could see he had no other weapons. Then he held it by the barrel and stepped fully into view.

"This is new for me as well," Trapp said.

"Then let us begin," Chao said and tossed the weapon.

57

L amar was unsure which way was up. Pain lanced through him as blood flowed between his fingers, but he was not dead. He'd been shot less than a week ago, and that gunshot wound to the arm hadn't just incapacitated the limb—it had sapped his energy.

Now a new wave of weakness washed over him. Fang had suckered him, stabbing him with a shiv. She had kicked his gun away, then frantically searched him, finding the thumb drive with the TIPTOE files. Even with Greaves' failsafe, Lamar had taken a huge risk today—one he couldn't have shared with Trapp.

Pressing his wound with one hand, Lamar pushed himself up with the other. No time to search for the gun. He propped himself on the sedan, twisted, and saw Fang running off. Always conscious of the sniper, having calculated the angle from earlier shots fired, he limped heavily after her, sticking to the channels that made a kill shot from the partly-constructed hotel difficult, if not impossible. Each footfall jolted the pain, as if he was being stabbed all over again, but he wouldn't let her escape.

Lamar lumbered past the minivan, his free hand slapping the window to reassure his wife inside, but leaving only a bloody handprint on the glass. He regretted it immediately.

No time.

Must run.

Fang was twenty yards ahead, maybe thirty; it was hard to tell. It felt like he was chasing her uphill as he stayed near the stacks of bricks and breezeblocks to keep from getting his head blown off.

She was slim but not athletic, and Lamar's legs pumped faster than his pulse. He was gaining on her but stumbled as nausea hit. He steadied himself and resumed his pace, willing his thighs to keep going.

The gap closed to ten yards. Nearing the construction site's edge, Fang glanced back, eyes wide, hair over her terrified face. She wasn't a pro, but she had thought fast, completed her objective, and escaped, now bouncing out through the chain-link gate left unlocked.

Lamar only thought about the files she carried.

Hoping any sniper was now blind due to the increasing angle as he neared, he crashed through the gate after her, not considering other dangers. Five feet and gaining.

A black car roared up ahead of her. She halted, giving him a chance to close the last few yards.

With his free hand, he grabbed Fang's elbow. She screamed, and a sting ripped through Lamar's shoulder, loosening his grasp. A gunshot crack followed a split-second later.

∽

"Got him," Jeffers said. "Want me to take the girl now?"

"Yes," Charlie said, his ears still ringing. "Wait 'til I finish my call."

"Hurry."

Charlie lifted his phone, dialed number 3 on his contacts, and when Joey picked up—a guy from his own crew waiting nearby with his two ex-con buddies—Charlie said, "Get in there. There's only two guys and a crippled bitch. Do them all and get gone."

∾

LAMAR'S HAND didn't work. The pain in his gut transferred to the gunshot wound, searing through his shoulder. He dropped to the ground and tried to roll, but was too disoriented.

The black car's rear door opened.

His mind whirred, his vision spun, and the last thing he saw before the world went black was Fang climbing into the limo.

Breathless, terror contorting her face, she had a smear of Lamar's blood on her dress. She stared down at him.

Her terror morphed into a tiny smile.

∾

"MISSED HER," Jeffers stated.

Charlie pushed himself up onto his knees. "You what?"

"More accurately"—Jeffers turned, propped on his elbow—"you made me miss her."

"Yeah?" Charlie had had a shitty couple of days. Maybe once he'd been a true believer in the Song regime. But he'd been in America years, working in the gutter to generate hard cash for his paymasters back home. Technically he was still a North Korean intelligence asset, but he'd figured as long as he sent enough cash home, he'd be forgotten about. And as the years passed, he learned to like America's freedoms. Maybe even begin to think that a man like him could go a long way. And then Hwa Yung-Gi had come into his life. He stiffened. "My fault, huh?"

"Yup." Jeffers spat over the edge, pointing at the other site. "You want me to keep backing up your other boys?"

Charlie had made a decision. "Yes, do that."

And as Jeffers turned his head back to the scope, Charlie Hu pulled out a gun and pointed it at the back of the veteran's head.

Jeffers rolled over onto his back with startling speed, whipping the rifle around, folding stand and all. The barrel flashed, and a huge bang assaulted Charlie's ears.

A thud hit his chest, followed by a piercing pain, like a knife sliding into his ribcage. He staggered, hearing Jeffers laugh, but as he fell, he managed to raise his pistol.

His finger squeezed, the weapon bucked, and the last thing Charlie Hu saw before he died was Samuel Jeffers' head blowing open.

LI CHAO EDGED FULLY into the square that would one day make up the foundation of a luxury condo block.

Trapp maneuvered into position on the balls of his feet, his favored boxer-style position. Chao sank into a low stance that looked exhausting, but also like he could leap forward or backward as if on a spring.

"So this really isn't about embarrassing the CIA," Trapp said. "You're going to kill President Kuk of North Korea before releasing the files. It's about destroying America's influence."

...what the Chinese and Koreans have always known...

That the Americans will assassinate whomever they choose.

"You have figured this out," Chao said condescendingly. "Very clever."

"I just want to know why." Trapp kept his distance from

Chao as they felt one another out. "You're allies. Why are you so paranoid about North Korea accepting Western help?"

Chao refused to speak, just shook his head derisively.

"The deal doesn't encroach on your borders—just the opposite," Trapp added. "It doesn't impact your security."

Chao bit at that, his frame angled for defense. "It is the phrase your media likes to use: the beginning of a 'slippery slope.' If our friends in the North succumb to American charity and accept you as a legitimate ally, you will take the first opportunity to 'help' China next. Your government wants to subjugate China to the same oppression that your civilians think is 'freedom.' But true freedom is when you have no concerns about your rulers, when you are free to go about your business however you choose, as long as you obey the same clear rules as everyone else."

Still no sign of Lamar. If Valerie had taken a turn for the worse, he would have prioritized her, and Trapp would not have blamed him. This meant, though, that Trapp had to improvise his way out of here, as he was unsure that he could keep Chao talking much longer. They had the confirmation that the summit was the target, Project TIPTOE the garnish, and Trapp was just gravy. Shooting Chao dead and burying him here was the next logical step.

"So the summit has to fail and the CIA takes the blame," Trapp said.

Chao ceased circling in his showy kung fu stance, a finger to his ear. "Oh, dear."

He smiled.

"What?" Trapp said.

"They have removed the comms dampeners."

"Why?"

"Can't you guess?"

Trapp felt his stomach dropping away, as if he was on a rollercoaster that had just begun a steep drop. "They have it."

Chao had his back to the wall, which was a cobweb of metal rebar poles for strengthening the concrete foundation. More of a speedbump than a stop sign. He'd eyed it a few times already, and Trapp expected him to make a break that way if he was losing. But they'd been cautious with one another, more a sporting bout than a life-or-death fight.

Were they *both* stalling?

No one else knew they were here except Timothy Greaves, but he would not act until at least 10 a.m., by which time the Chinese could have the leak secure in the embassy.

"Just one last piece of business then," Trapp said, re-firming his position.

"Sir," Chao said, his head tilted, still watching Trapp as he spoke to someone else, probably over an earpiece, "I can finish this."

Trapp threw a hard forward kick, having feigned a punch. Chao danced aside, thrust back with a rally of his own fists, and threw a kick which Trapp back-stepped from. Trapp launched his counter-punch faster than any civilian or gym-trained fighter would have been able to dodge, but Chao spun on the ball of one foot and crashed a hard heel into Trapp's chest, just above his solar plexus. It blew the air out of him, his diaphragm constricting and dumping him into a heap.

He rolled and covered his head, preparing for a further attack. But nothing came.

Chao was still in conversation with someone. "Sir, five minutes and I am done with him."

Trapp struggled for breath, regulating his intake to three seconds, then out for six, increasing each length as he regained his bearings and found himself on one knee.

Chao glared his way. "Yes, you are of course correct. There *are* more important things."

Chao lingered on Trapp for three seconds, his teeth pressed together, eyes boiling with hatred.

He said, "And do not think your pathetic virus on the thumb drive will save you. Our team will disable it offline before the summit."

Then Chao bolted, running upward to ground level and away from Trapp, forgoing the chance to finish him.

AFTER REORIENTING himself and reacquiring his firearm, Trapp took after Chao, only slowing to clear each area as he navigated the maze of half-finished structures and construction equipment. Fatigue nagged at him again, his tender knee jolting every few steps but still holding his weight. But finally he caught a stroke of unbelievable luck, something he had not encountered much over the past week or so.

As he rounded a corner, he spotted Chao moving through the site. He'd caught up somehow.

With the drive secure, he'd expected Chao to disappear, but here he was. And yet...

Was it luck?

Something was off. Chao moved cautiously, his usual agility tempered.

An ambush?

If so, why was he out there where Trapp could see him instead of hiding in one of the many—

Then Trapp saw them—two gangbanger-types, probably sent by the Koreans, since that seemed to be Yung-Gi's main resource. Closing in on Chao.

Trapp's pulse quickened. This was too good. Yung-Gi wanted Chao off the board, and Trapp was happy to help.

He raised his gun, steadied it.

Then a rush of footsteps and a cry of "Hey!" preceded a third gang member lunging at Trapp, a knife in his hand. Must have been sneaking around the side.

Trapp barely had time to react. He blocked the first blow by thrusting his forearm into his attacker's wrist, the blade slicing his sleeve and grazing his skin. Trapp twisted, over-rotated the guy's elbow, and pumped three bullets through his torso.

The other two now turned their attention to Trapp and advanced, guns drawn. Trapp dove for cover behind a stack of plywood sheets as bullets tore through the air. Wood splintered around him, fresh sawdust pluming.

Where had Chao gone?

Trapp fired back. His shots were precise but hurried. Only one of the gangbangers went down, clutching his shoulder, while the other kept coming. Trapp rolled to the other side of the pile, coming up in a crouch and firing. The second thug dropped, his gun clattering to the ground.

Trapp jumped back behind the plywood and waited.

Nothing happened, except the baggy-clothed man groaned a lot.

Trapp carefully edged out, his gun up, sweeping the scene.

Chao had taken his chance and slipped away, disappearing through the shadows and into the city.

Trapp forced himself to run, pain radiating through every part of his body, echoes of the firefight ringing in his ears. "God*damn* it."

58

B y the time Trapp made it back to the minivan and
sedan, the construction site was empty to the point of
eeriness. The three bodies Lamar had dropped
remained in-situ. There was a puddle of blood next to the open
car door and a trail leading to the minivan, where Trapp
opened the back door to check on Valerie.

"It's Lamar. He's hurt. He went after her," she said.

"After who?"

"The girl."

Fang Chen.

Trapp ran from the van, conscious that the sniper had not
attempted to take a shot at him. Had the sniper been one of
those he'd taken out just now?

Unlikely.

But there wasn't time to overthink it.

Spotting more blood droplets in the dirt, he followed them
out to the street, where his friend lay on the sidewalk, more
blood pooling beneath him. People surrounded him, good
Samaritans applying first aid and less-good Samaritans filming
it on their cell phones.

Trapp was about to rush in to help, but sirens rose in pitch, coming closer. Police mixing with an ambulance. They would administer far better treatment than Trapp could.

With his gut pulling itself apart over leaving Lamar, Trapp raced back to Valerie, who had propped herself up on one elbow. She was bandaged and gaunt-looking, though she was free of tubes and wires.

"He's alive," Trapp said. "He's getting treatment."

They could see an ambulance's lights flashing at the end of the row. Cops, still incoming.

Valerie's face knotted as she said, "Get me out of here, Trapp."

"No. We'll wait for—"

"I mean, take me where we can get these bastards. I want to help."

"You should be in the hospital."

"I don't need no damn hospital. My man is down. He might not survive. I can't help patch him back together, but I can sure as hell help you lay some pain down on whoever did it to him. So shut the fuck up and start driving. And fill me in along the way."

TRAPP DROVE them out of the construction site. The diplomatic vehicle's tinted windows hid them from the incoming cops, and the plates would deter any stops, but they'd likely be tracked by the Chinese. He risked the seven minutes to the strip mall parking lot where they'd left the brown panel van in a camera blind spot.

Witnesses gave them odd looks as Trapp carried Valerie to the van as if she were a baby and set her in the passenger seat. He'd offered to set up the gurney in the back, but Valerie insisted there was no time. Though doped up on painkillers, the change in position drew hisses of discomfort even as she insisted she knew her limits. Trapp couldn't deny her requests for information, given all she'd been through. If it became too much, he would drop her at the nearest ER.

Trapp spent twenty minutes filling her in as they drove toward the freeway. Valerie remained steadfast. He doubted anything could change her mind unless a doctor demanded a kidney to save her husband's life.

"That's where we are," Trapp said. "I've brought us to the brink. I'm not sure I can pull us back."

"Anyone else on the team?"

"An IT guy, but he'll stay out of it unless directed otherwise. He said the file would be corrupted on distribution, but I think they're ready for that. I need to warn him."

"That's it? No backup?"

"I fucked up, Val. I have to do the right thing."

Valerie gave a *hmm*. "Sounds like you're planning on giving yourself up."

"Considering it. Not planning. Not yet. But if that's what it takes, I will. I just worry the damage is already done. Feds'll focus more on me breaking into the listening station than anything I might have to say about the summit."

"They won't be that pig-headed."

"There's the question of credibility. I need to feel them out first."

Trapp couldn't repeat his covert meeting on the hiking trail. No time to set it up, and no one would trust him enough to appear. Even Mike Mitchell and Nick Pope couldn't risk associating with him now.

Trapp pulled the sat-phone from under the seat and switched it on. He dialed it one- handed, but Nick's phone only rang and rang, then cut off without going to voicemail.

He tried Mike. The woman who answered when Trapp had

called from Boston picked up. He asked for Deputy Director Mitchell, but she stonewalled him like a pro.

He couldn't drag Ikeda back in, and he'd burned Madison. There were others he could gamble on, but with TIPTOE out there, he wouldn't risk tainting any friends. That left one other number he had memorized.

He dialed, and the line connected on the second ring.

"Drebin."

"You know who this is?" Trapp said. "Don't say my name."

"I'm afraid I don't take orders from the CIA, Mr. Trapp. Although you're no longer affiliated with the Agency, are you? I understand they're not picking up your calls."

Trapp gripped the handset, unsure if Pope and Mitchell believed ill of him or were ghosting him to avoid incriminating themselves.

"Why do you think I'm calling you?" Trapp asked.

"Desperation?"

Valerie raised her eyebrows but said nothing, better not to identify herself on a likely-recorded line.

"I'm ready to come in."

A pause on Drebin's end, then, "Good. You know the address."

"I do. But don't brew a fresh pot just yet."

"You're a fugitive who wants to come in but not yet. If this is some negotiating tactic, save it for the lawyers."

"I need to know you've acted on my information first. Do you have a pen, or will you just play this back later?"

"Why not both?" A click on the line. "I need your whereabouts and assurances your accomplices are unharmed."

"You know exactly who my accomplice is, and he isn't unharmed. I'd appreciate any updates on his condition."

"You'll get that when you swing by Pennsylvania Avenue."

If Drebin knew Valerie was present, he might have softened.

But Valerie's commitment to Trapp meant she needed to conceal her presence. Speaking up was her choice.

Trapp said, "We've identified a Chinese operative under diplomatic cover in the DC area. His name is Li Chao. He is in possession of documents that may embarrass the US government and the CIA, as well as endanger lives. I armed it with a failsafe, but it's possible they will bypass it before releasing it to the world. They'll then use it to justify Chao's actions in New York City."

"This would be the classified files you stole using Madison Grubbs as a patsy?"

"First, I'm glad you know I used her. She didn't deserve that. Second, yes. Have you been briefed on the contents?"

"Above my clearance level. I don't care either. All I need to know is where you are and when you'll hand yourself in."

"No." Trapp kept his frustration in check. "What you need to know is that Li Chao plans to assassinate the President of North Korea, possibly President Son too. He'll use the documents to frame the CIA and—"

Trapp sensed a shift inside his chest, constricting his throat. Why hadn't they thought of that sooner? If Chao couldn't kill Trapp, he'd bring him out into the open, hence the Hangman leaks, knowing Trapp would follow Chao to New York, completing the circle.

"He'll frame the CIA and, if I'm still out there, me specifically. If a disgraced CIA asset were implicated in President Kuk's death, there'd be no clearing our names."

A shuffling and a pause. Trapp wondered if he'd been put on hold, then Drebin said, "How can one man expect to kill a dignitary at an event with more security than our own president?"

"I don't know yet," Trapp said. "But he doesn't lack ambition."

"Where is Li Chao at the moment?"

"Pass on what I told you to Mike Mitchell, Nick Pope, and anyone associated with the security operation. You'll have Li Chao on file, though his picture may be outdated. Take every precaution. When you've apprehended him, I'll come in."

Another shuffle and pause.

"You can't just dump vague clues and expect us to run with it. You took the files. How do we know you won't release more intel? How can we be certain it wasn't you who leaked details about yourself?"

"Maybe you have to trust that I'm on your side and the infamous Chinese assassin isn't."

Trapp hung up. No point in saying more. Either Drebin would act, or he would focus only on Trapp and others would die.

They drove in silence, stopping at traffic lights. There were signs to the hospital and the freeway.

"I'll drop you off, no point in you getting yourself—"

"There's every point. You..." She petered out, then perked back up. "You need another brain to bounce off. Besides..." She took a deep breath. "Besides, I know I'm not exactly sparkling company right now. But I can't be alone."

AFTER A SLOW, careful drive over the rutted approach, Trapp parked in front of the prepper hut canopied by the forest. He helped Valerie into the cabin and set her up on the couch, then found some hefty painkillers, though the brand name wasn't one he recognized. Sounded like it came from a veterinarian. Rather than risk side effects or an overdose, he offered her a combo of Tylenol and Advil before fixing them a chili con carne MRE. They drank from glass water bottles, although Trapp was tempted to break open the bourbon he had stashed on the top shelf.

"So how do you think he'll do it?" Valerie asked, her voice slurring a little. "The Shark. How will he take out the president?"

"No idea. The plan of action is probably out of date, but the section I contributed to for North Korea was basically the current scenario we have."

"The current scenario?"

"We brainstormed these ideas starting with unfriendlies, then added some friendlies. I was given North Korea, Iran, South Africa, and my favorite, New Zealand."

"Why was that your favorite?"

"It's the easiest."

Valerie laughed. "You want easy, you picked the wrong line of work. So how did you plan to kill the North Korean president?"

"First choice would be to persuade someone to do it internally. Failing that, a suicide drone strike. Their air defence bubble isn't exactly what you'd describe as modern. Do it right and it wouldn't necessarily point directly at the United States. But there'd be enough suspicion, so I ruled it out."

Trapp remembered the musty, windowless room where he and half a dozen other grounded operatives had been utilized.

"I suggested getting him out of North Korea. Bring him to America, if possible. We could blame it on a domestic terror cell if we used an IED, and we would stash those IEDs on every possible route, which would prove to the world that the killers didn't know exactly where he would be. But of course, we would. Another possibility was a contact poison, a shake of the hand, a smear left on his seat. It couldn't be something he would have to ingest, because he has all his food tested beforehand."

"Li Chao doesn't strike me as an IED sort of guy."

"Oh, if it worked, he'd do it. But since I contributed my

opinion, technology has moved on. I would bet my life that other people like me have updated the plan since."

Valerie gave him a kind smile. "I don't think there are many people like you, Jason."

Trapp sat back, his water drained, his MRE empty. "Want me to call some hospitals? Find out about Lamar?"

"No," Valerie said firmly. "If he's gone, there's nothing I can do, and if he's okay, there's nothing I need to do. But there's something I can do here."

"What's that?"

"I can inspire a guy who looks like he's about to give up. Whose bosses and colleagues don't trust him."

"For good reason." Trapp was again thinking of Madison.

"Honey." Her head leaned back onto the pillows, eyes hooded, ready to sleep again. "You don't have to figure out what Li Chao will do. There are only so many options. Maybe just one. So, Jason Trapp, who compares to no one when it comes to tracking down high-value targets and removing that target if required... what would he do?"

"What would I do?"

"Imagine President Nash has ordered you to kidnap or kill President Kuk, and you agree that killing him will save thousands of American lives. And you know where he's going to be." Her eyes closed. "How would *you* kill the president of North Korea?"

What *would* Jason Trapp do?

He mulled it over while Valerie slept. Eventually, he succumbed to temptation, cracking open the bourbon and pouring himself a swollen finger before stepping out onto the porch to drink it.

He had no inside information. There simply wasn't enough intel for him to create a thorough hypothesis.

He sipped and was transported back to the bar shortly before the shooting. He had relaxed more that night than he had for some time. It would have been nice to sit with friends, to laugh, to reminisce, to have nothing to do except simply... *be.*

Then everything had turned upside down.

He finished the bourbon before he realized that he was considering another, but that would mean dulling his senses.

If President Kuk were to die tomorrow, his daughter Myo Il-Song would take the reins alongside her husband, a high-ranking general. If she were to die too, they might install her teenage son with some kind of regent until he came of age.

Trapp opened his eyes.

North Korean leaders were like royalty, the presidency passing from parent to child along a preordained line. Although they were not keen on women in authority, Myo had clamped down on dissidents and voiced disapproval at any hint of compromise with imperialists. It was likely she'd passed that on to her sons.

If like-minded souls within China were to rid her of her father's softening influence, if he died before this summit became his legacy, it would be the perfect time to sour relations with the West even further.

Legacy.

Why was that ringing a bell?

Because, Trapp thought, that was how he was going to win.

He risked turning the sat-phone back on and rummaged through his pockets to find one of the numbers he had not yet memorized.

The line opened without a greeting.

Trapp said, "Have you ever been to the Big Apple?"

59

New York City had seen its fair share of security operations over the years, but President Nash was reliably informed that this was most certainly the biggest. His morning coffee was the rich, deep roast he favored, and he found his early hours oddly relaxing, watching the city wake up through the floor-to-ceiling window of the suitably named Presidential Suite. There were twelve snipers on the roof, and the floor below had been cleared, permitting no access except for those on the security detail or in the president's inner circle. Beyond the window was a ballistic shield that refracted the light ever so slightly without impeding his view, while the other side was mirrored, so he could stand here naked and no one observing the hotel would see him.

Not that he was naked this morning. He was dressed in his most presidential suit with his most presidential tie, anticipating the most presidential of days.

His chief of staff had turned down the offer of coffee, as she did not drink caffeine anymore, nor did she consume meat, or dairy, or anything animal-related. She did, however, plan every little step to the nth degree, which was the saving grace that meant he kept her around. She was also fond of recapping itineraries.

Every silver lining has a cloud above it.

"You've given all the concessions you're willing to, including moving the American naval drills farther south. Both presidents will sign the preliminary documents at the UN building, they will make their speeches, and the delegates will vote on the motion to ease agricultural sanctions. Once the initial agreement is in place, you can make your victory speech, thanking everyone, and the official signing ceremony will take place at the White House tonight, which will rubber-stamp the aid package. You just need Congress to agree to the budget, then we'll allocate the farming subsidies, and a new phase in cooperation commences."

"*A new phase in cooperation,*" Nash said. "Are you writing my speeches now?"

"No, Mr. President, but if you want..." She offered a little smile, which she rarely did. "The security operation appears to be a success. No incidents overnight."

"I should hope not." Nash had balked at the scale, but more than one agency had convinced him it was necessary—entire city blocks cordoned off just for the Koreans and an entire hotel for each of the presidents and their families. FDR Drive along the East River closed, then from East 37th Street, back to 3rd Avenue, and up to East 54th. "I can't wait to get the bill for this one."

A door opened. Nash was not unduly alarmed when the head of his Secret Service detail entered, a former Navy SEAL by the name of Powell.

"Marine One is ready for you, sir."

"I'll be right with you." When the veteran was gone, Nash faced his chief of staff. "Any word from Nick or Mike?"

"Only what Agent Drebin sent through yesterday. No whispers, nothing on the airwaves. The TIPTOE files will fire an alert as soon as it's accessed on an open line, so we'll know where to go and how to block it. Probably."

"I don't like the word 'probably.'"

"Nor do I, sir."

"They've brought Greaves in to help?" Nash asked.

"Yes. He analyzed the hack that piggybacked on Madison Grubbs' login details and recognized the code as Russian. We will be appealing for extradition shortly, not that we'll get anything from the Russians. How Trapp knows him, I have no idea."

JASON TRAPP'S aching body had sprouted several more kinks this morning, having woken on the bed of the van he'd driven from DC. He groaned as he turned over and winced as he stretched and twisted, then tested his injuries. He considered himself remiss for not establishing a safehouse in New York City. Maybe he should play the Powerball more often and set himself up in every major US city.

Better leave enough over for the world's key capitals while you're at it...

In the absence of a billion-dollar fortune, Trapp had driven down overnight from his bolt hole in Maryland. He'd allowed Valerie to keep the sat-phone at the shack, which she could use to call for help if her condition worsened. Otherwise, she'd be Trapp's contact, routing his calls to evade tracking.

Though he knew little about the security operation, he had Internet access via one of two new burners. The plans for the closed-off streets had been announced weeks in advance, allowing businesses to prepare for the forty-eight-hour disruption encompassing the blocks surrounding the delegates' hotels and the three possible routes to the UN Assembly Building. Four, if he included the East River.

Trapp figured most security would focus on those streets and adjacent ones, so he checked into a cash-only dive three miles away from the nearest cordon to assemble the meager equipment he could get. Coming here sooner risked discovery, which was why he'd slept in the van. Valerie had vouched for him with her contacts down south, who had connected Trapp with people in New Jersey. He used the last of his cash for a rifle, spare ammo for his Sig Sauer, and a combination of low-key supplies to flush out Chao.

Facial recognition might pick him up given a clear view, but witnesses would have seen him sporting thick stubble, close to a beard, which had helped him remain anonymous earlier. But since the authorities knew his previous look, he had to change.

He gave himself a close shave, then cut his hair close to his scalp with electric clippers, a touch longer on top than around the sides. Like a new recruit at basic training, just a tad older.

He inventoried what he'd need, laying the items out on the ratty bed. One of the burner phones pinged, a dumb-phone that only sent texts and made calls. The text came from an unlisted phone number.

We're here. Are you sure this is going to work?

Trapp replied:

If you do exactly what I said. Be ready. 2 hours

MADISON GRUBBS HAD ONCE CONSIDERED Jason Trapp a good friend. She'd hoped to work with him again someday—but his rare blend of compassion and competence had blinded her to his intentions. She knew people in this trade often lacked scruples, especially with foreign agents, but she never expected to be on the receiving end of it.

Though not officially suspended, she was sure it was imminent, with disciplinary action to follow. The only reason it hadn't happened yet was Paolo Drebin, the FBI agent who had interrupted the grilling from her supervisor.

Now she was riding with Drebin in an unmarked car, both their names on a special list that granted access through all cordons around the UN Assembly Building.

"How do you know he'll be here?" Madison asked.

"I'm good at my job," Drebin replied dryly.

"I'm sure you are. And I appreciate you giving me this chance. But I could do with knowing a bit more."

"I am not 'giving you a chance.' I'm utilizing a witness who has worked closely with my suspect. You might have some instincts that could help if he shows up."

"But why would he?"

Drebin halted behind a line of cars at yet another ID check. Madison thought it was security theater, as those who got this far had already been thoroughly checked.

"Because I don't believe he's a bad guy," Drebin said.

Madison looked at him dubiously.

Drebin eased the car forward. "There's nothing in his past to point at treason. He may have taken the files under duress. But the moment they're released on a live system, they're supposed to trigger a virtual alarm, or so the tech guy concluded. The bigwigs believe him. Think he's some sort of god in this field. But Trapp said the Chinese could have disabled it. They're certainly aware of it."

"Are you sure this tech isn't helping Trapp?"

"Not entirely. But without evidence, I can't act."

"What evidence do you have that Trapp will be here?"

"He insists this is where Li Chao will be. And from what I've learned about Trapp, he won't stand back. He's either coming here to stop this supposed assassination or laying low."

"Making him a good guy?"

"Making him well-intentioned. But his good intentions have made him dangerous. I need to bring him in. And I need you to help pre-empt him."

That was good enough for Madison. Even if Trapp was right and all this was for good reasons, he still deserved a punch in the mouth. If the punch came from a beefed-up inmate in a federal penitentiary, she would accept that.

"I'll sure as hell try," she said.

THE AMBASSADOR'S unreserved praise for Fang Chen upon her delivery of the files had surprised her, as she didn't think Ambassador Wen appreciated either Li Chao's operation or presence. It seemed a dutiful endeavor, simply following orders. But once Wen had the thumb drive, his enthusiasm for Chao's mission grew, particularly after he detailed a team of computer experts to examine the contents of the drive. She did not know what they'd found, but the ambassador had seemed troubled as he instructed her to take some time to recover, saying he recognized her stress and anxiety but warning that there was one last thing required of her.

She traveled in a limo from Washington that afternoon—a surprisingly short trip at just shy of four hours. They rarely ventured beyond DC, so this would normally have been a tantalizing treat: a luxurious American hotel, a huge bed to herself, and room service. Of course, she wasn't permitted to go sightseeing, and two security personnel were posted at her door for her safety.

Despite a fitful night's sleep, she now presented a professional appearance in a white blouse and black skirt, as Wen preferred, her special belt left behind so it set off no alerts. She joined him in the limo scheduled to carry them to the Assembly.

Ambassador Wen showed her the thumb drive, reminding her why they were here, but she still didn't know their plan. The death of Fabian Pincher had brought too much heat on their pet congressman, so they had to keep their distance.

Wen switched on a chunky laptop. "This computer has one purpose only. It is linked to a communications satellite and will download the contents of this drive, then transmit the files to every news outlet and consulate worldwide."

"Why must we wait?" Fang just wanted this over with. She could cope with illicit meetings, blackmailing American assassins, and even stabbing a man to escape. But Wen's change—from reluctance and skepticism to anticipation—was unsettling. "Ambassador, if we release it now and leave the computer to be found in a coffee shop somewhere, our hands are clean."

Wen smiled, and for a moment she thought he might pat her head like a puppy, but he kept his hands to himself.

"The file is infected with a virus. There were three stages to this—what our IT people called a 'flare,' an alarm to notify the authorities; a blocker; and corruption software. We believe we have removed the damaging sections, but the alarm is embedded in the data itself. They may intercept it, so we must wait for the right time, when it can reach our secure satellite *and* when it will have the most impact. The timing, Fang, is crucial. And it is almost upon us."

Hwa Yung-Gi patrolled the hotel room, wrinkling his nose at the strong floral aroma from the enormous bouquet on the central table, a request from Myo Il-Song. The president's daughter had claimed this huge suite, choosing the bedroom off to Yung-Gi's left for herself and placing her eight- and ten-year-old daughters in a smaller room with twin beds. Her husband had remained home with their sixteen-year-old son.

The main living area also had a gym station with a rack of weights and a bench—provided so Myo Il-Song could exercise safely in private, while the rest of the room had social seating, cabinets, and chillers full of soft drinks and alcohol, plus all the utensils and coffee-making paraphernalia they could wish for. They'd kept the adjoining room open, which housed Myo's father.

Yung-Gi was satisfied with his inspection. But not with himself.

He had failed, and his throat and chest felt heavy with shame. He'd faced his superior officer, who had arrived in New York with the presidential detail, and confessed that the potential threat he'd perceived in Li Chao, a former MSS operative well known in Korea, was still at large. But the evidence he'd presented was insufficient to convince the commanders to notify the president of Yung-Gi's speculation.

But they hadn't lived here the past few days. They hadn't followed the trails Yung-Gi had, from the Triads working for Li Chao to the Hangman operative. They hadn't seen the strange meeting at the former Chinese Embassy residence, which had looked—according to Charlie Hu—like an exchange of sorts.

The fact that Charlie was now dead, along with the lowlife killers he'd recruited, had also caused Yung-Gi to push back on his commanders' decision harder than usual. Harder than was proper.

Given that he could not promise to keep his theories to himself, Yung-Gi was taken off the primary detail and assigned to Myo Il-Song and her family, who went shopping and dining out on the eve of the summit and now planned to watch it on TV.

At least, Yung-Gi thought, they would see if he was correct, live on the news.

~

As Nash had done many times over the last five years, he climbed out of the White Hawk's sliding door, the wind blasting him the face as he placed his feet squarely on the ground, his head down. The mob of Secret Service agents escorted him under the buffeting rotors to a pair of doors leading into the UN Assembly building's roof space.

There was no postponing it, no suspending proceedings for a few hours. It all had to unfold as planned.

If Trapp was right that Li Chao had a feasible strategy for taking out the North Korean president, the summit would descend into madness. Accompanied by the release of the TIPTOE files, there would be no coming back for either the CIA or America's credibility on the world stage. No matter what evidence they presented to the contrary.

Nash's route was executed with maximum diligence and efficiency—through the utilitarian upper levels, metal doors clanging open as they took a circuitous route, into a freight elevator, then down and out through a catering store. Nash would have preferred to walk in through the main lobby, but the people paid to think about such things said Marine One was as good as a grand entrance, conveying strength and enhancing his presidential credentials.

The pace picked up as they entered a space with carpet and painted walls, portraits and sculptures, and Nash pulled ahead of his detail. Anyone ahead of him would be there by design.

They came to a halt facing two closed doors.

Powell, the former SEAL, listened to his earpiece and replied using his throat's mic. "Coming through now."

The doors opened, and Nash absorbed the barrage of

flashes and static lights bearing down on him from the wide, low-ceilinged hall hosting the welcome party. He walked out, practiced at not recoiling, smiling as if none of it bothered him.

The way parted, and before Nash stood a middle-aged woman, President Son Seo-Yeun of South Korea, and an elderly man, President Kuk Il-Song of North Korea. Back home he was the Supreme Leader. But that title just wouldn't fly with the American public, so the diplomats had fashioned a landing zone that left nobody's nose out of joint. It had been decided in advance that he would shake the hand of his ally first, so he extended it toward Son. She shook it and gave a shallow bow, which he reciprocated.

He then faced President Kuk, smiled warmly, and shook the hand of a man whose hubris had brought famine to his country and the deaths of tens of thousands—perhaps more. Both men remained upright as they held the pose for five seconds of camera flashes. President Kuk had dark eyes set deep in a wrinkled face. He looked gaunt. Nash had been prepped for this by the rumors of sickness in his intelligence brief; seeing him in the flesh only confirmed that it was worse than the spooks thought.

When the two presidents finally disengaged, Nash turned to the assembled press, sandwiched between both presidents, and waited for quiet.

"Thank you all for coming today."

He surveyed the other delegates, the ambassadors of two dozen countries present to witness history.

"Ladies and gentlemen, I'm sure you're all craving a juicy quote. But the big speeches will happen later. For now, let's just enjoy this moment as we welcome our guests and extend the hand of friendship. We are all on the cusp of a new era."

60

A disguise would only go so far, which meant Trapp could only expect to fool people in person for a short time. He had no such issue in his current bolt hole, where he had heard the same woman singing the "Oh My God" song to the tune of creaking mattress springs four times since he'd checked in that morning.

Before embarking on what could be his final mission, Trapp penned a note in case he died or was apprehended and accused of treason, espionage, and possibly murder.

He stated that he had been the instigator of all actions relating to the theft of the TIPTOE files and that Madison Grubbs was an unwitting participant. He claimed that any others who might seem to be involved were working under duress, although he did not name anyone.

His final point was that he believed he'd equipped the leak with sufficient failsafes and had been working in the best interests of his country, emphasizing that nothing he did was for personal gain.

Trapp sealed the letter in an envelope and addressed it to Paulo Drebin, who he believed would be the one mostly likely to search this room should Trapp not return—and the least likely to cover it up.

Then he was ready.

He pulled on the jacket and attached the necessary straps, belt, and weapons, then donned the distinctive hat: it was unlikely that he'd pass as a friendly if stopped at a checkpoint, but he didn't believe that would be a problem.

He set out and closed the door behind him.

ZHEN GUANYU WAS thirsty for revenge. Dennis could tell by the tension in his neck and his fidgeting fingers as he looked out the second-story window. They had set up in an art studio off 3rd Avenue in Manhattan, now cleared for the event that had sparked all this trouble. The studio owner was the hipster offspring of a millionaire, sympathetic to the Triad business model—especially where it helped him skirt customs rules that were crippling his business.

Dennis had delivered the tip that Jason Trapp would be in New York for the summit. When Zhen asked where he got this information, Dennis said it was from their employer, Li Chao— the man whose interference, Dennis believed, had led to Madame Guanyu's death.

"Li Chao is off the books," Dennis said. "There are factions back in China that don't agree with what's happening today, and I think he's working with one of them."

"What does that have to do with the bastard who killed my mother?"

Dennis pressed his tongue against the back of his teeth to avoid snapping. Zhen's ascent to head of the Boston chapter hadn't been made official yet, although it would be soon. At that point, Dennis knew, he'd be back on the job market.

I cannot work for this child.

"Trapp is going to try to stop Li Chao from completing his mission here," Dennis said, gritting his teeth. "He will approach from that direction and move through the streets. It's the only weak point."

Zhen looked out the second-story window. Three of the walls had windows: the rear facing Park Avenue, the longest side looking into a mall-like space, and the frontage over-looking one of the forbidden zones.

"We know the timetable," Dennis continued. "So we can make an educated guess at when he'll funnel through."

Zhen pulled back from the window and studied the foot soldiers. They had brought six from Boston, and four more had been drafted by their New York hosts. It wasn't a typical collaboration, but today was special. They believed Trapp had killed Madame Guanyu, who was one of their own. Even though Zhen's bullets had taken her life, he continued to blame Trapp; there was still no sign of conscience or guilt in the boy.

"He'll be here," Dennis assured him.

A couple of the Triad gunmen picked up on the tension and glanced their way but held their positions around the studio.

Dennis had never pledged loyalty to Zhen Guanyu. He had served Zhen's mother and would honor her legacy out of duty. Today, he thought, was a different kind of duty.

"Is that him?" one of the men at the back of the studio asked.

Zhen jogged over. Dennis joined him and tracked the police officer as he wound through the pedestrians. The covered space, once an entire street, was locked, but the cop fiddled with one of the doors for a few seconds. He checked around, nodded to a passerby, then entered.

"Okay," Zhen said. "We've got him."

∼

THE BUILDING WAS LOCKED on the west side and patrolled on the east. Trapp gained entry with a pick set and a sturdy screwdriver. He had borrowed the NYPD uniform from one of Valerie's contacts and arranged a photo ID that would probably hold up to a cursory check, but not the thorough scan he might face later. There would be lists and assignments, and Trapp was on none of them.

He used inserts in his shoes to disguise his gait. While he preferred not to alter his face as he had in Washington—it could fall apart under scrutiny—the cap should suffice for security cameras, which tended to shoot from above. He just needed one more element to slot into place.

The street-like mall was covered with a glass ceiling and lined with empty stalls, and was probably a bohemian paradise on the right day. This was the weak point that he believed offered him the best chance, but only if Dennis Rhee came through.

The Triads were scum, ruining the lives of all those they touched. But while Dennis was part of that world and had likely committed unforgivable crimes, he was still Trapp's best option to rid them all of Li Chao forever.

Trapp had been in tighter spots and tracked by more experienced goons than Zhen's people. He had spotted the shadows at the second-floor windows as soon as he closed the door and stuck to the far wall so they could watch him. The exit at the far end was tempting, but the likelihood of being surprised by a patrolman within the three-block UN cordon was too great.

He branched away from the line he had been holding, crossed the street, and slipped between two empty stalls. He shouldered out through a fire exit, entering a different building rather than exiting to the street.

The indoor market was a warren of corridors crammed with compact boutique stores not much bigger than the market stalls outside. He pulled his Sig Sauer, expecting that superior firepower was on its way, then tried two doors before finding a third unlocked. He secured a suppressor to his pistol and hid himself in the store, which appeared to stock traditional Kenyan formalwear.

It didn't take long for two men to appear outside the storefront, clearly mimicking the operators they saw in the movies, rather than knowing why they were doing anything at all. Their hand and arm positions weren't too far off, but their footwork betrayed a distinct lack of practice.

Trapp nosed his gun out and fired twice. Both heads expelled a mist of gray and red. They fell silently, except for their guns clattering to the ground. The suppressor didn't muffle the reports entirely but ensured the pops wouldn't carry far enough to betray his position.

Trapp was already moving as he heard reinforcements coming.

He sped out the door, slowed briefly to take out two incoming Triads, then pushed on through another branch of the rabbit warren.

He ran hard as others closed in behind him. One was up front. He raised the gun and fired twice. Double tap. The man fell before Trapp veered left into a fancy-dress shop. Then he continued out the back, making plenty of noise.

"Okay, okay. Which way?"

The plans were public record, so he knew where he wanted to go. He just had to be sure he picked the right corridor, as there were four of them. He counted them off: one... two... and moved to his left where he waited.

He heard yelling in Chinese, replies higher-pitched than the orders. Then he listened as the footsteps encroached.

Time for his big gamble.

He removed the suppressor, poked his gun around the corner, and aimed at the four approaching killers, firing until his gun racked empty, the din echoing around the passages. At least three of the incoming men fell; whether they were dead or not, he didn't know and didn't really care.

Trapp ejected the magazine while running down the corridor and reloaded within seconds, slipping the empty mag back into his police belt. He kicked open a door, splintering the lock, and emerged into a wide, narrow café. Wooden tables and chairs were arranged in singles, doubles, and groups of ten.

He pressed onward, taking cover behind the food counter, hit by competing aromas of coffee and disinfectant, as well as the odor of a fridge whose power had been cut.

Aiming at the entrance he'd come through, he kept the three other ingresses in sight. The windows overlooked the closed-off street that he needed to reach.

"We're coming for you," Zhen shouted from somewhere Trapp couldn't see.

"That's fine," Trapp called back. "I brought you a present."

"Come out and I'll kill you quick."

"Has that ever in the history of bad guy clichés ever worked?"

"Shut the fuck up and die."

Two young men breached the café with semi-automatics braced at their shoulders, firing indiscriminately. The cash register and bottles of syrup exploded, and a cart stacked with bussing trays was perforated with random fire.

Trapp could have picked them off, but as bullets struck the bright windows to the street, he turned his gun that way instead. He fired four times, spiderwebbing the glass first, then shattering it completely. Though he hadn't seen anyone outside, he knew help could not be far behind.

The two gunmen paused, and Trapp sidestepped out with them in his sights.

"Freeze! NYPD!"

The pair did just that, their eyes wide with surprise. More disposable assets, Trapp supposed.

Two more emerged from a different entrance, and Trapp eased back behind the cooler for cover. It would take a lucky shot for them to inflict any damage. But this pair was accompanied by Zhen Guanyu himself, wielding his .44 Magnum.

"You're cornered," Zhen bragged.

"Are you sure?"

Trapp had a clear shot at the first two, but a corner wall made it difficult to take out Zhen directly.

"Everyone unload on that bastard," Zhen ordered.

The four men started shooting, bullets battering Trapp's hiding place, the cooler that usually held sandwiches and pastries. It pinged and dented, the rattle of gunfire echoing all around. The wall behind him shredded, the floor torn up beside him, and he couldn't get a shot off as the four men spread out—they were better organized than their predecessors.

Then the gunfire stopped. Trapp peeked out, his adrenaline spiking hard. Two were reloading while the others held a bead on his location. A colossal boom thundered, and a fist-sized chunk of metal flew off too close to Trapp for comfort. Zhen was a better shot than Trapp had given him credit for.

"You're dead, motherfucker," Zhen boasted.

"And you talk too much," Dennis Rhee said, coming in behind Zhen.

Trapp peeked out in time to see Rhee holding a black duffel in one hand and a handgun in the other, aimed at Trapp's hiding place.

"What the fuck are you—" Zhen started.

Rhee switched his aim and pulled the trigger. Zhen's head burst with a spray of brain, blood, and bone, dropping him to the ground. The other four men hesitated, one lifting his gun toward Dennis, then back to Trapp, unsure where the danger lay.

But there was no danger. Not from Dennis. Not from Trapp,

unless they gave him a reason. Only Dennis had known the true plan, and he'd encouraged Zhen to go out guns blazing to seal his own fate. Trapp should have been the one to take him down, but Dennis had no qualms. Madame Guanyu had expressed a desire for Dennis to take over the Boston Guild, and with Zhen gone, he was her only legacy.

"Get out of here," Trapp said.

Dennis glanced at the men Zhen had been willing to sacrifice and said, "Wait here five minutes."

Rhee departed down the smaller passage via the kitchen, but there would be no five minutes. During the standoff between Trapp and the last four Triads, at least ten NYPD officers had assembled, accessed the building, and coordinated on their position. Four converged on the street outside the broken window while six more swarmed in from the street entrance, shouting warnings and surrounding the gunmen.

Trapp's backup, even if they didn't know it yet.

He remained hidden, adjusted his uniform, dusted himself off, and glided out from cover, his gun trained on the Triads. There were enough officers here for him to lose himself.

"Put your weapons down, hands on your head," the lead officer ordered.

The gangsters looked at each other, made a silent agreement, and raised their weapons. One of them even got a shot off. It was the last thing any of them would do before six cops opened fire, cutting them down where they stood.

Trapp broke free in the chaos, stopping only long enough to collect the small NYPD-branded duffel that Dennis had left for him before he exited into the street, mingling briefly with the cops arriving en masse before penetrating the first stage of the iron shield around the UN.

61

Looking out over the fan of seats radiating from the central podium, Nash finished his speech and absorbed the applause from the packed assembly. It never failed to prick the hairs on his neck—success where most had failed was his biggest thrill. With perhaps the exception of his opiate bill, this might be the finest contribution to his legacy to date. He just needed to get it over the line. And the delegations, each with six seats facing the rostrum and interpreters in booths farther back providing real-time translations, would be instrumental in the final phase. Each nation had a vote that—barring any last-minute hiccups—would go Nash's way.

He had a teleprompter but chose not to use it; he'd practiced the speech so many times he knew the pauses, intonations, and key moments better than anyone. He had made personal touches, veering off script twice to emphasize crucial points. His focus was not on himself or even the United States, but on President Son Seo-Yeon's magnificent proposal to aid their northern brethren, and Kuk Il-Song's bravery in reconciling with former enemies. On the fly, Nash changed a paragraph about nuclear "disarmament" to "de-escalation" when he saw Kuk's face harden.

The applause rose as the majority of nations stood, and Nash accepted their show of respect. He lingered just long enough to be polite, finishing with handshakes for Presidents Son and Kuk before leaving the floor to the gathered press.

Secret Service Agent Powell informed him briefly of a shooting two miles away, some local gang conflict that had been contained by NYPD. Nash thanked him and—having rehearsed this part of the day almost as much as the speech—faced the microphones, answering questions with the smoothness of a seasoned politician.

But the final question was unexpected.

"Mr. President," said a man with a Fox News lanyard, "can you speculate on the shootout we're hearing about? Is it related to your presence here today?"

"Well, Blake," Nash said, recalling the man's name, "I don't know if you've seen the operation we have here, but even I have to show my ID before entering the building."

A ripple of laughter.

Nash waited for confirmation they understood before concluding, "I am aware of the incident, and it has been handled. A local matter which the fine members of NYPD have resolved. Rest assured that if anything were to escalate, we have the best in the business monitoring and patrolling the city."

THE MOBILE MONITORING hub had arrived on the back of a heavy goods vehicle which Greaves had joked resembled Optimus Prime from *Transformers*. It was an open line, like a news gallery, with long desk benches down each side. And two distinct groups: the personnel charged with protecting President Nash and those monitoring for rogue agent Jason Trapp or suspected Chinese assassin Li Chao.

Madison and Drebin were granted a corner of their own and headphones with mics tapped into a five-way conversation. Joining Madison and Drebin on the line were Pope, Mitchell, and Greaves, who was waiting anxiously for the first hint that the tracker Trapp installed in the files had been detected.

Alongside Drebin were three others. Catherine Fernandez watched for incursions on the outskirts of the cordon, for vehicles or armed individuals who might attempt a forced entry.

Kamar Tucker was on the facial recognition scanners, which also automatically analyzed the manner of a person's walk, the shape of their body, and anyone displaying deception indicators, such as hiding within a hoodie or pulling their cap down low.

Finally, Laura Hart was a heavily-pierced and tattooed girl barely out of her teens, tracking comms and social media. When Madison said she doubted Trapp or Li Chao was going to release a TikTok of their intentions, Laura had given her a patient smile and stated that it wasn't their accounts she was monitoring but anyone in the vicinity who might incidentally capture someone they could feed into Kamar's software. She would also listen for keywords on cell phones and every satellite frequency they could breach. And Laura held a potent backup option if it was needed.

"He hasn't tried to make contact with me again," Mike Mitchell stated, leading off from the conversation.

Pope said, "Me neither, but you never know with Trapp. He'll either pop up when we're least expecting it, or he'll stay dark until it's over."

∼

No CAMERAS WERE ALLOWED in the conference room set off from the Secretary General's office. This was a formal meeting where declarations would be signed once a couple of final disputes in the wording could be worked out.

They had set up with a round table much like the knights in King Arthur's court. World leaders were a lot like children, Nash had long thought. They fought and squabbled over the tiniest indicators of status. God forbid another was given the seat at the head of the table. A little thing like that could start a war.

The documents came out, the respective presidents and advisors at their bosses' sides. Only Nash was alone, trusting the Korean translators. The mood was thick, and smiles were in short supply, although negotiations had been, if not friendly, then cordial. They had now arrived firmly at the business end of the deal, and the final opportunity to back out.

Nash had wrangled Congress to agree agricultural subsidies —enriching American farmers without lining the pockets of too many billionaire corporations, and in turn allowing North Korea to purchase what they needed at a discount. They were, as far as they were concerned, paying their way without charity.

In exchange for allowing the Americans to help feed their population, they would put their uranium enrichment programs on ice and disband two full divisions. In return, the number of American troops in South Korea would be reduced by twenty percent, with all future military exercises a minimum of a hundred kilometers from North Korean sovereign territory.

Most importantly, a pathway to full de-escalation had been drawn up. It would take years, if not a decade, for the planned sequence of bilaterals and military confidence-building efforts to pay off. But this initial offer was a small price to pay for a foot in the door, even though the Chinese objected to their neighbor cozying up to the feared imperialist Americans.

Ultimately, Nash was making the world safer for future generations of all their countries.

"Thank you, everyone," he said. "Let us begin."

62

Trapp kept his posture upright, duffel slung over one shoulder like a low-ranking patrolman on an errand as he strode forward. He was now on the inside, but a final checkpoint remained before he could access the UN Plaza.

No one stopped him.

The UN complex was situated on 1st Avenue, bordered by 42nd Street to the south and 48th to the north, with the East River patrolled by the US Coast Guard. The fastest route was up East 45th, but it was also the riskiest.

Trapp stiffened as he passed an NYPD officer, but the man simply nodded his way. He returned the greeting and kept going.

Ahead, barriers and cones marked the transition from safety to scrutiny. Secret Service agents and cops mixed with a heavy UN security presence. Anyone entering needed their name on a list.

Everybody except Trapp.

He turned right, toward the northern part of the five-story General Assembly Building, where flags fluttered above the sculpture dedicated to non-violence.

Then a commotion drew his attention. Suited agents at the top of East 45th touched their ears, looking around in not-quite a panic but a state of high alert. Men like this did not panic.

As if obeying the same radioed command the agents parted, and a unit of the FBI's Hostage Rescue Team poured out of the UN Plaza and onto the street.

INSIDE THE MOBILE MONITORING HUB, Madison was at the point in surveillance that always drove her crazy. Her fingers twitched, longing for something to do other than flicking between screens she couldn't control. She didn't expect to spot something the experts missed, but that fantasy kept her going as her latest caffeine buzz dropped off a cliff.

Fatigue was the absolute worst.

Jason Trapp could jump up at the camera and give a manic wave like Kermit the Frog, and Madison would groan, ease herself out of her chair, and go do her job. It would be a relief more than a rush at this point.

Just as she was about to suggest a coffee and donut run, Kamar sat upright, making a clattering noise that turned every eye in the hub toward him.

"I think I've got something," he said. "A partial hit."

Madison switched her view to mirror Kamar's, leaning forward. "Like the fourteen others?"

"Yeah, but this one's different." He switched from the automated software, keeping it running in the background. He brought up six artificially-generated photos of what Trapp might look like: shaved, bearded, mustache, glasses, cap, and a police uniform hat.

Kamar zoomed in, and Madison moved to watch over his shoulder. The two were virtually ear to ear as Kamar mapped several angles. He set a dot on the man's jaw, another on his lip, and two more from his lip to his chin. Enhancing that section, he fed it to the software before a box popped up and scrolled with data.

"It's him," Kamar said. "East 45th. He's coming right at us."

~

TRAPP MAINTAINED his path as the HRT guys sprinted his way. The team was well drilled and confident in their movement. Every fiber in him screamed for him to turn and run, but he ignored his instincts and pushed himself onward as his hand went to the butt of his gun in case it was needed, as did every other cop.

If he panicked, it was definitely over.

So don't.

~

MADISON AND DREBIN FELL BACK, the remote camera feed and two HRT body cams now cast into an iPad handed to Madison as the team of eight channeled out. Trapp had been marked on the screens attached to their arms, so they would laser in on him like a guided missile.

There!

Madison and Drebin watched the team surround Trapp in a semicircle, and Trapp started shouting back and stabbing the air with his finger. On the audio, the lead HRT agent ordered Trapp to get down on the ground.

They had him.

He refused at first, and for a moment, Madison wondered if he would attempt to fight his way out. The body cam streamed Trapp's face feigning surprise and confusion.

Something's wrong.

"It's a trick," Madison said. "He wouldn't be this easy to catch. Unless he wanted to be caught."

Drebin grunted something inaudible, clearly not caring much either way.

From their post, they watched the HRT lead reach for Trapp, grab him by the scruff of his vest, and drag him forward.

On the screen, Trapp seemed to give up; he fell to his knees, then to his belly, hands on the back of his head. Others moved in, disarmed him, cuffed him, and lifted him to his feet.

Madison radioed, "Trapp is in custody. We have him."

"Intact?" Mitchell asked.

"Unharmed." Madison watched them hustle Trapp up the street beyond the cordon. She progressed toward him, balling her right hand into a tight, hard fist. "He might have suffered a bloody lip during the arrest."

Drebin frowned at her. But as she squinted his way, he raised a finger and was clearly about to say something when the hostage rescue team delivered Trapp before her, and she clenched her fist as she wound up the hardest punch of her life.

But she did not hit him. Her throat tightened and a chill ran down her back.

The man in custody was maybe twenty-five years old, with green eyes and a pug nose. Although he had a decent build, he was most definitely not Jason Trapp.

"Greaves," she groaned, shock driving the air from her lungs. "Damnit, I was right."

TRAPP'S RISK had reaped its reward—a trick he had not been sure would work, despite huge advances in AI and Greaves' promise that his fingers were fast enough to keep up with the ever-changing camera angles. He was now in a shirt and tie, having removed his cop's jacket, vest, and utility belt. The tie had come in the duffel bag along with a blazer, which he also wore, and an ID acquired the previous night that identified him as an FBI Special Agent with the domestic terrorism task force. It was by no means perfect, but since the HRT had picked up the wrong person, he continued on his mission.

With the majority of personnel flocking to the security breach, he'd blended in with a crowd of onlookers and staffers and crossed the plaza to the five-story assembly building at an entrance normally used for tours and special presentations.

The guard, a UN employee, stopped him. Trapp handed over the wallet containing a fake ID and a real FBI badge, the latter stolen by elements best left unquestioned. The security guard, backed up by a Secret Service agent, scrutinized Trapp's face carefully.

Thick-framed glasses and his new haircut altered his appearance enough to pass muster, at least at first, before the guy brought up a list on his e-tablet.

"Just need to check this," the guard said.

The Secret Service agent was a stern-looking Black man who had watched from six feet back. They would all be equipped with photos of him and of Li Chao, and Trapp now regretted being quite so bold, despite the facial rec systems now failing to confirm his presence.

Another gift.

"What's your business here?" the guard asked.

"This." Trapp raised the bag, from which he had removed the NYPD branding on a tear-away strip after he'd donned his tie.

The guard needed to search it.

He rummaged through, bringing out a couple of tablets and some office equipment, legal pads, and a bulky blue pouch with the United States of America Department of State seal embroidered on the front. It was closed with a zip and plastic seal that would need breaking to open it.

"What's this?" the guard asked.

"It's a diplomatic pouch. Items needed for the conference."

The Secret Service agent now took more of an interest. "What's in it?"

"I'm afraid it's confidential. National security."

"I'm going to need you to open that, sir," the guard said.

"I can't do that, I'm afraid." Trapp eyed the Secret Service agent. "No one can open a diplomatic pouch. Right?"

"Right," the agent replied.

"Check my name. I'm expected."

"Scan his face too," the Secret Service agent said. "Make sure it's on the record."

The guard lifted his e-tablet and hit some areas of the screen that Trapp couldn't see. All he could do was hold still.

He waited.

Two possibilities. He would soon be under arrest or he'd be waved through with a smile.

"Agent Greaves," the guard said. "Thank you."

Nice touch.

63

Madison headed back to the mobile monitoring hub, leaving behind a police officer who was either an Oscar-worthy actor or who really didn't know what the hell was going on. But Madison believed him when he said he had never heard of Jason Trapp.

Inside the hub, Kamar and Laura confirmed that the man being released was definitely their target. On the screen, an angry Jason Trapp argued with Agent Paolo Drebin and the HRT lead, who held up appeasing hands.

"Who do we have on the line?" Madison asked. "Agent Pope, Deputy Director Mitchell, Dr. Greaves, are you receiving?"

"Mitchell here," the Deputy Director said. "I think Nick is here too."

"Yes," Pope said. "Following all this in real time. It sure looks like Jason."

"Dr. Greaves," Madison said, "are you here?"

"Greaves had to drop off for urgent business," Mitchell said.

Madison slumped into a chair. "I know it looks like we have Jason Trapp in custody, but that's not him."

"What are we looking at?" Pope asked.

Kamar answered, "The best deepfake I've ever seen."

"How can it be live?" Pope interrupted. "My understanding is that deepfakes take hours of editing."

"Not really," Laura said. "Think about Snapchat and TikTok filters. They're live. They can turn you into a cat or show you as a teenager. And you've probably seen those hologram tours of dead singers."

"But to fool facial recognition software," Kamar added, "it would have to be—"

"Greaves," Madison said. "Unless we've let foreign agents into our systems, it has to be him."

"Would Greaves really side with Trapp?" Pope asked.

"If he was convinced it was the right thing to do, maybe," Mitchell replied. "Greaves is... odd. Loyal, but odd. He'll do the right thing, even if it isn't legal."

"A perfect Trapp ally, then."

"Can we get a warrant for Timothy Greaves on this?" Madison asked.

"I'll get on it," Pope replied.

"You'll have to find him first," Mitchell said.

TRAPP DISCARDED everything but the diplomatic pouch and a small iPad once he'd made it into the service area. The bare breezeblock walls and metal walkways were a far cry from the luxury of the halls walked by diplomats, ambassadors, and world leaders. He had a map on the iPad in a hidden folder, hand-drawn and scanned since he needed to be in a specific place that wasn't in the public record.

Trapp advanced up to the second floor, where he was greeted by two armed Caucasian men—one middle-aged and bald, one gray and a little older. The bald guy pulled his

Glock and gave a firm "What the hell are you doing here? ID, now."

They were plain-clothes, but they lacked the bearing of a Secret Service detail—likely they'd been hired to patrol the back areas. Trapp slowly reached into his pocket, showing his gun but making no move toward it as he handed over his credentials. Though Greaves had added him to the building's access list, he doubted that would serve as an all-access pass.

The gray-haired guard checked the ID. "What's the FBI doing back here?"

"Long story," Trapp replied.

"Yeah, well, you'll have plenty of time to tell it in lockup," the bald guard said.

The gray-haired guard reached for Trapp's shoulder to spin him around like a cop about to cuff a suspect.

While he hated hurting people who were simply doing their jobs, time was running out; if he was here now, Chao could have penetrated the security even earlier.

Trapp adopted a submissive position, hands in plain sight. When the bald guard got within half an arm's length, Trapp pivoted, used his elbow to redirect the guy's aim, and pulled the man between himself and the gray guard. He twisted the bald guy's arm, palm-struck the gun to send it clattering down the stairs, and shoved him stomach-first into the edge of the guardrail, winding him.

To avoid excessive injury, Trapp went for the gray guard's wrist before he could pull his gun, gripped him by the neck, and waited until both hands were upon his arm before maneuvering him into a choke hold.

The bald one recovered and charged. Trapp threw his unconscious captive at the oncoming man, slowing him. He punched the bald guard in the jaw, then in the ear, then applied another chokehold, rendering his second victim unconscious.

Victim.

Good guys, just doing their jobs.

Trapp zip-tied the pair with their own equipment and assessed his options.

One black steel door led out to a gangway overlooking the General Assembly Hall for engineers, lighting and sound technicians—presumably why the two had been posted here. A second steel door led to an elevator shaft mechanism. He took a third option, a narrow gangway funneling between two walls. This was a new addition to the building, used to transport equipment during busy times so manual laborers didn't litter up the place while world leaders were in attendance.

He moved silently, rising to a mezzanine, ducking under cable trays and AC ducts as he went. If Chao was close, Trapp had to be careful.

At the mezzanine's end, Trapp descended a ladder and crossed two close-set steel beams, walking above what appeared to be floorboards but was actually part of the second-floor ceiling. He snapped open the diplomatic pouch and removed one of three plastic-wrapped packages. Biting off a corner, he squeezed the contents into a wide square, four feet on each side.

He then took out the remaining packages and a polystyrene box containing four detonators, which he slotted into place. Finally, he laid a charge wire in the gel-based square and retreated to the walkway's edge.

This *had* to work.

~

Li Chao was attired in black and white: white jacket and shirt, black trousers, tie, and shoes. The twelve men around him, chosen months earlier for this mission, were dressed identically. Though unaware of the exact date and location, Chao had embedded them—and dozens of others—in New York City, gaining experience and solidifying their covers while waiting tables, cooking, and working in the catering trade.

Their real jobs within the target building provided perfect cover. Even Chao, who had arrived three weeks ago, was welcomed on the recommendation of more embedded personnel. Trusted as in-house catering and agency workers, they hadn't needed to wait to smuggle guns in on this high-security day.

Chao led four men out of the kitchen, ostensibly for a break. They had been filtering in and out all day, repeating the same task each time. In a corridor reserved for security and staff, Chao tapped a baseboard and lowered it. While two colleagues kept watch, the other three knelt on the carpet as Chao removed an AK-47 from the hollowed-out space, passing it to Bolo Wang, who dismantled and sprayed the mechanism with oil, then reassembled it before Chao had removed the second assault weapon. They repeated the maintenance with six Type 56 rifles—the Chinese derivative of the stalwart AK-47—all of which had been smuggled in over several months, one innocent-looking piece at a time, and hidden away.

When ready, they loaded the guns and spare ammo into a laundry cart, which they trundled down the corridor and into an elevator.

Chao and his men gathered in the elevator, which rose smoothly. The doors opened to reveal the rest of the paramilitary unit, each with their own laundry carts. Five operatives wheeled out trollies, mixing with other staff transporting food and drinks to the room hosting their targets—people whose deaths would herald a new era in Chinese supremacy.

As their targets' security detail approached, Chao's men braced. He had complete faith in them. They knew what to expect, but the security detail would never be able to predict what was about to happen.

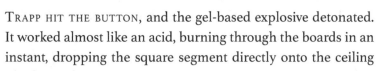

TRAPP HIT THE BUTTON, and the gel-based explosive detonated. It worked almost like an acid, burning through the boards in an instant, dropping the square segment directly onto the ceiling tiles beneath.

Trapp rushed forward and stamped on the debris. The plastic and foam tiles gave way in a burst of white. Trapp dropped through, holding the two blocks of explosives and landing in an office occupied by three women who had been eating sandwiches. They were stunned and terrified, huddling away from Trapp in one corner.

"I'm not here to hurt you. But get down and cover your heads."

Trapp's stomach clenched as they slunk lower behind the desk. He took no pleasure in frightening civilians. But it would be over quickly.

He ripped each of the explosive packets in two and attached the four chunks to the inner wall before stretching a detonator cord between them. He tipped over the desk and lay down behind it, near the women. A mere fifteen seconds had passed since Trapp had blown the ceiling out.

Trapp hit the remote detonator.

The directional blast filled the office with noise and smoke, leaving a gaping, ragged hole in the wall.

Gun out, Trapp dashed to the new hole and tossed in two grenades with the pins pulled. The "grenades" gave off a series of pops and sparks, like firecrackers but much less potent.

Trapp climbed through the hole to be faced with a conference room full of Korean presidents and their entourages, along with the President of the United States of America, Charles Nash. All had pressed back against the far wall with Nash out in front, ready to shield his guests from danger.

Trapp stood at the opposite side of the round conference

desk, placed his gun on the tabletop, and threw himself to the floor with his hands behind his head.

Secret Service burst through the main doors with their guns up and made a beeline for the president while others covered Trapp, who had made himself as non-threatening as possible. Or as non-threatening as any man who'd just blown up the world's most important conference *could* look.

As the Korean security personnel also piled in, Nash tried to shrug off his attempted saviors, but they were trained not to take shit from a president who did not want to be protected. It was the one time they did not have to take orders from their commander-in-chief.

As he was dragged out of the room, Nash's face bore a mask of pure confusion.

"What the hell is this, Trapp? What do you think you're doing?"

"I'm sorry, sir," Trapp said through grunts as an agent kneed him in the back. "But if I can get this close, I could have killed you all. And if *I* could do it, Li Chao can do it, too. He's here, I'm sure of it. You've got to find him."

64

The noise was the worst, Chao's ears throbbing even with the plugs. The battle through the lower corridors could have been an assault on some Islamist desert stronghold, of which Chao had led many—the gunsmoke, the cacophony of automatic fire, the sheer bloody claustrophobia.

The Korean security personnel pushed back valiantly against Chao's infiltration before digging in on the floor beneath their target. The Chinese patriots had yet to suffer a casualty.

Their training had been dynamic and thorough, even before they'd known their assignment. The months since Chao's superiors had learned of the summit were all they needed to plan this operation. And while Chinese diplomats whispered in North Korean ears to avoid Camp David, to push for the UN, Chinese sleeper agents had mapped every inch of every building the Americans might have used to host the Korean presidents.

Chao remembered a terror cell that wished to masquerade as freedom fighters, a group who claimed a small region of what some nations still called Tibet. The Uyghur Muslims, determined to defy the state and live as lawless mercenaries, had thought of themselves as a community and the buildings in which they prayed as "religious sanctuaries." They had armed themselves to the teeth and resisted when a search was ordered.

Chao had led the assault, clearing their places of worship as well as the tunnels they had dug under the streets, losing only three men while his unit killed fifty-six terrorists, crippled twenty more, and arrested the thirty-two who finally surrendered. They had gone on to liberate the families, brainwashed by a toxic culture of superstition and monotheism, then transported the survivors to deprogramming education camps before releasing *most* of them back into communities chosen for them by the state.

Chao had heard on the comms that an explosion had interrupted the signing of the sham of a Treaty, which pleased Chao no end. He could hardly wait for the Americans to fully understand what they were facing.

The resistance on this floor was almost at an end. He and his team were minutes away from progressing to their prize.

"Sir," Powell, the chief of Nash's Secret Service detail yelled over the roar of Marine One's engine noise. "You can resist all you want, but we'll carry you out if it comes to it. The Koreans are safe. Right not getting you out of here is my only concern."

They paused inside the exit to the rooftop helipad.

"If you won't let me stay," Nash said, "how about an update?"

Powell gave him a filthy look, before clearly remembering where he was and who he was talking to. He blinked away his displeasure at Nash's lack of cooperation.

"If Li Chao is here, he's hiding well," Powell said. "He wasn't on the conference room floor."

"Then where is he?"

"We have HRT and our best agents sweeping the building. Everything is locked down, no one in or out. The presidents are being evacuated, but the rest is at a standstill."

"And Trapp?"

Powell couldn't hide his annoyance.

"Update on the suspect," he said into his throat mic. He paused. "They have him secure, sir. He seems to be alone, but we're checking the back rooms. Looks like he neutralized a couple of security personnel."

"So is the danger past?" Nash asked.

"We're getting you out of here, sir." Powell listened again. "Marine One is almost ready. One minute."

"Agent Powell," Nash said, his tone commanding but calm. He glanced at the agents manning the door, then the ones covering their rear. "In your honest, professional opinion, is my life currently in danger?"

"Sir?"

"You heard me. Answer the question."

"Sir, we have to get you out of the building."

"You only override my orders when there's a clear danger to my life or well-being. Is that correct?"

"Correct, sir."

"Then look at me and tell me straight. With Trapp in custody and your best men and women sweeping the Assembly Building, is my life currently under threat?"

Powell licked his top lip and swallowed. "Unlikely, sir. But possibly. You must evacuate after an event like that."

"No," Nash replied. "If Trapp is right, an attack on our nation—and on the new peace I was trying to broker—is underway. I need to understand what we're facing. Now take me to him."

Powell looked like he was about to argue but thought better of it. He radioed orders to keep Marine One ready, then he and the team escorted Nash down two floors. Powell remained visibly unhappy, but at a sturdy walnut-patterned door, he knocked. It opened.

Inside resembled a police interview room. Present were Agent Drebin, CIA analyst Madison Grubbs, and an armed guard standing over Jason Trapp, who was cuffed to a chair beside the table.

"Hello, Jason," Nash said. "You're damn lucky those signatures were in place before you blew everything all to hell."

TRAPP SAT, stone-faced to disguise his fear that he had completely, monumentally, catastrophically fucked up.

"Sir, I know you could order one of these men to shoot me dead and no one would mourn my loss. But if I could get to Kuk and Son, and even you, then so could Chao."

"Li Chao doesn't seem to be here," Nash said. "What do you make of that?"

"This man is paranoid, sir," Drebin said before turning his attention to his prisoner. "Maybe you pissed off the wrong people in Rwanda, and all they're doing is yanking your chain."

"Unlikely," Trapp said. "The files they wanted point directly to the scenario I just played out. Only with a more permanent outcome."

"I suppose you think you were clever," Madison said. "But it hasn't gotten you any closer to recovering the files."

"There's a failsafe, but they could still do some damage," Trapp said. "Depends on how quickly they extract the data. I assume Greaves is on it?"

"What sort of damage are we talking?" Nash asked.

"Catastrophic," Madison said. "We haven't gotten ahold of

Dr. Greaves yet, but we think he was conspiring with Jason here. I also believe the Russian hacker was a distraction that allowed Greaves to analyze his own code and give us a fake interpretation. That's why he's so certain that even if they crack the corruption virus, the so-called 'alarm' will alert him. So I don't think the Chinese would risk that."

"Why not?"

"Because it's an obvious failsafe. A basic move. They'll have planned to counter it. Crack it offline and copy it, or just find a more secure uplink to stall Greaves. The only thing stopping them right now is the comms blanket over the site. They don't know what's happened yet. But that can't last."

Nash ran his hand over his face. "What the hell were you doing, Jason?"

"Helping, sir," Trapp said. "But you have to get Chao. Put extra men on President Kuk especially. If he's leaving in a convoy, that might be the vulnerable point of attack."

Drebin narrowed his eyes, and Trapp intuited that he was considering an alternative. "The Triads."

"Triads?" Nash said.

"NYPD stumbled across a Triad shootout. Initial reports were that a cop discovered them and came under fire. Only that cop is mysteriously nowhere to be found. The cops are concerned he was kidnapped, but I think he's sitting right here."

Nash looked down at Trapp with the disappointment of a father catching his son with stolen goods from a shoplifting spree. "Jason, is this true?"

"Sir, my tactics are a distraction. We've got bigger problems to worry about. They will have no part in Li Chao's operation. The new leadership wouldn't allow that."

"New leadership?" Madison said. "What, you've installed your own puppet snake head, have you?"

Something triggered inside Trapp. A shock of an idea, buried deep.

"*Puppet...*" Trapp mused.

The new leadership.

"He's only in place because..." Trapp thought about his words carefully. "Because... with Zhen gone, there's no natural heir."

"What are you talking about?" Drebin asked.

"Give me a second." Trapp regulated his breathing to counteract the hot jet of adrenaline that was trying to make his brain explode.

I got it all wrong.

"Sir," Trapp said, drilling his gaze at Nash. "Li Chao and his handlers want the summit to fail, but the signatures are already dry. All that's left is the ceremonial signing at the White House. Isn't that right?"

"Correct." Nash started pacing. "What does that tell us?"

"If President Kuk is murdered, then his daughter takes over. She and her husband. Right?"

"Correct."

"So it doesn't achieve Li Chao's ultimate goal," Madison said, heading down the same thought path as Trapp.

"He seems frail," Nash added. "Probably won't last much longer if the rumors about his cancer are true."

It all coalesced at once, Trapp's mind firing on all cylinders. His pulse took off, and his face flushed.

"Killing President Kuk does little for them. And he's toast anyway. But if Chao were to cut off all heirs, that's all it would take to eliminate the regime, to nullify the current president's legacy."

Trapp could hardly believe he had been played this way, but he had to say it out loud.

"He's going to kill the families."

65

Yung-Gi had ordered additional security to be posted throughout the hotel, ready to converge on some unconventional attempt on Myo Il-Song's life. Even in his wildest imagination he couldn't have imagined losing half those men in a matter of minutes. But this attack was more unconventional than he had ever feared.

As soon as the alarm sounded, Yung-Gi had secured Myo and her daughters in the safest room available, then assembled his dozen-strong detail to resist until they could bring in reinforcements. All elevators had been locked off, and they'd received confirmation of the incoming assault team heading away from the west stairwell toward the east one.

Yung-Gi dispatched four of his best to the stairwell linking to the floor below. Their orders were to hold off the incoming assassins, to protect the access point with all they had.

Knowing with all the certainty of his forty-plus years of experience that those men would not be returning, he set up a makeshift battle station, dragging out a file cabinet, a massive table, and all the other heavy items he and his remaining eight men could use for cover. The mess in the corridor outside the room resembled a barricade in a zombie movie, hastily assembled by panicked humans attempting to hold off hordes of the undead.

All they could do now was wait.

CHAO'S UNIT broke through the second wave of resistance at the hotel, which was deserted of all guests except President Kuk's family and his army of security. The armed personnel pulled back to secure their principals on the floor above where the family was staying, along with the usual attendants that North Korean leaders seemed to need in order to function.

It was amusing to Chao that a country as backward as North Korea could hold such power over its civilians. Their leadership envied the Chinese way, seeking to mimic the ideal balance of control and satisfaction. They had gotten the control part right, although they resorted to complete and utter fear to enforce it, while their failure to satisfy their own people saw thousands, possibly tens of thousands, fleeing the country every year and finding sanctuary with enemies.

North Korea was a loyal ally, but only while China was useful to them.

The droughts that had swept the region had left China as bereft as the Korean Peninsula, which had rendered Kuk's government vulnerable to revolution from either the civilian population or a coup from its own military. Somebody needed to take control. Somebody competent and willing to do the things that President Kuk would not.

With Kuk dying, leadership would pass to his daughter, Myo Il-Song, who would fall under pressure to maintain his legacy. If that legacy included détente with the Americans, she would be obliged to continue.

Chao and his right-thinking colleagues could not allow such a thing to happen.

He urged his still unbloodied unit onward, up the guest staircase usually reserved for exiting the building to the lobby, and left two men to alert them of anyone encroaching from behind. The stairwell was wide with a narrow central column —ideal for an incursion, difficult to defend.

Chao pressed his four lieutenants ahead and drifted in behind with the remaining troops at his back. Bolo Wang, whom Chao had selected personally, attached a tennis ball-sized plastic charge to the seam down the middle of the two doors and retreated to wait for his master's approval.

Li Chao nodded tersely. "Blow it."

TRAPP SAW IT ALL CLEARLY. "I have a new number for Dr. Greaves. He was supposed to go dark once it was obvious who was helping me. If a presidential pardon isn't in the offing, he's capable of engineering any number of new identities—"

"Why are you telling us this?" Drebin asked.

"He got me in. He has tentacles in every system in this area. The only thing he can't do is hack the building itself because of the digital lock-down; he can only hack the servers feeding it. I need to know, quickly, what's happening elsewhere."

"And you're sure about it this time?" Nash asked.

Madison was pacing quickly behind Trapp, ignoring the guard on duty. She shook her head. "Sir, you can't seriously believe a word—"

Nash held up his hand to cut her off.

"If they're not here, then they're somewhere else," Trapp said, shooting Madison an apologetic look that died in ice. *Deservedly.* "And it makes more sense. Like the Triads, the North Korean presidency is dynastic. They're more like royalty than a republic. If killing the president won't help him, then he'll do what has the most long-term benefit. That's taking out the daughter and grandkids."

"Children?" Nash said.

"He's done it before." Trapp looked up at the president and adopted his most apologetic expression. "When we drop bombs to protect our country, we know children could be caught up. Just because Chao has to look them in the face before he pulls the trigger doesn't make it any different."

Nash looked at the floor and appeared to consider the situation before addressing Drebin. "If Greaves can give us some sort of confirmation, I want it."

"Think you can let me out of these things?" Trapp rattled his cuffs. "I surrendered. I'm not going anywhere."

Nash glanced between the guard, Madison, and Drebin. All three shook their heads slowly.

"Let's leave it there for now," Nash said, clearly not wishing to alienate his advisors.

"Call him. I'm the only one who has the number." Trapp rattled off the digits for yet another burner phone, which Madison punched into her own phone before selecting the speaker function.

"Is that you, Jason?" Greaves asked.

"I'm here," Trapp replied. "I'm with a few others, including the president."

"You were successful?"

"Situation Normal, "Trapp replied dryly.

It took a beat for Greaves to get it. He let out a low chuckle when the penny dropped. "All Fucked Up?"

"You got it. Chao is playing by different rules. I think he's targeting the families. I need you to look for unusual activity around the hotels."

"On it."

As Greaves went silent except for a chorus of clicking and striking keys, nobody spoke.

"Good lord," Greaves said. "Yes, it's local, a brute force attack taking out amenities like traffic signals. It's playing havoc with some comms."

"Which comms?" Drebin asked.

"Random. Cell towers, Internet. They've redirected several cops to manage a traffic accident caused by the problems."

"What sort of comms are going to go down?" Madison asked. "Specifically?"

"Are you worried about any in particular?"

"The blackout over the assembly building," Madison said. "It's run through cell towers, like a negative feedback loop that stops them transmitting. But I don't know where the files are at the moment. They could be here with the ambassador or they could be with Li Chao. Could they be masking something?"

"Could just be a diversion, keeping the cops back." Drebin folded his arms to his chest, pinched his chin.

Greaves said, "Could be building to an assault on the power grid, trying to take it all down. Overloading might allow someone to bypass the jammers."

"Then we use the same tools against them," Drebin said, turning to Madison.

She said, "If we don't stop this and TIPTOE gets out, the Chinese will cripple the CIA."

"What is TIPTOE?" Drebin asked. "I know it's above my clearance level, but—"

Nash cut him off. "I'll declassify it for you, Agent Drebin. But I can see what they're trying to do: blame us for the deaths of the first family of North Korea, then install their own government. Just as China believes that America installs South Korea's leadership."

"I don't think Chao would have TIPTOE on him," Trapp said. "The danger of getting killed before he has a chance to release it is too great. Even if he has an over-inflated sense of his own ability, his superiors don't. They ordered him not to kill me because it would take too much time."

"Then who's behind this?" Madison asked.

"There's only one conduit to go through. And since I don't think Chao is working for the Chinese government directly, Beijing wouldn't let it out of their sight."

Nash chimed in, "Politically, they'd need to know that Chao accomplished his mission before taking the chance of releasing it. The fallout would be not in their favor if they released it after the assassination attempt failed."

"Which means," Drebin said, "it must be with someone who the Chinese trust implicitly. Not a former MSS agent."

Trapp jumped in. "That only leaves the ambassador. His secretary took the thumb drive off Lamar when she stabbed him. It must be with them."

"Is Ambassador Wen still in the building?" Nash asked.

Drebin moved for the door. "I'll find out. What are the rules of engagement, sir?"

"Whatever it takes. I'll deal with the diplomatic fallout." Nash stopped him. "Before you go, though…"

"Yes, Mr. President?"

"Trapp needs to get to the president's family."

"Sir?"

"Release Jason right away and get HRT to the roof of this building. My ride is already warmed up. Get over there and stop that bastard."

66

"He's gone," Drebin said, dropping his radio handset from his ear.

"Shit," Madison muttered. The way this tumult had exploded had smashed the footing from underneath her. She wasn't sure what to believe. The one thing she was certain of was that Drebin would not break the law, even at the behest of the president. Obeying an illegal order was still a crime.

She keyed a walkie talkie tuned to the command frequency and said, "We need somebody on Ambassador Wen's vehicle. Now."

"And watch out for that secretary of his," Drebin said. "From what Trapp said, she's very capable."

Agents parted the way for them all the way out onto the plaza.

The female Secret Service agent assigned to check Wen's parking space transmitted an update. "His car left four minutes ago."

"He's trying to get beyond the communications blackout," Madison said. "I'd put money on it."

"Agreed," Drebin said. "We need to slow him down somehow."

They crossed the plaza to the monitoring hub, which was now more sparsely manned, though the three principal experts remained as instructed.

"I need you guys to do something for me," Madison said, "and it's going to sound really strange."

THE HELICOPTER—NO longer Marine One, since Nash was not on board—banked sharply after taking off from the UN building. Its nose dipped, and it accelerated the half-mile toward the Norfolk Grand Hotel where President Kuk and his family had been told they would be safe.

Trapp looked around at the Hostage Rescue Team and asked for a comms check. Each of the eight responded in turn, ending with the lead, a veteran Army Ranger called Yardley Randolph. Although Trapp had been charged with coordinating the wider operation, Randolph retained control over his men.

"What's the plan when we get there?" Randolph asked.

"I hate going in unprepared, but all we know is that the targets are on the top floor, right beneath the penthouse. Reports we received before the blackout are that a gunfight was already taking place—with heavy casualties. The way I see it, the weakest entry point is a room on the corner farthest from the target zone. It gives us the best chance of surprising them."

Since their other option was to land on the roof and make a massive racket, giving the enemy time to shore themselves up, Randolph said, "I concur. Southwest corner."

"Thirty seconds," the pilot said.

Each of the team pulled their straps tight and secured their weapons. Trapp did likewise, although he was far less well-equipped. He'd snagged a ballistic vest and an MP5, and his Sig Sauer had been returned. Other than that, he was still in his trousers, shirt, and regular shoes.

"You should wait here," Randolph said. "We'll take them out, and you can bring up the rear."

The helicopter assumed a stationary hover, and Randolph was already halfway out the door with his rappelling gear.

"I know the principal," Trapp said as he attached his own carabiner. "My presence might give you a few extra seconds. It's better if I'm there."

～

Laura Hart frowned at Madison. "You want me to what?"

Kamar and Catherine also appeared bemused, but Catherine waved her hand in front of Laura's face to get her attention.

"It's possible," she said. "But it depends how much power they have."

"I know it's *possible*," Laura replied. "I'm just not sure it's legal."

"It's legal," Drebin said. "Orders from the president."

Laura frowned. "I can route it through the cell phone towers and other radio transmitters, but that will leave *all* comms down, not just sat-phones and cellphones."

"Do it," Madison said. "Drebin, we need a vehicle."

～

It had been fifteen years since Yung-Gi had fought in battle against anything more than a peasant uprising, and the sheer wall of noise and the stench of gunpowder brought it all back.

Fifteen, maybe sixteen men, exchanging fire in a hotel corridor could do nothing but assault the senses with the number of deafening shockwaves blasting from so many weapons. Even the sting of spent cartridges singeing his skin gave him a nostalgic if terrifying thrill.

The Chinese had broken through the outer cordon faster than he'd hoped, but he'd successfully pinned them back, positioning his men at intervals that would allow them to switch their defense to their rear should their enemy circle around.

A lull in fighting suggested to Yung-Gi that the invaders were preparing to try something new, maybe retreat, or maybe there were others coming in from the other direction that he had missed.

But their next move surprised even Yung-Gi. Three—no, four—Chinese operatives ran headlong toward the barricade, a howl tearing from their throats like a war cry.

Yung-Gi wasn't sure what the hell they were doing, but he didn't hesitate to shoot at their fast-moving torsos.

It was a good opportunity to press on, go on the offensive while they were rattled.

But then the fighting stopped dead for a moment as the beating *whump-whump-whump* of a helicopter buzzed the hotel, and Yung-Gi had to wonder if this meant reinforcements were incoming... and if they were for him or for Li Chao.

TRAPP and the team rappelled to the corner balcony and breached the empty room by crowbarring the French doors. After clearing the space, they progressed into the plush corridor lined with artwork and plants. There was no one here, but the blasts of close-quarters gunfire echoed from around the first corner. Smoke and cordite lingered in the air.

"Shit, they're closer than we thought," Randolph yelled.

"Security's pushing them back," Trapp said. "Good. It means they haven't gotten in yet."

"Sir." Laughlin, one of Randolph's deputies, presented him a ruggedized e-tablet with the hotel's plans on it. "This next passageway links around the back of the elevators and comes out halfway up that corridor."

"Sounds good," Trapp said.

Randolph nodded. "Okay, Laughlin, you're with Jones, Singh, and Ruiz. Don't move until my mark. I want flashbangs up the ass of every one of those motherfuckers."

IT MIGHT HAVE STRUCK Madison as typical, a macho male trait in Drebin compelling him to drive, but as the armored SUV tore out of the plaza, she was pleased to admit she was wrong. Drebin handled the vehicle much better than she ever could, despite being pretty decent behind the wheel herself.

They rumbled down three stairs to the main street as the signal came through for those manning the cordon to make way.

No one had stopped Ambassador Wen from leaving, since he had the correct documentation. He was very obviously heading toward the outer perimeter.

"The file was accessed," Greaves confirmed as Drebin pulled the SUV around in a skid that Madison felt might have overturned it had he not corrected at the last second. "The curtain came down before they got it out, though. They can't transmit it until they're outside the net."

"How long will that be?" Madison asked.

"Impossible to tell. We caught the alarm, but they still have the file. They were connected to the Internet via a sat-phone. If they get to a point where they can transmit it to a satellite, we are screwed."

"And you can't give us a location?"

"No. The comm net works both ways. Since it's killed all electronic signals in the area, we can't track them either."

"Laura, are you on the line?" Madison asked.

"Copy," Laura replied. "I'm scraping all social media and body cam caches. Everything in the last eight minutes to see if anything flagged before being blocked."

"Any sign?"

"Yes! The last location was along Third Avenue. Close to the Chrysler Building."

Madison snapped toward Drebin. "Can you get us there?"

"Of course," he said and fishtailed the vehicle onto Second Avenue, accelerating with a roar that startled a handful of cops.

"Idiots!" Li Chao swore, furious that four of his men had gotten impatient and rushed the enemy, getting themselves cut down like cannon fodder.

Worse, there was no missing the sound of the chopper vibrating through the walls of the hotel, way too heavy and low to be anything but reinforcements of one stripe or another. He had to end this, and end it quickly, but not in suicidal fashion. Secured down low with only ten feet between his front line and the presidential suite, closer than his impatient troops had been, Chao ordered two men to rush the security personnel holding them off.

They obeyed without question, blasting their rifles with abandon. They plowed forward through a hail of incoming gunfire, bloodying the Korean guards while a second wave brought up the rear, spraying bullets as if their magazines were infinite. It was impossible to see clearly through the smoke, but it looked like they'd gotten them all.

Li Chao's men died as heroes. Those they defeated were unworthy of such a title.

He now had a free run at the offspring of President Kuk.

The survivors of the assault party assembled forward as a unit and found the doors locked and barred securely.

"We have incoming," one of Chao's men reported, fear tingeing his face. "Americans."

"Hold them off," Chao ordered.

"Yes, sir."

Two of the remaining men took to shooting crouches and readied themselves.

Four cylinders jangled in from around the nearest corner.

Chao yelled, "Flash!"

The flashbangs detonated in a fury, pummeling his hearing and blotting out his vision.

This was surely the end. But he had never failed a mission. He could not fail here.

TRAPP BROUGHT up the rear as Randolph took point in a two-by-two formation, taking turns to tap the shoulder of the pair in front, then move ahead to lead the line. Two men dressed as hotel catering staff had already fallen to well-placed shots from the point man, in addition to those who already littered the ground.

That left four men recovering in the middle of the flash-bang smoke, and no sign of Li Chao.

The second half of the HRT unit prepared to breach while Randolph and company held their fire. The deputy, Laughlin, led his group in the same two-by-two covering tactic, using the ice machine and alcoves as cover. But the AC or some extractor fan must have kicked in, as the mist cleared momentarily. Chao's men reacted first, and Trapp heard the distinct, deafening cacophony of at least two automatic weapons discharging multiple rounds at once.

"Agents down!" Laughlin yelled through the comms net. "Ruiz is hit. Jones too."

"Move in!" Randolph ordered.

The four rearguard HRT operators kicked into gear, laying down covering fire to allow Laughlin and Singh to pull the fallen agents back into the branching corridor.

"You see him?" Trapp asked, squinting through the ever-thinning smoke.

"I got four," Randolph answered. "Wait. Five. I think he's setting a charge."

"Damn it. They're going in."

Trapp ran through his memory of the approach to the hotel from the air. He pictured the exterior, its windows, its balconies, the penthouse above. The Chinese were dug in deep, just like the Korean protection detail had been.

"We can't get there in time," Trapp said. "I'm going to circle around."

"We tried that already."

"Not that way."

Trapp fired at the nearest room door. He rammed it, shoulder-first, crashing through into a room bigger than his apartment and about fifteen times as luxurious. The couch alone probably cost more than the entire contents of his own home. He headed straight for the balcony, turned the lock, and stepped outside.

Ten stories above the street, he could see the balcony of the VIP suite about eight feet away.

～

Li Chao just needed a few more seconds. While the flashbang had momentarily rendered his senses null and void, he had much experience in dealing with sensory overload, as had each member of his team.

While they had to fire blind for a time, it didn't matter much. Their ammo was in no danger of running dry. He wasn't back to full capacity yet but good enough to lay another breaching charge against the door hinges and alert his men that he was going to blow it.

He retreated behind the wall and hit the detonator.

The explosives ripped the wood and metal apart. A firm kick completed the job, and Chao entered with his Makarov pistol raised, shooting the two remaining guards in the head where they stood, still trying to recover from the surprise of the explosion.

He was in.

∾

Hwa Yung-Gi had seen the end coming moments before it arrived. The Americans had arrived too late, so all he could do was position his people in stations where they could slow the incursion. There was chance of them stopping it entirely.

Now as he heard the door blow inward and the concussive thump of fresh gunshots, he held the younger of Myo's daughters in his lap, urging the older one to shush, for Myo to sob more quietly.

He promised them he would do all he could to protect them, but the first, primary goal was to ensure they did not give away their hiding spot. And for that, he needed silence.

With that, Yung-Gi could do nothing more than wait. And be ready.

He glanced down at the flash of pink peeking out from underneath the cuff of his shirt—the bracelet given to him by the young girl shortly before she'd been murdered by rebels. If Myo and her daughters died here on American soil, the treaty would fall apart, and every single villager who'd agreed to share their precious harvest would starve. And not just those villagers: millions of his countrymen would starve, too. They were all depending on Yung-Gi.

He could not fail them.

67

Drebin had transformed from a stoic, almost emotionally blank slate to grinning, manic thrill-seeker in a matter of minutes. Madison quite liked this version of the FBI agent.

Their comms were now dead, so they could not contact Greaves. They would not know for certain whether Wen and Fang had released the files.

"The perimeter is to prevent people getting in," Madison said, "not stop them getting out."

"And you can bet that damn limo is armored," Drebin said. "Probably not as tough as the Beast, but more than enough to make it through a few squad cars blocking the way."

Even with the absence of regular traffic, there were operational vehicles around, transporting staff and cops and other personnel. Drebin wound around them, coming up against a snarl of SUVs which he bypassed by careening onto the sidewalk.

Although the cops had been alerted to a pursuit, they were still mighty pissed at having to scatter as the SUV sped through. It glanced off a lamppost and almost crashed through a cell phone shop before Drebin corrected, and the mirror on Madison's side disintegrated in a shower of plastic, metal, and glass.

She looked at him sharply. "Well, this is an experience."

"Happy to oblige, ma'am," Drebin deadpanned. "I think I see them."

"They're a hundred yards from the perimeter. Look, that's why they chose this route. It's just a line of cruisers marking the edge of the zone."

They would have brought in concrete barriers for the innermost perimeter and for some of the main channels near the East River and close to Grand Central. But even an operation of this size had its limits.

"They'll crash right through those squad cars," Drebin agreed.

"I guess it's up to us then."

"Is ramming them a breach of international law?"

"Only technically."

"Fuck it," Drebin said with a snarl as he dropped a gear and accelerated with the loudest growl yet.

TRAPP HAD JUMPED this distance before but never with a drop of this magnitude waiting at the bottom. Taking a moment to judge the harsh breeze hitting him from below and from the north side of the hotel, he calculated the distance between the two balconies and concluded he couldn't make it from a standing start. He needed a run-up.

The stone balustrade was a foot wide, which would not be a problem if it were only a foot off the ground. Easy enough to balance on. But ten stories in the air with wind sweeping in from the river and the beating rotor wash of a circling helicopter made for a precarious balancing act.

He stripped himself of the ballistic vest, MP5, and spare magazines whose weight threatened to drag him to his death, keeping only the Sig. Then he climbed up onto the edge of the balcony. Starting on all fours, he zeroed in on the VIP suite's balustrade, its ornamental pillar-like struts holding it aloft.

He had no idea what to expect.

"This has got to be the dumbest thing you've ever done."

Trapp wobbled upright, finding his balance, as if on a tightrope. He took baby steps at first, the wind buffeting him. He lengthened his strides with only three more to go, pushing as fast as he could. The ball of his right foot pressed into the edge, knee bent, and he thrust off hard. He threw his arms forward, over his head, with all his weight behind him.

He was going to fall short.

Trapp reached his arms out and somehow hooked his arms over the balustrade as he crashed against the VIP suite's balcony. The impact knocked the wind out of him and might have cracked an already-bruised rib. He tensed his shoulders and arms, clinging to the stone railing, then heaved his legs around and touched a toe to the bottom of the promontory. Once he got enough traction, he pushed upward and rolled over onto the balcony.

He drew his Sig and moved to the French doors, flattening his body against the wall and taking the fastest of peeks into the room.

What the hell?

Chao appeared to be alone, his gun making arcs around the bedroom, searching.

Had he finished them already?

There was no time to wait to find out.

He stepped out, firing three times through the door. The panes shattered and fell out in massive shards. Chao stumbled backward before pitching out of the bedroom into which Trapp now threw himself as the remaining glass fell away.

Chao returned fire blindly, poking his gun around the door jamb.

Trapp dived to the floor, firing at the wall in the hope that it was a cheap construction his bullets could penetrate.

No such luck.

It was solid, a skin of plaster breaking off before the bullet died in the brick beneath.

Then Trapp was up and moving. He fired three more times, and the doorframe splintered, showering Chao's gun hand with wood. The hand withdrew.

Trapp had no time to mess around. He pushed forward and out into the suite's lounge area, firing after Chao, who ducked into a bathroom.

The bedroom he'd come from was palatial, but that paled in comparison to the main living area, which had a sunken couch, a dining section with a buffet laid out, a gym with weights and mats, and a door that probably led to yet another bedroom. Two dead men lay sprawled in suits, bullet holes in their heads, and under the stifling odor of gunsmoke was a flowery scent of cleanliness.

The bathroom Chao had retreated to would likely be impressive as well, and Trapp assumed the set of double doors led to an adjoining room.

He pressed himself against one of the walls, keeping an eye on the main entry point. The exchange of gunfire in the corridor sounded much like a stalemate, neither defenders nor attackers willing to commit. That left Chao alone with Trapp.

What was missing, though, was the North Korean family that Chao had come to kill—and Trapp was here to protect.

"You missed them," Trapp called.

"I did not miss them." Chao stuck his hand out of the bathroom and squeezed off two shots. "They moved to the adjoining room but left their guards in place. I will finish you, then I will be through."

"Not going to happen."

"You can't possibly know that." Then Chao yelled, "Wang! Get in here. Engage the enemy."

Trapp had only seconds to assess what that meant. He retreated from the door while improving his angle as a broad-shouldered Chinese man abandoned his post and ran in shooting.

Trapp barely made it to one of the colonnades, chunks of plaster and paint and brick becoming shrapnel as he hunkered down behind it.

He had no way out, and although the man called Wang would certainly run out of ammo in the next few seconds, that might be all Chao needed.

Sure enough, during the split-second that Trapp dared look out from his position, Chao darted out of the bathroom toward the double doors to the adjoining room where he figured the North Korean president's family had to be hiding. He kicked at the middle of the two doors. It didn't break open right away, but there was a definite crack.

Trapp had no room to aim and shoot, but he did have one live grenade. That would certainly cause problems, but it might also give him a moment of respite. Trapp unhooked the grenade, pulled the pin, and counted down before throwing it.

The grenade landed beneath Chao's legs.

Chao didn't even have to look at it. He leaped behind a hefty armchair and pulled it over him before the grenade exploded —destroying the only barrier keeping him from accomplishing his mission.

THE GRENADE'S explosion was enough to stun the gunman named Wang, so Trapp stepped out and shot him twice in the head.

Then he fired into the chair that Chao had used for cover, hoping to keep him away from the family's room.

Too late.

"Crap."

Ears ringing, Trapp kept low, duckwalked to the next pillar, and pinned himself there, estimating that Chao must have returned to the bathroom.

"I don't suppose," Trapp called, "you want to go for some more of that decadent Hollywood bullshit?"

Chao came out firing.

Trapp fired back. Three, four shots, all center mass, blowing Chao off his feet and into a tumble that drew a look of surprise.

Trapp's gun had racked empty, though, and as he was advancing to pump at least one more round in Chao's head to make certain, he ejected the magazine. It was only as reached to draw a spare from his belt that he remembered he had discarded them to lighten his load.

Shit.

A dinner plate frisbeed through the air and hit Trapp square in the face. Then a second plate knocked the empty gun from his hand.

Chao had fallen next to a dinner cart containing used crockery. His gun lay five feet away, as useless as Trapp's own, and the assassin was already ripping off his ballistic vest.

"I guess we get to indulge in that bullshit after all," Trapp said.

Chao tossed his vest aside, rubbing his chest where the bullets had impacted without breaking the skin.

"After I kill you, I'll finish that damn daughter and her brats."

∼

THE ARMORED SUV gained on the limousine, its massive horsepower able to top a hundred miles per hour, but they were cutting things mighty fine. The ambassador's car had reached the outer marker, and all that stood between them and the rest of New York City were two NYPD Dodge Chargers, nose to nose. A crowd of cops aimed their guns at the limo and opened fire. The bullets hit the windows and body and the run-flat tires, but nothing slowed it down.

"Definitely armored," Drebin said.

The sleek black vehicle sent the cops running and slammed into the two Chargers, spinning them aside as it flew past.

A couple of dozen yards and they would be clear.

AT THE MASSIVE lurch of the impact, Fang Chen almost dropped the laptop but managed to hold it securely to her.

"Is it done?" Ambassador Wen asked.

"No," Fang replied. "Redial please, sir."

The ambassador was sweating, his fingers shaking as he tried to reconnect the satellite phone.

Fang could see the file in front of her. She had read several entries, shocked at the detail with which the Americans had planned to murder various world leaders, even their allies. But there was no time for this. All their mission required was getting it to Chao's superiors.

Ambassador Wen had told Fang that although Beijing would have deemed this a reckless act, they would most certainly approve of the outcome. He had a certain amount of leeway in his decision-making, and it would only backfire if he got it wrong.

After the car survived the impact with the cops' vehicles, Fang was certain they would get through.

"It's connected," Wen said.

Fang scanned for the signal which would connect the laptop to the satellite and send the TIPTOE files into the ether faster than any 5G signal.

"It's there."

Fang dragged the file to the FTP server and hovered the mouse over the upload button. She was about to click when the car lurched upward and pitched sideways. She thought her head was going to come off as her neck jerked and the laptop fell to the floor. The Americans had rammed them into a brick wall, knocking the driver unconscious.

"Get the computer," Wen ordered. "Get the computer *now*."

Dizzy, her head and neck hurting, Fang reached for the laptop. But something was holding her back. She couldn't quite reach it.

The seatbelt.

They had buckled up in order to ram their way out of the dead comm zone. She pulled back, and the biggest jolt of pain yet shot down her neck.

She unfastened the seatbelt. The clasp came away, and she leaned forward.

Her hands grasped the laptop.

She picked it up, oriented herself with the mouse, and readied it.

Before she could hit send, the door flew open, and she was staring at a gun. Again.

A stern-looking Caucasian man said, "Move and I shoot."

Fang looked at the computer screen where the FTP server awaited the command.

"Do it. Do it now," Wen said.

Fang told herself she was acting on behalf of her country, that she would be remembered well, and her family rewarded.

She dropped her hand, and the gun fired.

68

Trapp and Chao circled each other, fists raised, eyes locked, the smoke from the gunfight and explosion lingering in the air around them like a wraith. The gunfire was background noise that Trapp forced into a faded soundtrack. Chao moved like a dancer, slow and graceful, feet gliding across the floor as he choreographed his stance.

"Always so direct, so brutish," Chao said.

Trapp remained silent, never wavering from his opponent. Chao was trying to bait him, provoke an emotional response. He would not expose himself again.

Chao lunged forward, his hands a blur. Trapp barely had time to react as Chao's palm struck his chest, then his elbow, followed by a rapid series of finger jabs to his throat and face. The blows were precise, delivered like a striking snake.

Trapp staggered back from the impacts, while Chao flowed into a sequence of circular arm movements and sweeping kicks.

"You can't match me," Chao declared. "Traditional arts teach grace, balance, and fluidity. Something you lack."

Trapp shook his head, clearing the fog, but kept on blinking to seem dazed. As a kick came in, he launched a counterattack, throwing a series of heavy punches at Chao's head and torso. But the Chinese assassin evaded the bigger blows, so Trapp only landed glancing shots as Chao's body twisted and turned like a leaf in the wind.

"And now, Wing Chun," Chao announced, his hands a flurry of rapid strikes, targeting Trapp's centerline. They came from all angles, Trapp's defense deflecting only a couple. "Direct, efficient, and devastating. If a little basic."

Trapp grunted, the punches having battered his ribs, sternum, and pecs. His strength was waning, his breath starting to labor.

Chao danced back with a look of pure arrogance. "Wushu, Tai Chi, Bagua—each art honed centuries before your pathetic country was even birthed."

Trapp spat blood onto the plush carpet, eyes narrowing. He couldn't match Chao's speed or technical mastery, but he'd be damned if he was going to listen to this smug bastard's lecture on hand-to-hand combat.

Trapp charged forward, fists clenched, ready to deliver some good old-fashioned American brutality.

His charge was met with a swift kick to the chest, sending him stumbling backward into the gym area. He didn't fall, although he could easily have sat down for a rest.

"You see, Trapp," Chao said, following with a casual swagger, "you are going to die at the hands of a superior warrior."

Trapp spotted a rack of medicine balls, dropped back and grabbed one, hurling it at Chao's face. The assassin ducked and came back up smiling, but the momentary distraction allowed Trapp to close the distance and land a solid punch on Chao's jaw.

Chao reeled back. Trapp thought he'd lifted his opponent off the floor an inch or two. But Chao landed, scuttled back, and quickly regained his composure. He retaliated with a series of lightning-fast strikes to Trapp's head and torso. Trapp managed to block some, but the speed and precision left gave him nowhere to hide.

Sensing his advantage, Chao leaped onto a nearby weight bench, using it as a springboard to launch himself into a graceful aerial kick. His foot caught Trapp in the neck, sending him crashing into a rack of free weights, gasping.

Trapp inhaled deeply and assessed himself—no major damage. He could taste blood in his mouth, and his ribs ached with every breath. Maybe even a spot of whiplash.

Chao stood over him.

Trapp's hand closed behind his back, around the cold metal handle of a dumbbell.

"You're pathetic," the assassin said. "A relic. Clinging to outdated notions of strength. Patriotism. Faith."

With a sudden burst, Trapp swung the dumbbell upward. The weight slammed the assassin's jaw with a crunch, sending him staggering backward.

Trapp pressed this shift in momentum, rising to his feet and unleashing a flurry of heavy punches to Chao's head and body —jabs, reverse, hooks, a knee to the gut. The assassin blocked some, but this time, Trapp's sheer strength and determination bulldozed through. Chao's underestimation of him had paid off.

But Chao was a master of his craft, using an instep-kick at Trapp's knee to flare the recent injury back to life, buying himself room to move to the buffet area. Trapp pursued him, wanting to keep him on the defensive, but Chao had recovered his composure. He seemed to flow like water around Trapp's attacks, his movements reverting to their effortless grace, even as he delivered another devastating elbow strike to Trapp's already-throbbing ribs.

Trapp grabbed a handful of cutlery from the floor and flung it at the man's face. The assassin batted the projectiles aside, but the momentary distraction allowed Trapp to land a solid kick to Chao's midsection, doubling him over.

Trapp was grateful for the momentary break as they both caught their breath.

Fights usually went one of two ways: over very quickly with one person incapacitated or grinding to a stalemate with both grappling on the floor, unwilling to risk breaking away.

That flicked a switch, drawing a smile from Trapp.

"Okay, then."

Trapp turned his back on Chao and raced for the bathroom door, where residual steam from the hot tub enveloped him like a warm, wet blanket. He searched for anything he could use, his one chance to hobble Chao, bring him down to Trapp's level.

There.

If this ploy didn't work, he was dead.

Chao followed, pausing in the doorway, a steamy mist passing like gunsmoke around him.

"There's nowhere to run, Trapp. You're finished."

Trapp, his legs against the deep hot tub so he could go no farther, was in a poor defensive position. He raised his fists. "Come on, then."

Chao, focusing only on his prey, charged forward. His feet flew out from under him as he hit the liquid soap Trapp had dumped over the floor. It could have been a Looney Tunes pratfall if he hadn't corrected enough to grab Trapp before he slapped to the floor in an undignified heap.

Trapp seized his chance, dragging Chao backward into the tiles. Chao thrashed and struggled, but Trapp's grip was unbreakable as he slammed the assassin into the wall, then used his bodyweight to fall sideways, hammering Chao's head off the step to the hot tub.

Trapp held him there, raining blow after blow, feeling one of Chao's ribs break. This close in, Chao could only slither free.

But as soon as he pushed up to one foot, Trapp tackled him like a linebacker.

They tumbled into the steaming water, clawing at each other like animals. Chao's elegant martial arts techniques were useless in here, and Trapp's raw strength and tenacity rose like cream. He wrapped his arm around Chao's neck, squeezing with everything he had, pushing away the pain in his ribs and knee.

Chao's eyes bulged, his face turning a deep shade of purple as he gasped for air. His hands scrabbled uselessly at Trapp's arm, trying to break free.

But Trapp was relentless. Even as Chao's struggles grew weaker and more feeble, he held on tighter. Trapp wasn't fooled. Finally, with a last desperate gurgle, the assassin gave up the pretense of unconsciousness, making one final bid to buck out of the hold. Trapp pulled him down under the water and held him there.

As Chao went limp, Trapp simply lay back, ensuring that Chao's face remained submerged longer than even the world's greatest free-diver could hold their breath.

Finally satisfied, he released his hold, letting Chao's lifeless body slip beneath the scented water as he crawled out of the tub, spilling water over the floor. The world seemed to tilt and sway around him, but he had work left to do.

As he stepped into the main room, Trapp realized that the gunfire had ceased and an eerie silence hung over the space. Only his breath and the hot tub jets could be heard.

The Hostage Rescue Team swarmed into the room. Trapp instinctively raised his hands, but as the agents took in the scene, their weapons went down. They spread out slowly, checking rooms and appointing guards at each.

"Trapp," Agent Randolph called out. "Are you all right?"

Trapp nodded, his voice rasping from the smoke. "The family... are they...?"

"Safe," said a man that Trapp recognized from the bridge. Hwa Yung-Gi emerged from the blasted-open door to President Kuk's suite, hands raised, then spoke to someone in Korean in a reassuring tone.

President Kuk's daughter emerged from the adjoining room, her face etched with a mix of fear and gratitude. She said something in Korean as she approached cautiously, as if unsure whether to embrace Trapp or keep her distance. Behind her, her daughters followed tentatively, their faces streaked with tears. The younger girl called to her mother in Korean, and Myo Il-Song replied with a gushing tone. Even though Trapp couldn't understand a word, he caught the meaning: *We're safe now.*

Trapp looked around the room, at the faces of the agents who had fought their way in, and at the family he had risked everything to protect. A wave of emotion crashed over him, and he felt his knees buckle beneath him. He caught himself on the edge of a nearby couch and leaned against it.

"And the files?" he asked. "Project TIPTOE?"

"I don't know yet," Randolph said. "Comms are still down."

Trapp sat there a long moment, wanting nothing more than to lie down, but said, "Let's go find Drebin and Grubbs. We might be needed."

"One moment please," Yung-Gi said. He came forward, extending his hand to Trapp. "Thank you."

Trapp shook the man's hand and said, "You're welcome."

But then a growl of fury raged from behind them. Turning, Trapp saw Li Chao, soaking wet. He slammed an HRT officer's head with his elbow, removing the guy's sidearm and using him as a shield to advance upon the family. He wasn't even trying to kill Trapp, he held the gun steady on Myo Il-Song.

Trapp moved.

Randolph moved.

Guns rose.

And Hwa Yung-Gi shoved Trapp aside, scooping up the two girls, angling them away from Chao and throwing himself in front of Myo.

His back was shredded under Chao's barrage of shots, the professional pumping round after round into him, until a torrent of bursts of three from the HRT forced Li Chao into the final, bloodiest dance of his life.

He slapped down, dead.

And Trapp found himself beside the Koreans, checking that the blood on the girls and mom were not theirs before rolling Yung-Gi off them. The FBI team now hurried the three females out, treating it like an evac, getting them to safety.

Trapp stared down at Hwa Yung-Gi. He had barely known this man who had employed scumbags and gangsters—much like Trapp had used the Triads in pursuit of a greater good—but in the end had accomplished his mission. And his final, bloody-tinged smile before the light went out in his eyes meant he knew it too.

He'd saved the people in his charge.

Now Trapp had to track down Madison and help her do the same.

MADISON SURVEYED the scene before her, taking in the battered limousine. One side of the once-sleek vehicle had crumpled when the SUV had rammed it, forcing it against the side of a building and shattering its reinforced windows.

A total of eight cops guarded Ambassador Wen and his driver, who were face-down on the sidewalk, hands cuffed behind them. Paramedics tended to them, ensuring that they were stable enough for transport.

Madison's eyes drifted to the limo's back seat, where Fang

Chen sat, her hands also restrained. The young woman looked shaken, her face pale and her eyes wet with fear.

Drebin approached, the laptop tucked under his arm, still shedding plastic flakes and chunks after his bullet had decimated it, blocking the transmission. He held up the thumb drive with a grim smile.

"It's secure," he said.

Madison sighed in relief, a weight lifting from her. "We need to get a message to the president," she said, her mind already racing ahead. "And to Trapp, I guess. They need to know the files are safe."

Drebin handed the laptop to a nearby agent, instructing her to secure the evidence, but kept hold of the thumb drive.

He turned back to Madison. "We'll get the news out. First, we need to deal with her."

Drebin nodded toward Ms. Chen, who seemed to shrink under his gaze. Madison approached the young woman, crouching down to her eye level.

"Fang," she said, her voice gentle but firm. "You have a choice. If you cooperate, we can help you."

Fang shook her head vigorously. "I am just a secretary. I didn't know what they were planning. I was only along for the ride."

Madison studied her face, searching for any sign of deception. All she saw was a young woman caught up in a scheme far beyond her ability.

"Okay," Madison said, standing up. "But you need to tell us everything you know."

69

Over the next five days, the news cycles raged with wild stories of betrayal, heroism, accusations, and commemorations. People had died, some of them bad, but other brave souls had given their lives protecting the innocent. It took time, but when the White House opened itself up to a transparent review by both Korean presidents, they were satisfied with the efforts of the security services and publicly thanked those involved in ridding the world of a rogue Chinese nationalist cell. President Kuk also acknowledged that he believed Beijing had played no part in the attempt on his family's lives and paid tribute to all those who had died protecting them. Hwa Yung-Gi's name was mentioned specifically, as Trapp had requested.

After the largely ceremonial yet deeply historic ceremony, Nash stood at the podium on the White House lawn, flanked by Presidents Kuk and Son, all three emanating pride at their achievement.

"Today," Nash said to the assembled press who beamed his words live to the nation and across the world, "we celebrate not only the signing of this groundbreaking treaty, but the bravery and dedication of those who made it possible. In particular, I want to praise the actions of a wrongly-accused CIA asset, known to the public as Hangman."

A murmur rippled through the press corps. The incident in New York had all but wiped the intelligence leak from the airwaves.

"This asset used the plot against him to uncover a rogue Chinese assassin, who aimed to sabotage these negotiations and sow chaos across the international stage," Nash continued. "The files are now known to be fakes, set up by our committed and expert technicians so our field operative could draw out the plotters."

Which was true, even though Trapp had been unaware of it at the time. Greaves hadn't told him until the files were recovered that only a handful of the assassination proposals on the drive were legit, enough to pass validation during the handover.

"I used to love fan fiction," Greaves had told Trapp later. "I've written more pages of Harry Potter than JK herself, and don't get me started on my X Files novellas. The night before we stole it, I made my own TIPTOE file, equipped it with the viruses, the alarm flare, and then switched it out with the original after we broke into the facility."

"Then why was I risking my ass and getting shot at?" Trapp had replied.

"Chao's handlers needed to believe you'd stolen the real thing—they wouldn't be convinced you were handing over the stolen files unless they saw evidence of an actual break-in." Greaves had smirked. "You don't think they have their own people watching? No one quite like me, but—"

"Definitely no one like you." Trapp was sure of that.

He brought his attention back to the present as Nash concluded his speech. "We have determined the Hangman execution video to be a so-called "deepfake", and under my instruction the Agency will be declassifying those files publicly to prove it."

The room erupted in in questions as Trapp shifted uncomfortably, watching from the sidelines. Although no attention would fall upon him from the press, he caught the eye of Mitchell, who gave him a small nod of acknowledgement from the other side of the stage.

As the ceremony concluded and the crowd began to disperse, Trapp slipped out. He had business to conclude.

~

LATER THAT DAY, Trapp found himself limping through a park, bruised and battered but healing. He approached a familiar figure sitting alone on a bench, eating an enormous Belgian waffle out of a bag. Fang Chen looked up as he approached.

"Mr. Trapp," she said, cool and formal. "I have nothing to say to you."

Trapp sat at the opposite end of the bench, his ribs, knee, and, well, almost everything aching. "I wanted to see how you were doing. I heard about your boss."

Fang nodded, her gaze fixed on the trees ahead. "He was sent back to China."

"And you?" Trapp asked. "What happens to you?"

Fang shrugged, uncertainty in her voice. "I am learning who my new boss will be later today, but I am not sure if I will be here when they take up their post next week. Perhaps your country will decide that I should follow Ambassador Wen."

Trapp nodded, understanding her position. "For what it's worth, I don't think you're a risk. You were caught up in something bigger than you could handle."

Fang's lips flickered into a humorless smile. "Tell that to the panel."

They sat in silence for a long moment.

"I can't tell them that," Trapp said. "But I know someone who might."

"Who?"

"Someone who would like to receive an anonymous tip-off."

Fang frowned. "A... what?"

"The Chinese agent who pressured you into those illegal acts of espionage..." Trapp watched her, reading recognition in her face. "I don't believe he dealt with a congressman's aide and no one else. I also know how Chao operates. He would need leverage. And I think you might know what sort of leverage he had."

Fang's expression was bleak, her lips tight. Her throat bobbed as she swallowed. "Leverage? You mean... proof...?"

"I mean if proof of Congressman Redman's treason were to arrive at the FBI headquarters on Pennsylvania Avenue addressed to Agent Paolo Drebin, there could be people in the federal government who would put a kind word in for you at your hearing."

Fang blinked a few times, then looked at the last of her waffle with bemusement, as if surprised to find she was holding it.

"I should go," she said, tossing the last of it into a garbage can and gathering her things. "I don't want to be late for my meeting."

Trapp stood, offering her a small nod of farewell. "Take care of yourself, Fang."

THE HSPCI HEARING had been in session for thirty-five minutes when the doors to the chamber opened, revealing Agent Drebin, the geek who had interviewed Jake Redman regarding Fabian Pincher's murder. He was flanked by a team of FBI agents. Redman looked up from his notes, ready to yell at the man for interrupting them, but as Drebin strode purpose-fully toward him, Redman could tell his intent.

"Congressman Redman," Drebin said, his voice carrying across the stunned chamber as he showed his warrant, "you are under arrest for violations of the Espionage Act."

Jake leapt to his feet, his face reddening.

As the agents handcuffed him and led him away, he caught sight of the journalists gathered outside the room, their cameras flashing and recording devices at the ready as he was manhandled out.

"No!" he bellowed. "I have done nothing wrong! This is political persecution, plain and simple!"

He was sincere. He really had done nothing wrong except try to help America. To build a stronger country.

Looking back, he found Rita Tarragona smiling—a happy-confused expression that just made him madder.

"President Nash is behind this!" he shouted at the cameras. "We are investigating his corruption and incompetence, and he's trying to silence his enemies... to hide the truth about his *own* treasonous actions!"

The journalists hustled back and forth, their questions overlapping in a wall of sound as Redman was dragged from the room while Drebin read him his rights.

WHILE THE CONGRESSMAN was being arrested, Trapp worked to repair the damage to Joshua's bar from weeks earlier. Joshua, freshly released from the hospital, sat in a corner, directing efforts with Valerie and Lamar by his side. Fresh sawdust danced in the air, and a drill hummed as it secured another panel to replace a bullet hole-riddled section of the bar.

"No, no, Jason," Valerie called out. "That board goes on the other side!"

Trapp looked up with a mock scowl. "I thought you were supposed to be resting."

Lamar chuckled, wincing as the jiggle of lungs pulled at his healing wounds. "You know she can't resist bossing a guy around."

That earned a gentle swat from his wife.

A knock at the door shut everyone up. Trapp felt a familiar tension creep into his muscles as he moved to lift the blind, his hand resting on the concealed gun in the back of his belt.

He peered through the glass, and a wave of relief washed over him. "It's Mike."

Trapp unlocked the door, and Mike Mitchell entered, somber as he took in the scene before him. "I come bearing news."

"Good or bad?" Joshua asked, levering himself up a grunt.

"A bit of both," Mitchell replied. "First, the good. Lamar, Valerie, Dr. Timothy Greaves—all have been granted presidential pardons. And Madison Grubbs will face no action for her involvement."

Although Trapp had been expecting this, a certain tension drained from the group.

"And Jason?" Lamar asked.

Mike turned to face Trapp, his expression unreadable. "Officially, you've been let go by the agency. A necessary step for all sides."

Trapp nodded, unsurprised by the news. "And unofficially?"

Mitchell motioned him to one side, where they could speak in private.

"Oh, now you don't trust us?" Valerie groused. "After all we've been through..."

"Unofficially, you've also been pardoned." Mike paused, letting the words sink in. "And you've been re-assigned. A highly classified cell, tasked with taking the fight to China."

Trapp's eyebrows rose, but he remained calm.

"They're a clear threat, Jason. But they prefer to operate in the shadows. The president doesn't want this escalating into another Cold War, or worse. You are to investigate the people behind Li Chao, neutralize them, and prevent anything like the TIPTOE leak from happening again."

Trapp nodded, wondering how long it would be before he set foot in here again.

"Your first stop is Nigeria," Mike added, handing him a thick file. "There's a suspiciously non-threatening project that the Chinese are pouring a lot of money into. You fly out tonight."

"Alone?" Trapp asked, accepting the file.

Mike's smile widened. "Not quite. Madison Grubbs will be along, too. To keep you in line."

A rueful grin spread across Trapp's face. "I can't wait."

70

The Chinese Embassy towered over Fang Chen, but as she approached for the first time since the chaos in New York, the edifice seemed less imposing than before, and her steps felt measured and purposeful. This might be the day that new management fired her, or she might return to business as usual. Either way, it wasn't a day she had been looking forward to.

Despite the repatriation of Ambassador Wen and a dozen other officials caught up in the joint NSA/FBI trawl of diplomatic visas, Fang had been deemed a victim, coerced into acting as she did, and she had managed to hold on to her status, thanks largely, she believed, to the deal she had struck with Jason Trapp. All it took was the audio that Li Chao had recorded during his meeting with Redman at the Smithsonian, a meeting the congressman still claimed was—alternately—a deepfake or a setup, depending which outlet he was ranting at.

As she entered the building, she gave the guards on duty a stern look, and they averted their eyes. She wandered up the office floor, greeted the people she knew and liked, and found the corner office frosted over in its privacy setting. Her friend Hei Lo whispered that "she" kept it like that often.

She.

Fang knocked on the office door, heard "Enter," and as she obeyed, she was greeted by a woman she recognized but had never met in person. The new ambassador, Lian Zhelan, looked to be in her fifties, her severe face framed by a sleek bob of jet-black hair. Ropy sinews tensed on her arms and calves, speaking of her military officer career; she clearly still maintained a healthy physical regimen. The woman indicated that Fang should close the door, then remained standing.

"Fang Chen," Lian said, her voice cool and appraising. "Ambassador Wen spoke highly of you. Your loyalty, bravery, and quick-thinking impressed him—and others."

Fang inclined her head, accepting the praise and meeting the woman's gaze with a small smile. "I only did what was necessary."

Lian nodded, a flicker of approval. "That is precisely why we will continue the work that Ambassador Wen and Li Chao started." Her tone grew more serious. "People back in Beijing, they have taken notice of you. They want you to play a role in what comes next."

People.

Not *the Party*.

A stirring of unease settled deep within her, tempered by a thrill of excitement in her veins.

"These people," Fang said slowly, "they are not the government?"

Lian's smile widened. "Very astute, Fang Chen. No, these people are not the government. Not yet, anyway. They are far more ambitious than our weak leaders who have to imprison anyone who so much as speaks out of turn."

Fang had seen firsthand what the government could do to individuals who dared row against the current and what a man like Li Chao could have done, had he succeeded. If not for Jason Trapp and his allies.

She had been disgusted by the way both men had treated her, a pawn in their big-boy spy games. There had to be another way.

"I will do whatever it takes to build a better world," Fang said.

Lian's satisfied smile stepped up in wattage to triumphant. She strode forward and clasped Fang's hand in a firm grip. "Li Chao's plot was merely testing the waters. Now the real mission is about to begin. When it is over, America will bend the knee to China, and to us."

Fang Chen's pulse quickened; she could not stop her mouth from turning up into a grin. Today was turning into a very good day after all.

America will bend the knee...

ALSO BY JACK SLATER

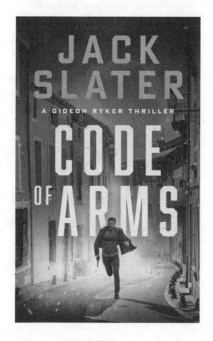

The first instalment in a new thrilling action series that fans of the Jason Bourne and Terminal List series will love.

He can't run. He can't hide. He can't *remember*…

Six weeks ago, Gideon Ryker awoke from a coma in the French chateau where veterans of the Foreign Legion live out their final days in peace. His body is a torturer's canvas, his mind an empty slate—except for haunting dreams of a young girl's face. He doesn't even remember his name.

But he knows that a legionnaire's life is a brutal struggle. The only reward: a new identity and passport. A fresh start. You'd only take that deal if you needed to forget your past life.

Or escape it...

Clearly Gideon didn't run fast enough. Someone caught up with him once. And when a CIA hit squad arrives at the chateau, he discovers that hunting season isn't over.

But where did he come from? Who is the girl that stalks his dreams?

And why does everybody want him dead?

FOR ALL THE LATEST NEWS

I hope you enjoyed *Eyes Only*. If you did, and don't fancy sifting through thousands of books on Amazon and leaving your next great read to chance, then sign up to my mailing list and be the first to hear when I release a new book.

Just visit www.jack-slater.com/updates to join!

Thanks so much for reading!

Jack.

AUTHOR'S NOTE

Hi,

Jason Trapp fans, it's been a while...

But Jason's back with a bang. I hope you liked *Eyes Only*! This book came in three months later and 20 chapters longer than I had planned, but I hope you found it worth the wait.

If you've got this far, then you know that Eyes Only is the first book in a new arc for Jason. A new power is rising in the East, and maybe, just maybe, the sun is starting to set on America's time as the only global superpower.

Or maybe Jason's going to have to do something about that, too...

As for what the next few months hold—I'm writing this from a mattress on the floor, with all my worldly possessions in boxes around me. Tomorrow we're moving house. About three months from today, I'll be a dad! As you can imagine, it's been a busy time and it's only going to get busier.

However... *Proof of Life*, Gideon Ryder book 3, is in progress. I'm really, really hoping to finish it before a newborn crows his way into my life and has me juggling diapers and my keyboard with the same hand. If he comes early, all bets are off... Ideally

I'd like to release end of January 2025, but if that doesn't happen, you know why.

Untitled Jason Trapp Book 11, the catchy working title for *Jason Trapp* book 11, is also underway and is due late Spring.

We're almost caught up in audio (all thanks due to my wife), and between Podium Audio releasing *No Loose End (Blake Larsen 4)*, and us getting *Test of Faith* out a couple of weeks back, we're hoping to have the whole catalog up to date in 2025. If you haven't tried the new multi-cast audiobooks produced by Graphic Audio, check them out. They're getting great reviews!

On a personal note, parenting tips will be very welcome from anyone who's braved the gauntlet before me.

And—as always—thanks for reading, and allowing me to do what I love.

Jack.

Made in United States
Cleveland, OH
09 December 2024

11578681R00267